LAST OF
THE MOJITOS

By

J.E. McBee

ALSO BY J.E. McBEE

For Laura Thorn, who challenged me to look within.

"Without music life would be a mistake."

- Friedrich Nietzsche

ACKNOWLEDGMENTS

I would like to thank an extremely talented and generous group of friends and colleagues who have provided significant contributions to this work of fiction – without their insight, knowledge and assistance, this story would never have reached the printed page.

Many thanks to Pete Malamas, who once again provided a brilliant and evocative cover design.

Thanks also to Linda Chamberlain, Pat Maher, William Lawson and Thomas Sharp for their early review and astute critiques of this work in progress.

Also of immeasurable help were Michael Lawley and John Richard Rodgers, who provided vital information concerning policies and procedures of the U.S. Army and Air Force, respectively. Many thanks also to Arne Becker, John Kux, John Lynch and Lipbone Redding, who supplied key information and insight into the world of music and musicians, Victor Parra Gonzalez, whose wizardry in the kitchen deeply influenced this work, and to Darla Moore of Rollins College in Winter Park, Florida, who contributed valuable historical perspective.

2018

1

Dealing with the death of a family member is always a tricky proposition, fraught with levels of emotional investment that can vary widely from moment to moment, day to day, year to year. There is no playbook, no manual, no guide for the suddenly bereaved, only the hope that whatever path is chosen will result in the least amount of damage possible to those survivors moving forward.

In the case of Marcia Alvarez, the death of her father from a stroke at 87 produced in her a range of emotions that fluctuated wildly, emotions that could be triggered by something as simple as a change in the weather. His only child, she had been Clement Harkins' caretaker since she had retired from the U.S. Army fourteen years earlier, a task that had exhausted her, leaving her resentful and frustrated more often than not.

Two years before suffering the stroke that would eventually kill him, Harkins had fallen and broken his hip. His slow recovery and resulting lack of mobility left him an angry man, prone to verbal outbursts that increased in frequency as the frustration over his condition mounted. This frustration was directed toward Marcia, his only child, who absorbed the attacks with difficulty, torn between her desire to hit back, to tell him exactly what she thought of him and his wild mood swings, and a familial obligation to stay the course regardless of the abuse he heaped upon her. She couldn't count the number of times she'd stormed out the door of the condo they shared in Dunedin, Florida after an argument, intent on packing her things, removing herself from the toxic drama for good. But she always came back, her anger tempered by the salve of time and a sense of duty forged from twenty years of military service rather than a deep-seated affection for her father.

She had sacrificed a life of her own to do the right thing. But now that her father was dead, she felt a sense of relief rather than grief. It was her turn now.

*****

Marcia Alvarez was Clement Harkins' only living relative at the time of his death. His wife Kay had died from a brain aneurism when Marcia was sixteen, and Clement's only sister Louise had died from breast cancer twenty years earlier. Two years with her father as a single parent was the primary reason Marcia had enlisted in the army as soon as she graduated from high school; she couldn't wait to flee the nest.

She had been an indifferent student, barely managing passing grades in most of her subjects throughout middle school and high school. But she had a natural affinity for foreign languages, and at her high school graduation had received an award from the Foreign Languages Department as the outstanding senior in both Spanish and French. She parlayed that aptitude in language skills on her Skill Qualification Test when she enlisted and was subsequently accepted in Linguist School, where she graduated at the top of her class. After graduation she was assigned to the elite Intelligence and Security Command (INSCOM) and was stationed at the joint operations base in Kunia, Hawaii as a linguistics analyst.

She could hardly believe her good fortune. When she'd enlisted, she'd given little thought as to what she might do in the army. She just wanted to get away from her father and his mercurial temper – she figured anything the army had to offer her would be a step up. But Hawaii? The base was only a half-hour drive from the north shore of Oahu and Waimea Bay, which attracted some of the finest surfers on the planet each winter. The lush vegetation and ideal climate were a far cry from the bleakness of Fort Sill, Oklahoma, where she'd undergone basic training.

It was on Oahu where she met a motor pool mechanic from El Paso named Javier Alvarez. It was lust at first sight – Marcia hadn't dated in high school, mainly because of her fear that her father's overzealous parenting style would intimidate any boy in whom she professed an interest. Freed from that sort of oversight, eager to realize her worth as a woman, Marcia was no match for the darkly handsome Alvarez, a first-generation Mexican-American whose family had emigrated from Ciudad Juarez when Javier was three years old. He was ten years older than she, cocksure of his attraction to the opposite sex. His unwavering confidence and smoldering sexuality lured the virginal Marcia Harkins to his bed without a hint of hesitation on her part.

Three months later, after a series of clandestine off-base meetings both in the wild and at a local hot sheet joint near the base, the two were married in a simple ceremony by a city court judge in Honolulu. As soon as they could manage it the couple moved into married personnel housing and began to adjust to their new life.

What Marcia hadn't known when she'd been swept off her feet by her new husband was his rejection of monogamy as a desirable lifestyle, even for a newlywed. The first time she'd confronted him after she observed him in the enlisted personnel bar on base, openly caressing the breast of an administrative clerk from the motor pool while kissing her neck, she exploded. She approached unseen from behind him, blood boiling

"What the fuck do you think you're doing?" she demanded when she reached him, giving him a shove.

He turned deliberately on his barstool, a smile on his face that displayed no mirth as he got to his feet and grabbed her firmly above the elbow, escorting her outside, away from curious eyes and ears in the bar. When they were far enough from the building that they couldn't be overheard, he spun her around so they were facing one another before releasing his grip. "What does it look like I was doing?" he said pleasantly, as though nothing was wrong. He lit a cigarette and exhaled toward her face.

"Trying to get into that slut's pants," she exclaimed hotly, fists clenched, resting defiantly on her hips.

He spread his hands to his sides, palms up in a gesture proclaiming innocence. "See? I knew it."

"Knew what?"

"That you'd get it wrong." He took another drag from his cigarette as he moved closer and bent down, his face inches from hers. "I wasn't trying to get into her pants. I already have. Wanna know how many times?"

She raised her arm to strike him, but he was ready. He grabbed her by the wrist and forced her roughly to the ground, the smile never leaving his lips. "That's the way it's going to be, because that's the way it's always been. I like women. Just because we're married doesn't change that, so get used to it."

She struggled to regain her feet, but his grip was strong. She was helpless. "Let me up, you motherfucker!"

"Are you going to be nice?" he asked, tone still pleasant.

"I'm gonna knock your fuckin' block off," she snarled, trying again to free herself, to no avail.

Suddenly he released her and took several steps back, still smiling. Marcia regained her feet and rushed him with a snarl, fist raised. He waited until she was within an arm's length, then took a quick step to the side to avoid her before uncorking a straight right hand to her nose. The force of the punch knocked her off her feet, onto her backside in the gravel parking lot.

Marcia was still conscious, but just barely. The pain was excruciating, and blood flowed freely from her nose, which she feared was broken. She cowered as Javier flicked his cigarette away and knelt beside her. In a tone soft enough to appease a librarian, he said. "Don't bother waiting up tonight." He stood up, still smiling, and reached into his pocket, retrieving a soiled handkerchief and tossing it onto her chest before turning and walking back into the bar.

It took her eighteen months after that incident before she was able to convince her superiors that she needed a transfer. In the interim, she did her best to ignore Javier's indiscretions, giving him a wide berth whenever possible. On those occasions when she voiced her displeasure at his alley cat behavior, his response was the same: he hit her until the protests stopped. She knew that she'd receive little support from the military hierarchy, which was overwhelmingly male, so instead of turning him in she did the best she could to hide the discoloration and swelling his rampages left behind with makeup and clothing with long sleeves.

By the time her transfer to Fort Benning was approved, she'd filed for divorce and was again living in the barracks, soured on men after only one, desperate for a new start where no one knew or cared about her past. Her commanding officer, Major Cornell Thomas, was bewildered by her desire to throw away a promising career with INSCOM, unable to comprehend her reasoning, repeatedly trying to talk her out of leaving without success.

He and the rest of the brass didn't know her focus had changed. She no longer had the desire to be part of the Intelligence Service. She wanted another challenge, one where the passion and conviction that had grown in her as a victim of abuse could be best channeled. She knew it wouldn't be easy, but she was determined to give it her best effort. Her naivete shredded by her disastrous marriage, she came to believe that her situation was far from isolated. She wanted to make a difference when it came to the dirty secret of female abuse in the armed services.

The best way she could do that, she thought, was by joining the military police, a subset of the army that was, like all other departments in the early 1980s, overwhelmingly male. Women in the armed services, the most vulnerable of all soldiers, deserved an advocate, someone who had experienced their pain and knew the best methods to combat and alleviate it. As an MP, she could be that advocate. She relished the challenge.

Her father had been bewildered by her decision making, from the quickie marriage to the subsequent divorce and her choice to throw away a career in Intelligence to become a military cop.

Marcia knew he struggled with it all, which was why she limited her contacts with him. She didn't tell him that she had been married until after her divorce was final, and she didn't tell him she'd left Hawaii until she was relocated to Georgia. And she certainly didn't tell him the reason behind her divorce, citing that old standby irreconcilable differences, that things simply hadn't worked out.

She completed her stint in the army as a member of the military police at Fort Benning, where she rose through the ranks, retiring after twenty years as a sergeant. After her retirement she moved to Tampa, where her father was living in a small apartment near MacDill Air Force Base. She used much of the money she'd managed to save during the last twenty years, along with some of her father's savings, to purchase a condominium in Dunedin where the two of them had lived for fourteen years before her father passed away two months after Hurricane Irma tore through the Keys.

After his death Marcia met with Judy Ruliani, her father's attorney, for a reading of the will. As sole survivor, Marcia knew that she would receive whatever her father had accumulated during his life, including the seventh-floor condo on the Dunedin Causeway that overlooked Caladesi Island and Clearwater Beach beyond that. That is, unless he decided to give it all to the Scientologists, which he had threatened to do several times in the past when they had argued. Knowing her father, anything was possible.

Ruliani was well known in the Tampa Bay area, her smiling face and oversized teeth plastered on billboards throughout the region and featured on numerous local television commercials. Her office was in downtown Tampa, in one of the high-rise buildings along Ashley Street, in the heart of the financial district.

Marcia spent the forty-minute drive from Dunedin that morning mulling her future. For the first time in her life, her father wouldn't be around to influence her choices. Even when she was in the army, the specter of his presence loomed over her like an ominous cloud teeming with thunder. Now that he was gone and she was on her own, she wondered what she might do with her life.

Often in her caretaker role, especially after he'd broken his hip, she had daydreamed about the day the old man would die. But she had never let her thoughts become too optimistic; her army pension was adequate but not excessive, so a life of leisure was out. She'd probably have to figure out some way to augment that pension moving forward. Unless she won the lottery.

When she arrived she was greeted warmly by the receptionist, who ushered her into Ruliani's office immediately. "Ms. Ruliani is expecting you."

After a brief exchange of pleasantries, the attorney got down to business. "The will is fairly simple. As the sole survivor, you have been designated both executor and sole beneficiary of your late father's estate." She paused, smiling before she continued. "The condo, which is fully paid for, is yours. In addition, your father had a savings account which contains $137,692, and a certificate of deposit with SunTrust worth $88,799 that matures in four weeks and three days." She pushed a small key across the table toward Marcia. "Your father also rented a safe deposit box at a SunTrust branch on Curlew. As executor of his estate, you're authorized to access the contents of that box at any time after today." She paused again, still smiling, her veneers blindingly white. "Any questions?"

Marcia was speechless. She had no idea the old man had squirreled away that amount of cash. And the existence of a safe deposit box was news to her. She wondered what could be inside. After a few moments she had a thought. "Will I be able to cash in the certificate of deposit at that branch on Curlew?"

"Of course. Just present them with the paperwork when you go there." She glanced at the clock on the wall, then back at Marcia. "Any more questions?"

"I don't think so."

Ruliani stood, offering her hand across the desk again. "If you do, don't hesitate to call me."

2

Despite her curiosity about the contents of her father's safe deposit box, Marcia decided to wait to check it until the certificate of deposit had matured. She had more than enough money to get by for the next month now that she had transferred the cash from her father's savings account into her own. She'd wait; the contents of the box would make for a nice gift before Christmas.

From time to time the matter popped into her head and she speculated what the box might contain but resisted the temptation to rush down to the bank. Again and again she came to the same conclusion: that it had something to do with her father's ludicrous claim that he was the real D.B. Cooper. She had humored him over the years publicly, while laughing off the notion in private that her father was the most notorious hijacker in U.S. history. Despite his claims, he'd never offered her a shred of proof that the was Cooper, and Marcia eventually came to believe that her father's fantasy had something to do with his Air Force career as a paratrooper. Because he had actually jumped out of planes during his military career, the old man had somehow convinced himself that he was the elusive and mythical Cooper. Wishful thinking on steroids, she concluded. She saw no harm in her father's claim, as long as it stayed between the two of them.

She'd slipped only once. She'd mentioned her father's claim to Gracie Fenton, the weekday bartender at Kitty Galore's Raw Bar in Ozona, where she had been a lunchtime regular for the last year. Their condo on the causeway was only minutes away from Kitty's via the Pinellas Trail bike path, so she rode her bike there and back, Monday through Friday. The hour of respite she received from having to deal with her increasingly unstable father was only possible through the kindness of Edith Zieman and Muriel Drake, two elderly widows from her condo complex who took turns watching Clement Harkins while Marcia decompressed at the bar.

The normally taciturn Gracie had disappointed her by mentioning her father's insistence that he was the real D.B. Cooper to Steve Morrison and Zach Rheinhart, two other lunchtime regulars at Kitty's. Luckily, both Morrison and Rheinhart had scoffed at the claim and hadn't mentioned it again, at least in front of Marcia. So far, the situation appeared to be under control.

During those times when she convinced herself that the contents of the safe deposit box had to be something unrelated to Cooper, her most frequent alternative to the Cooper hypothesis was that the old man had purchased some stocks and stashed them in the bank. Certainly plausible, except for one major hurdle: her father had been computer illiterate, so if he had purchased stocks, he would've needed her help, either with his order on the computer or to take him to a brokerage where he could make the purchase in person, since her father no longer drove a car. Neither of those things had occurred, which brought her back to Cooper.

She spent a large chunk of her time while waiting for the certificate of deposit to mature studying the stock market. Now that she had some disposable cash and was about to receive some more, she thought the market was the place where her money would do her the most good. Ever since Obama had bailed out the banks and rescued the world economy, the stock market had been on a bull run, rising to record heights, with no end in sight. If she wanted her money to work for her, she needed to learn about the workings of Wall Street, something she'd never had the luxury of considering before.

*****

Two days before Christmas, Marcia Alvarez drove to the SunTrust branch on Curlew and cashed in the CD her father had bequeathed to her. She'd been watching the stock market closely for the last month, educating herself on its nuances and pitfalls. She'd never had enough money on her own before to consider investing it, but she had some pretty concrete ideas on what to do with the cashier's check that one of the bank managers prepared for her while she waited patiently.

The manager, a well-dressed woman in her late forties with autumn hair and a mole on her left cheek, smiled as she reached across the desk to hand Marcia the check. "You know, we'd be happy to deposit that check for you if you'd like."

"Thanks," Marcia said, "But I'm planning on investing this in the market."

"That's pretty risky," the bank manager warned.

"Maybe," Marcia said. "But you're only young once, right? You gotta take your shot when it comes along. This is my last inheritance – I'm not getting another chance."

"Whatever you say, Ms. Alvarez. Is there anything else I can do for you today?"

She reached into her pocket for the key to her late father's safe deposit box. She passed it over to the manager. "I'd like to look in this safe deposit box."

"Wait right here," the manager said, rising to her feet. "I'll get the duplicate."

Marcia looked around the bank as she waited for the manager to return. There was only one other customer in the bank, an elderly man with a cane discussing something in earnest with one of the cashiers, their heads close together. Marcia couldn't hear what they were saying, but she saw the young cashier blush and smile, shaking her head. The old coot probably asked her for a date, she thought.

A moment later the manager returned. "Follow me."

24

Marcia trailed behind as they walked to a locked gate in the rear of the bank. The manager inserted a key into the lock, opened the door and ushered her inside to the restricted area, scanning the wall to her right, looking for the proper number. When she found it, she motioned Marcia over and handed her the second key. "You'll need to insert both keys in order to access your box." She smiled. "Would you like some help?"

"No thanks," Marcia replied, forcing a smile. "I can take it from here."

"Very well," the manager said. "I'll be outside in case you need any assistance." She turned and went out the door, closing it behind her.

Marcia was alone in the vault area. She took a deep breath to steady herself. Her father had rented one of the largest boxes the bank had to offer, big enough to stuff a small golf bag into it. What on earth was in it?

She inserted both keys, turned them a half turn and heard a click. She removed the box and laid it on a broad table nearby to examine the contents, hesitating to lift the lid for a moment before she gathered her nerve and opened it.

She gasped. Before her were bundles of twenty-dollar bills with bank wrappers binding them together, stacked one of top of the other, four deep filling the entire box. She picked up one of the bundles and examined it, riffling it like a deck of cards. The bills were old, all dated either 1963 or 1969, most of them from the Federal Reserve Bank in San Francisco. She eyeballed the stacks and did some rough math in her head. Must be at least a hundred fifty grand here, she thought.

She took a step back. She had been holding her breath; she released it now. She felt a little light-headed, like it was all a dream.

She stepped forward again to look inside, to see if there was anything else there. The only other item in the box was a business envelope, with Marcia's name printed on the front in her father's unmistakable scrawl. Holding her breath again, she tore the envelope open with one of her nails, careful not to disturb its

25

contents. She extracted a single folded sheet of paper, opening it and laying it on the table next to the safe deposit box, revealing a short sentence in her father's handwriting:

Do you believe me now?

She felt a sudden pressure in her chest as she read the note again, heart pounding. So it was true – Clement Harkins *was* the real D.B. Cooper and had been all along. She realized she had been holding her breath again and exhaled noisily. A flood of regret coursed through her being as she realized her father had kept the secret of the ages and had gone to his grave knowing that the only person he'd shared it with thought he was either a delusional fool or an outright liar.

She reached into the box and extracted all the bundles of cash and began to count. As she counted she periodically checked the series dates; they all were dates before 1971, the year the hijacking occurred, which told her the dates were in line with her father's claim.

Twenty minutes later she had the total: $194,200. Suddenly she felt faint. She reached out with her left hand to steady herself, trying to wrap her head around it all.

What should she do now?

3

As soon as she reached the condo, Marcia called Judy Ruliani's office. Her receptionist answered on the second ring. "Law offices of Judy Ruliani. How may I help you?"

Marcia tried to steady her voice. Her pulse was racing. "This is Marcia Alvarez. My father was a client of Ms. Ruliani's, Clement Harkins. I was in your office last month for a reading of his will."

"I remember, Ms. Alvarez. What can I do for you today?"

"I'd like to set up an appointment with Ms. Ruliani. The sooner the better."

There was concern in the receptionist's voice. "Is there something wrong regarding the estate?"

"No, no, nothing like that. I'd like to retain Ms. Ruliani as my personal attorney, and I have a matter of extreme urgency that I'd like to discuss with her as soon as possible."

"Ms. Ruliani is on vacation and won't be in until after the first of the year," she said regretfully. "Is there anything I can do for you now?"

"No."

"Would you like me to set up an appointment for you?"

"Please."

"Please hold a moment." She came back a minute later. "I have an opening for Wednesday January 3rd at 10:00 am."

A little less than two weeks. "I'll take it. Thanks very much, Ms.___"

"Madeline. Madeline Collins."

"Thanks very much, Madeline. I'll see you then."

Marcia hung up the phone and retreated to her bedroom. On the floor in the closet was a safe. She dropped to her knees and dialed the combination. When she felt the final number click she twisted the dial and swung the door open. She picked up an envelope marked **DBC** and carried it back with her to the living room, where she extracted three twenty-dollar bills, bills she had removed from the safe deposit box so she could check their authenticity.

She sat down at the dining room table and flipped open her laptop. When she was online she logged into Google and typed in "D.B. Cooper serial numbers." When the next screen popped up she noticed at the bottom of the page there were six pages of results. Methodically she clicked on each one, hoping to find a list of the numbers she could check against the numbers on the three bills on the table next to her, but found nothing of value, no list of any kind. Disappointed, she tried several other iterations of the same search message. On her third try, after plugging in "a list of serial numbers for D.B. Cooper" she reached a website which offered to check the serial number of any number the searcher wanted to input against the list of numbers from the ransom money.

Excited, she reached for one of the bills and started to enter the serial number. After inputting three numbers, however, she stopped. She had no idea who was behind this website. Also, there was no list of serial numbers anywhere on the website; she had hoped to find a list of numbers and check the three bills against the numbers on her list. By inputting the complete list of numbers, she could be giving her identity away to some scammer. Along with the fact that she was in possession of three bills whose serial numbers matched those placed in the ransom package that Cooper took with him when he leaped out of the plane.

She closed down the search and leaned back from the table. She needed a cigarette.

*****

On the morning of January 3rd, Marcia arrived at the offices of Judy Ruliani with fifteen minutes to spare. The suspense had been building over the last ten days, so much so that she barely noticed Christmas, which in Florida was a strange holiday to begin with, never any snow on the ground or even a nip in the air. She found a parking spot two blocks away and set off for the high-rise office building where Judy Ruliani conducted business. In her purse were the three bills she'd removed from the bank. She clutched her purse to her side like it was her child.

When she exited the elevator, Madeline Collins greeted her with a broad smile. "Nice to see you again, Ms. Alvarez."

"Please call me Marcia."

She gestured toward Ruliani's office door. "She's expecting you, Marcia. Go on in."

Ruliani looked up from a brief she was reviewing when the door opened. A broad smile creased her tanned face as she removed her reading glasses and stood up, extending her hand across the desk. "Good to see you again, Marcia." She gestured toward her guest chair. "Have a seat. What can I do for you today?"

"How was the vacation?" Marcia asked. "From the looks of your tan, it was on a beach somewhere."

Ruliani smiled. "You should be a detective. I was in the Maldives."

"Where's that?"

"A series of small islands off the tip of India. The best beaches I've ever seen."

29

Marcia smiled. "Business must be good."

Ruliani returned the smile. "I have no complaints. So, what can I do for you today?"

Marcia took a deep breath, then began. "Do you know who D.B. Cooper is?"

"I've heard of him. They never found him, did they?"

"No. After he jumped out of the plane he was never seen again. They never found a body, and nobody tried to spend any of the money. The serial numbers had been recorded by the FBI, and none of them have ever surfaced." She added hastily. "With the exception of three bundles of bills that were found on the banks of the Columbia River in Oregon in 1980 by a family out for a hike." She paused for a moment, then continued. "It was like he vanished into thin air."

"I assume there's more to the story."

"There is," Marcia replied. "My father, Clement Harkins, was a career Air Force man, a paratrooper during the Korean War who was stationed on the west coast, in Oregon, when the hijacking occurred."

Ruliani pulled out a note pad and a pen. "When did the hijacking occur?"

Marcia reached into her purse and withdrew a small notebook. She skimmed a few pages before looking up. "November 24, 1971, the day before Thanksgiving."

"Go on."

"My father was a bit of a character back then. A man's man, I think you'd call him. Loved to spend time with the other flyboys, more than he spent with us, it seemed. We didn't see him that much in those days."

"Who's we?"

"My mother and me. I was an only child. Anyway, that year I was six years old. As wild as my father could be, he never missed a holiday with us. Except for Thanksgiving that year."

Ruliani was scribbling on her pad. "That was 1971?"

"Yes. I remember I was really disappointed that he missed Thanksgiving dinner. Mom had to carve the turkey, and she made a real mess of it." She smiled, recalling. "It looked like it went through a shredder."

"So your father missed Thanksgiving dinner. Did he ever say why he missed it?"

Marcia shook her head. "He never mentioned it, but my mother told me he was on an assignment. A secret mission of some sort. I wasn't supposed to ask him about it or mention it to any of my friends, so I didn't."

"When did he come home?"

"The following Tuesday. He was all scratched up, his arms and the side of his neck, and he was walking with a limp, but he acted like nothing unusual had happened."

"And your mother never mentioned it again?"

"No. I was just a kid, so I sort of forgot about it."

"Did you ever ask your mother about it?"

Marcia shook her head. "No. It turns out now to be one of my biggest regrets. My mother died of a brain aneurism when I was sixteen, so I never did find out what the secret mission was." She smiled wistfully. "She took it to her grave."

"What about your father?" Ruliani asked. "Did he ever mention it again? Or did you ask him?"

Marcia nodded. "He did, but not until I got out of the army, in 2003. He was living by himself in a rundown apartment near MacDill then, so after I put in my twenty I moved to Tampa, and together we purchased the condo on the causeway in Dunedin."

"Put in your twenty?"

Marcia smiled sheepishly. "Army talk. I retired in 2003 after twenty year of service."

"The two of you lived together from then on?"

31

Marcia nodded. "We did. He was starting to develop some mobility issues, and he had no one else in his life. So I became his caretaker."

"That must've been a tough life for you," Ruliani said sympathetically. "You were still pretty young then to be a parental aide."

Marcia nodded. "I was 38. It wasn't bad at first, but as the years passed, he became more unhinged. Or so I thought."

"What do you mean by unhinged?"

"Started talking crazy shit about his past. He claimed he was D.B. Cooper."

Ruliani dropped her pen and looked across the desk at Marcia. She was starting to fill in the blanks. "How did you respond?"

"Not well," she admitted. "I called him a crazy old man and a lot of other things that weren't nearly as nice as that. Anyway, he kept it up over the years. Every time we got into an argument, which was pretty often, if he got too frustrated, he'd blurt out that he was D.B. Cooper, like it was some sort of defense mechanism. Usually I'd just throw up my hands and walk away from him, which would frustrate him even more. I was pretty shitty toward him."

"So....?"

"So that brings us to last November, when he died and I came into your office to find out what was in his will. That's when I found out about the safe deposit box." She paused, then continued. "I waited until the certificate of deposit matured and went to the SunTrust Bank on Curlew where the box was located. First I cashed in the CD and deposited it into my account, and then the clerk led me to the vault, where I checked the box." She stopped for a moment and withdrew the envelope from her purse and held it in both hands in front of her. "When I opened the box, I saw it was filled with money. Stacks of twenties, piled four deep, filled the entire box. After I caught my breath, I counted the money. They were all old bills, Series 1963A or 1969."

"How much?"

"More than \$190,000. I counted it twice." She withdrew the three bills from the envelope and placed them on the desk. "These are three of the bills."

Ruliani leaned in closely. "May I touch them?"

"Be my guest."

She picked up a bill and held it up to the light. Her knowledge of old bills was limited, but these felt right to her. If they were counterfeit, someone had done an excellent job. "Did you call the police?"

A look of horror filled Marcia's face. "No way. As soon as I got home from the bank I called you, but you were on vacation, so I went down to Haslam's in St. Pete and bought a book on D.B. Cooper. I took it home and read it, trying to verify my father's claim."

"Before we go any farther, was there anything else in the safe deposit box?" Ruliani asked.

Marcia nodded. "A note, in my father's handwriting."

"What did it say?"

"Do you believe me now?"

Ruliani wrote some more. "Did you keep the note?"

"Yes. I have it in my purse. Would you like to see it?"

Ruliani shook her head. "That's not necessary. But I'd advise you to put it in a safe place, somewhere where no one can get to it."

"I have a safe in my bedroom in the condo."

"That should be perfect." She jotted something down, then looked up again. "What about the book you bought? Did it help?"

Marcia nodded. "It did. One of the stewardesses on the flight described how Cooper acted on the plane. When I read that, shivers ran up and down my spine."

"What did she say?"

"That Cooper had a couple of drinks and chain-smoked during both flights, before he got the money and after the money was delivered. She said he was drinking bourbon and soda and smoking Raleigh cigarettes." She paused. "My father drank bourbon and soda. And he was a heavy smoker, three packs a day." Pause. "He smoked Raleighs."

Ruliani's mind was working at warp speed. Not so fast, she thought. Better make sure first. "Have you done anything else to try to verify that the money is genuine?"

"Yeah, I went online and Googled D.B. Cooper serial numbers, but didn't find anything I could use." She decided not to mention the suspect website she'd visited briefly. "That's where I hoped you could help. I was hoping you might know some way to check the serial numbers without alerting the FBI."

"I can certainly try. I have a few contacts that might be helpful." Another thought occurred to her. "Have you told anyone else about this?"

Marcia shook her head. "You're the first."

"Excellent. I suggest you keep it that way." Ruliani stood up. "Do you mind if I make copies of these bills?"

"Go right ahead."

She reached down and gingerly picked up the bills. "I'll be right back."

Marcia turned and watched as Ruliani exited the office, closing the door behind her. She had a pang of regret – was she doing the right thing, entrusting what could be one of the biggest news stories of the century to Tampa's billboard lawyer?

4

It took six days for Ruliani to get back to Marcia. When the phone rang on Monday morning after their initial meeting, Marcia answered it immediately when she saw who was calling. "Hello?"

Ruliani laughed. "You sound out of breath. Have you been jogging?"

Marcia, who had a two-pack-a-day habit herself, responded with a laugh of her own. "Not hardly."

"Is this a good time?"

"As good as it gets, I guess. Did you find anything out?"

"I did," Ruliani said reassuringly. "First, I can't emphasize enough that you can't mention what your father revealed to you to anyone, not even your best friend. If word gets out that your father was the real D.B. Cooper, your life as you know it will be ruined. The media will hound you everywhere you go: a restaurant, the movies, the mall. They'll camp out outside your home and follow you everywhere you go. It will be a nightmare for you."

Her words confirmed Marcia's worst fear. "I kinda figured that, with the Internet and all. Plus, cell phones all have cameras today. Everyone is a member of the *paparazzi* these days."

Ruliani's voice was soothing, full of approval. "Good. Mum's the word. Have you retained those bills like you said you were going to?"

"They're here, in the safe."

"Excellent," Ruliani replied. "I've been in contact with a client of mine who has agreed to examine the bills to determine if they're counterfeit. There's no need to proceed further if this whole thing is a hoax." Pause. "Is that something you would be open to, having the bills authenticated?"

"I guess so," Marcia answered haltingly, adding quickly. "As long as you can trust this person to keep a secret."

"That won't be a problem. He won't realize the significance of the bills, because we won't tell him. All he'll know is that we want to know if they're real."

"How long will that take?" Marcia asked.

"Once you give the go-ahead, it becomes a matter of getting the bills to him. Once he has them, he'll know immediately."

Marcia was reassured by that. She hadn't considered that the bills might be counterfeit, but once Ruliani mentioned it, she realized that their authenticity needed to be confirmed. "How should we do this?"

Ruliani was ready for her question. "I think the best way would be for the examination to be done on neutral ground. If you feel comfortable with that, I suggest we use the conference room in my office. Your identity will remain unknown that way – the examiner will only think I'm doing it for some anonymous client."

Marcia wasn't fully convinced. "What if this person gets curious about the fact that the money is old? Wouldn't he get suspicious?"

"I don't think so. But if he does, I can always tell him that a client found the money between an old mattress and box spring set and wants to know if it's real." Ruliani paused. "If you have doubts, give it a day, think about it a bit. There's no rush, is there?"

"No," Marcia replied, mulling the idea. "Why don't you give me a call tomorrow. Is that okay?"

"If it's okay with you, it's okay with me – you're the client."

After they ended the call, Marcia grabbed her cigarettes and took the elevator to the ground floor. She needed some fresh air, mixed with nicotine.

*****

While she waited for her attorney to get back to her, Marcia again returned to thinking about the road ahead, a process that had begun as soon as her father was laid to rest. Being her father's caretaker had been her job for fifteen years, no days off, no paid vacations and no chance of promotion or transfer. For the first time since she'd retired from the army, she had options.

Those options had increased significantly as soon as Clement Harkins' will was read. The surprising amount of cash he'd been able to save would provide a much-needed cushion to her pension, especially if she invested it wisely. She'd picked out a few stocks and a mutual fund that was highly rated by several of the brokers whom she had contacted and had moved swiftly, opening a self-actuated IRA with one of the discount online brokerages.

But now she was faced with a decision of a different kind: what to do with the remainder of the ransom paid to her father. Ruliani had been right; announcing to the world that she was the daughter of D.B. Cooper and was in possession of the cash from the hijacking would set off a feeding frenzy of publicity seekers, grifters and law enforcement, a perfect storm of scrutiny that would transform her life into a hellish nightmare, with no happy ending in sight. She wasn't about to let that happen, but she didn't want the cash to just sit there in the bank and gather dust, either. She needed another option, one that had yet to present itself.

The day after her phone call with Ruliani, Marcia rose early, puttering around the condo, taking several trips down the elevator so she could smoke in between checking her new portfolio

37

on her laptop. She was killing time, waiting for Kitty Galore's to open for lunch.

It was overcast, with a steady breeze from the north that made it feel cooler than it was. She opted for a pair of jeans and a light sweater, and at 11:15 unchained her bicycle and pedaled east on the causeway toward the bike path. Traffic along the causeway was light, but she knew that would change dramatically once the snowbirds began to arrive.

Twenty minutes later she secured her bike to the rack next to the front entrance of Kitty's and walked inside. Gracie Fenton was working alone, stocking the two ice-filled tubs behind the bar with beer when she arrived. Several tables were occupied, and there were two couples at the bar, studying menus.

Marcia took a seat at the end of the bar by the main entrance and announced cheerfully, "What's a broad have to do to get a drink around here?"

A pleasant blond with a trim figure and the ideal personality for a career in customer service, Gracie swiveled her head around at the sound of Marcia's voice and rose to her feet, a wide, welcoming smile on her face. "Well, well, well. Look who's back," she exclaimed. "How long has it been?"

Marcia thought for a moment. "Since I've been here? About two months, I guess. Since before my father died."

Gracie's tone was sympathetic. "How have you been doing?

She shrugged her shoulders. "Okay. I've been sleeping better lately, which is a plus. Other than that, not much has changed since you had me over for Thanksgiving." She smiled. "I haven't eaten that well since."

Gracie smiled as she poured Marcia a draft. "We enjoyed having you. We'll have to do it again soon."

Marcia shook her head. "No way. It's my turn; I'm going to take you and Hank out for dinner." Hank was Gracie's live-in boyfriend. "Have you been to Bern's lately?" she asked, referring to Tampa's world-renowned steakhouse.

38

Gracie shook her head as she handed Marcia her drink. "We've never been there."

Marcia took a long swallow before responding, savoring the cold relief the beer provided. "Never? How long has it been since you moved here from Boca?"

Gracie thought for a moment. "Has to be twenty years at least."

"Then you're way overdue."

Marcia looked around the bar. It felt good to be back. Before her father's stroke, Kitty Galore's had been a beacon of sanity for her, a refuge where she could escape the demands of her unpredictable father for an hour each weekday, reveling in conversation that rarely veered into batshit crazy territory. She hired two elderly widows from the condo complex to sit with her father each weekday for an hour while she escaped to Kitty's, and even that short, daily exposure to Clement Harkins had each of the ladies threatening to quit on multiple occasions. Now, with that chapter behind her, she looked forward to being able to enjoy life again on her own terms, at her own pace. "What's new here?"

Gracie deftly slid some recently washed wine glasses into an overhead rack before turning back toward Marcia. "Let me think... Morrison and Rheinhart broke up." Steve Morrison and Zach Rheinhart were fellow luncheon regulars at Kitty's who'd also attended what Gracie termed their orphans' Thanksgiving feast last November.

Marcia was confused. "Broke up? I didn't know they were gay."

Gracie laughed heartily. "They're not. They're more like Butch and Sundance. Trail buddies, I guess you could call them."

"What happened?" Marcia asked as she finished off her beer and slid the empty glass toward Gracie, who promptly poured her a fresh one.

"Rheinhart has a girlfriend now, which leaves Morrison the odd man out."

"Who's the lucky girl?"

"Her name is Gwen Westphal. She won a medal at the Olympics in kayaking about twenty years ago. These days she's a scientist working for the Clear Sailing Alliance, a clean water advocacy group. You've probably seen her on TV or read about her in the papers – she pops up whenever red tide appears in the Gulf." Gracie smiled. "It never hurts when your spokesperson is drop-dead gorgeous."

Marcia was struggling to put a face to the name. "How old is she?"

"Hard to say," Gracie replied. "She's one of those women who could be anywhere from thirty to sixty."

"I hate those bastards," Marcia said, a small smile belying her words. "How old is Rheinhart?"

"Late fifties, I think." Gracie indicated a menu. "Interested in lunch today?"

"I am. The new me is planning to drink less and eat better." She scanned the menu Gracie handed to her for a moment before looking up. "Give me a bowl of the gumbo."

"Coming right up."

Marcia reached for her cigarettes and lighter. "I'll be back."

Gracie smiled. "I'll be here."

5

Marcia's phone rang twenty minutes after she returned home from Kitty's. It was Ruliani. "Perfect timing. I just got home."

"Having some fun, I hope," responded Ruliani in her trademark nasal tone.

"I rode my bike down to Kitty Galore's in Ozona for lunch. It's one of our local gems."

"But you live in Dunedin…"

"The northern tip. It's only a ten-minute ride to Ozona from my house, close enough to consider it local." She shifted gears. "I think we should go ahead and have your guy check the bills to see if they're real. Once we know that, we can move ahead."

"I'll call him as soon as we hang up," Ruliani said. "Anything else?"

"Not now, but if I think of something else, I'll let you know."

"Okay. I think my authenticator has a lot of free time these days, so it may not take long to arrange a meeting. Probably sometime this week."

"I'll be ready," Marcia replied.

After she hung up she went into her bedroom and withdrew the three bills from the safe, gingerly placing them on her dining room table. She spent several minutes staring at them, wondering what to do with them. She was already convinced the bills were real – it would've been an extremely complicated task to fabricate counterfeit bills from more than fifty years ago with the identical serial numbers, and her father had never displayed that sort of initiative. He would've needed help from a forger who would have had to be let in on the secret. Knowing her father, she felt certain he wouldn't have taken such a risk. Plus, how on earth would he get his hands on a list of the correct serial numbers without alerting the FBI? The bills had to be real.

She removed a frozen dinner from her freezer, turned on the oven and set the timer. While she waited for her lasagna to cook, she scrolled through the music on her phone, selecting an older Canadian band, Martha and the Muffins. Her father had been born in Northbrook, a small town in eastern Ontario, which had sparked a curiosity about Canada during her early teens that led her to discover the Canadian New Wave music scene. She fell in love with Martha and the Muffins immediately, seduced by the irresistible beat and intelligent, sometime political songwriting, and the fact that the band's leader, Martha Johnson, was a woman. Joan Jett and Chrissie Hynde were the only other women she knew of who fronted bands at that time.

She picked out her favorite album by the group, *Danseparc*, and soon was dancing around the compact condo's living area to the album's title tune, belting out the lyrics she knew by heart as the aroma of lasagna began to fill the room.

When the song ended she checked the timer on the oven. Calculating she had enough time to have a smoke downstairs before her dinner was ready, she grabbed her cigarettes and walked to the elevator. On the way she noticed the stairs and thought back to Ruliani's comment the day before about her being out of breath. Maybe it was time for a cleanse, to cut back on smoking; the price of cigarettes had soared in recent years, offering her the perfect excuse. She'd read all the stories about people who gained weight

42

after quitting, which she'd used to justify continuing the habit when the subject had come up before. Taking the stairs once in a while instead of the elevator, getting some exercise other than riding her bike back and forth to Kitty's, might help keep those added pounds off if she did decide to quit. She wasn't getting any younger, and now that she was released from the burden of babysitting her father, she had choices. Life was getting better.

She hopped into the elevator, promising herself she would take the stairs on the way back.

*****

Ruliani wasted no time calling Ervin Howell, the man she'd selected to authenticate Marcia's cash. Howell was retired from the Bureau of Engraving and Printing in Washington, D.C., where he'd been a quality control supervisor in the production department. Ruliani had met him after he'd retired and moved to Oldsmar, where he fell victim to a particularly slick Internet insurance scam not long after he and his wife had arrived. He had contacted Ruliani, seeking legal assistance, after seeing her billboards around town. She found him rough around the edges, with a steel-gray military haircut and a direct manner she found refreshing. She'd managed to recoup the money he'd been swindled out of and charged him a bargain basement rate, so he owed her. It was time to collect.

"Judy, Judy, Judy," he intoned in a bad Cary Grant imitation, his usual greeting whenever the two spoke. "What a pleasant surprise – what can I do for you today?"

"How have you been, Ervin?" Ruliani asked sweetly. "And how's Martha?"

"Not getting any younger, neither one of us," he answered gruffly. "You call to shoot the breeze, or is there a purpose to this call somewhere?"

Classic Ervin. "You are indeed a man of few words."

"I wish you were," he complained. "The point….?"

"How'd you like to make a little extra cash?"

43

"You got my interest. Go on."

"I have a client who recently bought a furnished house at auction. There was an old bed in one of the bedrooms, and when they went to get rid of it, they found some old cash between the mattress and the box spring."

"How old?"

"Old. The bills are all either Series 1963A or 1969. My client needs someone to verify that the bills are real. They want to sell them, but not until someone determines they're authentic and what they might be worth on the collector's market." She paused. "That's where you come in."

"How many bills we talkin' about here?"

"I'm not at liberty to say, but I have three for you to look at. Shouldn't take you more than a few minutes. We're talking easy money here, Ervin."

"How much?"

"Well, they're pretty eager to move on this, so you're in a good position."

"I'll do it for a grand." Pause. "It'll be more if they want me to look at more bills," he added as an afterthought.

About what she had expected. "Let me contact my client and see what they say. I'll get back to you as soon as I can. What's your schedule look like?"

He snorted. "I'm free any time during the week, but I'd like to be home in time for supper and *Entertainment Tonight*. I just can't get enough of those Kardashian girls."

Ruliani couldn't tell if he was serious or not. "So this week?"

"The sooner the better. Remember, it'll be a grand."

"I'll get back to you. Nice talking to you, Ervin."

"I know." Click.

*****

"A thousand dollars? For three bills?"

Ruliani trotted out the voice of reason. "He's good, he's fast, he's reliable, and he won't talk. I think he's worth it."

"I don't know…"

"As your attorney, I'm advising you to accept the offer," Ruliani said. "You might find someone to do it for less, but I can guarantee you whoever that person is won't be as discreet as Ervin Howell."

"He's reliable?"

"Absolutely. He used to work for the Bureau of Engraving and Printing in D.C. And he's old – bills from back then won't be a challenge for him."

Marcia hesitated. "I wasn't planning on spending that much…."

"Well, you're always free to look for someone else. But remember – you get what you pay for. With my guy, you get one hundred percent reliability." Pause. "Think about it if you'd like. But the clock is ticking…."

There was silence at the other end of the phone as Marcia considered the offer. She had the money and she needed the expertise. After a moment she replied. "Okay. Set it up."

"You're making the right choice," Ruliani said reassuringly. "You'll have your answer by the end of the week. I'll call you as soon as I talk to my guy. Any time this week bad for you?"

"No."

"I'll get back to you as soon as I can."

6

The meeting with Ervin Howell was set for Thursday morning at 10:00. Marcia arrived at 9:15 with the bills to be authenticated and was ushered into a vacant office where Ruliani had set up a laptop with a video monitor so she could watch the meeting remotely. After a few simple instructions on how not to inadvertently interrupt the feed from the conference room, Ruliani left her alone, closing the door behind her on the way out.

Marcia filled the time before Howell arrived by playing Solitaire on her phone. Looking up occasionally to check the laptop, she wondered what Ervin looked like. Ruliani had said only that he was older and a man of few words, which didn't give her much to go on. Once again, she'd hoped she'd made the right decision. If the bills were fake, everything would end today. But if they were real, her next step would be to figure out some way to monetize them without alerting the world to their significance, a task far more difficult in practice than in theory. She was counting on Ruliani to point her in the right direction.

At five minutes before ten, the sound of a door closing brought her attention to the laptop screen. Marcia watched as Ruliani indicated a chair for the man who'd entered the room with her as she settled into one opposite him. Ervin Howell was

46

carrying a briefcase and was dressed casually in a white polo shirt and olive-green cargo shorts, typical Florida retiree attire. Marcia leaned forward as her attorney indicated an array of bottled drinks situated on the end of the table. "If you're thirsty," she said to her guest. "please help yourself."

"I'm good," he said.

Marcia was elated. The sound was crystal clear and the camera angle was sufficiently wide to encompass the entire conference room table. It was almost as if she were in the room with them.

The man opened his briefcase and removed several items, setting them on the table by his side. "Let's see those bills."

Ruliani handed him an unmarked envelope. Before withdrawing the bills from the envelope, Howell put on a pair of latex gloves, then gingerly withdrew the three bills from the envelope, laying them side by side on the table in front of him. He bent down, looking intently at the three bills, then straightened up. "They passed the first test. The serial numbers match the corresponding letter designations for that time period." He looked at Ruliani. "These bills are in excellent shape considering their age. You said they were found under someone's bed?"

"Between the mattress and the box spring."

From his array of equipment, he selected a small ultraviolet light and a device that resembled a thicker than normal monocle. Fitting the ocular device to his right eye, he scanned each of the bills slowly with the ultraviolet light. After a minute, he raised up and removed the device from his eye setting it back inside his briefcase along with the ultraviolet light. He turned back to Ruliani. "These bills are real. Your client is lucky because they're so old – there were only a few safeguards back then against counterfeiters, who didn't have access to the sophisticated color printers in the world today. The colored threads embedded in the bills when they were printed are in place, in the proper sequence. Together with the match between the letters and the serial numbers, I can guarantee you these bills are genuine U.S. currency."

47

Trying to keep her voice neutral, Ruliani spoke. "Any idea how much they might be worth?"

"That's a tougher question," Howell replied. "Depends on the collector, mostly. The bills are worth whatever the buyer is willing to spend for them. They're old, but not really old. If they were from, say, 1890, they would be worth a lot more, especially in this condition."

"But they're worth more than face value?" Ruliani asked.

Howell nodded. "Definitely. But like I said, it all depends on what the buyer is willing to pay. There are all sorts of currency collectors out there, all with their own priorities when it comes to assigning value. If your client isn't in a hurry and has some time to shop around, he'll be able to maximize his return."

Marcia was elated. The bills were genuine, which meant if the serial numbers matched those of the bills given to the hijacker, the mystery would be over. Clement Harkins *was* the real D.B. Cooper and had been all along.

In the conference room, Howell was speaking again. "You have a check for me?"

Ruliani nodded and slid a single sheet of paper across the table to him.

Howell looked at the paper, then looked up with a puzzled look. "This isn't a check."

"You're right, Ervin," Ruliani said. "That's an affidavit of authenticity that you need to sign so my client has proof the bills are genuine when they look for a purchaser. You sign on the bottom left; as a notary, I'll sign on the bottom right, then stamp the document, verifying its veracity. Once that's complete, I have a cashier's check for one thousand dollars, drawn on the law firm account, that has your name on it."

"Gimme a pen."

Ruliani slid a ballpoint across the table. Howell signed the document without reading it, then passed it back to Ruliani, who signed before certifying her signature with her stamp. She slid the document into a manila envelope, withdrawing a check and passing it across to Howell. He glanced at it briefly, noting the amount and the designee, and placed it in his briefcase. He stood up. "Anything else?"

"I don't think so." She stood and extended her hand across the table. "Always a pleasure doing business with you, Ervin."

He took her hand and gave it a firm shake before releasing it. He turned without speaking, heading for the door, calculating how long it would take him to get to his bank in Oldsmar to cash the check as he headed past Madeline's desk on his way toward the elevator. Marcia watched as Ruliani collected her file folder and turned toward the camera to give her a smile and a thumbs up before following Howell out of the conference room.

Ruliani tapped on the office door where Marcia was sequestered, then walked in. Marcia was all smiles as she got to her feet and embraced her attorney in gratitude. Ruliani returned the hug, then gently disengaged, keeping Marcia at arm's length. "One down, one big one to go," Ruliani said. "Getting access to the list of serial numbers we need to confirm that this is Cooper's loot won't be nearly as easy as this was."

Like that, Marcia returned to earth. "Any ideas?"

"A few, but I wasn't going to invest any time in pursuing them until we knew the money was genuine." Pause. "Do you have a moment?"

"You bet."

"Let's go back to my office."

Marcia followed her attorney and settled into the guest chair in her office. "What do you have in mind?"

"There are two ways to go at this," Ruliani stated. "With the knowledge of the FBI or without it. The first one is tricky, because the last thing we want to do is alert the FBI to what we're up to. It doesn't matter that they finally closed the Cooper case in 2016 – if they get even a whiff of our plan, that case will be active again in a nanosecond." She smiled grimly. "After the way the president has been going after the FBI since he was elected, you can bet the Bureau will jump all over a high-profile case like this to boost the spirits of the rank-and-file. So if we decide to go that way, we'll have to be very careful."

"Do you have any connections at the FBI?" Marcia asked hopefully.

Ruliani smiled. "I do. Colton Miller is in charge of the Clearwater office. He and I are both on the Board of Directors of Hearts Across The Bay. Are you familiar with them?"

Marcia nodded. Hearts Across The Bay was a non-profit organization in the Tampa Bay area supporting victims of domestic violence that was run by one of the area's top power couples, Walker and Julia Stevens. The husband and wife team also owned and operated Walker's Jewelers, a sprawling complex on Ulmerton Road in Clearwater whose local television commercials were nearly as prolific as Ruliani's. Because of her personal history with her ex-husband, Marcia had sent the agency a check shortly after she deposited the cash from her father's estate and had received a handwritten note from Julia Stevens thanking Marcia for her contribution that had touched her deeply. "I know them well."

Ruliani continued. "Knowing Colton Miller and pulling the wool over his eyes on something like this are two very different things. Approaching him would require a lot of planning, plus flawless execution."

"You don't sound too optimistic. How about Plan B?"

Ruliani leaned forward, forearms on the desk. "Trying to find the numbers without FBI support has just as many drawbacks, maybe more." Her tone was sobering. "First and foremost would be the absolute necessity of obtaining the numbers without leaving any sort of trail, paper or digital, behind. If that happens and your identity is revealed, your life would be over." She paused to let that sink in, then continued. "In order to prevent that from happening, you'd need to trust the person supplying the numbers. Whoever that person might be, he or she won't be stupid. They'll be able to figure out what's going on with no trouble at all. Which opens you up to the possibility of being blackmailed." Ruliani smiled sheepishly. "No easy choices here."

50

"You make it sound hopeless," Martha said dejectedly.

Ruliani shook her head firmly. "Not hopeless. Extremely difficult, but not hopeless. It will take some time, that's all. Are you willing to wait a bit while I look into it?"

"I guess I don't have much of a choice." She looked at Ruliani, trying to mask her disappointment. "How long will it take?"

Ruliani smiled. "That's one thing I can answer with certainty. It will take as long as it takes."

7

Ruliani smiled as she ended her call with Marcia on that cryptic note. She knew exactly how long it would take to come up with a list of the serial numbers needed to verify that Marcia was in possession of D.B. Cooper's ransom cash: within twenty-four hours of Ruliani being able to contact Headfake.

That was the only name she could apply to this mysterious figure, a hacker of legendary reputation who resided in the amorphous universe of the Dark Web. She didn't even know if Headfake was a man or a woman, although she reasoned the odds were higher that any hacker was a male rather than a female, simply because of her own anecdotal knowledge that more boys grew up drawn to the illicit joy of hacking than girls.

She'd discovered Headfake's existence and unique skills several years ago while working for the wife of a Tampa financial planner who, during their divorce proceeding, accused her husband of skimming cash from several portfolios of his investors to finance his relationship with his mistress, a local exotic dancer with expensive tastes. Somehow Headfake had become aware of the lawsuit – she reasoned through the initial public filing – and had contacted her by using a series of digital dead drops and false

IP addresses that kept his – or her – identity and location undetectable.

What Headfake provided to Ruliani was damning and included a supply of materials relevant to her client's case: multiple examples of video and pictorial evidence of the husband's infidelities, copies of electronic payments and credit card receipts regarding the expenses of the mistress, and copies of salacious text messages the unfaithful husband sent to his mistress from a burner phone the husband thought to be untraceable.

The preponderance of evidence was stunning. It wasn't until after Ruliani had shared the information with her client that she reached out to Headfake via their encrypted messaging service, inquiring as to why he – or she – had reached out to her, unsolicited, to provide such compelling evidence. Headfake's reply was characteristically concise and vague:

Some people deserve to be punished.

She hadn't been in contact with him – or her – since then, but she'd retained his contact info. She looked it up and sent a message:

Need some information. Can you help?

His – or her - reply came swiftly, in under a minute:

Yes. Send details.

She answered back:

Serial numbers for the bills in the ransom paid to D.B. Cooper, 1971.

The response was as swift as the first:

48 hours.

So she waited. Two days later there was a document addressed to her on the encrypted messaging service when she arrived at the office in the morning. She gasped in astonishment when she opened it. Before her was a listing of the serial numbers of the bills handed over to Cooper, on FBI letterhead to ensure the list's authenticity. Her eyes widened as she read the first page,

53

which contained a short statement of authorization from the director of the FBI at the time, J. Edgar Hoover.

Ruliani grinned in triumph. Marcia would be ecstatic when she heard this news. She punched a button on her phone; Madeline answered immediately. "Yes?"

"Get me Marcia Alvarez right away."

"Yes, ma'am." She was back in a moment. "Ms. Alvarez is on Line 2."

"Thanks, Madeline." She transferred the call. "Marcia?"

"Yes?" Her voice sounded tentative, hesitant.

Ruliani wasted no time with small talk. "I have good news. I have the list of serial numbers for the bills used in the ransom payout."

"Already? That was really fast." There was caution in her tone as she continued. "How do you know they're authentic?"

"Two reasons. My source is completely trustworthy." She paused for effect. "Plus, the list is on FBI letterhead, signed by J. Edgar Hoover. It doesn't get any better than that, my dear."

It took Marcia a moment to respond. "Holy shit."

"Indeed. Would you like to come into the office to pick it up?"

Marcia thought for a moment. "I can be there before noon."

"I have to be in court this morning at 11:00, but I'll leave the list with Madeline if you're not here before I leave," Ruliani said. "Is that all right with you?"

"See you then." Ruliani was about to say goodbye when Marcia spoke again. "I can't thank you enough, Ms. Ruliani."

"Sure, you can," Ruliani replied easily. "Just pay my bill."

Marcia stared at the phone in her hand after Ruliani ended the call. She was stunned by the swiftness of Ruliani's efforts on her behalf, but her surprise was blunted by a wave of questions forming in her mind. How on earth had Ruliani gotten her hands on an FBI document so quickly? Had she called in her favor with Colton Miller in Clearwater? If so, was there anything she would have to provide in return? She was uneasy about owing the FBI a favor, if that was the case, although she couldn't think of anything she might have that the feds would want.

The more she thought about it, the less likely it was that Ruliani had approached the FBI for the list. The agency was a hulking bureaucracy – any request going through official channels, especially one as sensitive as this, would take months to approve, if it was approved at all. No, Ruliani hadn't approached the FBI directly. Which meant Ruliani had some other method to access official FBI documents.

She wracked her brain as she showered and dressed. Did Ruliani have an informant in the Bureau, someone who could provide her with classified information in a couple of days? That at least seemed plausible to Marcia, especially given the public scrutiny and criticism aimed at the Bureau since the last presidential election. If you believed the current administration, the FBI leaked more than a bucket without a bottom. Marcia wasn't convinced that was the case, but it was enough to make her wonder.

Ruliani had left for court by the time Marcia arrived at her office in Tampa. Her assistant Madeline greeted her warmly as she got off the elevator, rising to her feet and handing her a manila envelope. "You just missed her," Madeline said. "She left less than five minutes ago. She'll be disappointed she didn't get to see the look on your face when you opened it." She handed Marcia another envelope, this one letter-sized. "She left you a note."

Marcia stared at the envelopes in her hand, heart racing. Should she open them here, or wait until she got home?

Madeline seemed to read her thoughts. "Take them home, put them in a safe place. Ms. Ruliani wants you to call her in the morning."

Marcia nodded numbly, mumbling her thanks as she wheeled and headed for the elevator, clutching the envelopes as if they were her children.

She had to remind herself to stay under the speed limit as she drove back to Dunedin, stereo blasting, win dows down. Mid-day traffic was light; she took solace in the fact that she'd hit most of the lights on her way home, considering it a good omen.

By the time she reached the parking lot at her condo, she could wait no longer. Still in the car, she opened the larger envelope first, scanning the cover page and marveling that she had a document containing the signature of J. Edgar Hoover before moving on to the list. There it was: a bundle of paper several inches thick, each sheet containing three columns of serial numbers. She'd done the math at home before she left, so she knew there were nearly a hundred sheets of numbers to be checked against the bills in the safe deposit box. It would be a daunting task, but she hoped the adrenaline produced as she verified the numbers against the bills would be plentiful enough to negate the boredom factor inherent in such a repetitive task.

She slid the serial numbers back into the envelope, and then checked the other, smaller envelope. Inside was a single sheet of paper, containing a sentence on Ruliani's letterhead that buoyed her spirits even more.

I know what to do next.

8

Marcia was showered, dressed and on her way to the SunTrust branch on Curlew by 8:45 the next morning. She called Ruliani just as she was pulling into the bank parking lot. "I'm at the bank with the list, ready to check the numbers. Are you available later today?"

"I'll have Madeline modify my schedule if necessary to fit you in," Ruliani replied. "Just call when you're on your way. Good luck with the numbers."

"Thanks."

Marcia knew that checking every number would be time consuming, mainly because she feared that the numbers on the list would be in a different sequence than those on the bundled bills. The prospect of having to check nearly ten thousand bills against a list of ten thousand numbers without any correlation between the two was frightening and had kept her awake most of the night.

She was the first person in the bank when the doors were unlocked at 9:30 and was quickly ushered into the vault by a pert young blond who seemed to sense Marcia's impatience and left her alone after a few routine questions.

As soon as the door was closed, Marcia unlocked her safe deposit box, set it down on the floor and pulled out the list of numbers, along with a ruler she'd brought from home to avoid confusion as she sat cross-legged on the floor next to the cash. She was comfortably dressed in a short-sleeved white blouse and a pair of navy blue shorts for the daunting task ahead. She sighed and removed the first bundle of cash from the safe deposit box.

*****

Ruliani knew it would take hours, maybe even a couple of days, for Marcia to manually check all the bills, so she wasn't expecting a visit from her until late afternoon at the earliest. She decided to reach out to Headfake, run something by him – or her – that had occurred to her the previous day, before Marcia had picked up the two envelopes from Ruliani's office. Assuming the bills were real, Marcia would have to decide what to do next. Ruliani had come up with three options while half watching a disturbing reality show called *Wives With Knives* two nights earlier: Marcia could do nothing, and the money would remain in the safe deposit box. Or she could go public with the news and then have to deal with the consequences that sort of revelation would have on her every-day existence. The final option was the one Ruliani favored – find a collector unconcerned with both the legal ramifications attached to being in possession of D.B. Cooper's ransom money and the resultant shitstorm of attention an announcement of that magnitude would release.

The person best suited to find that sort of collector was Headfake, who operated among the veiled, foreboding atmosphere of the Dark Web as easily as the rest of us navigate the aisles in a grocery store. Surely, Ruliani reasoned, there must be a person with enough money and enough layers of anonymity willing to purchase such a momentous prize, despite its notoriety. If anyone knew of such a person, it would be Headfake.

She sent him a message.

You there?

He responded within minutes.

Always.

She shook her head, smiling. No wasted words.

One more job for you. Interested?

He responded.

Depends. Related to other?

Ruliani replied.

Yes. Need discreet buyer for merchandise.

It was nearly a minute before he replied.

DBC merch?

So he'd figured it out.

Yes.

His response was immediate.

Timeline?

She was encouraged.

Irrelevant.

A minute later he responded.

Fee is 10% of sale price, in Bitcoin.

She'd never had a transaction involving Bitcoin, but was sure she could find someone to help her.

Let me check w/ my client.

He signed off.

Later.

Ruliani had no idea how much a purchase like that would cost. At least eight figures, which would be a nice payday for Headfake and would set Marcia up for life. She grabbed a yellow legal pad and began jotting down some notes, questions to raise with Marcia when they next spoke. Her excitement grew as she wrote – the illicit nature of such an undertaking was exhilarating, her endorphins popping as she added to the list.

Her phone buzzed. It was Madeline. "I have Mrs. Sharp on Line 2."

Camille Sharp had been injured in a collision with an armored car and was suing the company for damages. Attorneys for the armored car company had used every trick in their legal playbook to delay the proceedings, but at their last court session, the judge had expressed his frustration at their feet dragging and had ordered a trial date of February 27. "Put her through."

Time to get back to work.

*****

Headfake had guessed what he was dealing with concerning Ruliani's request as soon as she mentioned D.B. Cooper. Although he wasn't alive at the time, Headfake knew an enormous amount of information concerning the legendary hijacker. Among the hacking community Cooper was a god, a modern-day Robin Hood who'd bested the corrupt system that so many of his brethren battled each day. To be involved in the process of ending the mystery of his fate was a dream assignment, one that took his breath away.

Getting behind the FBI firewall had been a breeze, easier than he thought, and he had the list of serial numbers by midnight of the day Ruliani had messaged him. He then hacked into Ruliani's cell phone to discover that her client was Marcia Alvarez, whom he investigated thoroughly. He found that she was a veteran of the U.S. Army who had recently been in contact with Ruliani concerning the estate of her late father, Clement Harkins.

Intuiting that Harkins might be the mysterious Cooper, he switched his attention from daughter to father and dug deep into his military file. He discovered Harkins, Canadian by birth, had joined the U.S. Air Force as the Americans were entering the Korean War, his experience as both a pilot and paratrooper with the Canadian Forces his ticket to the big dance. He had the date of the hijacking in one of the early messages from Ruliani, so he compared it to where Harkins had been stationed at the time.

Bingo. Clement Harkins was stationed at the Mt. Hebo Air Force Base in Oregon at the time that Cooper leaped from the Northwest Orient Airlines' Boeing 727. He checked the distance between Mt. Hebo and Portland, where Cooper's flight originated, and smiled to himself when he discovered it was a two-hour drive. Easily manageable, plus Mt. Hebo wasn't far from the flight path of the second leg of his journey that had originated in Seattle, where Cooper had received the ransom and his requested parachutes.

It all fit. Marcia must've discovered some of the ransom, likely as a result of her father's death, since the correspondence between Alvarez and Ruliani began in earnest shortly after Harkins' death and the reading of his will. Alvarez was his only heir, so it seemed likely she had inherited some of the cash.

Which reminded him – he would need to check with Ruliani to find out exactly how much of the ransom Alvarez wanted to sell. The less of it she retained, the higher the price and the greater his fee. Headfake knew that a small portion of the cash had been discovered, badly decomposed, along the shore of the Columbia River in 1980 by a family on a hike. If Alvarez could prove she had the remainder, there was no telling how high the price might go.

D.B. Cooper. Far out.

9

By the time the bank clerk knocked on the vault door hours later, telling Marcia that the bank was going to close in ten minutes, she'd only managed to confirm eight hundred of the bills as genuine. As she had suspected, they were the real deal, the actual ransom paid to the infamous hijacker, but she was too weary after the exhaustive process to celebrate in any way other than to clamber to her feet, her legs stiff from her extended time on the bank vault floor, replace the safe deposit box and stumble to her car, thanking the clerk who had helped her along the way.

She did the math as she eyed the rush hour traffic in downtown Tampa while she waited to exit the parking lot. She was dismayed - at this rate, it would take her nearly two weeks to verify every bill in the vault.

She needed a drink.

*****

Shortly after ending his session with Ruliani, the hacker known as Headfake wasted little time in reaching out to a subset of the Dark Web known as the CG, or Collectors Group, posting this on a secure bulletin board maintained by the group:

Historic illicit cash for sale. Serious inquiries only.

He attached a secure address for interested parties to respond and then went to see what he had to eat in the refrigerator in his command post.

Let the bidding begin.

*****

Marcia stopped at Publix and purchased a carton of cigarettes, a couple of Lean Cuisine meals and a twelve-pack of Yuengling on her way home. It was dark by the time she pulled into her sheltered parking spot at the condo, lights on, illuminating the entrance. She opted for the stairs instead of the elevator, continuing her recent resolution to do what she could to get into better shape. She was breathing hard when she reached the seventh-floor landing.

She put the beer in the fridge, popped one of the meals into the oven and set the timer before grabbing one of the beers and a pack of cigarettes and her lighter and heading down the stairs again for a smoke, checking the time on her phone so she'd know when she had to return.

She walked around to the rear of the building and leaned against the fence surrounding the swimming pool, gazing at the lights of Clearwater Beach and several boats still on the sound, extending an unseasonably warm winter day. She cracked her beer and took a healthy swallow, then lit a cigarette. She'd considered and rejected just as quickly a phone call to Ruliani, who would be long gone from her office by now. Better to reflect on what to do next and come up with some options before getting in touch with her attorney again.

Ruliani's cryptic message, the one she'd inserted with the list of serial numbers, was intriguing. Marcia wasn't sure what her options were other than sitting on the cash to keep her private life private or coming forward publicly as the daughter of the real D.B. Cooper, which would thrust her into the international media spotlight. Neither of those choices appealed to her, so she was hoping Ruliani's teasing sentence was a viable alternative.

Her mind drifted to her father and the frustration he must've felt when his only living relative, his daughter, refused to believe the secret he'd maintained for nearly fifty years. She felt shame and remorse, especially now that she knew the truth. She had so many questions that could not be answered: why did he do it in the first place? For the sheer thrill of it, or as a method to improve their lives through use of the ransom cash? Had her mother known the truth, or was she as much in the dark about her husband's "mission" as was her daughter? If she was in the dark, why did her father keep the truth from his wife? And how did he manage to keep that large amount of cash hidden from her in their tiny apartment on the base in Mt. Hebo?

Her mind kept returning to the most burning question: did he have help from anyone else in pulling off the daring heist, or was it a solo operation? After reading several books on the hijacking and examining the timeline and the course of the Northwest Orient flight which offered key information indicating the time the hijacker had leaped from the plane, it seemed logical to her that her father's success in evading capture would've been aided by an accomplice on the ground, someone who could've assisted him in escaping from the hostile terrain into which he descended that cold November night.

But if that was the case, who at the base would he have trusted enough with that kind of secret? She could recall no one from those days who her father might've considered his best friend, no one who spent any significant amount of time in the presence of their family. And now there was no one to question on the subject. If that person existed, what had become of them?

She took a last drag on her cigarette and tossed it away in a shower of sparks before heading back toward the entrance to the building, depositing her empty beer bottle in a trash can just inside the main entrance and clambering up the stairs to rescue her dinner, her legs heavy as she ascended them for the second time in less than thirty minutes. She was feeling the burn in both her thighs and her lungs as she reached the seventh floor and entered her condo, reminding her there was much to do to increase her fitness level.

The smell of eggplant parmigiana filled the compact space as Marcia opened a second beer and set the table for one. She found the remote on the couch and turned on the television and watched *Jeopardy* while she ate, frustrated by the evening's categories, none of which she considered to be among her strengths.

When she was finished, she deposited the container for the meal into the trash, rinsed and placed her fork and knife in the dishwasher and moved to the couch, where she picked up the day's edition of the *Tampa Bay Times*. Her father had been a regular subscriber, but their subscription had run out in December. After mulling it over a bit, Marcia decided to renew the subscription, figuring it would be a small reminder of her father's presence moving forward. Besides, she hated the local news on television, which seemed to her to be exclusively stories on murder, lesser crimes and the weather. She could find out about the weather from her phone. She liked the depth and balance of stories in the local newspaper.

She checked the financial section first to see how her stocks were doing, a move that would've gone unconsidered just three months ago. But now she had a portfolio of her own for the first time and she preferred to check it in the paper rather than online. January had been a good month for her so far; she was riding the seductive high of asset appreciation during this extended bull market that had the investment community crowing daily on CNBC. It felt good to be a participant now instead of a spectator, another unintended consequence stemming from her father's death that she spent little time considering.

When she was done with the financial section, she read the first section from front to back, avoiding anything to do with local crime while at the same time being drawn to any story that had a connection to Florida Man or Woman, two genres of usually wacky tales distinctly unique to the Sunshine State and its eccentric citizenry. Her current favorite involved a middle-aged man who walked into a bank in Jacksonville recently wearing only a towel wrapped around his waist, demanding that the bank cash a personal check made out to "Jeff" for a billion dollars, despite the fact that "Jeff" had no identification and appeared to be highly intoxicated. Go big or go home.

When she was finished reading the paper she retired to her bedroom and tried to watch television, but her eyes, weary from checking serial numbers all day, refused to stay open. Within minutes she gave up, turning off the set and drifting off, her last thoughts about the call she planned to make to Ruliani in the morning.

10

Judy Ruliani lived on a quiet cul de sac in a gated community in Safety Harbor. Although she'd had the occasional lover throughout the years, she'd yet to encounter any man or woman – Ruliani batted from both sides of the plate – whose presence and affection were sufficient to overcome her reticence concerning commitment. It was her opinion in both her private and professional life that monogamy was a well-crafted fiction, much like religion, unsustainable in today's complex, speed-of-light society. The thought of sharing her hard-earned assets with another person galled her enough that she was known in local legal circles as the queen of the pre-nup, since that was always her first recommendation to any of her clients who were contemplating marriage.

She spent an hour in her backyard pool every morning, weather permitting, swimming laps and running through a series of aquatic exercises that usually left her feeling exhilarated, pumped with endorphins, possessing a ravenous appetite sated only partially by a breakfast consisting of half a grapefruit and two cups of coffee.

This morning was no different. Freshly showered and dressed in a navy power suit over a white blouse, she scanned the news on her phone as she ate. But her mind kept returning to Marcia Alvarez and the path that lay ahead for her. Ruliani was confident Headfake would be able to find a buyer for the Cooper ransom cash, someone willing to pay top dollar for the discovery of the century in the collectible world. He had an uncanny knack for being able to connect with the least connectable, to forge solutions in the most untenable of circumstances. In the legitimate sales world, he would've been a closer extraordinaire.

Ruliani knew Marcia wanted to offload the entire sum of the ransom in her possession, to be rid of any personal connection to the hijacking. Originally, Ruliani had agreed with her – best be done with it and move forward unencumbered by the burden of tainted history and the real possibility of jail time.

But the more she thought about it, Ruliani was less confident that was Marcia's best move. It might be prudent for Marcia to withhold a small number of bills from the ransom in case she needed another cash influx down the road. Once news circulated on the Dark Web that the Cooper ransom cash had been purchased by a collector, any subsequent knowledge that the bills missing from the first sale would be available for purchase would send the price of those bills sky high. She would sell it to Marcia as an insurance policy, a hedge against the uncertainty of the future.

By the time she reached her office she'd convinced herself that withholding some of the bills would be in her client's best interest. She emerged from the elevator with a wide smile on her face that was noticed immediately by Madeline. "Someone woke up on the right side of the bed this morning."

Ruliani's grin grew wider. "How does a child like you even know about a statement like that?" she said as she collected a series of messages from her administrative assistant. "How old are you, anyway?" she asked jokingly.

Madeline smiled. "I'm twenty-five, but I had a grandfather who was a fountain of knowledge when it came to 20th century axioms. If you hear them often enough, they stick."

Intelligent, attractive and ambitious, Madeline Collins had been a real find for Ruliani. The attorney had met her when

Madeline, a recent graduate of Carnegie Mellon with a degree in sports marketing who'd taken a job with the Tampa Bay Lightning, organized a cocktail party for suite holders at the Lightning arena prior to last season. Ruliani's first impression of the young woman had been sterling – she was poised, articulate and had a terrific sense of humor, moving easily among some of the wealthiest people in the Tampa Bay area as if she'd known them her entire life.

Ruliani observed her closely throughout the event and managed to grab her attention as the get together was breaking up. "Do you have a minute, Madeline?"

She smiled brightly. "Certainly, Ms. Ruliani. What can I do for you?"

Ruliani opened with her trademark bluntness. "Are you happy in your current position?"

Madeline's head swiveled around to see if anyone from the Lightning organization was within earshot. Satisfied, she turned back to Ruliani. "Don't get me wrong – I enjoy working for the Lightning. I've met a lot of really nice people, including most of the other staff."

"But…?"

Her face darkened. "I've been here for two years now, and some of the things they told me when I interviewed for the job weren't consistent with what I found when I got here."

"Such as…?"

"Well, the possibility for promotion, for one. Once I accepted the job and moved down here, my first friend in the organization was another member of the marketing department, Suzanne McCulloch. She was several years older than me, and she pulled me aside one day early on and told me some of the truths about the management." Pause. "She asked if I'd been told that the team was proud of their tradition of promoting from within. I told her that it had been one of their major selling points during my interview. She snorted and told me that wasn't true. What really has happened in the past is that the old boys' club in management –

her words, not mine – has a tendency to hire young women and work them to death, to the point that they leave on their own. Promoting from within was a ploy they used to justify a poverty-level initial wage offer." She shook her head sadly. "I fell for it, but Suzanne was right. Women aren't treated the same way as men here."

Welcome to the real world, honey. "Are you dissatisfied enough to consider a career change?" Ruliani asked.

Madeline seemed taken aback by the query. "I don't know. I haven't really thought about it that much. You see, I really like sports, especially hockey. I played on a woman's team when I was growing up in Pittsburgh. I thought this would be my dream job."

"Sounds to me like you've figured out that it isn't," Ruliani said. "What would it take to lure you away?"

Madeline looked closely at the attorney, sizing her up. "Are you offering me a job? I don't even know what you do for a living."

Ruliani laughed, a full-throated chuckle. "That's a refreshing response. You must not get out very much. Or watch much television."

"I don't. I spend all my time working."

Ruliani reached into her purse and withdrew a business card, which she handed to Madeline, who read it and looked up. "You're an attorney?"

"Not just any attorney, darlin'," she said. "I'm Tampa's billboard lawyer. My face is plastered on billboards all around the Tampa Bay area, and my firm advertises on the sideboards in the arena, right in front of the visiting team's bench."

"I don't know anything about the law," Madeline stammered.

"You don't have to – I already have all the attorneys I need. What I *do* need is a personal assistant, someone whom I can trust. I had to let my last assistant go because she couldn't seem to be able to get herself to work more than three or four days every week."

Ruliani smiled. "Most importantly, you won't have to worry about being exploited by men, because my firm doesn't employ any. It's all women, all the time."

Madeline still seemed hesitant, so Ruliani reached into her purse again, this time for a pen and note pad. She wrote a figure on the top sheet, tore it off and handed it to the young blond. "Would this be enough for you to start?"

Madeline gasped, her mouth agape. She looked at Ruliani in wonder. "That's three times what I make now."

"I figured as much. And that's just the start. All employees, not just the firm's partners, partake in our profit-sharing plan. Each quarter everyone receives a bonus check based on the firm's revenue from the previous quarter. We also have a great health plan which includes vision and dental."

Two days after their initial conversation, Madeline called the number on Ruliani's business card. "If the offer still holds, I'm ready to give the team my two-week notice."

Ruliani smiled to herself, delighted. "Of course it still holds. I'm surprised it took you this long to decide."

"I had to run it by my parents, see what they thought," Madeline explained. "My dad wasn't too pleased – he played college hockey at Clarkson – but my mom was thrilled, especially by the fact that I would be working for women instead of men."

"When can you start?" Ruliani asked, lowering her voice. "I have a temp now who's driving me crazy. I can't get her to put down her damn phone."

Madeline thought for a moment. "How about two weeks from Monday?"

"It's a deal."

Ruliani's initial impression had proven to be correct. Madeline assimilated into her new position without a hitch, absorbing the subtleties of her new job like a seasoned professional. By the end of her first year, she was Ruliani's most trusted confidante.

Ruliani looked up from the messages Madeline had just handed her. "My grandfather's favorite saying was `up, down and around like a fart in a mitt.' Ever hear that one?"

Madeline laughed. "Can't say as I have."

"Well, now that it's out there, you're free to use it any time." She smiled again. "Get me Marcia Alvarez. I have some information she's going to like."

11

Marcia was showered, dressed and having her second cup of coffee when Ruliani called. "Hi, Judy."

"Are you busy?"

"I'm just about to leave for the bank and another long day of matching serial numbers to twenty-dollar bills. Wanna help me out?"

"I'm glad I caught you in time," Ruliani said. "How'd you like to cancel that trip?"

"Why?"

"I heard from Headfake. He says he'll put together a program for prospective buyers to verify the numbers themselves. He thought they'd prefer that, given the high stakes involved. No offense to your integrity."

"None taken," replied Marcia, grateful not to have to spend another couple of days sprawled on the floor of a bank vault. "That'll save me a week of boring-ass work."

"He's also putting together a short list of potential bidders."

Marcia was dumbfounded. "How did he ____?"

"Know?" Ruliani interrupted. "He's a smart guy – he figured it out as soon as I mentioned D.B. Cooper. Why else would someone need his services to check those particular numbers?" Pause. "To sell them."

"He can't be *that* smart," Marcia declared.

"Why not?"

"If he was, he wouldn't have picked a lame-ass name for himself like Headfake."

*****

Freed from her need to go to the bank, Marcia finished her coffee, grabbed her cigarettes changed into shorts, a long-sleeved cotton T-shirt and sneakers and headed for the stairwell. It was a beautiful morning, seamless blue overhead and a gentle breeze from the west. Perfect for a walk along the causeway out to Honeymoon Island.

Traffic was light on the causeway as she exited the condo grounds and headed west. The sun felt warm on her neck as she walked purposefully, conscious of maintaining a steady pace, her spirits on the rise. She'd been dreading the days ahead and the mind-numbing monotony of matching serial numbers in a darkened vault. Now she was outside, breathing in the intoxicating, salty air of the Gulf of Mexico.

She waved to Omar, one of the causeway regulars who rented a fleet of paddleboards, kayaks and flotation devices from a small patch of sand along the road's shoulder. Omar, a good-natured, dreadlocked native of Ocho Rios, was talking to a young man on a bike who looked familiar to Marcia as she walked by. Omar interrupted their conversation to flash her a wide smile and wave back. "Good to see you, Mar-see-a," he called out in his cheery Jamaican accent. "Don't be a stranger, hear me?"

"I won't, Omar." She was trying to place where she'd seen this young man before. He was average height, thin, in his twenties, with dark hair and piercing dark eyes that seemed to warn her against further conversation. The bar at Kitty Galore's kept coming to mind as she continued on her way to the state park.

She walked all the way to the entrance to the park itself, where a man in a khaki shirt and shorts, wearing a ballcap with the state parks' insignia on it, stood outside a small roadside hut, handing out parking stickers to a line of cars in exchange for a parking fee. He smiled when he saw Marcia approach. "Two dollars for pedestrians, Marcia," he said, smiling. "I got change if you need it."

She smiled. This was their usual routine. "Just passing by today, Floyd. Save that change for a real customer."

Floyd handed two singles back to a man in a blue minivan sporting Minnesota plates and waved him on before responding. "You're nothin' but a tease, Marcia. When you gonna loosen up and stay awhile?" he said as the next car pulled forward.

She wiped a band of sweat from her forehead. "One of these days, Floyd. One of these days."

He faked a pout. "That's what you always say."

"At least I'm consistent." Before she turned around to head back, she added. "See ya later, Floyd."

"You, too, Marcia."

The breeze was at her back as she retraced her steps back toward the condo. It was two miles from the door of her condo complex to Floyd's toll booth at the entrance to the park, a round trip of four miles. Today she was determined to navigate the entire trip without a cigarette break; she was halfway there.

She idly scanned the license plates as she headed home, mentally tallying the different states as she did each time she walked to the park and back. Her concentration on that task was disrupted by seeing a car with Oregon plates, which reminded her of her looming decision of what to do with the proceeds from the sale of the ransom cash. It was too soon to tell how Arthur Glennie, the broker she'd selected to handle her new inheritance, was performing with his stock recommendations – it had been less than two months since her father had died, less than a month since she'd handed the wealth management keys for her rainy-day, nest-egg fund to the smooth-talking Glennie. Ruliani had recommended

Glennie as a man built for the long haul. "He's not one of those guys who's going trade, trade, trade to pump up his commissions," she'd explained to Marcia last month, just before Marcia had hired him. "You can trust him."

She'd been toying with another idea, something that had nothing to do with the stock market, poking around a bit, doing some research on a couple of things that interested her. Now that she was free from the responsibility of taking care of her father, she'd need something else, some other sort of activity to fill her days and nights. She knew if she didn't find something useful to do, she'd likely end up spending too much time down the road in Ozona at Kitty's. It wasn't that that option was unattractive to her; it was that it was too tempting, too easy - older woman, suddenly alone, turns to the bottle for companionship. An old story that rarely has a happy ending.

She had something completely different in mind.

2006

12

If it hadn't been for Hurricane Katrina, Lucien Devereaux would likely never have left his home in New Orleans, and his life would've continued on its comfortable yet unremarkable path until, sometime down the road, illness, violence or old age finished him off. But like so many others in that city, his modest shotgun house on North Galvez Street in the Seventh Ward was destroyed by flood waters in August of 2005, forever altering his destiny.

All he'd managed to grab before the river rose, engulfing both floors of the house and half the attic, were his three guitars and a backpack stuffed with clothes and his battered address book. All his music, albums, CDs and some old reel-to-reel tapes had been left behind in his haste to depart. He'd spent several tense days sleeping on the concrete floor of the Superdome before he was transported by bus to Houston, where he spent the next three months at the studio apartment of fellow musician Landon Farrell, sleeping on his couch.

When he finally returned to the Seventh Ward in December, the destruction he witnessed was heartbreaking. The first floor of his house was ankle deep in mud, the walls were covered in black mold, and the smell of death lingered in the humid air as he surveyed the damage. Within minutes he realized that there was nothing left for him to salvage, nothing to retain, so he left through the front door, closing it behind him for the last time, and walked down Esplanade to Liuzza's, by the fairgrounds, where he ordered a daiquiri and sat at one of the outdoor tables, contemplating his next move. He'd been born in Lafitte, in Jefferson Parish, and had lived his entire life in Louisiana, never contemplating a move. Until now.

His old neighborhood would take years to recover, even if the recovery process wasn't infected by the motives of the usual suspects, the politicians, grifters and scam artists intent on capitalizing on the misery and the hopelessness of those who had managed to survive the wrath of the storm. There wasn't a single house on either side of North Galvez that showed any sign of repair; only a few had chain link fences erected around the perimeter of their lot to try to prevent the incursion of looters. It was the most disheartening scene Devereaux had ever witnessed, and it left him feeling anxious and adrift, worried about his future and the future of his adopted city. Normal was light years away.

Earlier, while still in Houston, he'd anticipated that he probably wouldn't be returning to live in New Orleans very soon, if at all, so he'd begun to weigh his options. He was a musician, a guitar player, and in order to survive, he needed to be someplace where he could play music. He reached out to several of his closest musician friends, sounding them out about his situation. Most were sympathetic to Devereaux's plight but unwilling to extend the sort of helping hand he desperately needed, their voices filled with regret as they apologetically stated their positions and the reasons behind them.

After several futile attempts to find a new landing spot, Devereaux called Monroe Jessup in Nashville. He'd met Jessup, a native of Niagara Falls, forty years earlier through Blake Garrison, a guitar player and songwriter from the same area of western New York who'd been a member of a band called The Pharaohs that Devereaux had played with for a year during the 1970s. Garrison had been impressed by Jessup's singing and playing while a member of New River, an acoustic trio with a Jackson Browne/Eagles vibe that had attained modest regional success in western New York during that same time period. Buoyed by that success, Jessup left the area when New River disintegrated over creative differences, heading for Nashville, where he'd carved out a successful career as a songwriter and in-demand session player. They'd stayed in touch over the years, exchanging cards during the holiday season.

When Devereaux explained his situation to Jessup on that initial phone call from Liuzza's, the Nashville resident didn't hesitate. "You can come and stay with me for as long as you like, Lucien. I live alone, so there's plenty of room here as long as you don't mind dogs – I got three of 'em."

"Are you sure this won't be puttin' you out at all?" Devereaux asked, ever the pessimist.

"Nonsense," Jessup replied in a firm tone. "I look forward to playing with you. We should be able to get you some gigs, no problem."

Devereaux's sense of relief was immense. "I don't know how I'll be able to repay you…"

"Don't worry about that – just get your Louisiana ass up to Nashville. We can figure the other parts out later." Jessup paused as another thought occurred to him. "You need any money to get here?"

"I don't think so," Devereaux replied. "I got a friend here in town who is a dispatcher for a major southern trucking firm. If he's still in business, he should be able to hook me up with a ride to Tennessee."

"Well, you let me know if that doesn't pan out. I can front you some cash if you need some."

"I don't know how to thank you, Monroe…."

"I do. You can cook me some of your jambalaya and gumbo while you're here. Nobody in Nashville makes them like you bayou boys do."

"You got a deal."

Lucien was able to contact Lowell Joy, his dispatcher friend, later that day. When Lucien told him of his need to get to Nashville, Joy's voice oozed disbelief. "Y'all are leavin' New Orleans? Your house must've taken some hit – you just gonna walk away from it?"

"I didn't have no insurance, Lowell. My policy lapsed about a year ago when I was goin' through a rough patch. I never bothered to start up the premiums again when things turned around. You gonna be able to help me out here?"

"That's too bad about your house," Joy said. He thumbed through his traffic schedule. "I got a truckload of frozen shrimp and crawfish headin' out of here in the mornin'. You remember where our terminal is?"

"Over in Metairie, just off Causeway Boulevard?"

"That's it. My boy's scheduled to leave at six am. Where you stayin' tonight?"

Good question. Few of the hotels were back in business yet. Even if he did have the money. "Over here, by the fairgrounds," he lied. "I'll get a cab over early tomorrow mornin'."

"Don't be late," Joy warned.

"I won't"

When the call ended, Lucien checked his wallet. After paying for his daiquiri he'd have seventeen dollars left. A cab was out of the question, so he paid his bill, gathered his belongings and set out on foot to Metairie, six miles to the west. With luck he'd be able to get there before dark and find some place in an alley or doorway near the terminal where he could close his eyes for an hour or two without fearing for his life. Despite his bleak circumstances, there was a spring to his step as he navigated the post-apocalyptic landscape, heading for Metairie as he crossed town, a smile emerging on his face.

He was headed to Music City. He was on his way back.

*****

Monroe Jessup was at the freight terminal in downtown Nashville to meet Devereaux when the truck he was riding in pulled in late the following afternoon. He eyed Devereaux's guitars and backpack for a moment before asking, "That's it?" Devereaux nodded, embarrassed.

They were in Jessup's Subaru, on the way to his house, when he spoke again. "How bad was it?"

"Worse than you can imagine, worse than what you saw on TV," Devereaux said, staring straight ahead through the windshield. "It won't never get back to where it was before. Too many crooked politicians, too many shady construction companies, too much damage, too many lives destroyed. By the time they're done fleecin' the flock, what's left of 'em, New Orleans'll be on life support, if it hasn't already been killed."

Like most of America, Jessup had been drawn to the unfolding tragedy like a moth to a flame, unable to look away from scene after scene of devastated neighborhoods and the people who had somehow survived and were waiting in the brutal heat and humidity to be transported to higher, drier ground, the desperation on their faces gut-wrenching.

"How was Houston?"

Devereaux turned to look at Jessup. "I fuckin' hate Houston. You couldn't get me back there again if you had the winning Powerball jackpot ticket waitin' for me. Nothin' there except freeways goin' nowhere and roughnecks in pickup trucks. And the damn humidity is worse than New Orleans in the dead of summer." He shook his head. "If there's a hell on earth, Houston is it."

Jessup turned on the stereo as a way of changing the subject, inserting a CD he withdrew from a pile between the two front seats. "Ever hear of Dr. Dog?" he asked.

Devereaux shook his head. Jessup continued. "They're out of Philly. This is their second album, *Easy Beat*. It came out last March. Really talented guys."

Devereaux leaned back and closed his eyes. He usually listened to music with his eyes closed – it eliminated distractions and helped him concentrate on the structure and tempo of the songs. Like most musicians, Devereaux was always on the lookout for things he could steal, incorporate into his own playing. Nothing big – just a phrase or a chord progression that stood out. He liked the sound of these guys – very roots-based, Americana music, with interesting guitar interplay and intelligent lyrics. "How'd you find out about these guys?"

"I saw them on their first tour, supporting this album, at Vanderbilt. They opened for Dave Matthews. I thought they were better than DMB."

Rush hour traffic was thick as Jessup drove from the terminal to his house in Sylvan Park, on the city's west side, near the McCabe Park Community Center. Jessup's house was on a shade-lined street, with an open front yard and a backyard enclosed within a chain link fence where, he told Devereaux, his dogs spent most of their time.

Jessup pulled into the driveway and helped Devereaux carry his guitars inside, directing him to a pull-out sofa in the loft area over the family room. His tone was apologetic. "I use the spare bedroom as my studio. You can store your guitars in there if you like, or you can keep them here with you. Your choice."

The dogs, hearing the car doors close, were barking in the backyard, demanding attention. Devereaux turned to Jessup. "What kind of dogs are they?"

"All mutts, all of them rescues." He smiled sheepishly. "It used to get lonely here, just me and my guitars, so I decided to get a dog from a local shelter for a little company. Next thing I knew, I had three and my dogfood bill was going through the roof." He looked at Devereaux. "You a pet person?"

Devereaux had spent most of his adult life on tour, which made owning pets problematic. "I used to have a dog when I was a kid, back in Lafitte, but since I spend most of my time now on the road and the rest of it in a studio, pets don't work out too well." He added ruefully. "At least I used to spend my time on the road. This here is a whole new ball game for me. New town, new players. I'm startin' from scratch again."

"You're in the right place," Jessup says, grinning. "There's only two things that we have more of than musicians here in Nashville."

"What's that?"

"Waiters and waitresses who want to be musicians."

*****

Within four months Devereaux had saved enough money to get a small apartment of his own in the downtown area, thanks to a six-week touring gig of the Midwest he'd landed working with John Hiatt, who was promoting his latest album *Master of Disaster* and wanted an extra guitar to expand the sound on stage. He still didn't have a car, so Jessup helped him move, remarking on the amount of possessions he'd acquired in such a short time. "A lot different than the three guitars and a backpack you had when you got here."

Devereaux grinned. "Funny how that goes, ain't it?"

With his newfound wealth, however, came an age-old problem, one that had haunted him since his early days in the studio in New Orleans with The Meters: heroin. It had destroyed his marriages – all three of them. In the wake of Katrina he'd gone cold turkey and had managed to get clean, mainly because the supply and his funds had both evaporated at the same time. But as soon as he cashed the checks from John Hiatt, he found a dealer in Nashville as easily as a tourist looking for a liquor store.

Jessup noticed the change immediately. The two met for dinner at the Bluebird Cafe two weeks after the Hiatt tour ended and Jessup, who'd arrived first, waved to Devereaux as he entered and watched in dismay as his friend had difficulty navigating the narrow aisles between the tables before almost losing his balance and falling as he tried to settle into a chair. He flashed Jessup a lopsided grin, trying to laugh it off. "That was close."

Jessup wasn't smiling. "Are you feeling okay, Lucien?"

"Fanfuckingtastic, Monroe," he slurred, eyes barely open. "Never better."

They made it through the meal, but drifted apart after that, Jessup concentrating on his songwriting and session work, slowly erasing thoughts of Lucien Devereaux from his mind until it was as if he'd vanished without a trace. Jessup had a strict policy when it came to drugs and associating with those involved with drugs – he was a recovering alcoholic, thirty years sober, and he knew there was no place in his world for a junkie. No friendship, no matter how lengthy and treasured, was worth risking his hard-earned sobriety. From this point on, Lucien Devereaux would be the invisible man as far as Jessup was concerned.

13

As the word spread throughout the tightknit Nashville music community that Lucien Devereaux had once again embraced one of his old demons, a career that seemed to be back on track after the Hiatt tour nosedived into the gutter. After several disastrous studio sessions where he lost his place on several occasions and two where he failed to show up at all, the phone stopped ringing, the comeback halted.

Jessup phoned Blake Garrison in Muscle Shoals after hearing about the no-shows to share his concern about their mutual friend. "Remember the old Lucien, the guy who was either the greatest guitarist you'd ever heard or a mumbling, stumbling junkie who couldn't seem to hit the right note two times in a row? The second one's back, and I don't know what to do to help him."

Garrison, who was aware of Jessup's battle with sobriety, was sympathetic. "Nothing you can do, Monroe. You know the drill – you can't help someone who doesn't want to help themselves."

"Yeah, I know, but I was wondering if we both got together, both worked on him, we might be able to get him into that facility up in Pennsylvania, the one near Reading that Aerosmith supports."

Garrison was doubtful. "I don't know. He'd be a good fit, no question about that, but it's pretty hard to get in there on short notice. Plus, he's got to want to go. Have you mentioned anything to him about this?"

"No," Jessup admitted. "I've been steering clear of him since our last meeting at the Bluebird, but it's common knowledge all over town that he's getting worse. It's only a matter of time before something really bad happens."

"How about his family?" Garrison asked. "Doesn't he have a daughter somewhere who can help him out?"

"She's in Biloxi, with her mom. She doesn't want a thing to do with him, mainly because of his addiction issues. I made some calls, found out her number and called her yesterday; she hung up on me as soon as I mentioned Lucien's name."

"Do you have Lucien's number?"

"Yes."

"Send it to me. I'll see what I can do."

"Thanks, Blake."

"Don't thank me yet."

*****

Garrison made some calls to Pennsylvania and around the country during the next two days, then called Jessup back. "I called in some markers, and they said they would save a room for Lucien. They'll take him as soon as we can get him there."

"What about the cost?" Jessup asked. He knew this facility was known as the rehab facility of the stars and charged accordingly.

"Money won't be an issue," Garrison stated firmly. "You just worry about getting him to agree to go."

"I'll do my best."

As soon as his call with Garrison ended, Jessup dialed Lucien's number. After several rings, he heard a recorded message say that the number he had dialed was no longer in service. Jessup hung up, dismayed. It was the scenario he feared the most – that Lucien, in the throes of addiction, would stop paying his bills and lose his phone service.

After letting the dogs out into the backyard with a fresh dish of water, Jessup drove over to Lucien's apartment building, a rundown four-plex in East Nashville on the other side of the Cumberland River, a low-slung beige brick building sandwiched between a bail bondsman and a nail salon.

Jessup parked on the street. Outside the building's entrance, four doorbells were arranged vertically, with the tenant names directly opposite. Jessup shook his head, dismayed. Lucien's name had been covered with a strip of electrical tape. Not a good sign, Jessup thought. He tried each of the doorbells and waited after a moment a woman's voice came over the intercom. "Who is it?"

"My name is Monroe Jessup, ma'am. I'm looking for Lucien Devereaux in number 3."

The disembodied voice turned sour. "The gi-tar player? He don't live here no more."

"Do you know when he moved out?"

"Been gone a coupla weeks now. Wadda you want him for?"

Jessup ignored her question. "Do you know where he went?"

"Hell, no, and I don't want to," she answered succinctly. After a moment she spoke again. "He done something wrong?"

"No, ma'am. I'm a friend of his. Just checkin' in."

"Well, sonny, you ain't that good a friend if you don't know where he is, are ya?" The line went dead.

Lucien Devereaux was in the wind.

*****

89

Two weeks earlier, down to one guitar after he pawned the other two to buy drugs, Lucien Devereaux used the last of his cash to purchase a bus ticket to Biloxi. On the way south he slept intermittently, his constant shivering a symptom of withdrawal. Ten days since his last fix, close as he could recall; he hugged his guitar, trying to generate some heat, as he stared out the window as the bus rolled down I-65 toward Mississippi, hoping that somehow he'd be able to find his daughter Hazel. Without an address, he knew his best bet would be to try the casinos – they were the most likely places to attract Hazel Devereaux or her mother, Lily Verlaine.

Lily, especially. As far as Lucien knew, she'd never worked an honest day in her life. She'd been seventeen when they met; he was touring with Dr. John and she'd been a dirt-poor local groupie, hanging around the tour bus as soon as it pulled into Biloxi, hoping to seduce some rock star into taking her away from her shithole existence forever. Devereaux had noticed her perky tits and promising smile as soon as he descended the steps of the bus and invited her to the show that night as his guest.

After the show he hailed a cab for the two of them and directed the driver to take them to the nearest motel. As soon as they were inside Lily hopped onto the queen-sized bed with the remote in her hand, scanning the channels until she found what she was looking for: one of the nostalgia cable networks that featured television shows from the sixties.

Satisfied, she ripped of her top to reveal a beautiful pair of breasts, with erect, brown nipples that were as big as pencil erasers. She tilted her head to the side, hands on hips, and purred seductively. "What are you waitin' for, big boy?"

Lucien wasted no time shedding his clothes and hopped onto the bed beside her. He knew she looked young, but they were in Mississippi – girls were married as young as twelve down here. Any hesitancy about the possibility of her underage status had been overcome by the urgency between his legs. After a few hungry embraces, hands roaming as if their liaison was approaching a time limit, she positioned herself on her hands and knees, facing the television so she could watch, and instructed Lucien that she wanted to do it doggy style. "Make it hurt, rock star. Fill me up," she demanded.

Lucien did what he was told, slamming her from behind as she thrust her hips back against him, seeking more depth, more penetration. While her body responded perfectly to his pounding, her eyes never left the screen, avidly watching the show. Lucien managed to catch enough of the program through passion-shrouded eyes to recognize it was *Hazel*, an old sitcom about a domestic worker who ran the home of her corporate attorney employer with steel-eyed resolve.

Lucien's first climax occurred rather quickly, but after sharing a cigarette and a few swigs of Jim Beam, they resumed their lovemaking. This time it was more deliberate, because Lucien turned off the television over Lily's protests. "Sorry, babe, but we're doing it my way this time," he said as he tossed the remote beneath the bed.

They both came a second time and then drifted off to sleep. Lucien bought her breakfast the following morning, then slipped her two twenties as he paid the bill. "Cab fare, darlin'"

She looked at him, alarmed. "Where you goin'?"

He stood up, smiling. "We got a show tonight in Mobile. I gotta find a ride over there, 'cause the tour bus already left."

"But what about us?" she pouted.

He bent down to kiss her. "You're fantastic, darlin'. The next time you're in New Orleans, look me up."

She stared at him forlornly. "But what's your name?" The compulsion of their desire the previous evening had precluded introductions.

"Lucien. Lucien Devereaux, the best damn guitar player you ever heard of."

"I'm Lily. Lily Verlaine."

"Pleased to make your acquaintance, Lily."

And that was that. Their paths didn't cross for several years; Lily didn't go to New Orleans, and Lucien never considered returning to Biloxi. Since his one-night stand with her, there'd been so many other females eager to bed a rock star that he barely recalled the incident.

But Lily had a pressing need to track him down, which she did through the New Orleans' chapter of the musicians' union. Three years had passed from their night together when she finally reached him on the phone. "Lucien Devereaux?" she offered timidly when he answered the phone.

Immediately wary, he responded cautiously. "Who wants to know?"

"My name's Lily Verlaine, From Biloxi, three years ago."

Lucien searched his memory, but came up blank. "You'll have to do better than that. How do I know you from Biloxi?"

"Well, you fucked my brains out back then, after a Dr. John concert. Remember?"

If she was after money, this would be a short conversation. His voice turned syrupy sweet. "Of course I remember. How are you, darlin'? What can I do for you?"

"You can send me a check, that's what you can do. A big one."

"Why would I want to do that?"

"To help me raise our daughter. She just turned two a month ago, and that girl has some appetite."

Lucien was stunned, but recovered quickly. "I don't believe you," he stated flatly.

"Believe me, motherfucker," she snarled. "Her name is Hazel Devereaux, and you're her daddy."

"How do you know I'm the father?" His voice was defiant, unbelieving.

"I ain't that smart, but I did the math," she replied. "You were the second man I ever slept with. The first one was Darby

Tuttle, when I was fifteen. I was seventeen when we spent the night in that motel after the concert. I didn't sleep with anyone else after that night until the next year, and Hazel came along nine months after we met. Simple math, even for me." Pause. "Besides, your name is on her birth certificate. That's why she's named Devereaux instead of Verlaine."

Cornered, with no good way out, he took the coward's path – he hung up. He didn't answer the barrage of calls that followed for the rest of that day and into the night, and first thing the next morning he went down to the local Bell office and changed his phone number. He was very careful with whom he shared his new number, but it was some time before this nagging thought left his head.

He was a father.

*****

Lucien tried to remember how long it had been since he'd thought about his only child as the bus pulled into the Biloxi station. He slipped his backpack on, grabbed his guitar and descended the steps into the sultry heat of Mississippi in June. He walked into the terminal, his eyes struggling to adjust to the indoor lighting, looking for the chamber of commerce rack that adorned every transportation center. It took him a moment to find it, but it was in the lobby, next to the Coke machine. He was thirsty. He searched his pockets for change, but all he had was two pennies and a nickel. Disappointed, he shifted his attention to the rack of brochures hailing the attractions of Biloxi. He went through them methodically, picking out the eight casino pamphlets and carrying them over to an unpadded wooden bench, where he read them, one by one, looking for a clue he knew wasn't there.

How to find Hazel Devereaux.

14

Down to his last few dollars when he arrived in Biloxi, Lucien needed money fast. He realized his best option was music, so he found a spot close to one of the casinos but not so close that management would run him off and started busking, using a New Orleans Saints cap as his collection plate. He worked from dawn to midnight for three days straight, with little sleep, until he'd collected enough bills and change to afford a room in a downtown rooming house, formerly a majestic, three-story private home that now catered to transients and other down-on-their-luck folks.

The first night in his spartan room, he slept from midnight until five the following afternoon. Refreshed, he waited patiently until the shared bathroom was free and, once the door was locked, treated himself to a musician's bath – he filled the sink in the bathroom with tepid water and washed his face, under his arms and his crotch, drying himself with the shirt he'd worn the day before and putting on the cleanest clothes he had in his backpack before setting off in the direction of the casinos that stretched along the waterfront. Because he didn't trust the flimsy lock on the door to his room, he took his guitar and backpack with him, leaving his makeshift towel on the windowsill to dry.

He covered four casinos that first night, using the charm he'd developed on stage to get a few moments alone with floor managers and head cashiers, but none of them knew or had heard of Hazel Devereaux or Lily Verlaine. Disappointed and exhausted, he returned to the rooming house, collapsing on the bed fully clothed, asleep within minutes.

The next morning he was up with the sun, tired after only five hours sleep but determined to resume the search. He walked down to the waterfront again and played his guitar in front of one of the casinos until mid-afternoon, when he collected his money and continued his quest to locate his daughter. The first two casinos were washouts. By the time he arrived at the next casino on his list, he was famished, so he used some of his busking cash on the casino buffet, taking full advantage of their unlimited refill policy, filling himself with fried chicken and boiled shrimp, the first decent meal he'd had in over a week.

When he was done eating, he sought out the floor manager, an attractive thick-waisted brunette in her fifties whose name tag identified her as Daisy Stroud. She was walking toward him down the aisle between to endless rows of slot machines, observing the action, when Lucien stepped into her path. "Excuse me?"

"How can I help you, sir?" she said, a hospitality industry smile dominating her olive features while she continued to scan the slots.

"I'm looking for someone who works here or may have worked here at one time," Lucien said. "A woman named Lily Verlaine."

The floor manager's head snapped around. She looked at him intently. "Did you say Lily Verlaine?"

"Yes, ma'am, I did. Do you know her?"

The floor manager glanced at her watch. "I'm due for a break. Why don't we move into the lounge where it's a bit quieter?"

"I'll follow you."

A moment later they were seated in a booth in the otherwise deserted lounge. Behind the bar a lone bartender was washing glasses as the floor manager addressed Lucien in a reserved tone. "How do you know Lily Verlaine?"

"I met her back in '85, here in Biloxi." He indicated his guitar. "I'm a musician, and I was touring with Mac, er, Dr. John. I met her before the sound check and invited her to the show that night. She watched the show, and then we spent some time together before I left the next morning for Mobile." He looked at her earnestly. "I'd truly appreciate it if you could help me find her."

She studied him for a moment before speaking. He was about the right age. "What's your name?"

"Lucien Devereaux, ma'am."

She struggled to keep her emotions in check. So this was the deadbeat, the hit-and-run artist. She extended her hand across the table. "I'm Daisy Stroud," she said evenly.

Lucien took her hand and shook it firmly. "Pleased to meet you, ma'am. Do you know Lily?"

She withdrew a cigarette from her purse and lit it, turning her head to exhale. "We grew up together. She was my best friend back then." She pointed to her nametag. "They called us the flower girls. Lily and Daisy." Her eyes narrowed. "She told me a lot about you, Mr. Devereaux."

The elation he'd felt at finding someone who knew Lily evaporated as he evaluated her last sentence. Tentatively, in a small voice, he replied. "Somethin' good, I hope."

The smile vanished from her face. "Not hardly, Mr. Devereaux. I'd wager I never heard her say a kind thing about you, ever. Course, she had plenty of reasons to feel that way, didn't she?"

He tried to deflect the displeasure he viewed on her face. "Please call me Lucien."

"I think I'll stick with Mr. Devereaux. Why do you want to see Lily now, after all these years?"

"Actually, I was hoping to find her daughter." He looked at her hopefully. "Do you know her?"

"Hazel?"

"Yes."

"Why do you want to see her?" Her voice had a sharp edge now as she filled her lungs with smoke, this time not bothering to exhale in the other direction.

Lucien looked away for a moment, then shifted his gaze back. He took a deep breath. "Because she's my daughter."

"Aren't you a little late to come calling?" she asked angrily. "It's been, what, thirty-some years? Nobody's seen your sorry ass or heard boo from you since you left Biloxi that morning. Not even when Lily tracked you down in New Orleans to tell you the news." She stubbed out her cigarette. "She told me you were a deadbeat asshole motherfucker." She leaned forward. "Was she wrong?"

Lucien dropped his head. When he finally spoke he sounded like an apologetic child, full of contrition. "No, ma'am."

"There you go. We finally agree on something." Daisy looked at her watch. "I have to get back out on the floor, Mr. Devereaux. Please excuse me."

As she began to rise, he reached out, grabbing her arm and then releasing it just as quickly when he saw her reaction. "Please, Ms. Stroud, can you tell me where I can find my daughter?"

"What about Lily? Do you care what happened to her? Or are you just thinking about yourself, like the deadbeat asshole motherfucker you are?"

"Well, sure, yeah, I'd like to see her, too," he responded lamely.

"Too late for that," she spat out. "Lily's dead."

He slumped back in the booth, flattened by the news. When he spoke again he asked softly. "What happened?"

"Lily was my best friend – I loved her like she was my own sister, but she had godawful taste in men." Pause. "Like you, fer instance. She never could find a decent guy, one who loved her and treated her with respect. Someone to help raise that little girl of hers. Anyway, she hooked up with a long string of losers that she met in the bars and restaurants around town where she worked. The last of those losers was a piece of shit named Lyle Fremont. He was a union carpenter, employed by one of the casinos, I think. He had a gambling problem and also had trouble holding his liquor, and whenever he lost, which was a lot, he used to take it out on Lily with his fists. I begged her to leave him about a hundred times, but she wouldn't listen. Finally, after he'd lost a shitload of money on the Super Bowl, he lost it completely. He took it out on Lily, beat her to death in her own living room." She wiped a tear from her eye. "That was four years ago. Fremont's spending the rest of his days in the penitentiary over in Leakesville. Lily's in the Gate of Heaven Cemetery here in town." She gave him one final jab. "If you want to visit, I can give you directions."

Lucien's voice was barely a whisper. "I'm sorry to hear that. I truly am."

"You're sorry, all right." She adjusted her blazer and checked her watch again. "I've got to get back to work, Mr. Devereaux. I wish I could say it's been a pleasure, but I'd be lyin'."

"Ms. Stroud?"

"Yes?" she said impatiently.

"What happened to Hazel?"

"She stayed around for a few years, tryin' to hold things together, but there were too many bad memories for her in Biloxi. She left last December, just before Christmas." She looked at him defiantly, still bristling. "So you're too late all around, Mr. Devereaux. Seems like I detect a pattern here." She began to leave the booth, heading back to the casino floor.

Lucien followed her, tugging at her shoulder gently as the bartender, tuned in to the drama now, watched carefully. "Ms. Stroud?"

"What?" she barked, her patience gone.

"Do you know where Hazel is now?"

Daisy Stroud turned to face him for the last time. She wanted to remember what he looked like so she could describe him to her friend the next time she visited Lily's grave. She didn't see the attraction, what might've lured Lily into his bed, but she wasn't looking for his attributes, only his flaws. When she spoke, she sounded fatigued.

"Tampa."

15

At last he had a lead on where Hazel might be. He told himself to take it slowly, not get ahead of himself. While Daisy had revealed her location and the fact that the trail should be relatively warm – it had only been six months since Hazel had departed Biloxi for Tampa – he knew nothing about the city other than it was in Florida. How big it was, how daunting the task it would be to find her in a city he knew nothing about, especially if she didn't want to be found, were obstacles he'd have to somehow overcome.

It wouldn't be easy. The only person he knew in Tampa was Tom White, who owned the legendary Tampa music venue, Skipper's Smokehouse. Lucien had been introduced to White by Tommy Malone of the Subdudes, who appeared regularly at Skipper's and who'd played with Lucien countless times since he'd moved from Lafitte to New Orleans. What were the chances White would be able to help him find his daughter? Microscopic, but it was the only starting point he had.

Since he'd been able to make a few bucks after arriving in Biloxi by playing his guitar on the sidewalk outside of one of the casinos, he decided to stay a bit longer and bank some more cash before departing for Florida. He was paid up until the end of the month at the boarding house, which gave him two weeks before he'd have to decide whether to stay longer or head to Tampa.

Knowing what was riding on the next two weeks, Lucien summoned all the discipline he could muster, rising at dawn each morning, taking a bus to the waterfront and playing all day and into the evening until he caught the last bus of the night back to the boarding house. His resolve during that time to stay out of local liquor stores and bars, places that historically had swallowed up most of his income, was buttressed by his long work days – playing all day and into the evening without taking any breaks helped to prevent him from spending either time or money seeking out booze. Most importantly, it kept more of his hard-earned cash in his pocket when he really needed it rather than handing it over to various purveyors of spirits. The more he managed to save, he told himself, the quicker he'd be able to get to Florida.

The only time he spent money during those two weeks was to buy food and do his laundry, each on a limited basis. Because of his meager wardrobe and willingness to wear clothes for days at a time regardless of their condition, he visited a laundromat only once during his fortnight of busking, the day before he departed for Tampa. He limited himself to inexpensive junk food twice a day, bags of pork rinds and pretzels he picked up at the corner deli near the bus stop before heading to the waterfront each morning. Between eating less and avoiding alcohol, he lost weight and was forced to punch another hole in his leather belt with a fork purloined from a casino buffet table to help keep his pants up.

Healthy daily foot traffic coming to and leaving the casino combined with Lucien's prodigious talent on the guitar, evident even to the casual music fan during this stretch of sobriety, made for good business. Each night his totals were impressive; he went to extra lengths to make sure his daily take didn't provide temptation for those always looking to make their money the easy way, by taking someone else's. He emptied his Saints' cap whenever it started to look full to downplay his success, make him a less likely target for bands of restless youth constantly on the prowl in the area. He also thought the modest amount of money he left in the cap nudged some of those who stopped to listen to him play, shaming a number of them into reaching into their own pockets more often than they might have otherwise to support an obviously struggling artist.

By the middle of the second week it was clear he'd have enough money to depart for Tampa on schedule, so he informed his landlady he'd be leaving in a few days when the month ended. She was sad to hear that. He was her ideal client – only there long enough to sleep each night, and he paid cash for his room in advance. She was going to miss him.

Two days before he planned to leave Biloxi he called Lowell Joy, his dispatcher friend in New Orleans, and asked if he could line him up with a load heading to Tampa. "One thing – it has to be on Tuesday. That's when I lose the roof over my head."

Joy couldn't find a direct route from Biloxi to Tampa that day, so he offered the next best thing. "Can't find a thing going to Tampa on Tuesday, but I can get you on a truck to Orlando that morning. That leaves you a straight shot down I-4 to Tampa, two hours away."

"I'll take it."

An hour before dawn on Tuesday, Lucien arrived at the terminal and began looking for the Peterbilt that was taking him to Orlando. Joy told him the driver, Wardell Trent, was a solid sort "as truckers go these days", a family man originally from Starkville with a wife and three kids under the age of ten who made the Biloxi-to-Orlando run three times each week. He also warned Lucien that Trent thought of himself as an as-yet undiscovered songwriter. "If I was you, I wouldn't let him know I was a gi-tar player. He might never let you out of the cab."

Lucien was grateful for the heads up. "Thanks, Lowell. I owe you one."

"Better check your math, son. That number should be a whole lot higher."

*****

Joy was right. Wardell Trent was an amiable man in his late thirties with a pleasant smile who loved to talk. He was a bit overweight due to an addiction to Dr. Pepper, which he travelled with by the case. "It's my only vice," he said, hoisting a bottle he retrieved from a cooler next to his seat as soon as they pulled onto the on ramp for I-10. "The little lady is pleased about that."

Lucien would've preferred less talk as they headed east in the gathering daylight. He'd been anxious about the trip the night before and hadn't had much sleep, so he'd been hoping to get some shuteye as soon as they reached the interstate. Despite that, he didn't object to Trent's nonstop riffs on everything from his love for the current president to his analysis of SEC football. "Never been a better quarterback in the conference than Archie Manning. Not Namath, not Stabler, not even his boy Peyton at Tennessee," he intoned as they drove across Mobile Bay. "Don't matter none that I'm an Ole Miss fan. Old Arch was the gold standard, no matter where he played."

Lucien raised an eyebrow. "No disrespect, Wardell, but you look a tad young to know much about Archie Manning. Were you even born when he was playin'?"

"None taken. I was five when he was drafted by the Saints, but my daddy was the biggest Ole Miss fan in Starkville back then. He filled me in when I was a bit older. He always said more people would of agreed with him if Archie had played for Bear Bryant at Alabama." Wardell smiled, revealing a missing incisor. "It was tough, being an Ole Miss fan in Starkville. Our house was less than a mile from Davis Wade Stadium, and whenever Ole Miss played State, my father would hang a Rebel banner from a flagpole attached to the garage, which usually created some tension in the neighborhood, especially when they were playing in Starkville. He always preached to me that the ability to deal with tension creates character. I do believe he was correct."

It went like that for eight hours, Lucien slumped in his seat, eyes closed, feigning sleep while Wardell, thrilled to have an audience, scanned the highway and expounded on illegal shrimpers, mixed marriage, the next presidential election, Hurricane Katrina, the importance of unions, and his love for Dolly Parton. "Took the whole family to Dollywood last year for the first time. I been before, but never the wife and kids." He turned to look at Lucien. "You like country music?"

Be careful now. Without opening his eyes Lucien replied, "Some of it, yeah. The older stuff more than new country."

Wardell nodded vigorously. "I know what you mean. Give me Hank, Johnny and Waylon every day of the week over commie lesbos like them Dixie Chicks." He paused. "And Dolly, of course."

Lucien smiled, thinking Commie Lesbos would be a good name for a band. Wardell continued. "Who's *your* favorite?"

"That's a tough one," Lucien conceded. He thought for a moment. "If I had to pick one, I guess it'd be Kris Kristofferson."

Wardell took another swig of Dr. Pepper, then wiped his lips with his bare forearm. "Good choice. He ain't bad for a Texan."

As they passed one of the exits for Gainesville, Lucien wondered if Tom Petty still lived there. Probably not, he reckoned. Sooner or later all the big musicians move to L.A., and Petty had certainly outgrown Gainesville by now. Shit, he was best buds with Bob Dylan himself. He thought about Petty's Rickenbacker, how he'd always liked the tone those guitars produced. He remembered the first time he'd heard one, when the Byrds burst onto the scene in California back in the sixties. He was a teenager then, already passionate about music, spending hours each day playing scales on his Montgomery Ward guitar, hoping someday to make it to California himself. But when he moved from the delta to the Seventh Ward, all thoughts about heading west faded as he fell under the spell of New Orleans' colorful musical heritage and the irresistible characters that inhabited the scene. New Orleans was unlike any other place he'd ever been, which up to that time had consisted exclusively of Lafitte and the surrounding marshes. Being in New Orleans, close to the action, was the most intoxicating experience of his life thus far. For him, the grass was greener right where he was. He never wanted to leave.

Wardell interrupted Lucien's reminiscence. "You hungry?"

Lucien nodded. "I could eat."

"I know a place not far from where we're dropping this load that serves the best crawfish stew this side of Louisiana."

"I think I'd like that," Lucien said gratefully.

"Then it's settled." Wardell turned to look at Lucien with a gap-toothed grin. "You're buying."

Lucien smiled. "That's the least I can do."

"You got that right."

16

Wardell had dropped his trailer of frozen seafood at a cold storage facility and driven the two of them to the restaurant ten minutes away. He'd found a spot on a side street to park and the two of them had entered the unassuming wood-framed building and been ushered immediately to a booth against the far wall by a grateful hostess, who left them with a pair of menus and a promise to return shortly for their drink orders.

"What are you going to do next?" asked Wardell. His menu lay on the table; he knew what he wanted.

"First thing I have to do is find a place to stay." Lucien gestured toward the window by the front door. "It's probly too late for me to get a ride with anyone to Tampa tonight. Know anyplace that's clean and don't charge an arm and a leg?"

"I do," Wardell replied. "There's a motel on Orange Blossom Trail near 23rd Street called the Bit O' Paris. It's where I stay when I don't feel like drivin' home."

"You stayin' there tonight?"

Wardell nodded. Lucien continued. "Think they got a room?"

"I don't see why not. Tuesdays ain't exactly their peak nights. Leastwise, they haven't been when I stayed there."

The waitress, whose nametag identified her as Stella, returned, pen poised over pad. "Can I get you boys somethin' to drink?"

"You sure can, darlin'" Wardell said. "Bring me a big glass of water, lots of ice, and a Bud Light."

She turned to Lucien. "I'll just have water," he said.

Wardell gave him a look as Stella walked away. "You sure you don't want something stronger? That was a long day on the road."

Lucien smiled ruefully. "Me and alcohol have a complicated relationship. Right now we're separated, takin' some time off from one another." Pause. "Besides, I'm on a budget until I get to Tampa."

"What's in Tampa?"

"My daughter."

Wardell's face lit up. He was a firm believer in family values. "That's the best news I heard today. How old is she?"

It took Lucien a moment to answer. "She'll be twenty-one this year, in October."

"Just startin' out," Wardell observed wistfully. "What a great time in her life. What's she do in Tampa?"

"I'm not sure," Lucien said evasively. "She just moved there a few months ago. I think she's still lookin' for a job."

"Well, I'll bet she'll be happy to see her daddy. She know you're comin'?"

Lucien shook his head. "It's gonna be a surprise." That's the understatement of the year, he thought.

Stella returned with their drinks. Wardell ordered the crawfish stew he'd raved about earlier, along with a side of hushpuppies; Lucien made it easy for her by ordering the same. He watched as she retreated, savoring the rhythmic shimmy of her ass in the tight white uniform that hugged her hips as she walked away. He tried to remember how long it'd been since he'd sniffed his last pussy. Too long.

By the time their food arrived Wardell was on his third beer. He caught Lucien looking at him questioningly and deflected his concern. "I know my limit." He held up his glass. "This shit's like drinkin' water, anyway."

"That one better be your last, then. Ain't no way I'm drivin that cab of yours anywhere."

Wardell grunted. "Got that right."

When they were finished Lucien grabbed the check without protest from Wardell and calculated the tip. Orlando was probably a twenty percent town now, he thought, especially since Disney took it over. He decided on twenty-five and slid the money and the bill under his empty glass as they rose to leave. Not having a beer as he watched Wardell down three in rapid succession had been tough, but he was proud of himself for not giving in to his old nemesis. He hoped Hazel would be proud of the new Lucien as well.

It took them fifteen minutes to drive to the Bit O' Paris, a low-slung, vintage 50s motel whose large red sign had lost some of its paint and whose parking lot featured a single car when Wardell pulled his cab next to its office. Within five minutes a disinterested but efficient black clerk nearing the end of a long day had Lucien in a room two doors down from Wardell. "There ain't no continental breakfast here," she advised Lucien gruffly as she handed him his key.

"Good to know, ma'am. Thanks for the info." He turned to Wardell and extended his hand. "Thanks for all you done for me today, Wardell. I truly appreciate it."

Wardell patted his stomach and smiled. "I think we're pretty much even. Y'all tell Lowell Joy I said hey."

"Sure enough. Y'all have a safe trip back to Biloxi."

Lucien entered his room and was met by a fog of heat and humidity. No need to put on the air conditioning until you actually have a customer, Lucien thought ruefully. He found the unit below the window fronting onto the parking lot and turned it on full blast, then headed to the bathroom to take a shower. He hadn't had a bathroom to himself since he left Nashville, and he spent a full forty-five minutes under the lukewarm spray, trying to cleanse himself of his Biloxi experience with a half-used bar of Irish Spring.

He dried himself off with a towel that was too small to wrap around his waist, carefully pulled down the bedspread, and collapsed naked on the stiff, clean sheets. He grabbed the remote and checked the television to see if there was anything good on. He settled on a rerun of *Law & Order*, one of the early ones with the black prosecutor, and began to think about his trip to Tampa. Sure would be easier if that Daisy woman at the casino had provided an address for Hazel; he knew very little about the Tampa area, other than it had a Busch Gardens like the one in Virginia. Finding his daughter in a town he knew nothing about would be a challenge; he needed someone with local knowledge to help steer him in the right direction. Daisy had told him that Hazel worked waitress jobs around Biloxi before Lily died. It wasn't much to go on. Florida was a tourist mecca – there must be thousands of restaurants and bars in the Tampa Bay area.

His thoughts switched to Lily. Nobody deserved to die the way she had; he'd been feeling guilty about the way he'd shunned her, leaving her on her own with an infant child, not a dollar of his going toward their support during the last twenty years. Maybe if he hadn't been such an asshole and done the right thing when he found out he was a father, Lily might still be alive today. Coulda, shoulda, woulda was the story of his life, but as far as he knew, his hindsight-is-20/20 philosophy had never contributed to anyone's death. Until now.

He retrieved the phone book from the bedside table and thumbed through the yellow pages, trying to figure some way to get to Tampa that wouldn't cost much. His first impulse had been to call Lowell again, see if he could hook him up with a ride to Tampa, but then he'd backed off, thinking he'd asked enough of his dispatcher friend already. He found that the bus terminal was located on the other side of the interstate, about two miles from his hotel. He tried calling to inquire about their schedule, but received a recorded message telling him it was after normal business hours. He tossed the phone book aside. He'd try again in the morning.

He looked around the interior of his room, which was sparsely furnished with a guest chair but no desk, a set of drawers against the wall opposite the bed that doubled as a television stand and a collapsible bag stand with aluminum legs and canvas straps. He still had most of his busking money - he could stay another night or two at the Bit O' Paris without busting his budget, so he was in no rush to get back on the road. He tried to think if any of his musician friends lived in Orlando, but his memory, crippled by years of drug and alcohol abuse, provided no names.

His eyes began to droop as another episode of *Law & Order* followed the first. Ten minutes into the program he was snoring regularly, heading toward dreamland.

17

Lucien slept in late the next morning. It was nearly ten when he lurched into the bathroom for his morning constitutional. While sitting on the toilet, he tried to remember the last time he'd slept that late without being drunk or stoned the night before and couldn't come up with a date. The motel mattress was stiff, the way he liked it, much stiffer than the one he'd had in his room in Biloxi, and he'd been in no rush to relieve himself of that basic comfort.

His stomach growling, he showered and dressed quickly and strolled down to the motel office, noting that Wardell's rig was gone, on its way back to Biloxi. The black clerk from the night before had been replaced with a white man in his twenties, who was reading a tattered paperback copy of *Moby Dick* and idly picking his nose when Lucien opened the door, startling him. He tossed the book aside and sat up straight, forcing a grin. "You must be the guy in number six. Checking out?"

Lucien shook his head. "Not yet. The woman who checked me in last night told me y'all don't do breakfast here. I was

111

wondering if you could tell me where I might get a bite to eat that ain't too far away." He grinned sheepishly. "I'm on foot."

"You're in luck, old timer." Old timer? The young man continued, ignoring Lucien's frown. "There's a Waffle House about half a mile away on Orange Blossom Trail, same side of the street." He looked Lucien up and down, sizing him up. "You from around here? We don't get many guests without a vehicle."

You don't get many guests with a vehicle, either. "No. Just passin' through."

"Just so's you know, check-out time is 11:00 am." He pointed to the clock on the wall behind him. "You may want to check out before you go to breakfast, 'cause you won't be able to walk down there, eat, and get back here by eleven."

Lucien smiled. "I was actually thinking about staying another day or two. Y'all think I can stay in the same room, or will I have to move because of a previous reservation?" he asked, smiling.

The clerk looked at him incredulously. "In this shithole? Not hardly. You can have the fucking honeymoon suite if you want it. Course, there'll be a slight rate increase if you do."

"How much?"

"Seven dollars a day."

"What do I get for seven bucks?" Lucien asked.

"You get our only room on the backside of the place, facing away from the road and the sound of the traffic."

"Jacuzzi?" A soak in a hot tub would be nice, he thought.

The clerk snorted. "Yeah, right, just like the Marriott," he said, sarcasm dripping. "You want to move or not?"

"Well," Lucien said. "since I don't have a vehicle and I'm not bangin' somebody whose husband might come lookin' for her, I guess I'll stay where I am." He withdrew some bills, counted them, and handed them across the counter to the impatient clerk,

112

who counted it and shoved it into a cash box on the desk next to him. "That should be good for two more days, right?"

The clerk nodded. Lucien pointed at the book. "Any good?"

"Who knows?" said the clerk. "I just started it. It's for an assignment. I'm taking a summer course at the local J.C."

"Tell me how it comes out," Lucien said, turning away, heading toward the Waffle House.

*****

Lucien ordered the All Star Special – waffle, two eggs over easy, grits, toast and sausage – and took in his surroundings. He'd probably spent more time in Waffle Houses than any other restaurant, especially when he was touring in the South. They were as numerous as tattoo parlors and bail bondsmen below the Mason-Dixon line, and the food was consistent and decent wherever you stopped.

This morning the tables and booths were filled, so he took a seat at the counter, nursing a cup of coffee while he waited for his food. The counter person was a stocky woman whose nametag identified her as Earlene. Lucien figured she was in her fifties, with dark hair showing gray roots along her part gathered in her black visor, sporting a smile that somehow didn't seem forced. Maybe, he thought, she'd acquired enough seniority by now to avoid the midnight shift, when every flaming asshole who walked through the door seemed to have come from a bar where they'd been cut off before last call. The graveyard shift in an all-night diner was a tough way to make a living.

He grabbed a copy of the morning paper lying on the counter to his left and began to idly scan the want ads. Before he'd left the room earlier, he'd counted his cash and was thinking he'd probably need to replenish his stake before heading to Tampa, especially if he was going to take the bus and arrive with no one to greet him. He'd mentioned to one of the other sidewalk buskers in Biloxi that he was heading to Orlando, and the man had shaken his head. "Orlando's not a good place to play on the sidewalk. Disney runs that town like a corrupt sheriff – they don't like any competition for their entertainment options. Besides, you can't get close to the crowds going to either Disney or Universal because of the way they're set up. You have to take a train from the parking lot to the front gate at Disney, for Christ's sake."

Not being able to hustle for change by playing on the sidewalk was something he hadn't considered before that conversation. He scanned the columns of the paper, looking for ads for day laborers, but he could tell the jobs offered were the dregs – low pay, physical labor, young man's work. Lots of roofing jobs available. He shook his head; who wanted to be up on a roof during the summer heat and humidity in Orlando? Not many, judging by the surplus of ads from various roofing contractors.

He put the paper aside when his food came. Earlene stood poised with a coffee pot, smiling. "Refill?"

Lucien nodded. "Bless your heart, Earlene. I think I might be falling in love."

She blushed and wagged a finger at him in jest. "Don't you be playing with my heart, young man," she said as she refilled his cup. "Just be sure to think of me when you pay your bill."

Lucien glanced around as he ate. Not many people were leaving – most looked like what he termed squatters, the kind of customer who came in early, ordered some coffee and occupied their booth or table for several hours. The Waffle House was the highlight of their day; they had no place to go, so they were in no hurry to leave. At least it wasn't like Starbuck's – there wasn't a single person in the place pecking away at a typewriter, writing a novel or screenplay.

When he was finished, he attracted Earlene's attention and asked for the bill. She pulled it out of her apron and handed it to him. "Where you headed next?"

He looked at her, considering. "What makes you think I'm going somewhere?"

She gestured around the room. "All these other Crackers are regulars – I see their faces most every day. Anybody with a fresh face who wanders in here usually comes from one of the motels in the area."

Lucien smiled approvingly. "You surely are a wonder, Earlene. Whatever they're payin' you, it ain't hardly enough."

She smiled, revealing an even, white row of teeth that were her own. "I been tellin' management that for years now. Guess where it's got me?"

Impulsively, he pulled two twenties out of his wallet and slid them toward her with the bill, wildly over tipping her. "Keep the change, darlin'.

She smiled again. "Well, well, if it ain't Mr. Howard Hughes eatin' at my station today." She stuffed the bills into her apron. "Y'all take care of yourself, Mr. Hughes. You hear?"

"Same to you, Earlene," he said as he rose to his feet and walked into the midday heat.

Still no cars in the Bit O' Paris parking lot when he returned. He headed to the office. The young man had fallen asleep behind the desk, book in his lap, fan whirring behind his head. He jerked to attention when Lucien came through the door. "Just restin' my eyes."

"I can see that. What's your name, son?"

"Trevor. Trevor Potter."

"You own a computer, Trevor?"

He nodded. Lucien continued. "How'd you like to earn some easy money, Trevor?"

He eyed Lucien warily. "Depends what I have to do to earn it. I ain't no homo, if that's where you're goin' with this."

Lucien laughed, a full-throated guffaw. "Nothin' like that, Trevor – cool your shorts. I need to find some work, somethin' that'll pay me enough to keep my room here at the Ritz and have some left over to save so I can eventually leave. But I don't have a computer, and these days the want ads in the paper ain't worth shit. I'd be willin' to pay you if I could borrow yours, say tomorrow?"

"I got a laptop I could bring in tomorrow."

"This place got wi fi?"

Trevor looked around, to see if anyone else was listening. Lucien smiled to himself as the clerk bent forward and whispered conspiratorially, "We aren't supposed to tell the customers this, but, yeah, we got wi fi here."

"Your secret'll be safe with me."

Trevor looked at him more closely. "What kind of work you lookin' for?" Thinking, this guy's pretty old to be looking for a job.

"Somethin' that pays better than minimum wage, I guess. Nothin' too strenuous."

"Let me ponder that awhile. I think I might be able to help you out." He had a sudden thought. "Does it have to be somethin' on the right side of the law?"

"Well, I hadn't considered that option, to tell you the truth. Like you said before – it depends on what I'd have to do, how much risk is involved. But I suppose somethin' a little on the shady side would pay better than counter work at Mickey D's." Pause. "I wouldn't have to kill anyone, would I?"

Trevor recoiled in horror. "Jesus Christ, no." He saw Lucien's smile, realizing he was joking. He smiled himself. "You had me goin' there, old timer. Let me make a few calls tonight. And I'll bring in my laptop tomorrow so you can use it."

"Much obliged, Trevor."

18

When Lucien returned to his room, he turned down his freshly made bed and took a nap. Despite the rattling air conditioner, he managed to fall asleep, but not before pondering Ishmael, Ahab and *Moby Dick* as he drifted off, recalling an old line of graffiti from the boys' bathroom in high school:

Moby dick is not a social disease

He was thinking the quest to find his daughter was rapidly taking on aspects of the Melville novel, of Ahab's obsession with finding his mammalian prize at any cost. Would he be willing to go to any length to find Hazel, up to and including risking his life for her? Would he be possessed of the same determination that cost Ahab his life? Learning that Lily was dead had jarred his sensibilities, awakening some measure of paternal instinct from deep within that had never before been unsheathed. He was in uncharted territory, navigating by the seat of his pants as he came to the realization that finding Hazel and attempting to make amends might be a way to alter the sorry path his life had taken since that fateful one-night stand more than twenty years ago that had produced a child he had yet to see with his own eyes. If he did manage to locate her, how would she react to his sudden reappearance in her life? With a similar brand of disdain displayed in Biloxi by Daisy Stroud? Or with heartfelt gratitude at being reunited after all these years with her only kin, the ghost of a father her mother raised her to despise?

When he woke an hour later he felt as enervated as he had when he'd lain down. He plodded into the bathroom and splashed some water on his face, trying to juice his system, to get him going. His stomach was growling, reminding him he hadn't eaten since breakfast. He could try the Waffle House, but Earlene would be off duty by now, which made that particular restaurant less appealing to him. But there was rib joint called Harley's that he'd passed on his trips to the Waffle House that had a seductive aroma wafting into the street from an unseen smoker somewhere out back; it had been ages since he'd had some decent ribs.

He brushed his teeth, changed his shirt and ran a comb through his unruly hair, checking his appearance in the bathroom mirror. Good enough. He recounted the money in his wallet and calculated an amount he was willing to spend on dinner before heading out the door.

Harley's was a family operation run by husband-and-wife duo Harley and Chardonnay Jefferson, a black couple in their fifties whose two daughters, Alicia and Makayla, waited tables. It was a small place, only twelve tables in the narrow, rectangular space, and only two of those tables were unoccupied when Lucien arrived. It didn't bother him that he was the only Caucasian in the place – after all, he was a musician from Louisiana. His life had been largely devoid of distinctions drawn on the basis of race. People were people, he figured; differences in his world were determined through the actions of those around him, not the color of their skin. That philosophy on more than one occasion had resulted in Lucien being called naïve and worse by his Uncle Aristide, a member of the Ku Klux Klan hierarchy in Jefferson Parish whose harsh views on race relations only eased upon his death from congestive heart failure two years earlier at 73.

The younger of the two daughters, Makayla, brought him a menu and a glass of water with lemon. "Would you like anything else to drink?" she asked, revealing an adolescent smile dominated by braces.

"Water's fine," Lucien said. "Give me a minute or two with the menu."

"I'll be back in five," she said, smiling and moving quickly to another table that was finishing up.

Everything looked good to Lucien. After agonizing over several tempting choices, he opted for a half rack of ribs and a side order of collard greens. Makayla nodded with approval as she jotted down his order. "My mama makes the best greens in the state of Florida. Y'all are going to be pleased."

"I'm lookin' forward to it," Lucien said, smiling. He held up his water glass. "How about a refill, darlin'?"

"Coming right up."

While he waited for his food, he observed the other diners around him. There was plenty of conversation, laughter and earnest eating going on. The family of four next to him finished and paid their bill, and Lucien noted there had been little food left on their plates and no carryout containers when they rose to leave, which confirmed to him that Harley's had been the right choice.

The quality of his ribs and collard greens added to his conviction. The meat fell off the bones, with little fat or gristle to contend with, and the greens had just the right amount of bacon, onions and garlic to make him wish the portion had been larger. Like his neighbors, there was little left on his plate when Makayla returned to inquire if he wanted any dessert. "Specialty of the house is rice pudding."

"Another one of your mama's dishes?"

Makayla nodded. "My daddy handles all the meat. Mama cooks everything else."

"I think I have enough room left for some rice pudding," he said, patting his waistline.

Makayla returned in a moment with a dish of steaming rice pudding and a small container of reddish-black syrup. "It's her blackberry syrup. I think you'll like it," she said before gliding away again.

Lucien hadn't had food like this since leaving Louisiana. If he was sticking around, he thought, he'd be a regular at Harley's. After the last dollop of pudding was gone, Makayla dropped off his bill without a word and stood by the entrance to the kitchen, watching him intently as he extracted a handful of bills and placed them on top of his check. She returned and cast a raised eyebrow toward Lucien as she gathered them up. "I'll be back with your change in a minute."

"No need," Lucien said, smiling. "Y'all can keep it. That's the best meal I've had since I left New Orleans. Tell your mama and daddy I said so."

As he walked back to his motel in the gathering dusk, his mind shifted back to his main challenge – how to get to Tampa and find his daughter. He speculated how Trevor Potter might assist him in solving that dilemma. After all, he was just a kid, barely beyond puberty. How could he possibly help? Once again he briefly considered calling Lowell Joy to see if he could find a ride to Tampa with one of his truckers before rejecting it for good. Time to turn another new page, to move forward, maintain the momentum and the sliver of optimism he felt as long as he was on the move.

19

The following morning Lucien arose before dawn after another restless night of little sleep. After he showered he turned on *Good Morning, Orlando*, a newsy, gossipy two-hour show on the local ABC affiliate that concentrated on things to do in and around Orlando. He watched with amusement as a cooking section went awry when the male host stumbled while removing a pan of marinara sauce from the stove, spilling it all over the guest chef. The joys of live television.

He dressed and walked down to the Waffle House, where he exchanged pleasantries with Earlene at the counter while he ate his breakfast, relating how the *Good Morning, Orlando* host had botched the cooking segment earlier. "He was barely able to stay on his feet," Lucien said, shaking his head and chuckling at the memory. "You would've loved it, Earlene."

She smiled as she refilled his coffee cup. "I don't normally find humor in the misfortune of others, but I've met that chef before at a local function, several years ago. He's as full of himself as they come, a real know-it-all." Pause for effect. "It couldn't have happened to a more deserving fella." She looked at Lucien appraisingly. "You turnin' into a regular here at the House?"

Lucien shook his head. "I'm workin' on my getaway plan this very mornin'. Gotta get to Tampa to find my daughter. If that wasn't the case, I might just stay here in Orlando and fall in love."

Earlene laughed. "You are one sweet talker, that's for sure. Be sure to stop by to say goodbye before you go."

"You can count on that."

*****

Trevor was waiting for Lucien when he entered the office, his laptop set up on the desk next to him. "You ever used the Internet before?" he asked Lucien, motioning him around to his side of the counter.

Lucien shook his head. "Ain't never had a computer. Is it hard?"

"Not for someone who knows what they're doing," Trevor replied. He brought up the screen for Google and shifted the laptop slightly so Lucien could see it better. "This here is Google, the best search engine out there. All you have to do is type in whatever it is you want to find, and a bunch of results pop up on the screen. You click on whatever looks interesting to you and another window opens, with more information." He looked at Lucien. "What is it again that you want to find?"

"I'm lookin' to make my way to Tampa and maybe collect some cash by doing it."

"You mean like drivin' somebody's car from Point A to Point B?"

"Somethin' like that, I guess."

Trevor leaned forward, fingers flying confidently over the keyboard. "Well, your car idea is pure shit, seein' as how Tampa's only a coupla hours away down I-4. Nobody in their right mind would pay much for a job like that." A new screen popped up. "I can find you a ride to Tampa as long as you're willing to chip in for gas, but that's about it."

Lucien was disappointed. He was hoping to be compensated somehow during the journey and not have to shell out some of his dwindling cash supply along the way. "That's no good. Is there anything else out there?"

"Give me a few minutes."

A few minutes turned into thirty as Trevor searched for something that might fit into Lucien's plans. After one final search, he raised his head, disappointed. "I can't find anything that fits what you're looking for. You might have to suck it up and take the bus."

Lucien frowned. Trevor continued. "Unless..." He let it hang.

"Unless what?"

"Remember how I asked you yesterday if you'd be willing to do something a little shady?"

"You mean, against the law?"

"I might characterize it more like exploring a gray area of the law," Trevor said. "I have a friend who's in sales who might be able to help you out."

Lucien was immediately suspicious. "What kind of sales? Drugs?"

Trevor shook his head. "No. He, uh, brokers items of questionable provenance."

"What the hell does that mean?"

"He's a fence."

"Stolen goods?"

Trevor nodded. "He has a particular item for a buyer in Tampa that he's having trouble transporting. He's currently in the hospital, recovering from surgery, and can't do it himself. He reached out to me, but I have this job, plus school, so I turned him down."

"Any idea what this particular item is?"

Trevor shook his head. "As soon as I told him I couldn't do it, he clammed up. But it must be something big, because he was willing to pay me a lot of money to try to change my mind."

"How much is a lot?" Lucien asked. Now they were getting somewhere.

Trevor backed off. "This was a couple of days ago. He might've already found someone else to do it for him. I better check with him, see if the offer's still on the table."

Lucien looked at him in exasperation. "What are you waitin' for? Give him a call."

"Now?"

"You got a better time?"

Trevor was cornered. "I guess I could call him at the hospital…"

"Don't let me stop you," Lucien said. "What say I head back to my room so you can have some privacy? You can call me after you talk to him. How's that sound?"

"Okay, I guess."

Lucien stood up, preparing to leave. "I'm in number 6, in case you forgot."

"I haven't forgotten."

20

Lucien went back to his room and watched the *Dr. Phil* show and absently strummed on his guitar while he waited for Trevor's call. He was glad that this mysterious transaction wouldn't involve drugs, because he was fearful that the temptation to take the package and sell it on his own would be too much for him to resist.

Having the guitar in his hands again ushered in a sense of guilt for Lucien. He'd been avoiding it as if it were contagious since he'd arrived in Orlando. He needed to get back to it, to keep his fingers and his mind nimble and his calluses from fading away. He looked around the stark motel room. This was where he'd ended up without music as the central focus of his life, in a rundown motel in a rundown area of Orlando, hoping for some sort of miracle that would finance the next stage of his journey to find his daughter, a miracle that hinged on the connection between a pimply-faced college student he'd only just met and a purveyor of stolen goods he knew nothing about. He wondered if he could sink any lower.

*****

125

Trevor dialed the number of the hospital and was connected to the room he'd requested. It took a few moments, but a man finally answered the phone, his voice barely audible. "Hello? Who is it?"

"It's Trevor, from the motel," he replied. "How are you feeling?"

"Like dogshit," the man spat out. "No wonder nobody ever leaves the hospital alive. Are you coming to see me today?"

"Uh, I'm at work right now, but maybe I can stop by after I get off."

"I hope that doesn't ruin your day." Although the man's voice remained low, his sarcasm was evident.

"I think I have some good news for you," Trevor said, ignoring the dig. "Remember that item you were looking to move? I may have found a courier for you. If it hasn't been moved already, that is."

The man in the hospital was interested but cautious. "Have you changed your mind?"

"No," Trevor said. "but I've met someone who's traveling to Tampa and is desperate for money, desperate enough to take a lot less than you offered me, I'll bet."

"How long have you known this guy?"

"Not long," Trevor conceded. "but he's down on his luck and is looking for his daughter, who's missing. He told me he didn't mind if the work wasn't exactly legal."

"What's his name?"

"Lucien Devereaux. I did some research on him last night. He's a musician, somewhere in his sixties I'd guess, who's from New Orleans. He's played with a lot of famous acts: Dr. John, Elvis Costello, John Hiatt, the Meters, the Subdudes, even the Rolling Stones. Apparently, he's one of the world's best session guitarists. All the big boys have used him in the studio and on tour."

The man was doubtful. "Where'd you meet him?"

"Here, at the motel. He's been staying here the last couple of days."

More skepticism. "If he's so famous, what the hell is he doin' at that piece of shit motel you work at? That doesn't sound right to me."

"He's a bit down on his luck, I'll grant you that. But I have a good feeling about him."

"I can't tell you how much comfort your good feeling provides me," the man said acidly. "I suppose he's a Boy Scout leader as well?"

Trevor was getting impatient. "Look, either you still need a guy to take your package to your buyer in Tampa or you don't. If you have a better option, I suggest you exercise it. If not, I think you can get this guy for five grand." He paused for effect. "That's a third of what you offered me." He went on. "Besides, you won't be leavin' that hospital for some time, according to that doctor I spoke with when I visited you the other day. Looks to me like your options are limited."

There was silence for a few moments before the man in the hospital responded. "You come see me tonight and we'll talk about this some more." He lowered his voice again to avoid being overheard. "Bring me some Jim Beam. I'm dyin' for a drink."

"I get off at four," Trevor said. "I'll be over after I clean up and change my clothes, probably by six."

"I'll be here."

*****

Lucien was working on the Clapton solo from "Layla", his go-to busking piece, the one even the least musically inclined of his sidewalk audience was likely to recognize, the one that put real cash in his Saints' cap, when Trevor called him back on the room phone. "Hello?"

"It's Trevor, from the front desk. I talked to my guy."

"And…?"

"I think he's interested. I'm going to visit him at the hospital tonight after I get out of work to iron a few things out."

"What things need to be ironed out?" Lucien asked.

"Well, he's a little reluctant to offer this job to someone he doesn't know and has never met. I'll have to hold his hand a bit, I guess, make him feel more comfortable about trusting you on this."

"Do you think it would help if I came along with you?"

"I don't think so," Trevor responded. "He knows me – let me make a case for you. I'll call you after I talk with him, let you know how it went."

"What's he in the hospital for again?" Lucien asked.

"He had to have his spleen removed. He's recovering from surgery."

Lucien was hopeful. "Make sure you tell him I ain't got no car. I'm going to need wheels to get to Tampa."

"If he agrees to use you, I'm sure we can arrange for a rental. You do have a driver's license, don't you?"

"I do, issued by the state of Louisiana."

"Any outstanding warrants?" Trevor asked.

Lucien thought for a moment before answering. "I don't think so. There may be some minor shit, parkin' tickets and such, but they were a long time ago. The statue of limitations probably run out on them."

"Statute," Trevor corrected.

"Huh?"

"Statute of limitations, not statue."

"If you say so."

There'd been some indications of past substance abuse in the information he'd gleaned from the Internet about Lucien Devereaux the night before. He'd heard that musicians, especially the ones who grew up in the sixties, had been willing and eager participants in the drug world; from what he'd read, it sounded like Devereaux might've been one of the more eager of those participants. He wondered if this plan to use Lucien as a courier for something that valuable was a sound one but shelved his doubt almost as soon as it popped up. He was looking ahead to scoring a commission for himself on the deal. From what he'd seen so far, Lucien would be an easy mark. "I'll call you back tonight with the details, if I can convince him to hire you."

"I'll be waiting."

21

For the first time since he'd fallen off the wagon in Nashville after the John Hiatt tour, Lucien felt that things were finally looking up. He'd used the discovery that his only kin was living in Tampa as a sort of stimulus, a motivating force based on the slimmest of substance during his darkest days to keep his feet moving and to put his head back in the game. Buoyed by the hope that substantive help was on the way, despite its still-murky nature, Lucien felt like a new man, with refreshed purpose. A new man about to hit the road to finally meet his daughter.

He tried to take a nap after his conversation with Trevor, but he was too keyed up, so he picked up his guitar instead. He'd been working on a melody for his daughter, no lyrics yet, that he was now eager to expand into a full song. If he showed up with a tune he'd written especially for her, he figured there'd be no way she could turn her back on him.

He worked diligently, the time passing unnoticed as he improvised, trying to create a bridge following the intro of his work in progress. Maybe, he thought as he noodled, his imminent payday would allow him to get his other guitars out of hock in Nashville. If they hadn't been already purchased, that is. He made a mental note to call Monroe Jessup once he had the cash in his pocket to see if his friend would help, then put down his guitar and wrote a reminder in a small notebook he carried in his backpack because he was afraid the mental note might fade before he acted on it. He placed the notebook on the bedside table next to the clock radio, then leaned back, head on the pillow, and closed his eyes, anticipating what a reunion with his daughter might be like.

*****

"A musician?"

The disdain in the man's voice was tangible. Trevor moved quickly to reassure him. "He's a good guy. Plus, he's highly motivated to find his daughter. He claims he'll accept any conditions as long as he can get to Tampa."

Michael Garnett had been moved to a private room overlooking Lake Copeland since Trevor's last visit. It was a marked improvement over his previous room, more expansive than the smaller space which he'd shared with a chatty car salesman who'd had his appendix removed and was anxious to get back to selling cars, pestering Garnett daily, spewing the Oldsmobile company line about the need for every American to own a new car. The man's patter had become so unbearable that Garnett had requested to speak to a hospital administrator and had promised to make a sizable donation to the hospital's building fund, no strings attached, if he could be moved to a private room. Two hours later his wish had been granted.

Garnett wasn't convinced. "How long have you known this guy? A couple of days?" He gingerly raised himself up on his elbow in his bed and glared at the young man. "It's not like he's going to be delivering a pizza, for Christ sake. I have to *know* I can trust him."

"What are your options?" Trevor countered. "If you had any, the package would've been delivered by now. Right?"

A sharp pain in his midsection caused Garnett to recline again before he could respond. Why had his body betrayed him just as he was on the cusp of the biggest transaction of his career? He didn't smoke or drink and had avoided processed foods for most of his life. He didn't deserve to be flat on his back in a

131

hospital; he felt wronged, without recourse, at the mercy of a group of people he hadn't known two weeks ago. He'd been reduced to counting on a part-time motel desk clerk for both companionship and business advice – Trevor was the only person who'd visited him since he'd been admitted to the hospital. What did that say about his life?

When Garnett didn't answer, Trevor continued. "What kind of assurance are you looking for? Certainly not a signed document – that spells paper trail, which I'm sure you don't want."

As much as he hated to admit it, the kid was right. He had no better option – he'd been planning to make the delivery himself until he'd been sidetracked by his splenectomy. That's how he always conducted his transactions, person to person. But this time his client was growing antsy, getting cold feet during the delay caused by his medical emergency, making noise about finding another broker to handle the deal. "I just need to know that this guy isn't going to fuck up."

"Weren't you the guy who told me there are no certainties in this life? That you can take nothing for granted?" Trevor asked. "If you want the deal to go down before you get out of the hospital, Lucien Devereaux is the one to make it happen. You're going to have to trust him."

Easy for you to say, thought Garnett – you're not the one who stands to lose two million here if something goes wrong. There must be some way for him to cover his play – all he needed to do was to figure it out. "Let's say I agree with you. What would it take to make it happen?"

Trevor smiled, relieved that Garnett seemed to be easing his position. "Like I said before, the guy needs a car, a rental, I'd imagine. And you'd have to settle on a fee for his services."

"You mentioned something about five grand."

Trevor nodded emphatically. "I'm pretty sure he'd take that in a heartbeat. He told me what he really wants, after finding his daughter, is to get his guitars out of hock. He had to sell them a while back so he could eat."

132

Garnett was considering the five grand number, wondering if he could get it down a bit. "How many guitars are we talking about?"

"I think he said three."

"How much would that cost him?"

"Hard to say. This dude is a real player, one of the best. One article I read about him last night called him the Jimi Hendrix of Louisiana. I'm guessing he didn't buy 'em at Sears."

"What's his name again?" Garnett asked.

"Lucien Devereaux."

"Never heard of him."

"What have you got to lose?"

Two million, Garnett thought.

*****

It was nearly 10:00 when the phone in Lucien's room rang. He'd dosed off watching another rerun of *Law & Order* – it was his favorite show – but moved quickly to answer it. "Hello?" he responded eagerly.

"You've got a ride to Tampa."

Lucien was elated. "When?"

"As soon as we work out a few minor details," Trevor replied carefully.

"How much?"

"Three thousand dollars." Garnett had agreed to five, in cash. Trevor was taking his cut off the top. "Plus two hundred for you to get the rental. You're going to need a driver's license to rent a car."

"That's no problem," Lucien replied, failing to keep the glee from his voice. Three grand would get his guitars out of hock, no problem. "How soon can we do this?"

"Day after tomorrow," Trevor said. "I need to pick up the merchandise tomorrow while you arrange for a car. Does that work for you?"

"Like butter on bread."

"I'll call to you tomorrow when I have the merchandise." Trevor hung up without saying goodbye.

Lucien replaced the phone and let out a whoop before regaining his composure. First thing tomorrow he'd call Monroe and ask him to check on his guitars, see if they were still available.

He was headed to Tampa.

22

As soon as Trevor was out of his room, Garnett reached gingerly for the phone on the table next to his bed, the motion causing him sharp pain in the abdominal region, near his scar. He dialed a number he'd memorized and waited for recipient's voicemail to kick in. When he heard the recording of his client's voice, he left a message:

Being released in two days. Look for me then.

It was a message that his client and he had agreed upon before Garnett went into the hospital for his surgery, its true meaning lurking beneath the cheery wording, known only to the two of them. His client had been impatient when he'd heard of Garnett's scheduled surgery and had demanded that Garnett concoct a Plan B in case something went wrong while he was in the hospital or, more optimistically, if Garnett could somehow arrange for the transition of the merchandise before he was discharged. The message he'd just left was for the optimistic option, which Garnett felt would please his client.

He'd left the merchandise in a locked gun safe at his Mount Dora home, along with several bundles of cash, a portable GPS unit and a burner cell phone for the courier to use to contact his buyer as soon as he reached Tampa. He'd told Trevor that he would have instructions prepared detailing how to access the safe and the items inside when he returned to the hospital tomorrow. Using a notebook and pen that Garnett had asked Trevor to bring to the hospital today, he slowly copied down the instructions, wincing from sharp jabs of pain whenever he moved too quickly. Emphasizing the importance that Trevor not help himself to any of the additional cash he'd stored in the safe, his original thinking being that he'd have to pay the courier more than five thousand, was a brief note reminding Trevor that he knew exactly how much money he'd stored there. Any discrepancy in the total after Trevor's visit, minus the authorized five grand, would be dealt with swiftly and harshly.

When he finished the note he returned to his usual position, on his back, and closed his eyes. He was glad that this deal, the deal he had waited his entire life for, was about to be consummated. During his career as a freelance broker, he'd arranged a number of lucrative transactions between participants of dubious pedigree, but nothing approaching the scope of this.

Art history had never been his forte, so he'd had to do a lot of research to acquaint himself with the value of the merchandise currently sitting in his safe. The name of the artist, Raphael, and the name of the painting, *Portrait of a Young Man*, were both unknown to him, as was the mystery behind its circuitous route to his gun safe, but he soon grasped the basics: that the painting, completed in 1514, had been taken from the Czartoryski Museum in Krakow sometime in 1945 by Hans Frank, a high-ranking Nazi official stationed in Poland. Shortly thereafter Frank had been captured; the following year he went on trial in Nuremberg, where he was found guilty of numerous war crimes and executed. But he never revealed where he'd hidden the painting – it was a secret he took with him to his grave. This masterpiece from the Renaissance had been missing for sixty years. Until now.

Garnett had been recommended as a go-between for the transaction by one of his other clients, a more pedestrian thief who dealt in antiquities of much lower value and renown, someone who was acquainted with the seller but wanted no part of any deal that could be linked to Nazi war crimes. Garnett had been intrigued by the research he conducted after he was initially contacted and agreed to broker the deal with the buyer from Tampa. The buyer had insisted on verification of authenticity, which the seller provided through his association with a convicted art forger who now worked as a consultant for major insurance companies. The reformed forger had agreed to keep his mouth shut in exchange for an outsized fee and had provided a document that convinced the buyer that the painting was authentic.

It was easily the most complex deal of Garnett's career, and far and away the most lucrative – the kind of deal substantial enough to launch a person's retirement. That was Garnett's plan, even before the unexpected intervention of emergency surgery and the ensuing period of recovery, a time which had crystalized his conviction that it was time to get out of the brokerage profession. He'd negotiated a broker's fee with the seller that had him looking at beachfront property in Belize; he was ready to pull the trigger on the purchase of a home there as soon as his fee was deposited in an offshore account.

He was almost there, just one more hurdle to surpass. In a perfect world, he would've handled the transaction himself, but he was equally leery of being caught up in anything relating to Nazis, even before a defective spleen had betrayed him, so he'd decided to look for a dupe, someone who could fit the role of scapegoat should something go wrong. Trevor Potter had been his first choice, but the sallow desk clerk had stunned Garnett by refusing to take part, stalling the crucial final stage of the deal, greatly frustrating each of the principals involved in the negotiations, leaving Garnett despondent that the deal might fall through.

Enter Lucien Devereaux. The appearance of the musician at the Bit O' Paris Motel and his subsequent conversations with Trevor had provided Garnett with an unexpected lifeline, albeit a shaky and tenuous one. Under ideal circumstances, no one in their right mind, Garnett included, would pick an itinerant musician for such a crucial task, but the lure of this last, best payday had convinced the normally cautious middle man to take the advice of a part-time junior college student and trust that this guitarist –

someone he'd never met and likely never would - could deliver the goods without any mishaps.

It was the gamble of a lifetime.

*****

Lucien was asleep when Trevor called and reacted slowly to the phone. "Did I wake you?" Trevor asked, hoping he had.

Lucien blinked and shook his head for some clarity before responding. "Uh, yeah, I guess you did." He squinted at the clock on the bedside table: 10:21. "What's up?"

"The deal. The one where you get paid a shitload of money to deliver something to Tampa."

Lucien was paying attention now. "It's on?"

"It is if you agree to the terms. Want to hear them?"

"Shoot."

"We go the day after tomorrow---"

"You mean *I* go the day after tomorrow, right?" Lucien interjected.

"Yeah, yeah, you go," Trevor spit out. "You have two hundred dollars, cash, to rent a car. If I were you, I'd rent it for as long as I could, since you don't have a vehicle of your own. It's your responsibility to rent the car, in your name, with the money provided by my associate. I'll have the money tomorrow and will get it to you tomorrow night."

Lucien pressed. "What about the other money? For delivering the package?"

"You'll get three thousand dollars for delivering the package to the destination. To help you out, you'll also get a portable GPS unit to help you find the address and a cell phone to call the buyer once you arrive at his property. There's a security gate at the end of his driveway. Park there and tell him who you are. Someone will open the gate." Pause. "When it's over, you can keep the GPS if you want and the cell phone, since you don't have one. Just make sure you return the car on time." He paused again. "How does that sound?"

Lucien was giddy. Three thousand dollars would get his guitars back and leave a good chunk in his wallet to stake his claim in Tampa. And having a phone was the answer to his prayers. Without a phone, he'd never be able to find his daughter. Now he'd have a fighting chance. "Sounds good to me," Lucien said, trying to sound low-key. "The day after tomorrow, you said."

"Yeah," replied Trevor. "I have to pick up the money, cell phone and GPS tomorrow. I'll have it to you by tomorrow night at the latest. If I were you, I'd go to the car rental place about nine the next morning, so you can be on the road by ten. You'll be in Tampa by noon." Trevor gave Lucien a moment to digest it all before continuing. "As soon as you drop off the package, you can start looking for your daughter."

Lucien struggled to contain his excitement. The next phase of his life, a life shattered by Katrina and his recurring addiction to heroin, was trending upward for a change. After so much disappointment during the last two years, he was thrilled to be moving forward with purpose, on course to find the daughter he'd never seen or supported. He hoped she'd accept his late-stage quest to include her in his life as a noble one, his resurrected sense of family substantial enough to override the deep-seated resentment that had festered within her for years, fostered by a continuous series of vitriolic diatribes from her mother against an absent father that left him, in her eyes, viewed as inattentive at best and dismissive at worst.

He was looking forward to the challenge.

2019

23

Steven Morrison was beginning to lose patience. He glanced at his phone to check the time, then confirmed it by checking the clock on the wall behind him. He fumed silently while he waited for Gracie Fenton to return to his end of the bar so he could vent his frustration.

Gracie, the daytime bartender at Kitty Galore's Raw Bar, was busy chatting with a couple of snowbirds from New Brunswick who'd arrived from Moncton the previous week to begin a two-month stay at a mobile home park in Dunedin. It was their first time in Florida, and they had plenty of questions for the amiable blond bartender, who answered them as well as she could, even as she knew other customers were waiting. She discreetly looked away for a moment to see Morrison holding up an empty beer glass, which allowed her to excuse herself. "I'm sorry, but that guy at the end of the bar looks like he's going to burst if I don't get him another drink." She smiled. "I'll be back if you need anything else."

"Don't worry about us," the dark-haired husband said in a flat, down east accent. "We'll just read over the menu while you're gone."

Gracie walked purposefully to the end of the bar where Morrison's face remained dark. "Another beer?"

"Yeah, but I'm more interested in my food." He pointed to his watch for emphasis before continuing in an agitated tone. "It's been nearly forty-five minutes since I put in my order. What gives? Cook go out on strike?"

Gracie shook her head. "It's the new kid. He's training today."

The new kid was John Rucker, who'd started as an apprentice chef with the lunch crew two weeks earlier. He was in his mid-twenties, about five nine and stocky, with dark, close-cropped hair and two heavily inked forearms, a recent transplant from across the state in Boca Raton. He'd applied for a kitchen job and had been hired on the spot by Florence Leaf, the restaurant's owner, who later explained her impulsive decision by stating she had a "feeling" about John as soon as she met him. "I trust my gut."

"For Christ's sake, I ordered a sandwich. What's he doing, baking the bread?"

"You're touchy today," Gracie replied with a smile. "Besides, what's the rush? Where else do you have to be?"

Morrison, who lived within walking distance of Kitty's near the Crooked Snook Marina in Ozona, Florida, was retired from the film industry, living on Social Security and a small inheritance from his late uncle Merle Benson. He wasn't amused by Gracie's attempt at humor. "That's not the point. I'm a man with a delicate system that requires nourishment at regular intervals. My stomach is starting to rumble."

"I can call you an ambulance if you'd like, but if you can hang on for a minute, I'll go back into the kitchen and find out what the problem is," Gracie replied acidly, her smile widening. "Do you think you can last that long?"

Morrison was not amused. "Just bring me my food," he growled.

144

Gracie replenished his beer, then went back into the kitchen. The daytime chef, Nelson Gregory, was explaining to Rucker how to handle simultaneous orders. Gracie listened in. "Everything on the menu has a time stamp, the amount of time it should take for that particular item to be prepared and presented to the customer. You need to know that list by heart, so you'll know which item to begin to prepare first. You have a copy, right?"

Rucker nodded. "I've been working on it. It's pretty long, though."

"It is," Nelson replied. "But you have to put in the time." He noticed Gracie waiting patiently in the doorway, hands on hips. "What's up?"

"The guy who ordered the chipotle turkey avocado sandwich is about to explode at the bar. Is it ready yet?"

Nelson looked at Rucker, who replied meekly. "It'll be out in a minute. Just have to add the fries and pickle."

"Thanks," she replied. She returned to the bar and made her way down to Morrison. "It's coming right up. The kitchen got swamped all at once – what can I say?"

Morrison took a long swallow of his beer and looked around the bar. "It's only January. What are you going to do when high season really kicks in?"

"By that time, our new employees will be seasoned veterans." She looked at Morrison appraisingly. "You've really gotten cranky since you broke up with Rheinhart." She leaned forward, lowering her voice. "You could probably use some weed to mellow you out a bit. I know a guy, if you need some."

Gracie was referring to Zach Rheinhart, who had been Morrison's luncheon companion every Wednesday at Kitty's. That is, until a year earlier when he met Gwen Westphal, former Olympic kayaking medalist and current spokesperson for the Clear Sailing Alliance, a prominent water rights advocacy group throughout the state of Florida. Rheinhart had attended one of her lectures on red tide in Largo; shortly thereafter, they began to date, a relationship that had continued to blossom. In addition to having a girlfriend, Rheinhart, who had been unemployed when he'd met Westphal, now was working for Habitat for Humanity, a job he'd landed with the assistance of a local FBI agent. Special Agent Angela Threadgill had put in a good word for him after Rheinhart had provided the Bureau with critical assistance during an investigation that exposed a major Russian covert operation, an attempt to assassinate a sitting U.S. Supreme Court justice. Because of Rheinhart's increasingly cluttered dance card, most of Morrison's visits to Kitty Galore's now were solo efforts.

As always, Gracie's reference to the Rheinhart situation rankled him. "There was no break up because there was nothing to break up. We're still friends," he said exasperatingly.

Gracie looked him up and down. "I don't know. You're always irritable, hardly ever smile, just mad at the world in general. You sure act like you broke up with your lover." She softened her tone. "What bothers me now is how long your funk has lasted. What happened to Lauren, the gambler out at Fuego that you were seeing?" She gave him a knowing nudge. "She used to put a smile on your face."

Lauren Caputo was a resident at Fuego, Florida's largest clothing optional resort, located thirty minutes away in Land O' Lakes. "She cares more about poker than anything else. It seems she has less and less time for a side project like me," Morrison said. "Besides, she was never anything more than a port in the storm, if you get my drift."

"Aren't you the romantic?" Gracie teased, eyebrow arched. "With an attitude like that, it's a wonder you have any friends at all." She made a point of noting the empty barstools on either side of him. "Oh, that's right – you don't." She added a dollop of sympathy to her tone as she continued. "I guess that would make anyone cranky."

He stifled a heated retort when he saw one of the waitresses emerge from the kitchen with his sandwich, looking questioning for Gracie's direction. "Down here," Gracie called out. "That belongs to the guy here with no friends." When the sandwich was placed in front of Morrison, she had one final zinger. "Don't forget

146

to tip your server," she advised, dancing away before he could respond.

Morrison frowned but remained silent as Gracie moved away. He munched on his sandwich and thought: she was right. He had been a bit prickly lately, more sensitive to perceived criticism, especially when it concerned his personal behavior. And he hated to agree with her, but she was right about Rheinhart – he did miss his friend's companionship. Although it had been nearly four years since he'd moved to Ozona from Los Angeles, he could count the male friends he'd made in Florida on one hand, with several fingers left over. There was Rheinhart and DeWayne Bologna, who'd been his scuba instructor when he first moved to Florida. But Bologna was retired now, living the idyllic life on the island of Saipan, his once-thriving scuba business in Port Richey, one of Morrison's hangouts, shuttered for good. With Rheinhart spending less and less time with him since he'd begun a relationship with Westphal, Morrison lacked any male friends of consequence. He wasn't getting any younger, and the sense of solitude he felt was increasing. Not a good combination, under the best of circumstances.

He checked the fries and was surprised that they were hot, as if they'd just come from the fryer. This sandwich had been a suggestion of Gracie's when she'd mentioned earlier that he seemed to be in a rut as far as his menu choices at Kitty's were concerned. Like many of his elderly brethren, he'd grown more set in his ways as he aged, less prone to improvisation where his appetite was concerned. Gracie had been trying to get him to expand his menu choices for some time; this sandwich, he thought as he took another bite, was evidence that he needed to listen to her suggestions more closely.

The bar was half empty by the time Morrison finished his pickle and reached for the check. He confirmed the total out of habit, then added a generous tip despite Gracie's earlier disparaging remarks about his relationship with Rheinhart. She wasn't the enemy, he knew. But sometimes her mouth outpaced her intentions – when that happened, he needed to recognize that for what it was and not be so eager to take her bait. He promised himself he'd work on that.

He left cash and the check under his empty beer glass and waved to Gracie on his way out the door. She'd returned to the couple from Moncton, who were now peppering her with questions about the menu. She didn't look up.

The wind had picked up while he'd been eating, a steady breeze from offshore that he leaned into as he turned down Bay Street, heading for home. He passed Rheinhart's bungalow on his right; his car was gone. Morrison noted that both the front and back needed landscaping, overgrown saw palmettos shrouding the fieldstone path to the front door, bougainvillea overwhelming the frame of the carport. He looked around; Rheinhart was the bad sheep on the block, the rest of his neighbors' yards were well trimmed, weeds eradicated, bird feeders full, like the finished product from one of those home improvement shows.

Probably too busy building houses for the homeless and getting laid to care much about yard maintenance.

24

John Rucker berated himself silently as he drove home after his shift at Kitty Galore's. He was upset that he'd fallen behind on three orders today and that Nelson Gregory had been in his face about each of them. Gregory was the most demanding boss he'd ever had during the twenty-four years of his life, and the criticism, although justified, still stung.

Who was he kidding? Gregory was the *only* boss he'd ever had, aside from a disastrous three-day stint at the Apple Store in Boca Raton while he was a junior in high school. After graduating from the University of Florida three years earlier, he'd infuriated his parents by refusing to even attempt to utilize his degree in finance to find a job. Instead, he'd fully embraced the short-term optimism of youth and formed a punk band called Humongous

Fungus that, like most new bands in that genre, was known more for its enthusiasm than its musical expertise. Rucker had grown up as a passionate fan of the Sex Pistols, in particular Johnny Rotten. He so admired the Sex Pistols' lead singer that he adopted the stage name of Johnny Rattan when he recruited his friends to form Humongous Fungus. When asked by father Kirk Rucker, a well-respected certified public accountant with his own firm in Boca, why he chose the Rattan moniker, John replied with an impish grin. "I'm the Florida version, more Pier 1 than King's Road in Chelsea."

The band did well early on, managing semi-regular bookings in two local clubs and a number of gigs at frat houses at Florida Atlantic University, but the other three members of the band were less dedicated than Rucker and gave, as he saw it, less than their all, which infuriated him. The band imploded after thirteen months, torn apart by internal disagreements over just about everything. Rather than try to make another go of it in Boca Raton, an area with an uneasy relationship with any style of music that wasn't button down, Rucker heeded the advice of one of his high school friends, Kris Adamson, who had moved across the state to St. Petersburg and had told him about the exploding cultural scene in what used to be the shuffleboard capital of the South. "Dude, it's outrageous here. Clubs everywhere, bands, too. Lots of punks, a real scene. You gotta move here."

So he did, towing a U Haul trailer full of his possessions behind his weathered Honda Accord to the other side of the state. Rents were pretty steep in downtown St. Pete, so he settled for a studio apartment in an older section of Oldsmar, not far from Tampa Bay Downs. Music was still his passion, his main goal, but he was practical enough to know he'd have to find some sort of work to pay the rent until his music career took off, so he'd scanned the Internet for job opportunities before he left Boca.

That's how he found the apprentice chef job at Kitty Galore's Raw Bar in Ozona. He had no clue where Ozona was and had to look it up on Google Maps, discovering it was nestled between Palm Harbor and the Gulf of Mexico. He'd applied for the position via email and was called in the following week for an interview, the interview after which owner Florence Leaf had said she had a "feeling" about John Rucker and had offered him the job before he left the premises.

He knew his future wasn't in the restaurant business, but Kitty Galore's offered a distinct advantage for a musician – he'd been assured that his apprenticeship, his training, would occur exclusively during the lunch shift, leaving his evenings free for gigs and practice. He fully expected to pursue a career in music and planned to quit his job at the restaurant as soon as he could find a band and bandmates he could live with. In the interim, he'd be training as a chef, making enough to cover the rent until something better came along.

Every spare minute when he wasn't working, he prowled the streets of St. Pete, soaking in the positive vibe of the revitalized area downtown by the bay, on the lookout for like-minded youth with musical talent. Many of these sessions included his friend Kris, who was overjoyed when John moved to the west coast; he operated as John's tour guide and advisor as he sized up potential members for his new band like a Texas cattleman at an auction.

Within a month he'd found two kindred spirits: Kieran O'Shea, a drummer and native of Dublin who'd been recruited by the University of Tampa to play soccer, and bass player Evelyn Hall, who, depending on her mood that day, insisted she be called Lady Vulva while in musician mode. Both had recently left bands and were eager for a new start, and both were intrigued by John's concept for his new band. He wanted them to produce music in the spirit of Gainesville's Roach Motel, a pioneer of Florida punk that, along with the Sex Pistols, had inspired him to pursue a career in music. Ireland native O'Shea had never heard of Roach Motel, but Evelyn quickly clued him in in her best Lady Vulva voice. "Dude, they're legends. Fucking legends."

John Rucker wanted a fresh start, too. Afraid that his brief period in Boca as Johnny Rattan might somehow poison this new opportunity, he'd settled on a new name for himself as the front man for the new band, plucking two words out of the ether because he liked the way they sounded together: Tornado Jones. To be safe, he Googled the name to be sure some other musician or performer wasn't already using it. He was surprised to find that Tornado Jones was the protagonist of several young adult novels written in the 1950s by author Trella Lamson Dick. If she was still alive, he rationalized, she'd be too old to complain that he'd appropriated the name for his new band.

Evelyn lived in Largo with her parents and was able to convince them to allow the new band to practice in their detached garage. The three of them had to clear an area large enough for Evelyn's drum kit and a couple of amps and store what they'd removed in a crawl space above the garage. John, who was also a passionate believer in UFOs, had come up with a name for their new band: Alien Colonoscopy. He'd expected some pushback, but both Kieran and Evelyn had loved it. "Lady Vulva and Alien Colonoscopy," Evelyn had intoned, smiling and nodding her head at John's suggestion. "Goes together like Oreos and milk."

That first practice had been two months ago, and John was excited by the progress they'd made. Both Kieran and Evelyn were serious players; Kieran's playing was modeled after his personal hero, the late Keith Moon, and featured inspired runs more suited for the lead rather than the bottom. Evelyn – who insisted she be called Lady Vulva whenever she was within five feet of her bass – provided a steady if uncomplicated counterpoint to Kieran's thrash style, much like Tina Weymouth with Talking Heads.

The light at the corner of Alt 19 and Tampa Road was red as he slowed. He glanced at the clock on his dashboard: 5:37. Just enough time for a quick shower at his place before heading to Evelyn's to practice. He glanced at the Styrofoam container on the passenger seat beside him. Not having to cook dinner after a long day in the kitchen was another underrated aspect of working at Kitty's. Tonight's dinner was coconut shrimp and an order of fries. In rush hour traffic, he thought, they'll be gone before he reached McMullen Booth Road.

25

The sound of construction was driving Marcia Alvarez crazy. She rose from her desk and peered out the window, but couldn't see where the noise, a pulsing jack hammer, was coming from. She poked her head out of her office door and addressed her administrative assistant, seated at the reception desk in the compact office space. "Any idea where that noise is coming from, Colleen?"

Colleen McKinny shook her head. "I got here at 7:30 this morning and they were already at it, but I didn't see anything after I parked my car. Just heard it."

"Check with Pinellas County and see if they have any projects scheduled in the area. Find out how long this racket is going to last."

"Yes, ma'am. I'll get right on it."

Marcia returned to her office. She had a clear slate this morning, no appointments, which meant she had a chance to catch up on her paperwork, the least pleasurable aspect of her new career as a private investigator. Field work was one thing – she felt her endorphins kick in every time she was on the streets, working for her clients. Being tied to the desk, filling out forms required by state and county agencies, was the equivalent of bureaucratic waterboarding to her.

She knew when she took the plunge and opened Alvarez Investigations seven months ago that there would be some aspects of the job that were less desirable than others. But she also knew that this seismic event in her life, starting her own business after spending the last fourteen years of her life as sole caretaker for her ailing father, offered exciting challenges as well. During her twenty-year career in the Army she'd worked in Intelligence and the Military Police, two areas of expertise and experience that were ideal for her new career. Thanks to the connections and diligence of her attorney, Judy Ruliani, and the mysterious secret her father had kept for nearly fifty years until his death fourteen months earlier, she had a new lease on life, one dominated by hope instead of despair.

After signing a lease for the compact retail space in a strip mall on Main Street in Dunedin nestled between a Chinese restaurant and a laundromat, she toyed with the idea of hanging a framed sketch of D.B. Cooper on the wall of her office as a daily reminder of the life-altering effect the mysterious hijacker asserted on her new world. But in the end she'd backed off, rightly concerned about the questions clients would undoubtedly raise as to why there was a picture of the most notorious hijacker in American history prominently displayed on her wall. Instead, she opted for a colorful water-color painting by a local artist from Gulfport of a sailboat on the Gulf in brilliant sunshine and placed a framed photo of her late father that she selected from a scarce number that had survived his military days, a picture of him with his arm around his wife, her mother, while he was stationed in the Air Force in Oregon. No one would think that photo of her parents would be out of place in her office.

Finding Colleen McKinny had been another fortuitous step in her transformation to her new role as private investigator. She'd been the eleventh candidate Marcia had interviewed for the position of administrative assistant and Gal Friday for the fledgling organization, but the first one refreshingly lacking any sense of vapid entitlement that had permeated the first ten interviews she'd conducted, all with young women in their twenties. She'd been hopeful that Colleen's military experience – she'd spent four years in the army instead of attending college and had survived two tours in the Middle East as a communications specialist – would help her stand out, and she'd been correct. She was a woman among girls during the process, and Marcia had offered her the job, which she accepted on the spot, before she'd left the building on interview day.

The business had been slow to build at first as Marcia struggled with methods to get her name recognized in a crowded field. Her initial clients had been mostly wives who suspected their husbands were being unfaithful – she wasn't surprised that there were that many women in that position, but she was surprised that a large percentage of them had the resources necessary to discover the truth. Domestic cases usually involved extended periods of surveillance, and time was money.

Her big break had come when a reporter for *Creative Loafing*, the weekly alternative newspaper serving the Tampa Bay area, had interviewed her after she had investigated one of the members of the Tampa Bay Buccaneers football team and uncovered a sordid history of domestic abuse and violence that caught the attention of the national media and propelled her name and the name of Alvarez Investigations into the national spotlight. After that story broke, she'd been deluged with requests for media interviews, which afforded Marcia the unexpected luxury of being able to pick and choose the clients she preferred, rather than accepting the first person who came through the door simply because she needed the fees those clients would provide.

That publicity resulted in her introduction to her latest client, Lucien Devereaux, whom she'd first met five days earlier. Lucien was searching for his daughter, Hazel, whom he had never met. All he had to go on in his search was the word of the best friend of Hazel's late mother that Hazel had left her home in Biloxi, Mississippi for Tampa in 2006. Lucien revealed that he'd followed her to Tampa six months later, but with limited resources had been unable to locate her. Convinced she was somewhere in the area, Devereaux, a musician of considerable talent as she found when she ran a routine background check on him, had accepted a job with one of the cruise ship lines based in Tampa, playing in the cruise ship's band, his first steady gig in many years.

But Devereaux had miscalculated the time that he would be required to spend aboard the ship when he'd signed on, thinking he'd have ample time while off duty to search for Hazel. When he discovered that he would be working twenty-eight days straight, with seven days off before returning to the ship for another twenty-eight day stint, he'd rebelled, complaining to management that his contract, one he'd signed without bothering to read the fine print, amounted to legalized slave labor. Attorneys for the cruise ship company laughed at his objections, offering him a simple binary solution: either honor your contract or be fired on the spot, no severance, no extended benefits. It was the first time in his life that Lucien Devereaux had been covered by health insurance; he was fifty years old then, starting to experience some of the health-related consequences of a lifetime spent on the road, playing rock and roll. Access to legal medications and regular annual check-ups were luxuries he'd never enjoyed before and was reluctant to abandon, so he swallowed his pride and stayed on the job.

He stayed with the cruise line for eleven years until he self-destructed and was caught on board with enough cocaine to support a trafficking charge had the cruise ship line chosen to pursue it. He'd fallen into old habits, ones that he'd tactfully omitted from his resume when he'd applied for the job. His dismissal was swift; he was escorted from the ship immediately carrying his two guitars and a small box of personal items, relieved that there were no criminal charges filed against him, but worried about how he was going to support himself.

Desperate, nearly broke, he reached out to the best friend he had, the owner of Skipper's Smokehouse, one of Tampa's most eclectic music venues, who was able to steer him in the direction of other talented musicians in the Bay area, people who might be able to offer him some guidance on the local music scene, one he'd been largely insulated from while employed on the cruise ship. He was able make some connections that offered him small doses of hope, something he desperately needed.

In their last meeting two days ago, Lucien had told her that he had recently auditioned for a new band that was being formed in the area, but had yet to hear if he'd been accepted into the fledgling group. Lucien thought he was a shoo-in after delivering a sizzling array of fretwork skill on his guitar, saving his singular arrangement of Clapton's solo on *Layla* for last, which left the other three, Rick Manning, Gabe Templar and Tate Baggot, fawning in praise but unwilling to commit to Lucien on the spot.

Marcia wasn't convinced. Until Devereaux had some sort of revenue coming in, he was a risky client to take on. She certainly wasn't in a position, with less than a year of investigative experience on her own resume, to assume the risk of a deadbeat client. There might be some *pro bono* work in the cards for her in the future, but she was nowhere near that now.

What kept her from turning him away was the nature of his case. From her two interviews with Devereaux, his grief and regret over the choices he made back when Hazel was conceived struck her as legitimate. He admitted readily, eyes brimming with tears, that he had screwed up, many times over, but his determination to steer his life in a new direction, with his daughter as the focus, tugged at her heart. She knew what it was like to have an absentee father herself, how much damage that situation could wreak on the fabric of a family.

She wanted to be part of his happy ending, to change the course of his life for the better. No matter what it might cost her.

26

Just as the construction crew broke for lunch and the maddening sound of the jack hammer ceased, Colleen knocked and came into Marcia's office, holding an envelope. "Mail call," she said, a wide smile on her face.

Marcia looked up from the report she was trying to finish. "Who's it from?"

Colleen placed the envelope on the desk. "Check out the return address."

Marcia peered at the envelope. "Hearts Across The Bay." She looked at Colleen. "What's that?"

"It's a local charity in the Tampa Bay area, run by Julia Stevens. She's the wife of Walker Stevens."

Marcia was still clueless. "Am I supposed to know who they are?" she asked as she extracted what appeared to be an invitation from the envelope.

Colleen smiled. "You must not watch much television. The two of them own Walker's Jewelers in Clearwater. They run almost as many ads on local television as your attorney does. The wife, Julia Stevens, runs Hearts Across The Bay, a local charity that supports victims of domestic violence." She paused, allowing Marcia to finish reading the invitation before continuing. "You've been invited as one of their main guests to their annual fundraiser because of the work you did for that football player's wife."

Marcia finished reading and looked up. "Kind of late notice, isn't it? The event's two weeks away."

"You weren't famous yet when the original invitations went out," Colleen replied. "You've turned into the darling of Tampa Bay society after the *Creative Loafing* article. You're a hot commodity."

Marcia grimaced. "I suppose I have to go." She looked at the invitation again. "Sounds pretty fancy. I guess I'll have to get a new dress."

Colleen suppressed a smile – she had yet to see her boss in anything other than slacks. "Do you want me to respond? You're allowed to bring a guest…"

"A date? Where the hell would I find a date on such short notice?"

The exasperation in Marcia's tone made Colleen smile again. "I'll respond and tell them two will be attending. If you can't think of anyone, I'd be willing to go with you if you'd prefer not to go by yourself."

Marcia looked at her employee intently. "You'd be willing to do that?"

Colleen nodded vigorously. "I'd go in a second. It would be terrific exposure for Alvarez Investigations. Everyone who is anyone in the Tampa Bay area will be there. You could make some significant connections."

Marcia thought for a second, then handed the invitation back to her assistant. "Okay. Tell them I'll be there with an escort." She rose from her desk. "I think I'll get something to eat. Can I bring you anything?"

"Where are you going?"

"I thought I'd go to Kitty Galore's, in Ozona."

Colleen was familiar with Kitty's, having been there for lunch once before with Marcia. Apparently, she wasn't being invited along today. Which was okay, since she had some more research to do on Lucien Devereaux. "Bring me back an order of coconut shrimp." She turned to exit the office. "Let me get my wallet."

Marcia waved her off. "Don't worry about it. We'll figure it out when I get back."

"Which will be...?"

Marcia shrugged. "Who knows? That fucking jack hammer is driving me crazy. Can you last a couple of hours until you eat?"

"No problem. I think I can last that long without food. Just call me when you're on the way back."

"Will do."

*****

Marcia had been a luncheon regular at Kitty Galore's while she was caring for her ailing father. She'd arranged for two elderly women in the condo complex to watch her father for an hour each weekday while she rode her bike down to Kitty's for a much-needed break. But since her decision to become a private investigator, her visits had become less frequent. She missed the place, the convivial, laidback atmosphere of the restaurant nestled beneath the cypress and live oaks in sleepy Ozona.

She also missed her conversations with Gracie Fenton, the daytime bartender there during the week who had become one of her closest friends, her sounding board for all the complaints she had in dealing with an ornery parent whose health was failing. Gracie was the first person she'd told about her father's claim that he was the real D.B. Cooper; to her credit, she'd been a sympathetic ear, occasionally offering advice, but only when asked. If Marcia had to name her best friend, it would probably be Gracie Fenton.

Traffic was light as she navigated the short route between her office and Ozona. The parking lot was half full as she pulled in. The weather was unseasonably warm for Florida in January – her dashboard reported the temperature as 85 – with clouds just beginning to mass over the Gulf, a short distance to the west.

She lit a cigarette as soon as she exited her car, a white Lexus she'd purchased with some of the money from her late father's estate. She'd been trying to quit smoking and had made a pact with herself that she wouldn't smoke in the new car, thinking that would help. She'd been able to cut back a bit but was having difficulty quitting altogether. Old habits, she reflected, are indeed hard to break.

She glanced at the daily specials posted on a board by the entrance while she smoked, looking for something different that might entice her to vary from her go-to order, the Cobb salad, but finding nothing that interested her. She took a final drag, crushing the butt beneath her shoe before breezing by the hostess, heading for the bar.

Gracie spotted her immediately, a big smile creasing her face as Marcia strode in. "Well, stranger. Long time, no see."

Marcia slid onto a stool at the end of the bar next to the service area where the waitresses picked up drink orders. "Now that I'm a career woman, my schedule seems to have filled up. You won't hold that against me, will you?"

"You mean will any of the kitchen crew spit in your salad?" she asked impishly. "No need to worry – I'll alert them to stand down." She poured a Yuengling draft for her and placed it on a coaster in front of her. "You still like the Cobb salad?"

Marcia nodded, taking a sip of her beer. "I checked your specials, but nothing excited me."

Gracie turned to input the order on the touchpad. "Anything else?"

"I'll need an order of coconut shrimp to go, for Colleen back at the office. But not until just before I'm ready to leave."

"Got it," Gracie replied, turning back toward Marcia. "How's she working out?"

"Like a million bucks. You can't beat military training – it translates well to any civilian career a vet pursues."

"Glad to hear it." She checked the bar quickly, to see if any customers were in need, then returned her attention to Marcia. "I read about that case with the football player's wife. Nice work."

Marcia shook her head. "The husband was a real asshole, but lucky for his wife, he was also dumb as a rock. Too many hits to the head, I guess. He thought he could run around, screw anything with a pulse and then beat the shit out of his wife when she complained, all with no consequences." She smiled as she took another sip of beer. "You should've seen the look on his face when my client's lawyer showed him some of the video I shot." She smiled again. "My client said that it was the first time since she'd met the bozo that he'd been rendered speechless."

"How does it feel to be a star?" Gracie asked. "fending off the media and the *paparazzi?*"

"Funny you should ask. Just before I came over here, I got an invitation to attend some charity event. Have you ever heard of some organization called Hearts Across The Bay?"

Gracie nodded. "Yeah. It's run by that woman who's in those wacky jewelry store commercials. She and her husband. What's her name?"

"Julia Stevens."

"That's it. Brunette, really pretty, looks like a model. You can tell by her positioning in those commercials that she's had some modeling experience."

"I must be the only person in the Bay area not to know who these people are."

"You must not watch much television."

"That's exactly what Colleen said."

162

One of the waitresses appeared at the service bar, waiting patiently until Gracie saw her, then spit out her order. "Two Bud Lights, bottle, unsweetened iced tea with lemon and a diet Coke."

Marcia looked around the place. No new animal heads or fish mountings on the wall since her last visit. Owner Florence Leaf usually went on vacation once a year and returned with some sort of kitschy item destined for the wall or ceiling in the bar area. The year before it had been a moose head she found at a quirky roadside shop in Solon, Maine. Gracie had named it Moosey Galore.

When Gracie finished filling the beverage order she turned back to Gracie. "Any interesting new clients? Now that you're a star?"

Marcia grimaced. "I'm hardly a star."

"If you're going to the Hearts Across The Bay gala, I think that qualifies you as a star," Gracie countered. "Who's your next high-profile client?"

"I'm thinking about a missing persons case, some guy trying to find his daughter."

"Sounds like a nice change of pace from infidelity and spousal abuse."

Marcia nodded. "I was thinking the same thing. I've had enough of sneaking around hotels and motels with a video camera to last me a while."

"Anybody I know?"

Marcia shook her head. "I don't think so, but he's a musician who's toured with some pretty big acts. You might have heard of him."

"What's his name?"

"Devereaux. Lucien Devereaux. A pretty well-known guitar player."

Gracie looked at Marcia intently. "How do you spell that?"

"D-E-V-E-R-E-A-U-X. Devereaux."

163

"That's funny," Gracie replied. "There used to be a waitress here a few years back with that name. Worked here for about two years, I think."

Marcia leaned in. "You had an employee here named Devereaux?"

Gracie nodded. "I remember her because she had a real southern accent. The other girls used to tease her about it a lot. From Mississippi, I think."

It couldn't be, thought Marcia excitedly. "What was her first name?"

"Hazel. Hazel Devereaux."

27

"You're sure it was Hazel Devereaux?"

"Pretty sure. I could ask Nelson if he remembers. They were kind of friendly."

"I'd appreciate that."

"Be back in a minute."

As Gracie hustled into the kitchen, Marcia tried to compose herself. She thought back, trying to remember if she'd ever encountered anyone at Kitty's with a southern drawl, but she was at a disadvantage. All of her visits involved sitting at the bar, chatting with Gracie. She'd never had a waitress during any of her previous visits.

Gracie returned in a moment, nodding, as she handed Gracie her salad. "Nelson says she worked here from January of 2015 until May of 2017. He says she left before hurricane season, so she missed Irma."

"Did she have any other friends, people she was close to, on the staff?"

"I could ask around," Gracie offered.

"One more thing. Could you put in that coconut shrimp order? I want to get back to the office, work on a few things."

Gracie nodded and whirled to the touchpad. "Done."

Marcia gobbled down her salad, her mind racing, as Gracie moved off to service other customers. She knew she had to take Lucien on as a client now, despite his uncertain fiscal situation. Now that she knew Hazel Devereaux had worked at Kitty Galore's, there'd be a paper trail she could follow: W-2 forms, her resume, payroll records and work schedules. That is, if Florence Leaf allowed Marcia to copy a few of those documents. The case had life now, breathed into it by a random visit to a favorite haunt. Was it karma? Was she meant to take Lucien on as a client? It sure seemed that way.

Just as Marcia polished off her salad, her to-go order emerged from the kitchen in a Styrofoam box. Gracie tallied the bill and Marcia dropped two twenties on the bar, grabbed the box and headed for the door without saying goodbye, her mind formulating what she planned to tell Lucien about the information she'd discovered. She barely avoided a collision with a man entering the bar area as she scooted past, heading for the parking lot. The man gave her a nasty look and continued into the bar where he plopped himself onto the seat Marcia had just vacated. "What's the big hurry with Gumshoe?" the man asked haughtily as he removed his ball cap and set it on the bar next to his phone.

"She had to get back to work, Reb," Gracie replied. "Speaking of which, you're running late today."

"Had a clogged toilet to fix at 11:45. Who the hell takes a monster shit right *before* lunch, anyway?"

Reb Jadel was another one of Gracie's lunch regulars. He worked as a maintenance man at one of the condo complexes in Palm Harbor. In his late fifties, with thinning, reddish hair and a grin missing several teeth, he was a fifth-generation Floridian who drove a Chevy pickup with a Confederate flag on the rear window and a recently applied "Trump 2020" sticker on his rear bumper. He was the type of customer Gracie loathed: crude and cruel, with a mouth that never seemed to take a rest. It was a chore to serve him.

"Bud?" Gracie asked, reaching into the tub for a cold one.

"Does the pope shit in the woods?"

Reb Jadel had been an indifferent student during his abbreviated involvement with the public education system in Pasco County. Most folks knowledgeable of details regarding his past sensed that the scattershot arc of his life thus far could be directly linked to that indifference. He was ignorant of many social norms, profane at an alarming level, resentful of the chain of command and heavily armed - the kind of person Gracie never wanted to piss off on the highway. She tried to give him a wide berth whenever he came into the bar.

He'd been particularly contemptuous of Marcia Alvarez's new career – hence the derogatory nickname Gumshoe. The two knew each other through brief encounters at the bar but were not friendly. After the third time she'd refused his offer of a date – "Dinner at my place, darlin'. Nothin' could be finer." – she moved to the top of his shit list, becoming an object of constant derision, her sexuality openly questioned behind her back as the reason she'd repelled his advances.

Gracie placed a cold beer in front of him. "Interested in a menu, Reb?"

He held up his beer, his grin a leer. "Just keep an eye on the bottle, darlin'. Liquid lunch today."

*****

Marcia dropped the coconut shrimp on Colleen's desk and barked "Get me Lucien Devereaux on the phone!" as she strode into her office, closing the door behind her. Too stunned to reply, Colleen briefly weighed whether the growling in her stomach should override her boss's uncharacteristic demand, then rationalized: what's five minutes? Get Devereaux on the phone and then gobble down her shrimp. She dialed his number, transferred the call as soon as he picked up, then settled in to eat her lunch.

When the call came through, Marcia wasted no time. "I have two pieces of news for you today, and both of them are good."

Lucien's pulse quickened. "You're going to take my case?"

"I am."

"What about your fee?" Lucien asked cautiously. "The retainer you mentioned the last time we met is something beyond my reach." He quickly added, "At the moment, anyway."

Marcia dismissed his concerns. "We'll work something out. I just want to make sure you haven't hired anyone else since we spoke last."

"I haven't. You're the only person I've talked to about this."

Marcia was relieved. She thought he might've gone bargain hunting for a more affordable investigator. "That's good." She paused for effect. "Which brings me to the second piece of good news. Are you sitting down?"

He nodded, even though she couldn't see him. "I am."

"I have a lead on your daughter," she said breathlessly. "I know where she worked from January 2015 until May 2017. I have proof."

Lucien was stunned. In a moment, in a voice barely audible, he managed a single word. "How?"

"Do you believe in karma, Lucien?"

He hesitated. "I'm not sure I know what that is, exactly."

"It means this is your lucky day. I was having lunch today at a restaurant where I eat often. During a conversation I was having with one of the employees about the case I just completed for the football player's wife, she asked if I had any new cases coming up. I told her I was thinking about taking on your case, and she asked me your name." She added quickly. "I hope you don't mind."

"I don't."

"Good. Anyway, when I mentioned your name, it struck a bell with her. She remembered the name Devereaux, said there was a woman by that name who worked there from 2015 till 2017. She said she had a thick southern accent – she thought she was from Mississippi. When I heard that, I asked if she could confirm with anyone else on staff what she suspected. The cook confirmed it – the name of that employee was Hazel Devereaux."

"My God." Lucien felt like he was in a dream, floating above the earth, weightless. Tears began to well in his eyes as his mind raced ahead immediately to an image of a joyful reunion he'd conjured in his mind many times before.

Marcia continued, interrupting his reverie. "So if you agree, I'd like to start tracking her down immediately," she said. "We can work out the money side of this down the line. I don't want to waste any more time – she has a head start of a year and a half." She paused. "What do you say?"

His voice was strong, without reservation. "Let's find her."

28

When his call with the private investigator ended, Lucien had a powerful urge to get loaded to celebrate. It was the way he's always reacted to good news in the past – get high, and then get higher. He got to his feet and paced around his tiny apartment, a space barely big enough to house him, his guitars and his amps, his mind racing. Was she still here in Tampa? Had she made any friends while she was here that might know where she went after leaving that restaurant?

He caught himself. He'd been so stunned by the news that he'd forgotten to ask Marcia what the name of the restaurant where she had worked was. He grabbed his cell phone and was about to punch in her number when the phone rang. An incoming call from a local number. Maybe it was more good news. He answered eagerly. "Hello?"

A male voice that was vaguely familiar. "Lucien? Is this you?"

"Yes."

"It's Rick Manning. The bass player from your audition. Remember me?"

"Of course I remember you, Rick," he replied. "What's up?"

"I talked it over with the other guys, and we'd love for you to join our band. We were all blown away by your skill and speed. You're exactly what this band needs," he offered hopefully. "As long as you're still interested, that is."

"I'm definitely interested, Rick. I'd love to play with you guys." Could this day get any better?

Relief flooded into Rick's voice. "Excellent. We were hoping you hadn't found a better offer. The guys will be thrilled."

"When do we start?" Lucien asked.

"Right to the point. I like that. We've planned a rehearsal for this Friday at my house in Carpenter's Run, off State Road 54, near 75, where you auditioned the other day. Can you make it?"

"I'll be there," he said, adding. "Thanks for taking a chance on me."

Manning, a music fanatic with an encyclopedic memory, was having none of Lucien's humility. "Are you shitting me? What band wouldn't want to have Lucien Devereaux on lead guitar? I can't believe how lucky we are. Do you remember how to get to my place?"

"It's only been a few days, Rick," Lucien responded pointedly. "I think I can find it."

"Well, just in case I'll text you the address."

"What time?"

"I told the guys to be there by 7:00."

"See you then."

*****

The jack hammer had resumed work, but Marcia barely noticed. She had a yellow legal pad out, jotting down notes, possible angles to pursue in her quest to locate Hazel Devereaux. Her adrenaline was pumping as she compiled the list. She briefly considered turning around and returning to Kitty's to interview the

171

cook and anyone else who might've worked with Hazel, but after some thought decided to concentrate on creating a to-do list to guide the investigation as it moved forward. Better to have as many options as possible to pursue before returning to Kitty's when they opened tomorrow.

She was especially hopeful that the trail would begin with Hazel's restaurant connections. Those who work in the restaurant business – dishwashers, wait staff, cooks, bussers, bartenders – all share a common bond, almost as if they are part of a union. They're loyal to their fellow workers, wary of management and mindful of the cooperative nature of the work, especially in establishments like Kitty Galore's where tips are shared among the entire staff, not just the waiters and bartenders on the front line. Even when minor jealousies flare up, usually having something to do with complicated personal relationships, the common good – more money for all – usually prevails.

Marcia wanted to see whatever documents the restaurant had retained concerning Hazel Devereaux's tenure at Kitty's, but what she was really hoping to find was evidence of a best friend, the kind of friend with whom a young woman is willing to share her most intimate personal secrets. She was hoping to find Hazel's best friend; the fact that she had lasted on staff for more than two years, beyond the average tenure of what Marcia had anecdotally noted during her numerous luncheon visits was typical for wait staff, was especially encouraging. Someone who knew where Hazel traveled to next.

Another less savory thread to pursue was any connection Hazel might've had with county, state or federal law enforcement agencies. Had she broken any laws, served any time? Did information that Marcia could use to find her exist in any of the criminal justice files, on any level?

Housing was another key issue. Did she live alone, or did she have a roommate or boyfriend? Was there anyone in Hazel's sphere of influence that could point Marcia in the right direction, freshen a trail that at the moment looked cold? There was work to do, and Marcia was eager to get started.

She buzzed Colleen. "I'd like you to run a criminal background check on Hazel Devereaux to see if anything pops up. County, state, local. All the databases we have access to."

"How far back?"

Marcia consulted the notes she'd made during her initial interview with Lucien. "We think she arrived in Tampa in 2006. Let's start with that. If we need to go back further with Mississippi officials, we can do that at a later date."

"I'll get right on it," Colleen asserted. When she ended the call she popped the last shrimp in her mouth, savoring the crispy coconut coating. Dinner, she thought, might be a long way off tonight, as she wiped her hand on a paper napkin and tossed it along with the Styrofoam box into her trash can.

*****

Gracie sneaked a peek at the time on her phone. Nearly 3:30, that time of day when there was usually a welcome respite between the lunch and dinner surges. The bar was nearly deserted; only Reb Jadel still remained. Apparently, he was taking the afternoon off – he was on his sixth Budweiser, showing little signs of slowing down. The more he drank, the more he pestered her, mostly with questions about Marcia.

She rued her current fate. Reb was the sort of Floridian any local chamber of commerce wished could be prohibited from contact with the tourist population. He had the charisma of a neglected litter box, his breath horrid, the teeth that remained brown, disfigured by a lifetime of tobacco use and poor hygiene. No wonder she'd never seen him in the company of a woman, or even a male friend. These factors and more had resulted in a life based on solitude. Gracie thought he could've been the Cracker standard bearer for that odd niche of modern society that had been gaining notoriety in the media during the last few years, the involuntary celibate population. Alone and angry seemed to describe Reb Jadel to a T.

He was still grousing about being snubbed by Marcia as she rushed back to the office. "Who the hell does that bitch think she is, anyway? Just because her daddy went and died and left her a bunch of money doesn't give her the right to treat me like that."

"I don't know that you should take it personally, Reb," Gracie offered cautiously. "She just found out some important news about a new case and wanted to get back to her office as quick as she could. You just happened to be in her way."

Jeb tilted the bottle to his lips, draining its contents, and placed it in front of Gracie, his sign that he wanted another. Gracie looked at him closely. "Are you sure you need another? You still have to drive."

"If I wanted your fuckin' advice, I'da asked for it, darlin'. Bring me another one." His voice was tinged with menace, daring her to disagree.

When Gracie hesitated, he reached into his pocket and tossed a key ring the size of softball on the bar. "Here's my keys. Now bring me another beer."

Gracie experienced a huge sense of relief that Reb had offered her an unexpected way out of her personal sense of liability as to his degree of sobriety. She snatched the key ring and tossed it beneath the bar before popping another Bud and placing it on the bar in front of him.

Reb smiled. All was right in his narrow world again. "Now, darlin', howsabout you tell me about this new case of Gumshoe's that's so damn important?"

29

Gwen Westphal was pondering the same sort of dilemma Marcia Alvarez was currently facing. Holding up her invitation to the Hearts Across The Bay charity event, she queried her dining companion. "I suppose I should look for a dress for this. What do you think, Zach?"

Zach Rheinhart hesitated, buying time by exaggerated chewing motions, the last section of warm bread still clutched in his hand, the rest in his mouth. After swallowing, he responded. "Whatever you think, honey. You know your wardrobe better than I do."

She looked at him across the table. "What are you going to wear? You don't own a tux, do you?"

He shook his head. "Not anymore. I donated it to Goodwill last year. I figured I wouldn't be wearing it again. Guess I'll have to rent one." He smiled. "Since I won't be sitting with you at the head table, it probably doesn't matter what I wear." The invitation to the event specified that Gwen would be seated at the head table, while her companion would be seated at a table designated for those accompanying the stars of the evening. Zach had jokingly referred to it as being relegated to the kids' table when the invitation had first arrived.

They were having dinner at her favorite restaurant, Esoteric Fish in Palm Harbor. Gwen had introduced Zach to the intimate spot nestled incongruously in a strip mall on Tampa Road shortly after they'd started dating a year earlier. Although he didn't like it as much as Kitty Galore's, he conceded that the menu was more daring, the atmosphere more upscale than Kitty's. It certainly wasn't a hardship to dine there.

Gwen's invitation to the chic charity gala organized by Julia Stevens arrived as a result of her very visible local and national profile. Having a former Olympic medalist on the dais was a coup for any non-profit; the work she'd been doing throughout the state in her position as the public spokesperson for the Clear Sailing Alliance and their mission to provide clean water to all residents of Florida was icing on the cake. Her stunning looks, buff physique, and presentation skills comprised an ideal combination for loosening the purse strings of potential donors. Zach expected her to be the evening's star.

"Nonsense," Gwen replied, frowning. "Appearances matter a lot, especially to the major players. If you don't wear a tux, you'll be the only one there without one."

He smiled as the waitress brought their meals, waiting until she had departed before replying. "Don't worry. I'll rent one. But I'm going to count on you to keep me from looking like an overdressed clown, like I did at the senior prom."

She gave him a quizzical look across the table, shaking her head. "If your fashion sense hasn't advanced beyond that of a high school senior by this point, I'm afraid there's little hope."

*****

The following morning Lucien arrived at Marcia's office at 9:15. Colleen smiled as he closed the door behind him. "She's waiting for you. Would you like something to drink?"

"Coffee would be nice," he said gratefully, adding. "Black."

"I'll bring it right in."

The door to Marcia's office was open. She rose to her feet as he entered, gesturing toward a chair directly opposite hers. "Thanks for coming in on such short notice, Lucien."

He waved her off as he sat down. "No need to waste any more time. I been guilty of that for years where Hazel's concerned. No more."

"Good."

"Before we get started, can I ask you a question?"

"Of course."

"What restaurant was she working in?"

"Kitty Galore's Raw Bar. It's in Ozona."

"Where's that?" he asked.

"The western edge of Palm Harbor," she said. "on the other side of Alt 19. Unless you know it's there, it's pretty hard to find."

Colleen brought in his coffee, turned on her heel and left, closing the door behind her. He took a sip and placed the cup on Marcia's desk. "Never heard of it."

"It's definitely a hangout for locals, but they get a lot of tourists during high season, so they get the word out pretty well."

Lucien made a mental note to check it out. "What's the plan?"

Marcia leaned forward eyes bright. "I'm going back there today to interview some people, see if I can find anything out from any of the employees still there who might've known her."

"Can I come along?" he asked eagerly.

Marcia was ready for the question. "I think it would be best if I go alone this first trip. Of course, I can't stop you from going – it's a free world. But I know how these things work. These folks will be more liable to talk freely if the father of the subject isn't in the room, hanging on their every word. Potential witnesses tend to get squirrelly, less open, with relatives." She could see the

177

disappointment in his eyes. "Trust me on this – don't take it personal."

"How about after today?"

"I think it would be a good idea for you to go in, on your own, after me. Again, it's up to you, but I have no problem with you trying to dig up some information, too. The parent of a missing friend or colleague usually gets a lot of sympathy. Maybe you'll be able to turn up some valuable information."

"What do you suggest I do until then?"

"I'd just stick to your normal routine," she said. "Did you hear about your audition yet"

Lucien nodded. "They called me back last night. I'm in."

"Terrific!" she exclaimed, thinking: he's going to have a revenue stream. "When do you start?"

"We have a rehearsal on Friday."

"Are these guys any good?" she asked.

"The keyboard player, I think his name is Gabe, is really good. He used to tour with Koko Taylor and some other people you might've heard of."

Marcia had no idea who Koko Taylor was; she doubted she'd know any of the others. "I think that's great, Lucien. Tampa is a pretty good area for live music. There should be a lot of places the band will be able to play."

"That's what Rick, the bass player, told me. Lots of geezers like me, in their sixties and seventies, who still think that they're teenagers. Never gave up the sex, drugs and rock and roll lifestyle." He smiled. "Should be good for business."

"I agree," Marcia said, pulling out her file folder and the yellow legal pad. She picked up a pen and looked at him. "Is there anything else that we didn't cover in our initial interview that you can think of that might help find Hazel? Anything at all, no matter how small you might think it is."

Lucien closed his eyes reflexively, thinking. In a moment he shook his head. "Not that I can remember right now, but if I do think of something, I'll give you a call."

"Anytime, night or day. You have my number – use it." She almost added "because you're paying for it" but held back. She knew her fee was a sensitive subject for him.

"So how will this work?" Lucien was a fan of crime dramas on television, but he wasn't convinced that they depicted what actually happens during a real investigation.

"Well, the best-case scenario would be to find someone who was her friend at the restaurant, a confidante she might've told her plans to when she left Kitty's. If such a person exists, it'll save us a lot of legwork and time."

Lucien liked how Marcia was using the collective us. It made him feel like an active participant, rather than a passive bystander. "I wish I knew more about her," he said wistfully. "Contribute more to the cause." He looked at her. "What's the worst-case scenario?"

Marcia shook her head. "We're already beyond that – we found a previous employer, one from not too long ago. Don't waste time dwelling on the negative."

"If you say so…" His voice trailed off, laced with doubt.

She looked him in the eye, forcing him to match her gaze. "We're going to do everything we can and then some. If she's out there, we'll find her."

30

Marcia spent the rest of the evening compiling notes for her interviews with employees at Kitty Galore's tomorrow. Because she was energized by the prospect of generating more leads at the restaurant tomorrow, she wanted some upbeat music in the background. She looked through her CD rack for a few moments before finding what she wanted: Martha and the Muffins' *This is the Ice Age*.

She smiled to herself as she slid the disc into the player. If it hadn't been for her late father's Canadian heritage, she never would've known about this band. Clement Harkins had been born in the tiny town of Northbrook, Ontario, and the tales he'd told of an idyllic childhood spent in the forests and around the rivers and lakes in the sparsely populated tourist region known as the Land of Lakes had created indelible impressions in his only child. When Marcia was old enough, she began to learn more about Canada; a major part of her learning curve was the discovery of a vibrant music industry north of the border that was largely undiscovered by its neighbors to the south. Bands like Teenage Head, Rough Trade, Spirit of the West, the Northern Pikes, 54-40 and the Tragically Hip became the soundtrack of her life as a young adult.

But none was more meaningful to her than Martha and the Muffins. Maybe it was the female vocalist, Martha Johnson. Maybe it was the pointed lyrics, some of which were ahead of their time in feminist political content. Maybe it was the infectious, up tempo beat this pioneer Canadian punk band favored.

It was a cut on this very album, "Women Around the World at Work", that had guided her through her darkest time, when she had been married to Javier Alvarez and had suffered from unimaginable physical and psychological abuse. She'd always liked the beat of the song but had never really listened much to the lyrics before then. Closer examination, based on countless plays, revealed in the words a dark history of female exploitation, some of the victims as young as twelve. It turned out to be a dark anthem of protest shrouded beneath an infectious, danceable pop beat. Then as now, it was her favorite song by the band.

As the music filled the condo, she began to compose a letter to the restaurant's business manager, Betty Duval, asking if she could provide Marcia with a complete list of employees who had worked at Kitty's between 2015 and 2017, along with their contact information. No doubt some if not most of that information was likely to be outdated. Except for cell phone numbers – people tended to hold onto what was familiar to them and their friends. If Betty agreed to share those numbers, it would really jump start the search for Hazel Devereaux.

Gracie had mentioned on several occasions that Betty, whose office was in a white frame building directly across Orange Street from Kitty's, often walked across the street for lunch with owner Florence Leaf and her husband Walter. She might get lucky and run into Betty tomorrow, but in case she didn't, she'd leave the request with Gracie to pass on the next time the two met.

She picked up her phone to check the time: 8:27. No wonder she was starving; she began to root around the meager contents of her refrigerator, looking for something to eat. She selected a plastic container of leftover soup and heated it in the microwave, making a note to go shopping tomorrow, after her trip to Kitty's.

*****

Back at his apartment, Lucien put on Little Feat's *Waiting for Columbus* and pulled out his battered laptop, the one he'd purchased using the money he'd received for transporting that mysterious package from Orlando to Tampa fourteen years ago, and Googled Kitty Galore's Raw Bar.

He marveled at the genius of Lowell George as he scrolled through the rather basic website for Kitty's, skimming through a group of photos showing various staff members and smiling customers before settling on a brief history of the building that houses the restaurant. Formerly owned by one of Tampa Bay's most notorious bootleggers who made his fortune smuggling rum from Cuba during Prohibition, the building had changed hands several times before current owner Laurel Flowers purchased the two-story home in 1985 and converted it into a restaurant and raw bar with a laidback, Key West vibe.

The bar area reminded him of one his favorite bars back home in Louisiana, the Chart Room in New Orleans, with its nautical theme and collection of kitsch attached to the walls and ceiling. Even though he knew little about his daughter other than her name, he felt that Kitty's was the kind of place she would like. According to a brief bio of the place, it attracted a mixture of locals and snowbirds drawn in by one of the area's best selection of fresh, local seafood dishes and a lively bar trade. Its location a stone's throw from the Gulf of Mexico would also have attracted Hazel, who grew up similarly close to the Gulf in Biloxi.

Hell, it looked like a place *he* would like himself. He smiled at pictures of the annual Ozona Christmas parade, an event consisting entirely of locals driving cleverly decorated golf carts through the streets of the tiny community, the local open-bottle ordinance obviously suspended for the event. Everywhere he looked on the website, people were laughing, having fun, radiating a "wish you were here" attitude that the establishment seemed to foster.

182

His cell phone chirped, interrupting his virtual tour. He smiled when he saw the Caller ID: Monroe Jessup. He answered eagerly. "Monroe! How ya doin'?"

"I'm well, Lucien. You?"

The two had reconnected when Lucien had reached out to Monroe to see if he could help in getting Lucien's guitars out of the Nashville pawn shop where he'd sold them when he'd resumed his love affair with heroin. Both of the guitars were gone by the time Lucien inquired, but Monroe, buffered by the distance between the two, gradually assessed through their remote conversations that his old friend was on the rise again, which pleased him enough to resume their friendship. He'd been disappointed when Lucien had accepted a position with the cruise line, a job Monroe called "working for the dance band on the *Titanic.*" But he understood that a job was a job. At least Lucien was playing music again on a regular basis and being paid for it. It was a big step in the right direction.

"I'm doin' great, Monroe," Lucien gushed. "Everything is finally falling into place for me." Pause. "About fuckin' time."

"That's good to hear. What sort of things are you talking about?"

"Well, I landed a gig with a local band here in Tampa. I auditioned for them last week, and we're having our first rehearsal tomorrow night."

"That's great," Monroe enthused. "These guys any good?"

"One of 'em is. Gabe, the keyboard player, used to play with Koko Taylor. He's a real pro."

"That does sound promising. What about the others?"

Lucien hedged a bit before replying. "Well, they ain't terrible. Rick, the bass player, is decent. He was a big fan of Jaco Pastorius. Tries to model his playing after Jaco's style. The other guy, Tate, is our drummer. He'll do, but if someone better comes along…" He let the sentence hang.

"How's the audience for live music in Tampa?" Monroe asked. "I've never been there. I've only heard some things."

"It's pretty good," Lucien replied. "It ain't Nashville – what is, besides maybe Austin? – but it's pretty good. There's a place down here called Skipper's Smokehouse that Rick says might give us a weekly gig, every Wednesday night. They used to have a reggae band there on Wednesdays, but the locals didn't support them much. A lot of big acts play Skipper's – the Subdudes and Tab Benoit play here, and Donna the Buffalo plays every New Year's Eve."

"What kind of music will this new band play?"

"Mostly southern rock, I think, Allman Brothers, Lynyrd Skynyrd, which should be right up my alley. Rick says, and I believe him, that I'll have plenty of opportunity to shine. Maybe some Little Feat and Widespread Panic. Give me a chance to improvise a bit."

"Sounds promising," Monroe said approvingly. "This band got a name yet so I can follow you on YouTube?"

"Nothin' official yet, but I got an idea. Came up with it the other day after they told me I was in. I gotta run it by the guys tomorrow night."

"What is it?"

"Last of the Mojitos."

184

31

John Rucker and Nelson Gregory were already in the kitchen, prepping for lunch, when Gracie arrived the next morning a little before 10:00. Nelson looked up from the order of oysters that had been delivered earlier as she breezed in. "You're early today," he said in mock amazement. "What gives?"

"You make it sound like that's a rare occasion," she replied defensively.

Nelson gave her a sly smile. "You don't really want to go there, do you?" The bartender had a well-deserved reputation for running late.

"Not really." She reached into her purse and withdrew a sheet of paper, handing it to him. "Remember when I came in here yesterday afternoon, asking about a waitress who used to work here named Devereaux?"

Nelson nodded. "Yeah. Hazel, right?"

"My friend Marcia, the private investigator, is working for her father, trying to find her. She sent me a text last night, saying she'd like to speak to anyone who might've worked with her while she was here. I'm not sure if Betty's going to be in today – normally she'd be the one I'd talk to about this. I was wondering if you could jot down any names you might remember who was working here at the same time Hazel Devereaux was."

Nelson glanced at the list briefly, then folded it and put it in his back pocket. "I'll look at it today, when we get a lull."

Gracie continued. "Marcia said she was going to come in today, so this is a heads up."

"I'll get to it as soon as I can," Nelson said reassuringly.

John Rucker, who'd been feigning indifference to the conversation but was in fact hanging on every word, spoke up. "What's her father's name?"

They both looked at the young apprentice, startled. He rarely opened his mouth while at work. Gracie was the first to recover. "Lucien."

"Damn!" he exclaimed.

Nelson looked at his young protégé. "You know him?"

John shook his head. "Not personally, but, dude, Lucien Devereaux? He's one of the best guitarists in the world, right up there with Clapton and Joe Bonamassa. He's played with everybody!" He paused for a moment. "I can't believe it. Lucien Devereaux," he breathed reverently.

"Try not to pee your pants, rookie," Gracie advised. "My friend told me he'll probably show up here, looking to talk to some of the waitresses who knew her, so pull yourself together."

"Lucien Devereaux…here?" John couldn't wait to tell Kevin and Evelyn. He wished he'd brought his guitar to work today.

Gracie shook her head, then looked at Nelson. "Try to keep him in line, will you?" she instructed as she turned and walked out of the kitchen.

*****

Marcia arrived precisely at 10:50, just enough time for her to have a cigarette on the bench outside before the restaurant opened. When she was finished she plopped herself down on a stool next to the service bar, grinning widely. Gracie was slicing limes and lemons and looked up. "Just like the old days," she said, referencing Marcia's daily lunchtime visits while her father was still alive. "You turning into a regular again?" she asked as she drew a Yuengling draft and put it on a coaster in front of Marcia.

"You never know," Marcia replied with a smile. "Two days ago I would've bet against it, but a lot has changed since then." She took a full sip of her beer, savoring the cold liquid as it slid down her throat.

Gracie reached beneath the bar and placed a menu next to Marcia's beer. "Well, if you are, you need to keep your eyes open for Reb Jadel."

"That Cracker asshole? Why?"

"When you went racing out of here yesterday, you practically bowled him over while he was coming in."

"I never even saw him," Marcia offered in defense.

"That's what I told him," Gracie replied. "That you were in a hurry and he shouldn't take it personal that you didn't say hello."

"Why would I say hello to that moron? He couldn't pour sand out of his shoe if the instructions were printed on the heel."

Gracie laughed. "Well, you must've done something to piss him off. He calls you Gumshoe now, and it's not in a flattering manner."

Marcia had never mentioned the offers of dates she'd refused from him to Gracie. No need to share now. "He still come in for lunch a lot?"

"Most every day. The place where he works is only five minutes away." She leaned across the bar, continuing in earnest tones. "You really struck a nerve with him yesterday. He never went back to work. Stayed here all afternoon, draining Buds like they were oxygen. I threatened to cut him off until he handed me his keys." She shrugged. "I have no idea how he got home. His truck is still out back, in the corner."

"Not my problem." Marcia looked around the empty bar. "Think the manager will be in today?"

"Hard to say," Gracie said. "She doesn't have any set schedule. It usually depends on Florence's mood. Betty does whatever Florence tells her to." Florence Leaf was the owner of Kitty Galore's Raw Bar. "Walter's been under the weather lately, so I haven't seen them much." Referencing Walter Smart, Florence Leaf's second husband. Gracie went on. "I shared your list with Nelson in the kitchen when I came in this morning. He's been here a long time and has a good relationship with the waitresses. He told me he'd put a list together of women who worked here while Hazel did."

"That would be nice," Marcia said, treading cautiously. "But he wouldn't know their contact info, would he?"

"Probably not," Gracie conceded.

"That's the kind of stuff that I really need to see." She reached into her purse and withdrew a sealed envelope. "It's all laid out in this letter."

Gracie took the envelope and put it in her own purse. "If Betty doesn't come in today, I'll drop this off at the office before I go home tonight." She looked at Marcia. "Funny thing. I mentioned the name of your client when I was talking to Nelson, our chef, in the kitchen this morning, and his apprentice piped up, said he knew him. By reputation, anyway. Said he's one of the greatest guitar players in the world." She looked at her friend inquiringly. "That true?"

"He *is* a musician – that much I know. But I never heard of him before he showed up in my office."

"I guess the Rucker kid – the apprentice – is a musician, too. Plays guitar in some punk band called Alien Colonoscopy."

Marcia screwed up her face in disgust. "Nice image. Who came up with that name?"

"He said he did. Said it's meant to make you think."

"Of what?"

Gracie shrugged. "Who knows? He's just a kid. I never had one of my own, so I don't have anything to offer about what goes on in the minds of today's youth." She smiled, then continued. "I *do* remember that when I was a teenager, I'd say all sorts of things, trying to piss off my parents, especially my mother. Maybe he's just trying to be a smartass, the same as we were."

Gracie nodded sagely. "Some things never change." She pointed to the menu. "Do you want to order some food?"

Marcia pushed the menu back across the table. "Grouper sandwich, blackened. And another beer."

32

Lucien Devereaux's childhood had been far from idyllic. He'd grown up in the bayou country near Lafitte, Louisiana, the youngest of Antoine and Evangeline Devereaux's four children. His mother had died while giving birth to Lucien, and his father had never seemed to forgive his youngest son for the part he played in his mother's death.

Antoine was a shrimper like his father before him. He worked long days and nights, often in the wee hours, which meant the four children were often left to fend for themselves. He worked hard and played hard; he was rarely out of reach of a beer or some bayou everclear when he wasn't on the boat. As soon as Lucien was old enough, he grasped the key to staying safe in their volatile home from watching his older siblings. Whenever they could, they'd steer clear of the old man. The farther away they were from him, the less likely it was that they'd turn up in school the next day, sporting visible bruises. His oldest brother Jean-Luc referred to that ploy as survival of the fastest.

Lucien was a particular target of his father because of the manner in which his mother had died. But Jean-Luc and his other brother Fabien were nine and eight years older than him, respectively, and they did their best to shield their younger brother from the horrors they themselves had endured in the aftermath of their mother's death, each of them willing to absorb more than their share of liquor-fueled abuse to keep Lucien out of it for as long as they could. It wasn't until years later that Lucien began to comprehend the extent of the personal sacrifices his brothers had made to keep him safe.

Despite the outbursts of domestic violence at home, Lucien admired his father for his skill on the guitar. The family never had much in the way of material wealth, but music was their sanctuary; what little money there was left after purchasing food and clothing went toward strings for their instruments. Antoine played guitar, older sister Ameline was on the fiddle, Jean-Luc on banjo and Fabien on the mandolin. In a perfect world Lucien would've fleshed out their bayou family band on the stand-up bass, but since he was the youngest, too small to handle such a ponderous instrument, he was allowed a rare moment of free choice to pick the instrument he wanted to play.

Because his daddy was his hero, despite his tendency to use his fists on his family when inclined, all Lucien wanted to do was play the guitar. Not just play it, but play it better than his father, better than anyone else. His single-minded drive, so rare in one so young, served a dual purpose – it kept him safe from his father, whom the children knew was less likely to fly into one of his dark rages if they were practicing their instruments, and it resulted in Lucien's amazing proficiency. Although he never learned to read music until he was much older, in his twenties, he was a natural, enthusiastically playing scales, sometimes until his fingers bled, completely absorbed in the process, a perfectionist always in search of the perfect note, the perfect chord, the perfect progression. That ability to tune everything else out in the quest for musical proficiency had unintended consequences – it kept him, for the most part, from serving as his father's punching bag on the darkest of nights. It also offered him a path out of Lafitte, one that didn't include a life in the family business as a shrimper.

He jumped at the chance to escape that fate, leaving the bayou for the big city lights of New Orleans when he was seventeen. He'd been a horrible student, absent more often than not, opting to stay home to play his guitar rather than wrestle with the vagaries of book learning. He was never going to college, so why stick around?

He found work in a restaurant in the Garden District, riding the streetcar to and from the tiny apartment on Canal Street he shared with one of his co-workers, playing his guitar on vacant street corners in the French Quarter, where on most weeks he made more than he did at his dishwashing job. Between work and busking, he had time for little else. But he didn't care – the way he figured it, he was now a professional musician. People were paying to hear him play. He couldn't be happier.

It was during one of those busking sessions that he got his first real break. He was ripping through a frenzied version of "Foggy Mountain Breakdown" one Monday evening near Jackson Square, fingers flying, but the streets were mostly empty, his audience chased away by a steady rain that night. He was almost finished with the song when a black man in a fedora and raincoat stopped to listen. When Lucien had finished, the man placed a five-dollar bill in his donation cup and looked at him intently. "Not bad, whitebread. Can you play anything else?"

Lucien was staring at the five-dollar bill. No one had dropped a bill of that value in his cup before. He peered up at the man, the only other person on the street as far as he could see. "You bet."

Without hesitation he broke into "Black Mountain Rag", a favorite of his daddy. The black man watched in silence, listening intently as Lucien sped through the intro, into the middle bars usually handled by a fiddle, mimicking the longer, drawn-out notes with some impressive fretting and improvisation before finishing up with up with a blazing run of finger picking. He looked up at the black man expectantly when he finished.

He was nodding in approval. "Don't know that I ever heard Doc or Chet play that song like that. Where'd you learn to play, whitebread?"

"Lafitte, Louisiana, sir," Lucien replied. "Down in Jefferson Parish."

"How old are you?"

Lucien tried to make himself look taller, even though he was in a sitting position. "Seventeen, sir."

"How long you been playin'?" he asked as he withdrew another bill from his wallet, a ten this time, and dropped it into his cup."

Lucien was stunned. Two songs, and he'd made more money than he took home from the restaurant in a week. "Uh, since I was seven, sir."

"Self taught?"

Lucien shook his head vigorously. "No sir. My daddy taught me. Antoine Devereaux."

"He done a real good job. What's your name?"

"Lucien. Lucien Devereaux."

The black man smiled. Indicating the empty streets with a sweeping gesture, he said, "What do you say we get out of the rain, get something to eat?"

Lucien was on guard. He had no idea who this black stranger was. He wasn't sure he should trust him. Although he hadn't been in New Orleans long, he knew that the streets, especially in the Quarter, always held an element of danger

The black man saw him hesitate and moved quickly to reassure him. "I just want to talk a bit, Lucien." He extended his hand. "My name's George. George Porter, Jr. It's a pleasure to meet you."

Lucien, hesitated, then extended his hand. Porter looked him in the eye. "I know one of the best gumbo shops in the city, not two blocks from here. Where do you live, son?"

"On Canal Street."

Porter lit up with a luminescent smile. "Perfect. Should be an easy walk home from there." He indicated Lucien's guitar. "Pack that up before it gets any wetter. Let's get something to eat."

Lucien followed his benefactor over to St. Peter Street. The two headed west on St. Peter as the rain began to ease. Midway between Royal and Bourbon, Porter ducked into an unmarked doorway almost directly opposite Preservation Hall. If he hadn't been with Porter, he never would've known the place existed.

Inside, Porter led him to an open table against the far wall. Lucien looked around. It was a small place – he counted seven tables, four of which were occupied by diners enjoying a late supper. His pulse jumped – his was the only white face in the place. He took care to stand his guitar case against the wall behind his chair before double checking to make sure the money he'd collected was safely in his pocket.

When they were settled, a broad-hipped woman came over and, without saying a word, planted a kiss on Porter's lips. Porter smiled and turned to Lucien. "Lucien, meet the greatest cook in New Orleans, Annamae Cantrell. Annamae, this here is Lucien Devereaux. I expect you're going to hear a lot about him one day."

Annamae looked at the guitar, then at Lucien's youthful face. "He a player?"

Porter smiled. "You could say that. If I didn't want him to get a big ole head, I'd say he was already better than Leo."

Annamae viewed him with renewed interest. "You don't say. What you boys gonna have?"

"Two bowls of gumbo."

"Coming right up."

Lucien watched her disappear behind a curtain, then turned back to Porter. "What's the name of this place?"

"Annamae's," Porter replied.

"Who's Leo?" Lucien asked.

Porter smiled. "Leo Nocentelli. He's in a band with me, but he got hisself drafted a month ago. So we got ourselves an opening, at least for two years. Maybe longer, if they send his ass to Vietnam."

Lucien looked at Porter. "You play an instrument?"

Porter nodded. "Bass guitar."

"Stand-up, or electric?"

"Electric. Can't get no funk out of a big ole stand-up."

"My daddy wanted me to play the bass," Lucien said as Annamae brought them both a glass of water. When she was gone, he continued. "What's funk?"

Porter leaned back and guffawed, a full-throated sound that had every eye in the place shift in their direction. He rubbed an imaginary tear from his eye before he continued, still chuckling. "Leave it to whitebread to ask a question like that. You ain't never heard of funk?"

Lucien shook his head. Porter continued. "How about James Brown? Heard of him?"

Lucien nodded. "Who hasn't?"

"Well, Mr. James Brown is the king of funk. Ain't nobody else do it the way he do."

Lucien leaned forward eagerly. "Your band plays with James Brown?" he gushed.

"Not hardly. For one thing, we ain't got no horn section. Just guitar, bass, keyboards and drums. Plus, James Brown wouldn't give us the time of day." He winked at Lucien. "Not yet, anyway." He looked at his young companion. "You follow music at all?"

Lucien shook his head. "Not really. We had a record player back in Lafitte, but not much money. My daddy had a few records, Ralph Stanley and Bill Monroe mostly."

Porter nodded approvingly. "So you cut your teeth on bluegrass music. No wonder your fingers move the way they do." He changed gears. "What is it you do at this restaurant you work at?"

Lucien's head drooped. "I'm a dishwasher."

Porter smiled. "Good, honest work. People gotta eat and somebody gotta clean up their mess afterwards. You like it?"

Lucien shook his head. "It's boring. But it pays the rent."

Porter leaned forward, his eyes shining. "How'd you like to quit that job?"

Lucien was confused. "What would I do for money?"

"You'd play in my band, at least until Leo gets out of the army. You ever play an electric guitar?"

"No sir, never."

As Annamae brought two steaming bowls of gumbo to their table, Porter continued. "Well, we're gonna have to change that. You gonna need an electric guitar if you want to learn how to play funk."

Lucien bent down to smell the gumbo. The aroma was intoxicating. He looked up, face filled with wonder. "You offerin' me a job, Mr. Porter?"

"If you want it."

"For money?" Lucien couldn't believe what he was hearing.

"It won't be no fortune, but yeah, for money. More than you're makin' at that restaurant."

Lucien wanted to pinch himself. Was he dreaming? "You want hire me to play for money after hearing me play two songs?"

Porter smiled. "Those weren't just any songs. Both of 'em have a lot of bite. You played the hell out of 'em, whitebread. Of course, the rest of the boys will have to sign off on you, but that won't be no problem once they hear you play. I know my boys pretty well." He looked at him critically. "Can you read music?"

Suddenly Lucien's hopes went down in flames. He hung his head, avoiding eye contact. When he spoke, his voice was barely audible. "No, sir, I can't."

"That don't matter none," Porter said. "Woulda been nice, sure, but it ain't necessary."

Lucien looked up, hope restored. "Really?"

"Really. You got any money saved?"

Lucien's hopes were dashed again. "No, sir. I can barely pay my share of the rent. If I wasn't workin' in a restaurant, I wouldn't have enough money to eat."

"That don't matter," Porter said. "We'll get you an electric guitar. You can pay us back out of your share of the take."

"The take?"

"What the house takes in chargin' for admission. We usually get a percentage of that, plus a percentage of the bar take if the owner ain't too smart. Split four ways, of course. How does that sound?"

"If you wanna know the truth, Mr. Porter, it sounds like I'm dreamin'."

"You ain't dreamin', whitebread. It's as real as it gets. There's no better place in this country to make music than N'Awlins." Pause. "And the name is George. Mr. Porter is my daddy."

"Yes sir, George." It felt strange to call an adult by their first name. It was something he'd have to get used to. "Mr.,er, George?"

"Yes?"

"What's the name of your band?"

Porter smiled. "If I tell you, will you shut up long enough so we can eat this gumbo before it gets cold?"

Lucien nodded vigorously. "I promise."

"The Meters."

33

Marcia was finishing the last of her fries when Lucien Devereaux walked into Kitty's. He stopped next to her, blinking several times to help adjust his eyes to the indoor lighting after the brilliant sunshine of the afternoon, unaware that his investigator was beside him, within arm's reach.

She waited a moment, then reached out and tapped him on the thigh. "Can I buy you a drink, sailor?"

Lucien instinctively backed away from Marcia's initial contact until he saw who she was. Grinning in relief, he slid into an empty seat next to her. "You half scared me to death."

"You need to get out in the public more, get acquainted with people," Marcia suggested with a smile. "Would you like a drink?"

He struggled against his instinct to default to alcohol before speaking. "I will, thank you. Sweet tea with lemon, if they have it."

Gracie had noticed his arrival and leaned in, smiling. "It's one of our specialties." As she poured the tea from a chilled pitcher

Marcia continued, addressing Gracie. "This is the guy I was telling you about. Lucien Devereaux, this is Gracie Fenton. The best bartender in Florida."

Lucien nodded toward her. "Pleased to meet you, ma'am."

Gracie placed his tea on a coaster. "Same here, Lucien. Welcome to Kitty Galore's."

His eyes finally adjusted, he took in the bar area, noting several stuffed fish, a deer head and the moose head, and license plates from all over the country. "Interestin' place you got here."

Gracie smiled. "We like it. Can I get you anything to eat?"

Lucien had skipped breakfast earlier, too excited by the prospect of seeing where Hazel had worked to eat. He was hungry. "I think so."

Gracie handed him a menu. "Take your time. I'll be back in a minute." She headed to the other end of the bar to check on customers.

When she was out of earshot, Lucien spoke. "Nice lady," he said, nodding in Gracie's direction.

"She's one of the best. Worth getting to know, that's for sure. She and her boyfriend invited me over for Thanksgiving right after my father died a couple of years ago. Salt of the earth, Gracie Fenton."

"I'm sorry to hear that," Lucien offered sympathetically. "About your father."

"Thanks. It was a rough patch, that's for sure," she said as she popped the last French fry into her mouth and swallowed the last of her beer. "But it's in the past now."

He looked at the full bar, conversations buzzing, satellite radio tuned to a station from the Eighties, five televisions above the bar featuring various sporting events, their volumes muted. He tried to envision the daughter he'd never met working here, wearing one of the Kitty Galore tank tops that all the waitresses were wearing. Had she made any friends here? Where did she go when she left?

Marcia interrupted his reverie. "I have to get back to the office to work on your case. Enjoy your lunch."

Lucien had been studying the menu. He looked up. "What's good here?"

"I've been comin' here for a bunch of years, and I've never had anything that *wasn't* good." She pointed to the soups. "They even have a pretty good gumbo. At least for Florida."

"I was wonderin' about that," he said, smiling. "I might just have to try it."

Gracie returned to their end of the bar to mix two drinks. While she was at it she said to Lucien. "If you're ready to order, I'll be right back after I deliver these drinks."

"Yes, ma'am."

Marcia spoke. "You can cash me out as soon as you get a chance." She looked at Lucien and winked. "Some of us have to work today."

Gracie frowned, feigning offense, as she cashed Marcia out and handed her a bill. "Well, don't let me hold you up. Better get back to the No Tell Motel with your camera and kneepads." She winked at Lucien. "For crawling around in the dirt outside the afternoon delight love nest."

Marcia rose to her feet and dropped a twenty on the bar. Addressing Lucien again, she cautioned. "She's just kidding - I never use kneepads. Make sure to double check the total on your bill before you pay."

Lucien shook his head as Marcia turned and headed out the door. He looked back at Gracie, puzzled. "Y'all are really friends? You sure have a funny way of talkin' to one another."

Gracie smiled widely. "Not just friends. Best friends." She refilled his tea glass. "What can I get you?"

"I'll try a bowl of your gumbo."

"I'll put the order in myself. Be right back."

Nelson and John were scrambling to finish off an order from a group of ten women who worked at an accounting office in Dunedin when Gracie came into the kitchen. "Here's your big chance, fanboy," she intoned, looking at the young apprentice. "One bowl of gumbo. For Lucien Devereaux."

John's head shot up. "He's here? Now?"

Gracie nodded. "He is. Says he hasn't had any good gumbo since leaving New Orleans." She smiled, adding. "No pressure," as she returned to the bar area.

Nelson brought him back to earth. "Finish this order first, okay? All we have to do is ladle the gumbo out of the pot for your hero."

John nodded. "Sure thing, boss."

*****

When Marcia returned to the office, Colleen handed her a pink phone message slip. "Get anything good at Kitty's?"

"The grouper sandwich was delicious," she said as she examined the message, noting the time of the call: 11:20.

"That's not what I meant," Colleen said.

"I know," Marcia said, entering her office, closing the door behind her.

She dialed the familiar number herself. After exchanging perfunctory niceties, Marcia spoke. "What can I do for you, counselor?"

Judy Ruliani responded in a cheery tone. "I'm just calling to congratulate you. Not everybody gets to sit at the head table at the Hearts Across The Bay gala. You've really hit the big time."

Marcia frowned. "Is there anyone who *doesn't* know about this?"

"I doubt it," Ruliani replied archly. "You're really taking advantage of your fifteen minutes of fame. You're the Tampa Bay "It" girl, Marcia, until someone hotter comes along. Better get used to it."

Marcia paused, her response temporarily muted by her attorney's characterization. No one had ever referred to her as being hot before, not even obliquely. "How did you find out?"

"I ran into Walker Stevens and his wife this morning when I was shooting a new ad. We use the same ad agency in Tampa, and they were there, doing the same thing. I asked Julia how things were going in preparation for the event, and she mentioned you'd accepted their invitation to attend." She paused before continuing. "What are you going to wear?"

"Good question," she replied ruefully. "I have to get something. Maybe this weekend."

"If you're interested in avoiding a wardrobe clash, I'll be wearing a striking mid-length gown, sort of a cross between violet and indigo."

"You're going, too?"

"Of course I am. What kind of charity gala would it be without the Tampa billboard lawyer?"

34

As soon as the group from the accounting firm had been served their lunches, John turned to Nelson with an imploring look, who responded in a somber tone. "Five minutes. No more."

John peeled off his gloves. "I'll be right back, boss."

Lucien Devereaux was engaged in conversation with another customer at the bar when John emerged from the kitchen. He looked vaguely familiar: dark hair graying at the temples, average height. Gracie was lingering near the two, engaged in the conversation. Bad timing, John thought as he returned to the kitchen.

Nelson looked up from the triple tail special he was dousing with cilantro aioli. "That was fast. Stage fright?"

"No," John answered sheepishly. "He was talking to some guy I've seen before who comes in for lunch. Gracie was talking with them, too. It would've been impolite to interrupt."

Nelson tried to recall the last time he'd heard a person John's age defer from doing anything because it would be impolite. Maybe there was hope for this kid yet. "You might get lucky." He smiled. "I could be the one to change your luck."

John was lost. "How?"

"He didn't just wander into this place by accident," Nelson explained. "He's looking for his daughter. She used to work here as a waitress. Out of the staff who are here today, I worked with her more than anyone. If I know Gracie, it won't be long before she pokes her head in and asks me to speak with him." He smiled. "Play your cards right and I'll introduce you. Until then, you can take this triple tail out to Gracie," he said, handing the plate to his young trainee. "Maybe you'll get lucky."

John smiled, nearly running out of the kitchen to deliver the dish to Gracie. She'd moved from her spot in front of Devereaux and the dark-haired man to a position in the middle of the bar. He approached her with the special. "Who gets the triple tail?"

Gracie pointed to the man in conversation with Devereaux. "The dark-haired guy at the end of the bar."

"Haven't I seen him in here before?" John asked.

"You have. That's Steve Morrison. He lives here, down near the marina. He comes in a lot for lunch."

"Thanks." He headed for the two, who were deep in conversation as he approached.

Morrison was speaking, the enthusiasm in his voice evident. "Dick Dale was the man, especially after I moved to California. Nobody played the guitar like he did." He saw John standing by, plate in hand, and smiled. "Must be my lunch," he said, reaching for the plate. "Thanks."

"You're welcome," John replied. Turning to Lucien, he took advantage of Morrison's distraction. "Mr. Devereaux, I'm a huge fan. It's really a pleasure to meet you."

Lucien responded in his measured Louisiana drawl. "What's your name, son?"

"John Rucker, sir."

Lucien's face creased into a warm, inviting smile. "How is it a young fella like you knows an old coot like me? Y'all a musician?"

John nodded vigorously. "I am, sir. I play guitar," adding quickly, "not anywhere near as good as you." He pointed to Lucien's empty bowl. "How'd you like our gumbo?"

"Pretty good, the best I've had since I left New Orleans." He eyed the young apprentice chef. "Y'all play in a band?"

"Yeah, but we're just starting out," John said. "We haven't played a gig yet."

"Well, John, that means we have something in common. I just joined a band this past week."

"Here?" John asked. "In Tampa?"

Lucien nodded. "I live here now. Been here for, oh, nearly thirteen years, I guess." He smiled again. "Time flies when you're having fun."

The last thing John wanted to do was break off this conversation, but he knew Nelson had him on a stopwatch. "Uh, it was a pleasure to meet you, Mr. Devereaux, but I have to get back to work before my boss kills me."

Lucien extended his hand. "Never do anything that puts your day job in peril. Being a musician is a tough way to make a living. This band of yours got a name?"

John shook his hand. "Alien Colonoscopy."

Lucien threw back his head and guffawed. "You young'uns are so creative – I love it! If you get any gigs, you'll have to let me know." He gestured around the bar. "I think I'll be spending more time in this place from now on." He smiled again. "Glad I finished my gumbo before you put that image in my head. See ya around, John. Nice to meet ya."

Morrison looked up from his triple tail, mouth full, as John mutely retreated to the kitchen. "Didn't know that kid was in a band. According to Nelson, he's pretty talented in the kitchen."

"Nelson?"

"Nelson Gregory, the chef. Says he's had a lot of apprentices come and go during his time here, but that kid's the best."

Lucien picked up on the inference, leaning toward Morrison. "How long's he worked here?"

Morrison laid down his fork. "Nelson? Let me see...I moved here four years ago and he was the chef then. You'd have to ask Gracie how long he was here before that."

Lucien did the math in his head. "Did you know my daughter, Hazel Devereaux? She worked here as a waitress from 2015 to 2017."

Morrison shook his head. "Sorry. I really don't pay that much attention to the wait staff. I always sit at the bar when I come here. Besides, they seem to turn over a lot. Hard to keep track of 'em."

Gracie returned, smiling approvingly at Lucien's empty bowl. "I guess you liked it."

Lucien nodded. "Coulda been a little spicier, but it wasn't bad for Florida."

She smiled. "I'll take that as a compliment. Can I get you anything else? Dessert?" she asked.

He looked longingly at the draft beer by Morrison's plate. There was nothing more that he wanted at that moment – to feel the cold, soothing effect of alcohol sliding down his throat, the companion that had comforted him to the point of abject despair on too many occasions in the past. He fought off the urge and nodded back toward the kitchen. "If it's not too much bother, I'd like to chat with your chef, Nelson. Doesn't have to be today. But sometime soon."

"It probably wouldn't be a good idea today," Gracie advised. "Marcia just gave him a list of questions of things he might be able to help her with during the investigation before she left. Give him a day or two to sort that through first." She smiled. "Nelson's a good guy. He'll get right on it. Except for Betty, he knows more about our staff than anyone."

206

"Betty?"

"Betty Duval, our business manager. Marcia is trying to get her to provide personal data for anyone who worked at Kitty's the same time as your daughter." Pause. "She left a letter with me to give to her, detailing exactly what she's looking for. I'm going to drop it off later this afternoon before I head home."

"I guess I'll have to come back, then," Lucien said with a smile. "You can give me the check whenever you get a chance."

As Gracie turned to total his bill on the touchpad, Lucien turned to Morrison. "Pleasure talkin' to ya. What did you say your name was?" he asked.

"Steve Morrison."

"Pleased to meet you." He stared closer at Morrison's features; there was something about him, a sort of *deja vu*. "I have the strangest feelin' that I know you from somewhere. You look awful familiar. What do you do for a livin'?"

"I'm retired," Morrison asked cautiously. He wasn't sure he wanted to get too chummy with this guy – they'd just met.

"How about before that, when y'all were still workin'?"

"I was an actor."

Lucien tapped the bar with his closed fist. "I knew it! I musta seen one of your flicks!"

Gracie handed him his bill, giving Morrison a wink that she concealed from Lucien. "If you're lucky, you haven't."

35

After Lucien paid his bill and walked out, Morrison addressed Gracie. "Thanks for not blowing my cover. He's an interesting guy. Sounds like he might be coming back, at least until he finds his daughter."

Gracie looked at him primly. "You mean you're hesitant to reveal your true identity as the star of such cinema classics as *Debbie Does Des Moines, Jurassic Pork* and *The French Erection?*"

Before he'd moved to Ozona several years earlier, Morrison had lived in Los Angeles and worked for more than thirty years in the adult movie industry, using the stage name Biff Bratwurst. Only a few close friends in Florida knew the truth concerning his previous life, a life he was anxious to keep under wraps for a variety of reasons. Gracie held that knowledge over him like the sword of Damocles. He ignored the dig. "He might be a good replacement for Rheinhart, now that he's in love."

"As a lunch partner, you mean?"

Morrison nodded. "Sure. I'll bet he has a lot of good stories. Sex, drugs and rock and roll, baby."

Gracie smiled. "You mean as opposed to sex, drugs and more sex?"

Morrison grimaced. "Don't remind me."

*****

Lucien was so excited about the progression of his case, he called Monroe Jessup in Nashville to report the good news. It took Jessup a long time to answer; Lucien was about to give up when he came on the line, breathing hard. "Lucien. Sorry I took so long to get to the phone." He sounded like he'd been running to answer the call. "You'll never guess where I am."

"Hmm, that leads me to believe it ain't Nashville."

"Yep."

Lucien waited a few moments before realizing Monroe wanted him to guess. "We gonna just sit here, growin' old together, or are you gonna tell me?"

"Guess."

"I got no idea," Lucien snapped impatiently. "Geography ain't my long suit these days. Just tell me."

"Okay." He sounded disappointed that Lucien refused to play along. "I'm in Muscle Shoals, at Blake's studio."

"Blake Garrison? Tell that Yankee I said hi."

"I will," Monroe replied. "He invited me down. He and a bunch of his buddies from high school are all down here, laying down tracks for a CD. You know Walt Timmins?"

"The name sounds familiar."

"He was Blake's best friend back in New York when they were kids. They played in the same band together in high school, and they're having sort of a working vacation down here along with some of the other guys from the old days. Turns out, a bunch of them go back to New York for a weekend every July to reform the old band. A lot of their friends come back – it's like a reunion. They call it Riverstock. They're making a CD to sell this summer

209

and giving the proceeds to the high school music department where they all got their start."

"You and him are from the same place up there, right?"

"Almost," Monroe replied. "I'm from Niagara Falls. Blake and Walt are from Riverton, a small town a few miles away. Back then, my band used to play a lot of the same places as they did."

"What was the name of your band again?" Lucien asked

"New River. Me and Pierce Caldwell and Henry Williams."

"I remember Henry. He played with Firefall for a while."

There was nothing wrong with Lucien's memory, Monroe thought. "That's right." Pause. "Would you like to say hello to Blake?"

"I would," Lucien asserted. "Put him on."

In a moment Blake came on the line. "Lucien! How the heck are you?"

"Hangin' in, Blake, hangin' in. Sounds like you got a houseful."

Blake laughed. "Just a few old friends. And Monroe."

Lucien chuckled. "Same old Blake. Monroe tells me y'all are makin' a record."

"Yeah. We're recording some of the tunes we used play when we were in a band together in high school, plus a new song that Walt wrote called "Floatin' Down the River." It's part of a fundraiser for our old music department back in New York." He paused before continuing. "Monroe told me you're pretty busy these days down in Tampa. Too bad – we could've used you on guitar."

"Sounds like you got plenty of players already. Besides, it's Muscle Shoals – you can't walk ten feet without running into a session man down there."

"That's true," Blake conceded. "But it would be nice to play with you again, Lucien." He hesitated a moment before continuing, lowering his voice. "Monroe tells me you're sober these days. I think that's great."

"Thanks, Blake. One day at a time. You know the drill."

Blake knew all about Lucien being tossed off the John Hiatt tour when he was living in Nashville. "Still, I'm proud of you."

"Thanks, Blake." Time to change the subject. "What are y'all doin' besides havin' a high school reunion? What keeps you busy these days? Or are you still milkin' that Grammy for all it's worth?"

Blake laughed again. "That Grammy bought me my studio. Best thing that ever happened to me. Once these guys are gone, I'm going on tour with Marie Osmond as her musical director. She's playing some dates out west, ending up in Las Vegas. Should be a lotta fun. Then I head back to New York for Riverstock."

"Y'all sure are one busy fella. Couldn't of happened to a nicer guy."

"Thanks, Lucien. I am truly blessed." He dropped his voice again. "Monroe told me about your daughter. I hope you're able to find her. If there's anything I can do for you in that regard, name it. Anything you need, understand?"

"Thanks, Blake. I truly appreciate it. I got a real good detective workin' on the case, Marcia Alvarez. You mighta heard of her after her last case, the one with that pro football player's wife. Anyway, she's real good. I got a lotta confidence in her abilities. But thanks for the offer."

"It's always there, anytime you need it. All you have to do is call."

"Sounds like a line from a song."

"I do believe it is," Blake replied. "I'm going to give you back to Monroe now. It was great talking with you, Lucien. It's been too long."

"Same here, Blake. You take care."

"You, too."

In a moment Monroe was back on the line. "Blake tell you about his son?"

"He never mentioned his family. How they doin'?"

"His youngest, Brent, just graduated *summa cum laude* from Northern Alabama. Plus, he was a four-year starter on their baseball team. A second baseman, I think." Pause. "He's a great kid."

Lucien had no idea what *summa cum laude* meant, but it sounded impressive. "Blake still a Yankee fan?"

"Diehard. I think he wears pinstriped pajamas. He told me he met Derek Jeter a few years back, during his farewell tour."

Lucien shook his head in wonder. "It's amazin' what winnin' a Grammy can do. Derek Jeter, huh?"

"Derek Jeter."

36

It took a week for Betty Duval to respond to Marcia's request for contact information regarding former employees of Kitty Galore's. Gracie called Marcia to relay the news. "It's here, at the bar, in an envelope with your name on it. Betty told me to say she was sorry it took so long for her to get back to you."

Marcia was elated; now she would have something concrete to move on. "Hell, a week is nothing. Tell her I really appreciate it."

Instead of letting her impatience over the slow rollout of the investigation dominate her thoughts, she used the time to knock some items off her to-do list. With the help of Colleen, she picked out a dress for the Hearts Across The Bay gala, keeping in mind her attorney's warning not to duplicate her violet gown. She'd selected a sleeveless teal gown that extended just to her knees, with a scoop neckline designed to draw some attention. Once again, she was grateful she hadn't adorned her arms with tattoos when she was in the army like so many of her fellow soldiers.

Colleen was amazed by the alacrity of the process, which involved a single stop at a shop that Marcia had researched online. "That was really fast," Colleen marveled as Marcia stood in line, waiting to purchase the first dress she'd tried on. "It usually takes me a week before I find anything I like."

Marcia explained her shopping philosophy succinctly to her young assistant as the cashier packaged her purchase. "That's because I'm a buyer instead of a shopper, which is the opposite of what most women are. I figure out what I want and then go get it. For me, hanging out at the mall or any other retail outlet is torture. I'd rather undergo surgery without an anesthetic than spend time shopping."

Because she was a reluctant participant on social media, Marcia gave Colleen the assignment of pouring through Facebook, particularly the page set up by Kitty Galore's, for any photos that might have included Hazel Devereaux. Colleen quickly discovered that Hazel didn't have a page of her own, which disappointed Marcia, who thought that most if not all women in Hazel's demographic – she was thirty-four – were slaves to social media. Hazel Devereaux was the exception to that rule, which would make her harder to find.

Colleen unearthed a number of group photos that included staff members of Kitty's, mostly taken during their annual anniversary celebrations throughout the years. Because most of the photos weren't tagged, there was no way of knowing whether Hazel was in them until they were shown to someone from the restaurant. Colleen printed copies for Marcia to circulate among employees at the restaurant; by the time Gracie phoned with the news that Betty had compiled a list of names and information, Marcia had a stack of photos on her desk providing vital context to the information Colleen had compiled thus far.

As soon as she finished her phone call with Gracie, Marcia called through her open door to Colleen. "I'm going to Kitty's to pick up the list. Can I bring you anything back?"

Colleen thought for a moment, mulling her options before replying. "Bring me a Cobb salad. Last time the French fries that came with the coconut shrimp didn't age well."

*****

It was more difficult for Lucien to wait for information to come from Kitty Galore's. Although he couldn't afford to eat there on a regular basis – his band had yet to play their first gig, so he was relying mainly on his Social Security payments to survive – he stopped by several times in hopes of discovering some new nugget of information that might be important enough to advance the stalled investigation. Twice he ran into Steve Morrison, whom he found to be an engaging and interesting guy. He also enjoyed chatting with Gracie, whose tales of tavern follies made him laugh, helping to ease the disappointment that no additional information had yet been uncovered as to his daughter's location.

Most of all, he enjoyed talking with John Rucker, advising him in unvarnished terms of how difficult the life of a musician would be while at the same time not wishing to extinguish his enthusiasm for music. The kid was sharp and clever – he asked all the right questions and didn't shrink away from the answers that fell outside his own narrative. Because Nelson would only allow him to leave the kitchen for brief intervals, John's questions and remarks were pointed and never wandered. He made good use of the time he spent with Lucien.

Lucien's band had also established an ambitious rehearsal schedule which occupied most of his evenings. Three nights a week he headed to Rick Manning's house as they continued to become more familiar and comfortable with one another's abilities. An unexpected bonus derived from the formation of a band comprised of senior citizens was a total lack of ego on display during these rehearsals. The other three had enthusiastically accepted Lucien's proposal to name the band the Last of the Mojitos during that first rehearsal; if that suggestion had been offered by an incoming band member when all of them were in their twenties, the debate would've raged for weeks. Now, Tate, Gabe and Rick were relieved that someone had taken the initiative – it was one less thing they had to worry about.

215

He continued to struggle with the temptation of alcohol; each of the other members of the band were enthusiastic drinkers, beers plentiful during their rehearsals. Lucien hadn't mentioned his struggle with his addictions to any of the other three, although he suspected Gabe, because of the time he'd spent touring with some major blues' artists, might be aware of it. The coconut telegraph that ran through the music industry was as efficient as they come - substance abuse had derailed a lot of promising careers and the reporting of those flameouts had an insatiable group of followers. He was grateful that no one had yet questioned his avoidance of beer during those sessions.

Lucien had resisted a bit when they began to discuss what their playlist might be. The other three were all in agreement that, because of Lucien's skill and knowledge, southern rock would be the foundation of the band's setlist, but they also agreed with Rick's suggestion that they include some Jimmy Buffett tunes in their repertoire, citing their location. Tate said it best: "We're in Tampa, man. Gotta play some Buffett if we want to get any gigs outside of Skipper's. If we're gonna be called the Last of the Mojitos, people are going to expect us to play Buffett." Rather than oppose the majority on this subject, even though he considered most of Buffett's songs the equivalent of musical cotton candy, Lucien capitulated without much of a struggle.

It felt good to be back in a band, to experience the sort of camaraderie that develops when a group of like-minded folks unite behind a shared purpose. Rick had stated that purpose clearly during Lucien's audition: "We're here to enjoy ourselves, have a little fun playing music. If we can make some money at it, all the better. But it has to be fun."

It was also after that first audition that Rick, after the other two had left, retreated to the house and returned with some weed and a small pipe. "We have a friend out at Fuego who grows their own. He gets his seeds from a major grower in the Denver area. It's pretty good shit."

Lucien watched as Rick fired up the pipe and inhaled deeply. He offered the pipe to Lucien, who turned it down with difficulty. Rick's wife Elaine came into the garage then, accepting the pipe while mockingly accusing her husband of smoking behind her back. She winked at Lucien. "He does this to me all the time."

"I'm only thinking of your best interests, honey," Rick protested. Explaining to Lucien. "She still gets drug tested where she works."

"I'm an adult, dear," she stated. "You need to allow me to make my own decisions." She inhaled deeply, held it in for a minute before exhaling and offering the pipe to Lucien.

His resolve had evaporated. It had been a couple of years since he'd smoked weed, before the cocaine bust that cost him his job with the cruise ship line. He accepted the pipe and inhaled tentatively, unsure of the quality. Rick noted his timid intake and commented. "It's pretty good, but not killer. You can take a full hit and not hallucinate," he said with a wide smile on his face. "Take another."

Rick was right – it was good shit. Lucien's second hit was more robust, filling his lungs before he handed the pipe to Rick. Flavorful, but not harsh. He felt relaxed already, tension flowing from his body as the pipe made another round. When his turn came again, Lucien demurred. "I haven't done this in a long time, plus I still have to drive home. I think I'll pass."

Rick didn't argue. He took a final hit and tapped the ashes into a small trash can next to the door which led to the house, putting the still-warm pipe into the pocket of his shorts.

One item from before was puzzling Lucien. "What's Fuego?" he asked.

Rick looked at him in surprise. "You don't know about Fuego?"

Lucien shook his head. "I don't get out much."

"Fuego is a resort over in Land O' Lakes for nudists and swingers," Rick explained with a smile. "Would it shock you to know that Elaine and I are members out there?"

Lucien blushed. He couldn't help stealing a glance at Elaine, wondering what she looked like naked. After a moment he

217

turned toward Rick and answered. "Not really, I guess. But it is a little weird…for me, that is."

Rick smiled. "Weird clings to Florida like unwanted cat hair. Get used to it."

37

Steve Morrison was in deep conversation with a man at the bar when Marcia arrived. The Friday afternoon lunch crowd had filled the bar, leaving no unoccupied bar stools. She stood by the service bar, surveying the situation, shaking her head. Gracie caught her eye from the other end of the bar where she had just delivered two lunch orders, holding up a finger. Be with you in a minute.

Marcia observed a couple several seats down who were examining their check, preparing to leave. They counted out their cash, placed it under an empty glass along with their bill, and rose to leave. Marcia had spotted another couple sitting at a two-top against the wall further down the bar who were also eyeing the departing couple. As they reached their feet, Marcia darted from the end of the bar and managed to claim one of the recently vacated seats. She resisted the temptation to turn and look at the couple whose shift to the bar had been preempted by Marcia's quickness off the mark as they returned, disappointed, to their small table. You snooze, you lose, she thought.

Gracie had noticed Marcia's dash for a seat, nodding in approval as she drew Marcia a draft and placed it in front of her. "You move pretty good for an old broad."

Marcia took a sip of her beer. "Who you callin' old?" she asked with fake belligerence.

Gracie smiled. "I have no control over the calendar," she said as she grabbed the envelope from beneath the bar and handed it to Marcia. "I just call 'em as I see 'em."

Marcia noted the envelope was still sealed. "You didn't open it?"

Gracie shook her head. "Doesn't have my name on it. Since you're in law enforcement, I didn't want to get arrested."

Marcia tore open the envelope as Gracie leaned over the bar to get a closer look. It was a neatly compiled list of employee names, email addresses and telephone numbers for each employee who was working during Hazel's time at the restaurant. There was an asterisk next to several of the names. Marcia checked the bottom of the page and found that each asterisk denoted an employee who was still employed at Kitty's. She looked at Gracie, beaming. "This is perfect. Exactly what I need."

"Betty's a whiz at Excel," Gracie said. "She uses it all the time to keep track of inventory. Putting together the list you wanted was a snap." She reached beneath the bar again and withdrew another envelope. "I have a bonus for you. Nelson knew that you were looking for stuff about Hazel, so he spent one night, on his own time, going through the restaurant's Facebook page in depth. He found something you're going to like."

Marcia looked at the envelope, then at Gracie. "What's in it?"

"Open it and find out."

Marcia tore open the envelope. Inside were two pictures, candids snapped during what appeared to be some sort of celebration. Each of the pictures featured two young women with their arms draped over their companion's shoulder. One woman was common to both photographs: a dark-eyed brunette with straight hair to her shoulders, an average build and a tattoo just below her left shoulder, in the area of her bicep. In each photo her expression was dour, unsmiling.

Marcia grasped the implication immediately. "Is that her?"

Gracie nodded. "That's Hazel Devereaux. Those pictures were taken at our staff Christmas party three years ago. Nelson found them when he was looking through a photo scrapbook Florence put together of the party. He scanned the originals, so you can keep those."

"Who are the other women in the photo?" Marcia asked eagerly.

"The other brunette is Florence's daughter Alexandria," Gracie replied, referring to the owner of Kitty Galore's. "She worked here for a while before she moved to Atlanta with her boyfriend."

"Was she friends with Hazel?"

"Not really. I think Florence had them pose for a picture. Hazel doesn't seem to look too pleased about it."

Marcia shifted her focus to the second picture. "What about the other one? She doesn't look much happier there." Meaning Hazel.

"She never smiled much at all, as far as I can remember," Gracie said. "Although she should've been smiling more in that one."

Marcia looked at the blond bartender intently. "Why is that?"

"Because she's with her BFF in that one. Faye Tompkins, the weekend bartender here. She and Hazel were pretty close."

Marcia took a closer look. Faye Tompkins was strikingly attractive, several inches taller than Hazel, with dirty blond hair and an impressive multi-colored tattoo on the upper right portion of her back that peeked out from beneath the Kitty Galore tank top she was wearing in the photo. "She still work here?"

Gracie nodded. "Faye works tonight, after I leave, and from open to close on both Saturday and Sunday."

Marcia winced. "Sounds like a brutal schedule."

"Not for Faye," Gracie said with a shrug. "She likes the long hours, plus she has four days off every week."

Marcia stared at the photos, pointing at Hazel's tattoo. "Do you know what that says?" she asked Gracie. "It's too small for me to read."

Gracie smiled. "I thought you might ask that. I couldn't remember myself, so I texted Faye and asked her. She says it's a name. Lily."

Marcia looked up at Gracie. "That's her mother's name. Lily Verlaine." She made a note to follow up with Faye. "Do you have Faye's telephone number?"

"Sure," she said, reaching for a pen and a piece of paper from next to the cash register. She pulled out her cell, called up her contacts, and jotted down Faye's number before handing the slip of paper to Marcia. "She knows you'll probably want to speak with her – I gave her a rough outline of what was going on."

Marcia's heart raced as she considered this unexpected good news. Things were finally starting to move – if they were lucky, Faye would still be in contact with Hazel and know where she was. She thought of how thrilled Lucien would be when he heard the news. After thirteen years of operating in the dark, there was a glimmer of light illuminating the road ahead.

She slipped the photos into the manila envelope containing the spreadsheet of employees, heart still pounding, adrenaline flowing, the world a brighter and better place than it was when she walked in. She drained her beer and indicated her empty glass. "Another, please."

"Coming right up."

As Gracie replenished her drink, Marcia nodded toward Morrison. "Who's that guy Morrison is talking to? He looks familiar."

"He is. Remember Guido?"

Recognition dawned on Marcia's face. The dark-haired, swarthy man talking with Steve Morrison at the end of the bar had been one of Gracie's mystery customers two years ago. He'd shown up one Friday and proceeded to come into Kitty's every Friday after that, always alone, always ordering the same dish and same glass of wine before paying his tab and leaving. The taciturn man had resisted Gracie's attempts to elicit any personal information, which resulted in Gracie deciding he was an ex-Mafia figure currently in the Witness Protection Program. She called him Guido Vaticanini.

It wasn't until six months later that Morrison, during an innocent luncheon conversation, had discovered the man's real name and background. Rather than the exotic fantasy Gracie had concocted around the mystery man, the reality of his true circumstances was rather mundane. It turned out Guido Vaticanini was actually Arnold Berman, a resident of Southold, Long Island who'd retired to Florida with his wife Charlene a few years earlier. His wife had been killed in an automobile accident, and his silent grief had been wildly misinterpreted by Gracie as some sort of attempt to avoid attracting any attention from any Mafia types who might be looking to settle a score.

Marcia gave him a long look. "I remember that story now, but he looks different to me. What changed?"

Gracie smiled. "About sixty pounds. That's how much he's said he's lost since last year."

Marcia looked down at her own waistline glumly. "Wonder what his secret is?"

"I can introduce you if you like."

38

Instead of going back to the office and then returning once Faye Tompkins started her shift, Marcia decided to spend the afternoon at Kitty's. That way she could kill two birds with one stone – she could talk to Nelson once his shift ended to pick his brain some more, and she could question Faye in depth, as long as the late-afternoon bar crowd didn't preclude their opportunity to chat.

She phoned Colleen and told her of her plan. "Unless there's anything that needs my attention before the weekend, that is."

"What about my Cobb salad?" Colleen asked in mock indignation.

"Shit," a crestfallen Marcia exclaimed. "I forgot all about your lunch. Guess I will be coming back to the office, after all."

Colleen laughed. "Don't bother. It certainly wouldn't hurt me to miss a meal or two. I think I can survive."

"Are you sure?"

"Positive. I think I have a package of cheese and crackers somewhere in my desk. Besides, it's only a salad, right?"

How had she been so lucky to find a gem like Colleen? "If you don't mind…"

"I don't," Colleen said firmly. "But I *will* add it to the growing list of things you owe me."

*****

Gracie overheard the end of Marcia's conversation and prepared to draw her another Yuengling, but Marcia waved her off. "I've decided to stay and talk to Faye when she comes in, so I better take it easy. Give me an iced tea, unsweetened, instead." She scanned the bar area – there were only half as many customers now as when she arrived. "Does it always slow down like this between lunch and dinner?"

"Usually it does, but Fridays are funny," Gracie replied. "Sometimes it never lets up. Depends who's here." She pointed to the end of the bar. "See those two old guys sitting next to Morrison and Arnold?"

"The bald guy and the guy with glasses?"

Gracie nodded. "They come in here every Friday between November and May, like clockwork. Both of 'em claim to be married, although I've never seen their wives in here."

Marcia was confused. The two men Gracie had pointed out were engaged in conversation with two women to their left, who responded periodically with bursts of laughter. They looked to be the right age to be married to the men. "Those two aren't their wives?"

"Nope. But they're usually here with them, laughing at all their jokes, knocking back the drinks the men buy for them." She smiled at Marcia. "If those guys weren't so old, I'd say they were chasin' a little on the side. But I know they're not. The women

225

always leave together; the guys always stay for another drink or two before they leave."

Marcia watched the group, her investigator's genes kicking in, idly wondering how much Viagra cost for Medicare patients. Next to them, Arnold Berman was getting to his feet. He caught Gracie's eye and waved before heading out the door at the far end, the money for his lunch beneath his empty wine glass. Morrison rose with him, clapping him on the shoulder before heading in Marcia's direction, beer in hand. He pointed to the empty barstool next to her. "Anybody using that?"

Marcia smiled. "It's all yours."

Gracie leaned in, a smile playing on her lips. "She doesn't believe Statler and Waldorf aren't married to those babes. Must be her private eye instincts."

Marcia interjected. "Those are their names?"

Morrison laughed. "No. I think their names are Joe and Mark. But Gracie thinks they look like those two old guys on *Sesame Street* who sit in the balcony and offer unsolicited social commentary, so she calls them Statler and Waldorf." He looked at the clock by the cash register, then at Marcia. "Taking a long lunch today?"

"Yeah. I want to talk to Faye about a case I'm working on, so I decided to hang out till she gets here."

Morrison leaned forward eagerly. "The Devereaux case?"

Marcia nodded, wondering: is there *anyone* in this place who doesn't know her business? "According to several sources, she was Hazel Devereaux's closest friend while she worked here. I'm hoping she can help me find out where Hazel might've gone after she left Kitty's."

"Can't help you there. But if the trail leads to LA, that'd be a different story." He finished his beer and addressed Gracie. "Cash me out when you get a chance."

"Time for your nap?" Gracie asked teasingly. "Must have a big weekend ahead."

"Not that it's any of your business, but yeah, I do."

"What's her name?"

Morrison ignored Gracie's probe, answering only with a smile before turning to Marcia. "Good luck with Faye. Gracie's right – if anyone here knows where the Devereaux girl went, it would be Faye."

Gracie dropped his bill on the bar in front of him. He gave it a cursory glance, retrieved a ten and a twenty from his wallet to cover it and got to his feet. "Take it easy, you two." Looking at Marcia, he added. "Good luck with Faye. Let me know how it works out."

Gracie busied herself washing beer and wine glasses and serving other customers as Marcia watched a succession of fishing shows on the television above the cash register. She glanced at the other sets, which were tuned to a golf tournament and a NASCAR highlights program and decided to stick with the fishing shows. She was watching one located in the Keys when Faye Tompkins came into the bar at two minutes past five.

Gracie nodded toward the clock by the cash register and crossed her arms in a mock gesture to indicate her disapproval at her friend's tardy arrival. "Traffic jam?" Faye lived five minutes away in Palm Harbor.

Tears welled in Faye's eyes, and her lip trembled as she struggled to respond. Gracie noticed her distress, dropping her sarcastic tone as she moved to her friend's side and put her arm around her. "What's wrong?" she asked with concern.

Her voice caught as she answered, thick with emotion. "They canceled the trip."

The trip. For over a year, members of the current senior class at Palm Harbor University High School had been raising funds to help finance a senior trip for the ages: two weeks in the Galapagos Islands. Faye's son Seth was a member of the senior class and had poured his heart and soul into the effort, raising the second-highest amount of any senior in the school. Faye was planning to go with her son and had been as excited about the

227

prospect of this once-in-a-lifetime opportunity as Seth, offering animated weekly updates to Gracie as they neared their departure date. Gracie had never seen her friend as enthusiastic and upbeat as she'd been during the past year. But somehow, now, the bottom had fallen out. "What happened?" Gracie asked gently.

Sniffling, Faye managed to get it out. "Mr. Macaluso, Seth's biology teacher, organized the trip. Two days ago his mother, who's in her late eighties, had a massive stroke. She's a widow – her husband died about ten years ago – and Russ, Mr. Macaluso, is her only child. He didn't feel right trying to arrange for someone to attend to his mom while he was away on a school trip and decided it was his responsibility to care for her. So he talked to the tour group organizer and decided to cancel the trip. He had to decide right away because the deadline for cancelling the trip and getting our deposit back is next Wednesday." Her body shuddered. "Seth is crushed." She wiped away a tear. "So am I. I was so looking forward to this."

Gracie gave her friend a gentle squeeze before releasing her. "Do you want me to take your shift? I will if you want me to."

Faye shook her head. "No. I need to stay busy. If I went home, all I'd do there would be think about it and cry." She squeezed her friend's shoulder. "Thanks for offering."

Gracie noticed the unease on Marcia's face, as if she'd intruded on someone's confession to a priest. Maybe the investigation would provide another diversion for Faye, another way to keep her mind from pondering the cruelty of her fate. She indicated Marcia. "I'd like to introduce you to a friend of mine. Faye, this is Marcia Alvarez. She's a private investigator trying to find Hazel Devereaux. She has a few questions to ask you about her."

Faye looked at Marcia for a long moment before she spoke. "You're looking for Hazel?"

Marcia nodded, feeling foolish at having interrupted at such an inopportune moment.

Faye almost managed a smile. "Join the club."

39

The next evening, on her way to pick up Colleen, her date for the Hearts Across The Bay charity event, Marcia went over the scant information Faye had been able to provide her concerning Hazel Devereaux. She'd worked at a number of restaurants in the Tampa Bay area, never staying very long in one place before moving on, arriving at Kitty Galore's in January of 2015. She was a hard worker from the start, never shirking a shift or showing up late, but her success was hampered by an inability to exhibit any sense of joy. She rarely smiled, and when she did it was in the company of others on the staff. Her customers noticed; at the end of her shift her tip totals were usually dwarfed by the totals of her coworkers. "She just looked sad all the time, as if she was about to burst into tears at any moment," Faye had said. "Customers want a little smile, a little flirting to make them feel better about themselves. Hazel usually looked like she was planning her own suicide. Looking unhappy all the time cost her money."

Faye went on to say that they had socialized together on several occasions – going to the beach on their day off, going out for a drink after work – but Hazel was reluctant to talk about herself, deflecting any attempts by Faye or anyone else aimed at penetrating the barrier she'd erected around the details of her personal life. As far as Faye knew, with the exception of those few outings, Hazel spent her time away from Kitty's at her apartment, an apartment Faye had never visited, sulking and feeling sorry for herself. Faye had no idea that Hazel's mother had died, a victim of domestic violence, or that she'd never met her father – she knew nothing of Hazel's past. All she knew was that Hazel seemed to be the saddest woman she'd ever met.

Things changed one afternoon in March of 2017 when Roberto Salazar stopped into the restaurant for lunch. Hazel was next up in the rotation that day and was dispatched to his table to take his order, anticipating a subpar tip because he was by himself. After a minute or two of idle chatter he ordered a drink, and when Hazel came to the bar to give Gracie the order, she was smiling, chuckling to herself according to Gracie. It was the first time Gracie had noticed any joy in Hazel since she'd started more than two years earlier. It was such a seismic shift in her demeanor that Gracie had mentioned it to Faye during changeover the following Friday. "Not only was she smiling, she was actually laughing!" Gracie had marveled at the time.

Salazar was darkly handsome, of Latin descent, a stylish dresser whose fashion sense stood out among the usual array of T-shirts, cargo shorts and flip flops worn by the restaurant's clientele. He was older than Hazel – both Gracie and Faye calculated that he was in his mid to late forties – with a seductive smile worthy of a toothpaste commercial that oozed charm.

After that first visit Salazar became a regular, but only when Hazel was working, always requesting her as his waitress, willing to wait until she was available. On those occasions, Faye said, both she and Gracie would try to pry information from the charming mystery man. They each noticed that he wore no wedding ring, nor was there a tan line visible to indicate that a ring might have been removed before he entered the building. But the women were frustrated when they tried to get him to talk about himself; he was content to parry their questions with that brilliant smile until Hazel became available.

The change in Hazel was astonishing. According to Faye and confirmed by Gracie, Hazel began showing up for work wearing makeup on the days Salazar would visit, something she'd rarely done before. Both women surmised that Salazar's visits were coordinated with Hazel's schedule. Were the two an item, or merely friends without benefits? The rumor mill at Kitty's wasted no time in concluding the two were sleeping together, a notion Hazel repeatedly laughed off when needled by other members of the staff. But it was the fact that she dismissed the rumors in such a jovial manner that convinced her coworkers that those rumors were likely true. The woman who not long ago had been the poster child for depression had changed radically since the arrival of Roberto Salazar.

Then things changed again. Near the end of April, after Salazar had been coming into the restaurant for more than a month, Hazel missed a Friday dinner shift and didn't call in to explain her absence. Both incidents were firsts for Hazel – unlike many of her coworkers who had come and gone during her tenure at Kitty's, she'd never missed a shift because of illness or any other reason.

When she arrived for her shift the following afternoon, Faye noticed that she looked different – she was jumpy, twitchy, easily irritated by things that hadn't bothered her before, reluctant to make eye contact during conversations. Faye thought she looked tired, as if she hadn't slept. She feared that her friend was displaying signs of recent drug use.

For the next three weeks, Salazar came into Kitty's every day that Hazel worked. Her fellow employees watched as the telltale signs of drug use became more prevalent: circles under her eyes, weight loss, disinterest in most things not having to do with Roberto Salazar. Like most restaurant staffs, the one at Kitty's was no stranger to the world of recreational pharmaceuticals. They picked up on the clues immediately, because they'd seen this movie before.

On the Thursday before Memorial Day weekend, she showed up for her scheduled shift in bad shape and at the end of the night handed Shelly Fairweather, the evening bartender, a sealed envelope addressed to Florence and walked out without saying a word. It was the last time anyone at Kitty Galore's saw Hazel Devereaux.

By the time Faye came in for her shift on Friday, the news was out: Hazel had given her notice. Faye immediately tried calling Hazel, but the call went to voicemail. Faye left a message, then continued to try to reach her, calling and texting her several times over the weekend and again the following week, each call followed by a message until her voice mailbox was full, unable to accept any more messages. Hazel never responded.

Roberto Salazar had also disappeared. It was too much of a coincidence to believe the two departures were unrelated, Faye concluded. There were only two reasons Hazel would leave so abruptly, without warning, at the same time as a man she hadn't known three months earlier. Faye narrowed it down to two choices: either Hazel was in love with the mysterious Latin, or he was the one supplying her with the drugs. Her greatest fear was that both were true.

She continued to reach out to Hazel for several months, mostly through texts. Hazel never responded. By the time Hurricane Irma arrived in September Faye had given up trying to reach her friend. After the hurricane Hazel became an afterthought for Faye and the rest of the crew before finally slipping away altogether. Out of sight, out of mind.

Marcia had latched onto the connection with Roberto Salazar, racing home the night before to try to find out more about him. She was aided by a photo of Salazar that Faye had snapped surreptitiously one evening while he waited for his dinner. She'd texted it to Marcia before she left Kitty's last night, along with the following plea: "If you find her, please let me know. I can't help thinking something bad has happened to her."

Marcia has spent the rest of that evening on Google Images, trying to find Roberto Salazar, using the photo Faye had texted her to corroborate his identity. She had no idea there were so many Roberto Salazars out there – she figured the name must be the Latin equivalent of Bob Smith. She worked until 2:00 am, until her eyes could stay open no longer, then started in again as soon as she woke, fueled by two pots of coffee and a dismaying number of cigarettes.

She also ordered five prints of the photo of Salazar that Faye had texted her and picked them up from the CVS at the corner of Curlew and 19 on the way to Colleen's home to pick her up for the charity event. According to Faye, Salazar was a big spender. If he was a local, chances are one of the other high rollers at the event tonight might recognize him.

Colleen McKinny lived in a small one-story frame house on a shaded side street not far from the business district in Safety Harbor. Traffic was moderate on Curlew as Marcia turned south on McMullen Booth Road, her mind more on Hazel than the traffic around her but began to become more congested as Marcia approached Main Street in Safety Harbor. Must be an event tonight at Ruth Eckerd Hall, she decided. She waited patiently for two light changes before turning left on Main toward Colleen's house.

She was ready as Marcia pulled up, emerging from her front door dressed stylishly in a form-fitting silver sequined gown, carrying a matching clutch. As soon as Colleen maneuvered herself into Marcia's Lexus, a difficult task in the tight dress, Marcia handed her a picture of Roberto Salazar. She looked at it for a moment before looking at Marcia. "Am I supposed to guess who this is?" she asked.

Marcia smiled. "That's Roberto Salazar." She explained what she had learned from Faye about Hazel and her connection to Salazar, adding. "He's your new assignment. I want you to dig up anything you can find on him."

Colleen studied the photo; in it, a man was examining a menu at a restaurant. She noted his olive complexion and dark eyes and hair before speaking again. "How old is this photo?"

"About two years," Marcia stated as she looked both ways and pulled away from the curb. "Show it around tonight, if you get a chance. Maybe we'll get lucky."

"So while you're hobnobbing with the rich and famous at the head table, I'll be working?" she asked dejectedly.

"At least you won't be bored."

40

The Hearts Across The Bay event was being held at the Jonas Salt Academy in the tony Hyde Park area of Tampa, not far from the University of Tampa campus. A crew of glum-faced parking attendants, work-study students resplendent in orange vests, directed Marcia and Colleen to a spot in the rapidly filling parking lot. The gala was being held in the prep school's cavernous athletic facilities building, which dominated the rear of the campus and had been transformed into an elegant dining area for the evening.

Looking around in awe as they entered the vestibule, Colleen remarked, "I've never been here before. Have you?"

Marcia shook her head. "I'm not the prep school type."

They were directed by an usher in a tuxedo to the welcoming area, where their identities were confirmed before they were handed the evening's program. In it was a listing of each attendee and the table number where they were sitting, as well as a schematic showing the layout. As they walked away from the reception area, Colleen's tone was subdued "I should've brought my binoculars. The kids' table is way in the back, against the wall. I'd need cab fare to get to the head table from there."

Marcia nodded toward a bar area set up along one of the expansive side walls. "How about a drink instead?"

"I'm right behind you."

The place was abuzz with chatter as members of Tampa Bay's upper crust filed in. Marcia recognized several faces: the mayor of St. Petersburg, the former manager of the Tampa Bay Rays who also owned a swank Italian restaurant near the Riverwalk, a female anchor from one of the local Tampa television stations, a famous former pro wrestler known for his bleached blond hair and impressive handlebar moustache. They were playing in the big leagues tonight.

She also spotted Walker and Julia Stevens, the hosts for the event, circulating among the early arrivals, pressing the flesh as they worked their way through the room, stopping to chat at every table along the way. For a moment the two were beside one another as they passed each other, heading in opposite directions; Marcia was surprised to see that Walker was decidedly shorter than his wife but dismissed the difference after noting the length of heels Julia was wearing.

Colleen felt strange, out of place as she waited for Marcia to return with her martini. As an insatiable consumer of local news and sports, she recognized more people than Marcia, which left an uneasy feeling in the pit of her stomach. She didn't deserve to be here among the local elite; if it was any other Saturday night she'd be home alone, wearing a T-shirt and a pair of shorts, popping popcorn in anticipation of the Saturday night movie lineup on TCM. She hoped that she wouldn't do or say anything to embarrass herself tonight. More importantly, she didn't want to embarrass Marcia or the firm. Lay low, enjoy the entertainment and escape unscathed. That was her plan. Until Marcia handed her the photograph of Roberto Salazar. Now, mute anonymity was no longer an option.

Marcia returned with her drink, which Colleen gratefully accepted. "What time does this thing start?"

"Seven, I think." Marcia glanced at her phone. "In ten minutes. I better get to my seat. I'll see you later. Don't forget to show that photo around."

"I won't," Colleen replied, wondering if she should get another drink before heading to her table. "Have fun."

In ten minutes the lights in the room flashed on and off, signaling the crowd it was time to find their seats. Another five minutes passed before everyone was seated and Julia Stevens stepped to the microphone. "I want to thank everyone for coming out tonight. As you know, this gala is our main fundraiser for the upcoming year, and we're counting on the generosity of everyone in this room to make this our best year ever. Domestic violence is a formidable foe, one that never sleeps or takes a day off. But with the help of people like you, our programs are designed to empower the survivors of domestic abuse, to protect them from further abuse and to help them re-enter society with renewed purpose, without fear."

Marcia, because of her late invitation, was in the last seat at the end of the head table, sitting next to a striking redhead, one of those beauties who could be anywhere from forty to seventy. As soon as Marcia sat down, the redhead turned to introduce herself. "My name's Gretchen Schiller, Marcia. It's an honor to meet you."

Marcia was stunned. How did this woman know her name? Seeing Marcia's confusion, the redhead explained. "You're wondering how I know your name. There's no mystery – I read that story about your work with that pro football player's wife in the *Times* and then looked you up on your website." She looked her up and down, smiling with approval. "You're more attractive in person than those photos on your website. You should think about getting a real photographer to give you some honey shots. I have a few names, if you're interested."

"Thank you, Ms. Schiller," she stammered. "That's very kind of you."

"Call me Gretchen, please." She withdrew a business card from her purse and handed it to Marcia. "You can reach me at the number on the card. Anytime."

Marcia looked at the card before sliding it into her purse. Gretchen Schiller, CEO of the Seneca Falls Capital Fund. "Are you here with your husband?" If she was, Marcia doubted that he was sitting at the kids' table with Colleen.

"I'm divorced," she stated plainly. "I usually attend functions like this alone."

Marcia blushed. Five minutes in and she had already put her foot in her mouth. "I'm sorry."

"Don't be. I'm not."

While Gretchen and Marcia were speaking, introductions were underway at the kids' table. There were eight of them at the round table, six women and two men. The two men interested Colleen the most – unless one or both of them were gay, their significant others were also women seated at the head table, where the women outnumbered the men by two to one. The older of the two was sitting next to her and introduced himself as Zach Rheinhart. He asked, "Who are you here with?"

Colleen pointed to the end of the head table. "With Marcia Alvarez," she said, quickly adding. "I'm not her date. I'm her employee."

His eyes widened. "Marcia Alvarez, the private investigator?"

She nodded in wonder. "You know her?"

Rheinhart laughed. "I do. I met her before she became famous, two years ago at Thanksgiving."

Colleen digested this news for a moment before continuing. "Who are you with?"

He pointed toward the center of the head table. "My date is the woman with light brown hair, two down from Walker Stevens. Her name is Gwen Westphal."

"The Olympian?"

Rheinhart nodded proudly. "That's her. These days she's a spokesperson for the Clear Sailing Alliance, a water rights advocacy group here in Florida." He turned the focus back on Colleen. "How long have you been working for Marcia?"

"Since she started."

"Has she taken you to Kitty Galore's yet?"

Colleen looked at him, amazed. "You know about Kitty's?"

"My house is right around the corner from there, about a five-minute walk."

"You live in Ozona?" She couldn't keep the envy out of her voice.

"I do. What about you?"

"Safety Harbor. And no, she hasn't taken me to Kitty's yet. The closest I've come is the takeout she brings back when she goes there for lunch. Coconut shrimp, usually."

"You need to check it out on your own sometime. It's a great place."

"That's what Marcia says."

Colleen turned her attention to the head table as Julia Stevens ended her introductory remarks and the wait staff began to emerge from the shadows with platters of dinners. Julia waited for the noise to subside before introducing the main entertainment for the evening, a young comedian who'd just filmed her first hour-long special for Comedy Central. "Ladies and gentlemen, please give a warm round of applause to Gay Morgan!"

The room filled with applause before the crowd turned their primary attention to their meals. Colleen thought it was a tough room for the young woman; they were more interested in the filet mignon and the Chilean sea bass than they were in her act. But she plowed ahead, relating anecdotes concerning her upbringing in Indianapolis, her father's alcoholism, her boyfriend's disdain for kinky sex, Internet dating, the disadvantages she faced as a woman in a man's world and her fascination with sex among farm animals in a forty-five minute set that was well received by the distracted crowd. Half the crowd stood and applauded when she finished; the other half still had their mouths full.

Marcia loved the brassy young woman's balls and applauded loudly when she finished, still chuckling at her unvarnished description of sex between a goat and a hyena. Gretchen approved as well, clapping politely as she polished off her bass. "That young woman has a future," Gretchen predicted.

A string quartet followed the comedian's set, which Marcia thought would've been better suited to the dinner hour than a raunchy comedy act. Not that she was against raunch – she was a twenty-year veteran of the armed services, a female who'd heard much worse from her male cohorts in uniform. But there were a number of people in the room who had gasped audibly during her raw description of the goat/hyena liaison.

Dessert – vanilla ice cream with fresh blackberries, crème brulee and a black forest torte – was served while the quartet played, followed by an orchestrated mingling session, where diners from the head table circulated among the tables on the floor, soliciting pledges of support for the cause. Marcia hung back. No one had told her about this portion of the evening.

Gretchen noticed her reticence. "What do you say we sneak outside for a little while and take in some fresh air?"

"I was thinking the same thing," Marcia said, reaching for her purse, which contained her cigarettes and lighter. "I could use a smoke."

Gretchen smiled. "I'm right behind you."

The pair weaved their way through the crowd, passing close to the kids' table. Marcia held up her cigarettes and pointed outside as they passed. Colleen nodded – got it.

Darkness had moved in, but the air was pleasant, in the low seventies. A full moon unobscured by clouds bathed the ground in pale light as Marcia bent to light her cigarette before offering one to Gretchen.

Gretchen shook her head. "Twenty years ago I would've said yes. Tonight I'll just breathe in your second-hand smoke. No need to exhale away from me."

Marcia exhaled. "I wish I could quit. How did you do it?"

"Cold turkey," Gretchen said. "I woke up one morning after a night on the town and the entire room smelled like a used ashtray. Including my hair. Each of my husbands smoked, so they never complained about how I smelled."

"Each?"

Gretchen nodded. "There were three. The first one died and I divorced the other two. I've been single now for fourteen years and loving every minute of it."

"Interesting," Marcia replied. "I was married once and swore I'd never do it again."

Gretchen shook her head in mock disapproval. "Never say never. But in the meantime, you can always date."

"I've been thinking about that lately," Marcia admitted. "Since my father died. I took care of him for a lot of years. That was a full-time job."

"I'm sorry to hear that," Gretchen said sincerely. "Losing a parent is tough. My father didn't die when I was young, but he was a doctor. He was never home. He might as well have been dead as far as I was concerned."

"Mine was in the Air Force. We moved around a lot, until my mother died. I was sixteen." She took a final drag and tossed her cigarette away. Remembering where she was, she quickly moved over to stamp it out. "Maybe we should head back in."

Gretchen smiled. "What's the rush? Nobody will miss us in that crowd. It's a beautiful night. We might as well enjoy it a little longer." She looked at Marcia. "Who's your date tonight?"

"I brought my secretary," she admitted, blushing. "I haven't dated for years."

Gretchen frowned. "You ought to get back out there, now that your father's gone. It's a brave new dating world, just like that comedian said. Internet dating is the rage."

Marcia looked at the redhead curiously. "Have you tried it?"

She nodded. "It's the only way I roll now. I can't be bothered by any of the traditional methods. I'm too old for that. Internet dating is perfect for my needs."

"What are those needs, if I might ask?" Marcia queried.

"I have simple needs when it comes to men," Gretchen replied with a provocative smile. "I like them young, well-mannered and hung like a thoroughbred."

Marcia stared, her mouth open. Gretchen noted her discomfort and continued. "At this stage of my life, dating is all about the bedroom. I don't need somebody to accompany me to charity events like this or the opera and the theater. The kind of men I prefer would be uncomfortable in those situations and so would I. I need somebody who can make me see stars with their tongue and their dick."

Marcia gasped. Gretchen's philosophy about dating was revolutionary to her. She made Internet dating sound very enticing, with minimal attachment and maximum pleasure. Wham, bam, thank you, young man. She finally managed to find her voice. "That works for you?"

"Like a charm," she replied. "When I decide on a guy and tell him it's all about the sex, usually I've vetted him enough by that point to know that he's going to love that arrangement. All he has to do is show up with an erection. No flowers, no dinners or introductions to anyone's parents. Just sex."

"What site do you use?"

"MeetMarket.com. It's more of a fucking site than a dating site. For consenting adults only. Less bullshit, more orgasms." She smiled before continuing. "How can you go wrong?"

Marcia couldn't argue with that. In her limited experience, usually it was men who were advocates for relationships like that, where biological urges trumped emotional commitment. It was refreshing to hear such frank talk about sex from a woman of Gretchen's stature and age. "You make it sound easy."

"Easier than sitting at a hotel bar, hoping that the guy who looks attractive and wants to buy you a drink isn't a rapist or some other kind of criminal. Internet dating takes a lot of uncertainty out of the process, as long as you're willing to be patient." She smiled again. "Having your own money helps a lot, too. Not having to depend on a man for support is the ultimate freedom."

41

Marcia wanted another cigarette before they went inside but was hesitant to display the level of her addiction to her new friend. Gretchen seemed to read her mind, nodding toward the pack Marcia clutched tightly in her hand. "Go ahead. Have another. I'm in no rush to get back. To tell you the truth, I asked Julia Stevens to seat you next to me tonight. I wanted to talk to you about your business. It's much easier to do that out here."

Given permission, Marcia lit another cigarette and sucked in the smoke hungrily. Exhaling, she said, "What would you like to know?"

"Your business, being a detective, fascinates me. How did you decide that that was what you wanted to do? Especially now."

Marcia hesitated for a moment. No one had asked her that question before. "You really want to know?"

Gretchen looked at her expectantly. "I do."

Marcia started at the beginning, with her disastrous marriage to Javier Alvarez and how the abuse she'd suffered at his hands had been so impactful that she'd given up a promising career in military intelligence to instead join the military police, where she thought she might be an advocate for those women who had suffered similar fates at the hands of their male partners. She related how her responsibilities in caring for her infirm father had superseded any post-military ambitions she might have had, pushing them to the back burner until her father had passed away. Freed from the adult daycare she was providing by her father's death, she used some money from her father's estate as seed money for Alvarez Investigations.

Gretchen interjected here. "You used your own money? No loans or lines of credit from a bank or venture capital firm?'

Marcia laughed. "Venture capital firm? You're joking, right? What firm in their right mind would invest in someone with no experience running a business, someone who hadn't even held a job for the last fourteen years?"

Gretchen's eyes caught Marcia's and held them. "Mine would. I started the Seneca Falls Capital Fund expressly to invest in women-owned businesses, the kind of businesses that used to never get funded by the old-boy banking system. Alvarez Investigations is *exactly* the kind of company I like to back – you've proven that by the work you did for that poor woman married to that football player."

Marcia looked at her in amazement. "Are you serious?"

"Very. You have my card. Call me on Monday if you're interested."

Marcia took a last drag on her cigarette. She felt light-headed, as if she were dreaming. "We should get back."

Gretchen gestured toward the entrance with a flourish. "After you."

*****

When they entered the building, Walker Stevens was chatting with a pair of women seated at Colleen's table. Marcia turned to Gretchen. "I'm going to see how my associate is doing. See you back at our table."

Gretchen shook her head. "Look for me at the bar." Before she left, she added. "I really enjoyed our chat. Don't forget what I said about Monday."

"I won't."

Walker, noticing that Marcia had come in with Gretchen, broke off his conversation with the women and viewed Marcia appraisingly. "What do you think of Gretchen?" he asked.

"I think she's wonderful," Marcia gushed.

He chuckled. "She is a smooth talker. And very generous – since she moved to this side of the state, she's become one of our most reliable and generous supporters. A little wacky politically, but she writes a mean check."

"Where did she come from?" Marcia asked.

"She used to live in Palm Beach for about thirty years. But after the 2016 election, she got so fed up with the horrendous traffic situation whenever the president visited Mar a Lago, which soon became every weekend, she decided she couldn't take it anymore and moved over here, to Tarpon Springs." He chuckled again. "At least that's her story."

"What do you mean?"

"She didn't tell you about her golfing date with the president? She loves to tell that one."

"We just met tonight," Marcia said in explanation.

"I'll give you the short version," Walker said. "Although she tells it much better than I do. Gretchen Schiller was born in Georgia and spent most of her childhood playing golf at the local country club. By the time she graduated from high school she was good enough to win a golf scholarship to Rollins College, up in Winter Park."

"Flash forward to two years ago, shortly after the election. She was invited to a charity function at Mar a Lago – she's always been very generous with her contributions to worthy causes – where she was introduced to the president. A third party mentioned that Gretchen used to be a top golfer, number one on her team at Rollins. The president, who as we know loves golf, was intrigued and invited her to play a round with him. I think she surprised him when she accepted; he expected her to be too intimidated by the occasion to say yes. Anyway, they set up a date and she showed up in a sleeveless blouse and a golf skirt that barely covered the goods. She knew he'd notice her outfit – she told me she wore it in order to distract him, throw him off his game. The woman is one serious competitor when it comes to golf."

He continued. "It must've worked, because according to Gretchen's scorecard, when they reached the turn, she was two over on the front nine. The president had struggled to keep the ball in the fairway and had putted poorly, so she figured she was well ahead of him. When she asked how he'd done on the front nine, rubbing it in, he leered at her and told her he was two under." Walker shook his head, chuckling. "I wish I was there to see her face when he told her his score. According to Gretchen, she managed to hold her tongue, not saying a word as she turned and removed her clubs from her golf cart. One of the Secret Service agents accompanying them asked her what she was doing, and she told them she was done for the day. According to her, her exact words were 'I don't play golf with cheaters'. The president was right there, heard every word, but all he did was watch as she walked away, too stunned to reply."

"She called the president a cheater? To his face?" Marcia was astounded by the move.

"Yep," Walker said with a wide smile. "Needless to say, it was the last time she was invited to Mar a Lago." He shook his head. "She told me later her only regret was not turning around to see the look on the president's face as she walked away."

The rest of the table was trying hard to pretend they weren't eavesdropping on the conversation but failing. When he'd finished the story, one of the women reached out, touching his hand to get his attention. She was in her sixties, overweight but fashionably dressed, with a diamond necklace that looked to Marcia's

246

untrained eye to be worth as much as her condo. "What is it, Margaret?" he asked.

"I'd like to hear a story, too," she pouted, crossing her hands in her lap, looking at him expectantly.

With Margaret Woodard's check not yet in his possession, Walker was accommodating. "What kind of story would you like to hear?" he asked.

"Oh, nothing to do with politics. There's way too much of that kind of talk already." She looked at him, still holding his hand, a mischievous grin on her face. "There must be a fascinating story behind how you decided on the name of your jewelry store."

Stevens was lost. The name of his store was Walker's Jewelers. There was no mystery why he'd chosen that name. "I don't understand."

She squeezed his hand. "I think you must've had many options that were much better than that, dear."

He offered some pushback. "Walker's Jewelers is pretty self-explanatory. What would you have me call it? Walker's Laundry?"

"Don't be silly. I was wondering why your lovely wife doesn't share the billing with you."

He realized she was trying to get a rise out of him. He tried to sound patient. "You know why, Margaret. She wasn't my wife when I started the business back in 1986."

"But she is now. And you must admit – she's a lot better looking than you are. Everybody remembers your commercials because of her, not you." She smiled, releasing his hand with a wink. "I'd think about it if I were you."

42

Lucien Devereaux was home, practicing his guitar, when Marcia phoned the following morning. Because he was a musician, she waited to call until eleven, figuring he probably slept in late. Weren't most musicians night owls? What she didn't know was that her client was having difficulty sleeping and had been up that morning before the sun rose and was finishing up his second pot of coffee when the phone rang. He skipped the preliminaries completely when he saw who was calling. "Got any news for me?"

There was a moment of hesitation before Marcia responded. "Good morning to you, too, Lucien."

"Sorry," a sheepish Lucien replied. "I figured because you were calling me so early on a Sunday that it was good news about the case." Pause. "Is it?"

"It could be," Marcia replied cautiously. "But I don't want to get too excited over this just yet. The bartender from Kitty's, Faye Tompkins, supplied some interesting information on Friday. She told me that, about six weeks before Hazel left, she met a guy, a new customer at the restaurant. Faye thinks the two of them became close because he became a regular and asked for Hazel to be his server every time he was there, which was almost every day she was scheduled to work. Faye figured it was just a snowbird romance – she told me they sometimes happen when single men come down for the season. Because they're by themselves and lonely, they become emotionally attached to a certain waitress or bartender - they hang out together, might even date. But the relationship usually ends when the customer goes back north."

Lucien was still trying to wrap his head around the concept of a snowbird romance. "She thinks that's what happened with Hazel?"

"She does," Marcia affirmed. "As soon as Hazel gave her notice and left, the man disappeared. Never showed up again. Faye figures – and I agree – that the two of them leaving at the same time was no coincidence."

"She give you a name for this man?"

"She did. Roberto Salazar. We're trying to identify him right now – I have Colleen on it full time. It's a common name, might take a little time to find the right guy, but it's a solid lead. I thought you'd like to hear a little good news for a change." She decided to withhold Faye's speculation that Hazel had started to take drugs after she met Salazar. No need to worry Lucien until there was some solid evidence to back up her guess.

"Well, I'll be," replied an exuberant Lucien. "Gettin' this kinda news on the Lord's day has to be a good omen, don't you think?"

Marcia had never known Lucien to express any interest in religious faith before now, but she wasn't going to say anything to diminish this small moment of optimism in her client. "It *is* good news, Lucien. We're going to use it to help track down your daughter."

"You get any other clues from that bartender?" he asked hopefully. Things were finally starting to move.

"I saved the best for last," Marcia said. "Faye gave me her cell phone number. If she's like most women her age, that phone will never be more than an arm's length away from your daughter."

"Did you try the number?" he asked expectantly.

"I did, first thing. She didn't pick up – probably because she didn't recognize the number that I was calling from. The call went to voicemail, but her mailbox was full, so I couldn't leave a message."

Lucien's knowledge of cell phones was scant. "Did you try her again?"

"Several times, all with the same result."

Lucien drew on the knowledge he'd gleaned from hundreds of hours of watching *Law & Order*. "Can we trace her phone, find out where she is?"

"Not unless she actually picks up when one of us calls her. We need a connection to trace her location. Or a warrant issued by a judge."

Lucien had another idea. "What about her friend, Faye? Can we ask her to call Hazel? She'd probably pick up if she recognized who was calling."

"She told me she tried calling for a week and Hazel never picked up. She left a couple of messages before the mailbox filled up, but Hazel never called her back."

Lucien was deflated by that news, but tried to rally, remain positive. "So what's next?"

"We need to find Roberto Salazar."

*****

John Rucker was having trouble sleeping as well, for a different reason. Tonight, Alien Colonoscopy was playing their first official gig at a dive bar in St. Pete called The Shed, and he'd been up most of the night, nerves jangling, going over the setlist. The band had been practicing for two months and had been having trouble deciding what songs to play. Both Evelyn and Kieran wanted to stick with songs they felt the audience would recognize, safe covers of previous hits from other bands, but John wanted to play two original songs he'd written, one as a member of his former band Humongous Fungus called "Eat This," and one he'd

250

written last week called "Nips Don't Lie" of which he was particularly proud. Although the title was a nod to the 2006 Shakira hit, the lyrics were starkly different: in short, staccato bursts they reduced the mystical notions surrounding the elusive concept of the female orgasm and how to recognize the real thing during the fray.

When the idea started to blossom in his head, he'd approached Evelyn during one of their rehearsals and asked if the suspicion he'd held since puberty was true. She looked at him for a moment, trying to figure out if he was teasing her or not before responding. "Speaking from personal experience as Lady Vulva, I can confirm your hypothesis." She quickly added, "Not that *I've* ever faked one..."

In his thick brogue, Kieran, who'd overheard John's question, addressed his bandmate's response with his usual succinct candor. "I call bullshit on that, m'lady."

Now, as their initial public appearance loomed, he reached for the piece of paper he kept in his guitar case that contained the original handwritten lyrics and went over them one more time.

Nips Don't Lie

Pigs don't fly

Boys don't cry

Scotch ain't rye

Don't ask why

Nips Don't Lie!

Money can't buy

Fish won't fry

All things die

Don't ask why

Nips Don't Lie!

Say goodbye

To apple pie

Just say hi

To Semper Fi

Nips Don't Lie!

Nips Don't Lie!

Nips Don't Lie!

Played in a furious manner, three-chord guitar progressions between each line, the song was, in John's opinion, destined to be the band's signature tune, the one the crowds would remember and clamor for. The other two required some convincing, and although Evelyn liked it, Kieran hadn't yet come around. John offered a compromise: he'd drop the idea of the band including "Eat This" in their setlist for now if they agreed to play "Nips Don't Lie." After a day or two of pressure from the other two, Kieran caved, but with a caveat. "If it bombs, we drop it. Agreed?"

John smiled. He was ready. A little nervous, but ready. He glanced at his phone for the time: 12:15.

He had eight hours to morph into Tornado Jones.

43

After ending her call with Lucien, Marcia pulled out the Hazel Devereaux file and began to sift through the new material she'd received from Betty Duval and Faye Tompkins. She selected a Spirit of the West CD for background music and made another pot of coffee in lieu of lunch. It was a pleasant morning, slightly overcast, a whisper of breeze from the south; she heard the joyful sounds of some youthful swimmers frolicking in the pool seven floors below through the open door to her balcony as she pored over the material.

In addition to the name Roberto Salazar and Hazel's cell phone number, she also had copies of credit card receipts for all of Hazel Devereaux's customers during the twenty-eight months she worked at Kitty's. Marcia marveled at Betty's ability to have tracked down and copied such a vast amount of material in such a short time. Gracie had said she was a real whiz in the office; the mounds of paper scattered on the dining room table in front of her proved it. Pouring herself a fresh cup of coffee and placing an empty waste basket by her feet, she began to wade through the receipts, hoping to find the name Roberto Salazar.

*****

"You should've seen the look on Walker Stevens' face when that woman told him his wife was better looking than he was. He *so* wanted to strike back, but he didn't have her check yet. It was priceless."

Zach Rheinhart smiled as Gwen Westphal shuffled through the Sunday *Tampa Bay Times*, looking for the Floridian section. They were in Rheinhart's cozy kitchen; Gwen had surprised him the night before as they left the Hearts Across The Bay event, suggesting out of the blue that she spend the night at his bungalow in Ozona. Sleepovers at his place were rare – she usually preferred the comfort of her own bed, without company – so Rheinhart had leaped at the opportunity, giving himself a virtual pat on the back for having the foresight to clean his house yesterday morning.

She found what she was looking for and looked across the table. "What was her name again?"

"Margaret something," he replied. "She's on the Board of Directors at The Straz and the Tampa Theatre. Her husband must've been at the head table – did you meet him?"

She shook her head. "I might've, but if I did it didn't stick. The only person I remember from last night was Charlotte Linderman. What an interesting woman she is."

He reached for the sports section. "How so?"

"She's a psychologist by trade. She teaches up north at Pasco Community College and has a small clinical practice one day a week."

"She give you any free advice?" Rheinhart joked.

Gwen looked at him narrowly. "Are you implying something?"

He leaned back, raising his palms in defense. "Not at all. What does she teach?"

"She's head of the Human Services department there. But that's not what I found interesting."

"What was?"

"She belongs to a group called Bikers Against Domestic Abuse, BADA for short. What a remarkable organization."

The organization was unfamiliar to him. "What do they do?"

"They provide support, mostly for children who are survivors of domestic abuse and violence in the home."

He looked up from the paper. She had his attention now. "What kind of support?"

"She told me it varies. Could be anything from stopping by to take the kids for a ride on her motorcycle to showing up in court with some of her colleagues to provide support when they have to face their abusers in court."

"She's a biker?"

Gwen nodded. "She has a 1957 Indian Trailblazer. Showed me a picture of it. What a beautiful machine. Looks like it just rolled out of the showroom." She continued. "Like most motorcycle clubs, the members all have road names. But in BADA, those names serve a different purpose."

"How so?"

"To protect the kids whenever they have to go to court. Since the members all go by their road names, no defense attorney can subpoena them to testify in any court proceeding, because they can't attach a real name to any court order. That allows the members the ability to show up in numbers to support their kids without fear of retaliation. Quite clever, actually."

"What's this woman's road name?"

Gwen smiled. "Headmaster." She gave it a moment. "Because she's a psychologist."

"Huh," Zach grunted. "I woulda thought it'd be Shrink."

"That was my thought, too. I asked why it wasn't and she told me that someone down in their Sarasota chapter already had that road name when she joined."

"They're a statewide organization?"

"International. They have chapters in more than twenty countries."

He shook his head. "Sounds like you had a much more interesting time than I did last night. At least you met more interesting people."

She smiled across the table at her lover. "That's why they call it the head table."

*****

Gretchen Schiller slept until nearly nine on Sunday morning, extremely late for her. Usually she was up with the sun, but last night had taken a lot out of her. Although she hated to admit it, she wasn't as young as she used to be. Missing her usual bedtime of ten o'clock by two hours carried a cost.

She had to admit it felt good to sleep in for a change. She was still getting used to her new neighborhood, and although she was sleeping in the same bed as she had in Palm Beach, the morning traffic patterns and noises around her new home overlooking Clark Bayou in Tarpon Springs weren't yet regular routine for her. Her sprawling new two-story home, which she helped design herself, was much closer to the road than her home had been in Palm Beach, which meant that early morning traffic headed to Howard Park could cause more of a disruption as she sat on her second-floor balcony.

She was sipping a cup of tea, reading the Sunday paper, thinking back to the previous evening. She'd prepared herself for the usual excruciating affair, the hosts circling like vultures, urging the wealthy marks to loosen their sphincters and put some big numbers on a check, but she'd been pleasantly surprised. The entertainment provided by the young female comedian had been funny and dirty, making more than few of the attendees, most of them Republicans, a bit uncomfortable, which pleased her immensely.

But her biggest surprise had been Marcia Alvarez. She'd spoken to Julia Stevens a week earlier and in the course of their conversation, Julia mentioned that the Alvarez woman had been a last-minute addition to the head table. Gretchen had followed the news reports of the work she had done for the football player's wife closely and had cajoled Julia to adjust the seating chart at the head table so that she and Marcia would be seated next to each other, suggesting that the two of them be placed at the end to facilitate conversation. Julia, having up-to-date knowledge of Gretchen's net worth, had no problem making the change.

Marcia had been even more impressive than she had hoped. Her military background was a plus, as was the way she had rebounded from an abusive marriage that could've scarred her permanently. She'd been able to alter the course of her life, first as a military policewoman, then as a caretaker for her unpredictable and volatile father, and finally as a licensed private investigator. She'd been through the wringer and come out looking like a shiny new penny. She still had some rough edges, but in her current line of work, those edges were a plus.

Before the evening had ended, before she'd given Marcia her business card, Gretchen had decided that she was going to invest in Marcia's company. It was exactly the kind of woman-owned enterprise that Seneca Falls Capital Fund had been created to support. If she could help her navigate those first few lean years every startup has to face, she was confident that Alvarez Investigations would bloom like magnolias in the spring.

She was looking forward to tomorrow like a child anticipating Christmas.

44

Colleen was already in the office Monday when Marcia arrived at 8:45, working on narrowing the search for Roberto Salazar. She looked up briefly from her monitor when Marcia walked in, indicating the coffee station against the wall with a nod. "Just brewed a fresh pot."

Marcia looked at her young charge with admiration. "How long have you been here?"

"Couple of hours, I guess."

"Any progress?"

"Some, but not enough," Colleen said before returning her attention to the monitor.

Marcia grabbed a cup and closed the door to her office behind her. She dumped out the copies of receipts on her desk – she'd managed to work through half of them yesterday at home before her eyes began to glaze over and she'd forced herself to stop – and began to check them as she sipped her coffee.

About an hour in, she hit paydirt, a Visa receipt for a single diner with a stylish signature that clearly read Roberto Salazar. She checked the date: April 13, 2017. He'd had the broiled grouper dinner and two glasses of wine and had left an enormous tip, equal to the bill. She checked the server's name; the receipt said Hazel. Marcia set it aside and was about to return to the task when her office phone rang. It was Colleen. "Judy Ruliani on Line 1."

She tried to keep the irritation at the interruption from her voice. "Good morning, Judy. What can I do for you today?"

"Just checking in," her attorney replied in her trademark nasal tone. "We didn't get a chance to talk the other night."

There's a reason for that, thought Marcia. "I'm sorry, Judy. I was pretty overwhelmed at the number of people who wanted to talk to me. I wasn't prepared for that."

"Get used to it, my dear. You're a media darling now, as hot as they come in Tampa Bay. People want to get a look at the woman who took on the National Football League and kicked their ass."

"I wouldn't put it like that," she demurred.

"I would," Ruliani replied firmly. "When the Players' Association declines to back one of their own in favor of his battered spouse, that puts you, as the one who discovered and brought the abuse to the attention of the public, in a position few people, let alone women, have enjoyed. You should be proud of yourself." She paused for a moment before continuing. "That's not why I'm calling, however. I had a very interesting phone call from Gretchen Schiller this morning. I trust you know her?"

"We met Saturday night," Marcia said. "We were sitting next to each other at the head table."

"Well, whatever you said, it impressed the hell out of Ms. Schiller. She said she gave you her card on Saturday."

"She did." Marcia was confused. "How did she find out that you were my attorney? Your name never came up Saturday."

"I asked her the same thing when she told me what she wanted. She must have some top-flight connections – she told me she got my name from the articles of incorporation I drew up for Alvarez Investigations." She paused for effect. "On a Sunday, no less."

"What did she want?"

"She said she told you about her company, Seneca Falls Capital Fund, how its primary focus is providing funding to businesses run by women." She paused again. "She wants to invest in Alvarez Investigations. She wanted me to approach you to set up a meeting where we can hammer out the details. Are you interested?"

Marcia was speechless. When she found her voice, she asked, "Why didn't she call me herself?"

"That's the best part. She told me you hinted about having just started a new investigation and she said she didn't want to interrupt you at work." She chuckled. "Somehow she knew I wouldn't have the same problem. So she asked me to call you to set up a meeting, at your convenience."

"I'm definitely interested," Marcia blurted.

"I thought you might be, so we checked our calendars. How does 10:00 on Friday at your office sound? She wants to get a look at your operation, see where her money's going to go."

Although no one could see her, Marcia nodded vigorously. "That works for me."

"I'll call her back and set it up."

*****

Lucien Devereaux spent Monday morning and half of the afternoon on his laptop, looking for information on Roberto Salazar. Marcia was right – there were a lot of Roberto Salazars out there. Doing something was better than sitting around in his depressing apartment waiting for the telephone to ring. He had no specific plan in mind; he pressed on because that was the only name he had to go on.

Beside Hazel's, of course. Soon after his conversation years ago with Daisy Stroud in a Biloxi casino, he'd tried to find her through Google, without success. He'd figured she was the right age to participate in social media and was disappointed when several attempts came up empty. Just his luck that his daughter was one of the few people in her generation to shun those social platforms.

He was frustrated and hungry when he finally quit at three. He looked in the refrigerator, but its contents included two cans of Dr. Pepper and half a jar of mayonnaise. Not nearly good enough.

He checked his wallet to see how much cash he had left. It was still ten days before his Social Security check would be deposited, so he was running low. The Last of the Mojitos was scheduled for their first gig Wednesday at Skipper's, but he wasn't sure how or when they'd be paid. Rick Manning was handling all the administrative items for the band, and whatever he knew he was keeping to himself.

He did, however, have enough money for a sandwich at Kitty's, so he drove over to Ozona, hoping to get there before John Rucker left for the day. His band, Alien Colonoscopy, played for their first time in public last night, and Lucien was anxious to hear how it went. He liked young Rucker – he saw a lot of himself in the kid's determination to make it as a musician. He felt the two were growing closer, as each drew strength from their relationship to the other.

After a quick shower, he pulled into the parking lot at Kitty's at 4:30. Gracie Fenton saw him as soon as he came in. "Lucien! How they hangin'?"

"Low, loose and full of juice," he replied pleasantly as he slid onto a vacant bar seat. "John still here?"

Gracie nodded. "He's just wrapping up for the day. You want me to tell him you're here?"

"If you don't mind."

She stood expectantly by the taps. "What can I get you to drink?"

"Just sweet tea, with lemon, please."

She delivered his drink and disappeared into the kitchen. He looked around; the bar was nearly deserted. She returned in a moment. "He'll be right out."

Five minutes later John Rucker emerged from the kitchen and walked over to Lucien, who indicated the seat next to him. "Take a load off."

"Don't mind if I do," Rucker replied tiredly. "Lunch was insane today."

Lucien looked around the bar in mock amazement. "Don't look too busy to me."

"You should've been here at one." Gracie arrived with Coppertail tall boy and set it in front of John, who disdained a glass and instead took a healthy slug directly from the can.

Lucien shifted slightly, eyes bright. "So tell me about last night. How did it go?"

John hesitated. "Okay, I guess. We were opening for Herpes Cineplex, so they only gave us forty-five minutes onstage. I didn't know that The Shed closed early on Sunday nights."

"How was the crowd?"

John laughed ironically. "You mean besides our friends and relatives? Pretty light and pretty talkative."

Lucien nodded. "Par for the course. Did you get to play that song you wrote?"

John nodded. "I did. It was the only original we played. The crowd was, uh, mostly indifferent."

Lucien broke into a broad smile, raising his glass. "Welcome to the music industry, Tornado."

45

When Lucien saw John's face sag, he quickly added. "Don't let it get you down. All musicians run into that problem sooner or later. When it happened to me, in Louisiana, me and the boys had to dodge longnecks, what we used to call roadhouse grenades. Some of 'em were still full." He went on. "Just keep playin' and believin' in yourself. That's all you can do."

John still wasn't convinced. "I hope you're right," he said, voice laced with doubt.

"I am," he replied emphatically. "Were you nervous at all?"

"I was all day, but once we got there and set up and I noticed how little people were paying attention to us, I got pissed off and sorta forgot about being nervous."

"That's good," Lucien said. "As long as pissed off means that you aim to show the audience they're wrong not to be payin' attention. All you can do is play your best – you'll never have control over how the crowd reacts."

"Do you still get nervous?" John asked.

Lucien smiled. "Sure do. In fact, I'm nervous about Wednesday night. Our band is playing for the first time in public, just like you guys did last night. You always get butterflies, no matter how long you been playin'."

John had been so consumed with preparations for the initial Alien Colonoscopy gig that he'd forgotten about the upcoming local debut of Last of the Mojitos. "What time do you start?"

"Doors open at seven, we go on at eight."

His face brightened. "I might be able to make that."

"Hope to see you there."

*****

Late Tuesday, just before five, Colleen burst into Marcia's office. She was exuberant, her face glowing. Several sheets of paper were in her hand. "I think I found him!"

Marcia's heart leaped. "Salazar?"

Colleen nodded. "I think so." She came over and laid the papers out on Marcia's desk. "I'm pretty sure this is him."

Before her were three pictures of a man in his forties, with dark, longish hair swept back, dark eyes and an earring dangling from his left ear, taken from three different angles. "Based on the written description Faye Tompkins gave us, I think this is our guy. He's the right age and the right size. Plus, he has a Florida driver's license – that picture to your left is taken from his license."

Marcia was dumbfounded. She had performed several searches and had been overwhelmed by the amount of Roberto Salazars had emerged. "How did you come up with these pictures so fast?"

Colleen smiled. "The old-fashioned way, by calling in a favor. I spent two days eliminating suspects because they didn't fit the description Faye gave us, but then I hit a dead end. That's when I reached out."

"To who?"

"I have a friend in the Pinellas County Sheriff's Department. She owed me a favor, so I asked her to check for any outstanding warrants or ongoing investigations in the FDLE database for anyone named Roberto Salazar. She sent me a list of twelve names. I followed up, running down the promising leads, which led me to these," she said, indicating the photos. "I sent electronic files of these pictures to Faye Tompkins by email to see if she could confirm that we found the right guy."

"What did she say?" Marcia asked excitedly.

"Nothing yet. I sent the email just before I came in here." She indicated the copies. "These are your copies. As soon as I hear back from Faye, I'll let you know."

"Good work, Colleen," Marcia said excitedly. "Anything else for me now?"

"No, ma'am."

"Close the door on your way out."

Marcia stared at the photos after Colleen departed. She'd also provided a photocopy of his driver's license, which she'd blown up enough so that Marcia could read the address: Cudjoe Key, Florida.

If he turned out to be the Roberto Salazar they were looking for, now they had an address.

*****

When Steve Morrison walked into Kitty's for lunch on Tuesday, Reb Jadel had Gracie cornered. He could see by the look on her face that she needed to be rescued, so he sat down on a bar stool and looked at her patiently while Reb continued to go on about his latest pet peeve: boat prices beyond his means. "Here we are in Florida, water everywhere, a goddamn outdoor wonderland, and a guy like me can't even begin to think about buyin' a new boat. It just ain't right," he whined.

Morrison turned his head so Reb couldn't see his smile as Gracie moved over to draw a Yuengling draft for Morrison. As he took a sip, Gracie winked at Morrison and slipped out from behind the bar and into the kitchen, leaving the surly maintenance man in mid-sentence. Not breaking stride, he turned his attention to

Morrison. "Wadda you think, porn star?" he asked defiantly, spoiling for a fight. "You think I'm wrong?"

About nearly everything, he thought. But when he spoke he tried to sound conciliatory. "I know what you mean, Reb. Everything costs an arm and a leg these days. I can barely afford to eat."

Jadel nodded approvingly. "That's what I'm talkin' about. All them Brazilianaires out there don't need all that cash. Why not share the wealth a bit, spread it around to folks who need it more than they do?"

This time Morrison had to feign a cough to hide his amusement. When he composed himself, he said, "Be careful what you wish for, Reb. Sounds like you're leaning in a socialist direction here. That doesn't sound much like you."

Jadel finished his beer, counted out a combination of bills and coins and left them on the bar. "Tell Gracie to keep the change. We can pick this up next time."

Morrison watched as Jadel stalked out of the bar. Gracie returned from the kitchen as soon as he was out of sight. "Pick what up?" she asked.

"Reb's conversion to socialism," he said with a straight face. "He's tired of being dirt poor and figures it's time for him to get a fairer share."

"That man is eleven inches short of a foot," Gracie said, shaking her head. Changing her tone, she continued. "Thanks for coming to my rescue."

"How about a free drink to show your gratitude?" Morrison inquired with a smile.

"Come back on February 30. Beer's free all day then," she fired back. "Your buddy was in yesterday."

"Rheinhart?"

"No," Gracie said. "Your new buddy. Lucien Devereaux. Poor guy. I hope Marcia can help him find his daughter."

"Any luck with that?"

Gracie nodded. "Faye and Betty Duval put together a boatload of information for her. In the meantime, I *do* have some news I think you'll like. Lucien's band is playing their first gig tomorrow night at Skipper's."

That was interesting. "You planning to go?"

"I asked Hank if he wanted to go last night, but he never answered me." Hank Milosic was Gracie's live-in companion. "John, the kid from the kitchen, is gonna go. You didn't know about it?"

Morrison shook his head. Gracie continued. "I figured you'd know about it for sure, since one of your poker buddies from Fuego is in the band."

Morrison had forgotten that Rick Manning played bass in Lucien's band. "I haven't been playing cards much out there lately," he offered in defense. A moment later he perked up. A trip to Skipper's would be a nice change of pace. He hadn't been out for some time.

Gracie interrupted his thoughts. "You plan on eating, or are you just here for the scenery and the booze? If you're hungry, the oysters are outstanding today. Came in this morning from Louisiana."

"Bring me a dozen."

46

Faye Tompkins' reply to Colleen's email arrived mid-morning on Wednesday. She confirmed that the photos of Roberto Salazar that had been sent to her were of the mysterious diner who had demanded that Hazel Devereaux be his server at Kitty's.

Colleen shared the news with Marcia immediately, who responded with a broad smile. "See if you can find me a place to stay on or near Cudjoe Key that isn't too expensive."

"For when?"

Marcia thought for a moment, then responded. "Two days ought to do it. Make it for Thursday and Friday."

"What about your meeting on Friday with Judy Ruliani and Gretchen Schiller?" Colleen asked. "Should I reschedule?"

Just as quickly as the momentum had built once Salazar had been identified by Faye Tompkins, it deflated. She'd forgotten about the meeting with her newest friend during the excitement that had built during the confirmation of Salazar's identity and address. She knew she couldn't miss that. No matter how hard she tried to convince herself that she'd be able to drive down to the Keys, find out what she needed to know and then drive back in time for the meeting, she knew she would need more time. Reluctantly, she changed course. "No. Keep the meeting when it is. Better make those reservations for Saturday and Sunday night."

"I'll get right on it."

*****

Upon seeing Skipper's Smokehouse for the first time, blues legend Lonnie Mack characterized the ramshackle architectural style of Tampa's most iconic music venue as "the club that washed ashore." He wasn't alone in that assessment. Lucien Devereaux thought that the main structures on the property – the kitchen area, the Oyster Bar, the dining room and the outdoor stage and seating areas - all looked like they had been cobbled together by earnest would-be tradesmen using scrap lumber and driftwood.

He was the first member of the band to arrive for sound check on Wednesday, an hour before the time they'd agreed upon at their final rehearsal. He unloaded his guitars backstage and wandered into the Oyster Bar, where a hardcore group of wizened customers occupied a majority of the barstools by 3:00. He smiled; happy hour in Florida was a fluid event, restricted by no artificial time constraints. Reflexively, Lucien's eyes were drawn to the beer taps and the variety of national and local craft beers they represented. He wiped his lips; he wanted a beer so badly he could almost feel the cooling hops and barley in his mouth and throat.

Instead, he stepped up to the bar next to a man with a grey ponytail wearing a faded Grateful Dead T-shirt who was devouring a plate of chicken wings while ignoring the replay of last night's Lightning game on the television suspended above the bar.

It took several moments for Lucien to attract the bartender's attention. He waited patiently while the man, a balding, broad shouldered, dark-haired man in his forties, finished washing some beer mugs. When he looked up, a broad smile broke out on the bartender's face. "Lucien Devereaux, right? What can I get you?"

Lucien was stunned. "Do we know one another?" he asked, perplexed by the identification.

The bartender shook his head. "You don't know me, but I know you. I've been a big fan of yours for a long time. The staff here has been real excited ever since Tom told us that you were in the band that's going to be playing on Wednesday nights." Tom was Tom White, the owner of Skipper's. "How long's it been since you played here last?"

Lucien searched his memory. "Probly more than twenty years, easy. Last time was when Derek Trucks played when he was just a kid." He smiled sheepishly. "My math ain't too good."

"Well, welcome back. Now, what can I get you?"

He took a breath. "Tonic and lime."

The bartender nodded knowingly, aware of Lucien's battles with substance abuse over the years. He placed the glass on a coaster in front of Lucien. "How about something to eat?"

"I think I'll wait on that till me and the boys finish our sound check," Lucien said, grabbing his glass.

"Good luck tonight," the bartender called after him as Lucien turned to leave the tiny bar area. "There's gonna be a big crowd."

Lucien stopped and turned back. "Really? How do you know?"

"Advance ticket sales have been through the roof," the bartender said. "Usually we only sell that many tickets ahead of time when Tab Benoit or the Subdudes are playing here. Plus, there's no rain in the forecast. We'll get a good walk-in crowd, too. Tom has been advertising the shit out of your gig, in the papers and on the radio. Should be packed in like sardines tonight."

Lucien hadn't considered the size of the crowd, assuming it would be sparse because it was Wednesday. His thoughts had centered on refining the band's setlist. "Thanks for the heads up…."

The bartender thrust his hand forward. "Carl. Carl Perkins."

Lucien shook his hand, a quizzical look on his face. The bartender, reading Lucien's expression, continued. "I know, right? My dad played guitar. Probably woulda named me Carla if I'd been a girl."

"See ya later, Carl."

He walked outside and sat at one of the tables near the entrance to the Skipperdome. He knew a bunch of his new friends would be there tonight – Marcia Alvarez, John Rucker, Steve Morrison and Gracie Fenton from Kitty's, along with a bunch of people from the nudist resort where Rick Manning lived – but he'd never considered that there would be widespread appeal from the folks in Tampa Bay to see a bunch of old guys trying to recapture moments from their musical youth. Of course, shrewd fans like Carl the bartender might also recognize Gabe Templar's name from his days with Koko Taylor, but he had to believe that folks like that were scarce, even among the geriatric-heavy population of Tampa.

He felt the familiar nervousness beginning to build in the pit of his stomach, that good kind of nervousness he usually felt before a show, sparked by thoughts of a capacity crowd in the Skipperdome tonight. He finished his drink and headed to the stage to warm up, already in the performance zone, so focused on tonight's gig that the issue that had been dominating his thoughts for the last few weeks, the quest to find his missing daughter, had been temporarily shelved in another area of his brainpan. Tonight was all about the music.

*****

Eleven hundred miles away, Roberto Salazar emerged from the shower in his spacious loft in Soho, toweling his sleek black hair as he looked at himself in the mirror. No crow's feet yet around the eyes, his olive complexion unmarked, his recently whitened teeth in a self-satisfied smile that faded as he thought of the girl.

What had he been thinking? He'd been enjoying a rare vacation eighteen months earlier when he'd stumbled into a sleepy restaurant that had been recommended by one of the staff at the resort where he was staying, looking for some fresh seafood. When his server arrived after he'd been seated at a table on the patio by the hostess, everything changed in an instant.

It wasn't her bubbly personality – she'd arrived at his table in a sullen mood that was apparent to him despite her half-hearted effort to mask it while she waited for his order with a forced smile and a falsely cheery "Can I get you something to drink to start?"

It was her face, a face that he had known intimately and adored during the best years of his life. This server, who identified herself as Hazel, was the identical image of his late wife Cherise, the only woman he'd ever loved. She'd died six days before her twenty-eighth birthday of a brain hemorrhage she'd suffered while showering in their home before a dinner date scheduled to celebrate her recent discovery that she was pregnant with their first child. Hazel could've been her twin.

He managed somehow to stay composed and not blurt something out foolishly like an impulsive school boy during that first visit, asking only her opinion about the day's specials, heeding her recommendation to try the hogfish, tipping her lavishly and exiting the restaurant before she had a moment to digest what he had done.

His obsession with her was all-consuming. He called the restaurant as soon as it opened the next day, asking if Hazel was on the schedule, delighted when told she was. When he showed up for dinner that night and asked specifically that she be his server, her demeanor had undergone a major makeover as soon as she saw him once again sitting alone on the patio. She was full of warmth and charm, much more attentive than she'd been the night before, thinking she'd found the equivalent of a culinary sugar daddy – a generous tipper who wasted no time coming back for more. As for the handsome tourist, he'd fallen hard.

But then things changed.

47

By the time the band was ready to take the stage, the Skipperdome was packed, shoulder to shoulder, standing room only. Rick Manning had requested that the raised section in the back behind the mixing board be reserved for friends and family of the band and management had complied, using yellow police tape to cordon off the area and escorting the special guests to the temporary VIP section. Manning thought the uncharacteristic decision was a tip of the hat to Lucien's musical reputation.

John Rucker was sitting at one of the round tables with Marcia Alvarez, Gracie Fenton and Steve Morrison, scanning with envy the sold-out crowd. One day, he thought, this would be him. Maybe not with Alien Colonoscopy – his first band failure was a textbook example of the best musical intentions spiraling wildly out of control – but he hadn't yet lost the cocksure conviction borne of youthful optimism that he was destined for success as a musician. His plan tonight was to observe Lucien closely, to see how a veteran of the stage handled himself, to take something away that he could use at his band's next engagement.

Marcia tapped him on the shoulder and leaned in so she could be heard above the pre-show excitement. "Gracie tells me you're in a band, too. What's your band's name?"

"Alien Colonoscopy," he replied, continuing in explanation. "We're mostly a thrash punk band. Right now we're starting to play in some small clubs in St. Pete, but I'm hoping that'll change soon as the word gets out."

Marcia had no idea what thrash punk meant and decided to keep her ignorance to herself. "I hope it does, too. Good luck."

Backstage, Tom White tapped Lucien on the shoulder and nodded encouragingly as he walked out to the front of the stage and waited patiently until the crowd noticed his presence. When he began to speak his voice was clear and strong. "Welcome to Skipper's Smokehouse. We have a special treat for you tonight, a new local band that we hope to showcase every Wednesday from now on. Let's give a warm Skipper's welcome to the Last of the Mojitos!"

A generous wave of applause met the band as they emerged from backstage. Lucien leaned into the microphone as he surveyed the crowd, smiling. "Hope you brought your dancin' shoes tonight." He stepped back, nodded to Gabe on keyboards, who burst into the intro to the Allman Brothers' "Jessica", joined immediately by Lucien on guitar. They'd chosen this number to open because of Lucien's uncanny ability to replicate the sound that two guitars had produced on the original on his Stratocaster and because they wanted to get the crowd engaged from the start. They were confident most of the crowd would recognize "Jessica."

They were right. Those on the dance floor in front of the stage, which had been crowded before the show started, started moving as soon as they played the signature intro. Lucien, inspired to be back on stage again, was on fire, responding to Gabe's flying fingers on the keyboards with incendiary guitar riffs as the two played off each other like they'd been doing it for years.

When the song ended the crowd erupted in wild applause, whistles and shouts of delight. Rick looked over at Lucien, smiling, and winked. Good choice. Back in the VIP section, Steve Morrison was on his feet, applauding vigorously, taken aback by the musical expertise exhibited by the band during their opening number, shaking his head in amazement, raising his voice so Gracie, seated next to him, could hear him above the noise. "Wow!" John Rucker detected the familiar aroma of America's most beloved illegal substance in the vicinity, nodding his tacit approval as he scanned the crowd, looking for the source.

Rick and Lucien had taken extra care in assembling the setlist for the kind of crowd they knew assembled at Skipper's: older hippies, mostly, who cared deeply about music and whose knowledge of the tumultuous 1970s music scene extended far beyond Jimmy Buffett. They followed "Jessica" with another guitar anthem with local roots, "Green Grass and High Tides", from Tampa's Outlaws, which elicited another frenzied response from the overflow crowd.

When that song ended, Lucien knew he had this audience in his pocket. He and the boys could do no wrong tonight – over the next two hours they ripped through several songs from another Florida legend, Tom Petty, as well as two obligatory Buffett songs, a rousing version of Neil Young's "Like A Hurricane", a nod to Lucien's musical roots with "Cissy Strut" by The Meters and a smoldering take of the Grateful Dead's "Bertha" to close out the show. When the crowd refused to stop applauding after the final notes faded away, they returned with a withering ten-minute rendition of "Whipping Post" that had everyone on their feet.

As the crowd, reluctant to leave, shuffled off to the crushed shell parking lot, Rick drained a backstage beer in two gulps before starting to pack up their equipment. Because they were a brand-new band, with no discernible following, they had yet to attract any road crew volunteers. Even Gabe and Lucien, who were both accustomed to traveling with professional road crews, pitched in without complaint.

By the time the equipment was back in Rick's Econoline van, the only people left in the place were Skippers' employees policing the Skipperdome, picking up cans, bottles and other trash, and Elaine Prescott and Steve Morrison, who was leaning against the van, drinking a glass of water and offered his hand to a grinning Lucien. "Great show! I had no idea you were so good. Where'd you learn to play like that?"

"Louisiana," he replied. "Down on the bayou. Later on, in New Orleans."

Morrison shook his head in admiration. "No wonder. That's some of the best guitar playing I've ever heard. I thought Dick Dale was the tits until tonight."

"He wasn't too shabby," Lucien conceded with a smile. "A real original."

After a few moments Lucien managed to extricate himself from the small group and bid each good night. "Y'all come back next Wednesday, you hear?"

On the drive home Lucien went over the setlist, one by one. He'd been right to resist Tate's suggestion that they throw more Buffett songs into the mix, especially with this crowd. Each of their songs had been received with enthusiasm, but Lucien knew they could do better. More practice would help, obviously, and he knew he'd hit a couple of sour notes during their version of "Sultans of Swing", but he doubted many in the crowd had noticed. All in all, it was an excellent night; the adrenaline was still pumping. He knew he would have difficulty getting to sleep tonight. In the old days he would've self-medicated and been asleep minutes after his head hit the pillow. He'd felt that old familiar urge come roaring back when he'd smelled weed near the front of the stage – right now he'd kill for a joint.

Traffic was light at this hour as he cruised down U.S. 41, heading for home, but he knew that the cops would be out in force, despite the late hour in the middle of the week. He'd never seen a state with so many cops before – at least three vehicles and sometimes more whenever someone was pulled over on the side of the road. He'd read an article in the *Times* last Sunday lamenting the difficulty Florida was having attracting teachers. No wonder – everyone in this state wanted to be a cop so they could drive fast and carry a gun, two activities some Floridians revered more than an active sex life. He glanced at the speedometer, making sure he wasn't exceeding the limit, before checking his mirrors. Better to be safe than sorry, especially after midnight.

At home he made himself a cup of decaffeinated tea as he continued to try to wind down from the evening's excitement. Realizing he was still too wide awake to consider sleep, he scrolled through the channels on his small flat screen, settling on an old Marlon Brando movie, *On The Waterfront*. Not for the first time, he marveled that Karl Malden, owner of one of the oddest shaped noses God had ever created, had been able to craft a successful career during a time in Hollywood when good looks routinely superseded acting ability.

When the movie ended, he took a shower and crawled into bed, hoping for at least a few hours sleep. His schedule tomorrow was wide open, as it was on most days, so sleeping in would not be an issue. For the first time all day, his mind released from its fixation on the night's performance, his thoughts drifted to Hazel. He wished she could've seen him tonight, seen that the old man still had plenty of licks left in his guitar. Did she even like music, he wondered; his knowledge concerning anything related to his only child was scant. Lily had given him a chance to be a part of his daughter's life when she first told him of Hazel's existence, but he'd declined, doing everything he could to prevent that from happening. He'd been a fool, too self-absorbed with his own success to do the right thing thirty years ago, to step up and accept his parental responsibilities.

He hoped it wasn't too late to make amends.

48

Water had seeped through cracks in the subterranean wall, pooling in the low areas near the corner of the basement. She heard sounds in the dark, a creature she was convinced was a rat scurrying through the standing water. Reflexively she lifted her legs off the floor and onto the couch that was her makeshift bed. She was afraid to turn on the flashlight she gripped tightly in her hand, afraid of what it might reveal.

She closed her eyes and wondered what day it was.

*****

By the time Gretchen Schiller and Judy Ruliani arrived at Marcia's office on Friday morning, Colleen had collected a trove of information on Roberto Salazar. She spent an hour going over the material her assistant had accumulated on the mysterious Salazar before Colleen buzzed her on the phone, announcing that both women were outside in the reception area. She replaced the papers in the file folder and dropped them into a desk drawer as she intoned. "Send them in."

Colleen had somehow dug up an extra guest chair for her office which Marcia discovered when she arrived earlier that morning. Ruliani and Schiller settled into the two seats, each dressed as if they were headed to a fashion shoot. Colleen was right behind them with a fresh pot of coffee and two fresh mugs for the visitors. Without a word she withdrew, closing the door behind her.

As she waited for her coffee to cool, Ruliani looked at Marcia intently. "How was the show on Wednesday?"

Gretchen looked at Judy, then at Marcia. "What show?" she asked.

"My client, Lucien Devereaux, plays in a band," Marcia explained. "They were at Skipper's Smokehouse Wednesday night."

"I've heard about Skipper's," Gretchen remarked, "but I haven't been there yet." She looked at Marcia. "Is it worth a visit?"

"I haven't been there that much," Marcia conceded. "I think this was only my second time. If you like classic rock, Lucien's band is pretty good. He told me they'll be playing there on Wednesdays from here on."

"It's the perfect place to flaunt your thrift store wardrobe," Ruliani advised. "And whatever you do, don't wear heels. They'll be ruined before you get out of the parking lot."

"So noted." Gretchen smiled at Marcia. "Did Judy tell you why I wanted to see you today?"

Marcia knew, but she wanted to let the conversation come to her. "Not really."

Gretchen passed a shiny brochure across the table to Marcia. "This is a copy of the Seneca Falls Capital Fund's annual report, for your reference. When you get a chance to look at it, you'll be able to see what kind of ventures we invest in. I think Alvarez Investigations is exactly the kind of business my company was created to support. I've put together a rough outline for your attorney of how we'd like to proceed." She looked at Ruliani, who withdrew an offer sheet and passed it across the desk to Marcia. Gretchen continued. "Look it over and see what you think. Talk with Judy about it. We can work out the finer points at some later date, but if you're agreeable to the general premise of outside

279

investment in your company, I'd like to start with an immediate cash infusion, some working capital that doesn't come out of your piggy bank." She shook her head. "I still can't believe you self-financed your company. Nobody does that anymore. What you want is OPM."

Marcia was lost. "What's OPM?"

Ruliani broke in. "Other people's money. That way, if something goes wrong, some unexpected calamity, your personal capital won't be at risk. Without going into too much detail, I've informed Gretchen that your present financial situation is quite solid, more so than the average start-up."

"But even if it wasn't," Gretchen said, "I'd still want to invest in your firm. The fact that you spent twenty years in the military and were specifically trained to provide the type of services Alvarez Investigations offers says it all for me. The way I see it, the risk on my end is little to none. And the rewards could be spectacular." She paused. "For both of us."

Marcia scanned the offer sheet while Gretchen made her pitch. The amount of initial investment Gretchen's firm was willing to provide was significant, if she was reading the numbers correctly. She looked at Gretchen. "I'd like to go over this with Judy. When do you need an answer?"

"Whenever you feel you're comfortable with the terms," Gretchen said. "There's no rush on my end. The last thing I'd like to do is pressure you into agreeing to something you're uncomfortable with."

"It shouldn't take too long," Marcia said, glancing at her attorney, who nodded in affirmation. "No more than a week or two."

"Like I said. Whatever works for you," Gretchen said. She looked at Ruliani. "What do you say we get out of Marcia's hair, let her get back to work?" She turned to Marcia. "You *are* working on a new case, aren't you?"

Marcia nodded. "A missing persons case. Someone trying to find their daughter." She thought it would be prudent to refrain from offering any information on Lucien's case until she read the offer more closely.

Gretchen stood and extended her hand, which Marcia shook. "I hope there's more domestic bliss involved in your new case than there was in your last one."

Marcia smiled ruefully. "So do I."

49

As soon as the two women had departed, Marcia summoned Colleen, who showed up with a pen and pad of paper. Marcia motioned to the guest chair. "Where are we with accommodations in the Keys?"

"I found a nice room in Old Town in Key West, at a cozy B&B," Colleen said. "You're booked for two nights."

"Excellent," Marcia said approvingly. "How far is that from Cudjoe Key?"

"Thirty minutes, in normal traffic."

"Good." She looked intently at her assistant. "Tell me what you've learned since yesterday about our friend Mr. Salazar."

*****

Roberto Salazar had been born in Santa Ana, El Salvador and had immigrated to Monterrey, Mexico with his family when he was eleven. Shortly after arriving in Monterey, he'd been recruited by a local drug merchant as a courier, the standard entry-level position for someone aspiring to enter the drug trade because the *policia* hesitated to charge underage minors with serious crimes, even drug-related offenses.

Young Salazar was a quick study and rose rapidly in the organization. By the time he was twenty, he was running a crew of his own modeled after the Colombian kingpin Pablo Escobar according to a report compiled by the DEA detailing the various players involved in illegal drug trafficking in Nuevo Leon. Four years later he emigrated from Mexico to Miami, and by the time he was thirty he had purchased the land in Cudjoe Key that would later become his home.

Marcia looked up from the report at Colleen, her voice laced with amazement. "Where'd you get this stuff?"

"I got lucky," Colleen admitted. "I was running a search on one of the federal databases we subscribe to and it linked me to a FOIA request that had been submitted by a reporter from the *Miami Herald* who was working on a story linking drug activity in Mexico to similar activity in southern Florida. Roberto Salazar's name was prominent in the unredacted portions of the file."

"But if the DEA knew about Salazar's connection to the drug trade in Mexico, how could he possibly have been granted legal status to enter the country?"

"Two reasons, I think," Colleen replied. "The natural tendency among federal agencies to avoid sharing information with one another – the DEA and Immigration and Naturalization Services, in this case – and good old-fashioned bribery. I'd wager someone at the INS was paid a lot of money to look the other way when it came to judging Roberto Salazar's application for citizenship."

Shaking her head in wonder, Marcia returned to the report. After building his home on Cudjoe Key, a holding company under his direction began investing in bars and restaurants in the Miami area, later expanding his empire to New York and San Francisco, according to his current LinkedIn profile. It made sense – if Salazar was still involved in the drug trade, what better way to launder the illegal proceeds than through a collection of cash-based businesses such as bars and restaurants?

Another document from the file, this one from the Automated City Register Information System – ACRIS – in New

York City indicated that Roberto Salazar, through a second holding company, owned the No Name Bar in the East Village, Café Tulum in Lenox Hill and Isla Martinique in the West Village as well as a loft on Wooster Street in Soho. Marcia looked up again. "Seems our Mr. Salazar has built a nice little real estate empire," she said, adding. "Without acquiring a criminal record."

Colleen nodded in agreement. "So far, anyway. I reached out to the head of the FBI office in Miami – Carlos Gutierrez is the special agent in charge down there – and they are aware of the suspicions surrounding the legal status of his income sources, but so far haven't been able to accumulate enough evidence to file charges. According to the agent I spoke with down there, he's been on their radar for years."

Marcia extracted the most recent picture of Salazar and gazed at it. To her he resembled a young Antonio Banderas, a real Latin heartthrob, attractive, wealthy and possessing a smile that could melt the hearts of any number of women or men on several continents.

What was his attraction to Hazel Devereaux?

*****

Marcia had decided to drive to the Keys, overruling Colleen's suggestion she take a flight from Tampa. "I haven't been down there since the hurricane blew through a couple of years ago – I want to see how they've recovered," Marcia explained in her defense. "Besides, if I flew I wouldn't be able to stop for lunch at Mrs. Mac's Kitchen on the way."

She left at six Saturday morning and had I-75 to herself until she reached Naples, where she encountered a cluster of truckers headed across Alligator Alley. She fell in with them, set the cruise control and selected the Tragically Hip channel on Sirius, her mind sorting through the various scenarios she might find when she arrived on Cudjoe Key. Had Salazar's home been able to withstand the fury of Irma? The hurricane had made landfall on Cudjoe Key; from pictures she had seen, the storm had obliterated the sand and limestone hummock, leaving few structures behind. It wouldn't be much of a trip if his home hadn't survived.

She white-knuckled her way around Miami, her least favorite leg of the journey, breathing a sigh of relief once she reached Homestead, the gateway to the Keys. By the time she got to Key Largo at half past noon, the parking lot at Mrs. Mac's was overflowing, many of the cars and trucks bearing out-of-state plates. She decided to stop anyway, cajoling the hostess who wanted to seat her inside to get her a conch republic sandwich to go. She was finishing her third cigarette by the time the hostess returned with her order, which she snatched with a grateful smile, slipping her a ten for her efforts.

It was a clear day, with wispy cirrus clouds dotting the highest elevations, temperature in the upper sixties as she cruised through Marathon and across the Seven Mile Bridge. As she always did, she marveled at the distinct hues of the water, a heady mix of pale blues and brilliant greens dotted with several varieties of pleasure craft, enjoying another ideal day in paradise.

She decided to take a peek at Salazar's house before checking in to her room, so she turned right on Cutthroat Drive, just before the Square Grouper, heading north toward the Gulf side of the island. Most of the other residences on the key were on the southern shore, facing Cudjoe Bay, many of which she could see were still being repaired more than two years after the hurricane. Several mounds of building materials that used to comprise condos and trailers were still scattered along the side of Cutthroat Road, beyond the critical gaze of the tourist population.

She slowed as she checked Google Maps on her phone, verifying the address. Salazar's home was about a half mile beyond his nearest neighbor, a three-story fortress that appeared, on the surface, to have suffered little damage in the storm. From what she'd observed so far, Salazar owned the largest house on the key, a fitting waterfront palace for an international drug merchant.

She pulled off to the side of the road, checking before she exited the car to see if anyone was around. Satisfied she was alone, she snapped several pictures of the house from a number of angles before she returned to her car and headed out the way she came in, turning right on the Overseas Highway, heading for Key West.

Her accommodations were in Old Town, not far from the Ernest Hemingway House and Museum, steps from Duval Street. Colleen had promised off-road parking; Marcia pulled into the tight lane in front of the office and was checked in by an amiable lesbian named Marissa, who took down her information and directed Marcia to her room. "It's the one on the end, next to the pool. You can park your car in front of the room," she said, handing Marcia her key with a smile. "Enjoy your stay."

The room was perfect, spacious enough for her to spread out a bit, with a four-poster bed and water colors from local artists filling the walls, a small flat screen television and a compact kitchen area with a microwave, refrigerator, stove and a small circular table with two chairs. She unpacked, grateful that she had remembered her swimsuit. Even though the air was cool, the pool was heated. Marcia thought a swim was in order.

Marissa had informed her that there was no smoking allowed on the premises, so before she changed into her suit she grabbed her cigarettes and walked out to Duval Street, where she found a sliver of shade beneath the awning of a small real estate office, lit a cigarette, and watched the tourists stroll by, each involved in their personal version of the Duval crawl. She loved to people watch, and there was no better place for that in the Lower 48 than Key West.

When she'd finished her cigarette, she returned to her room, changed clothes, grabbed the Salazar case file and a towel and found an empty lounge chair in the shade of a saw palmetto by the pool. Within minutes, she was immersed in some of the more interesting details of Roberto Salazar's existence, prepping herself for what she hoped to be a revealing conversation tomorrow with her quarry.

50

After digesting the report Colleen had compiled on Salazar and a quick dip, Marcia took a shower and headed out for a bite to eat. Two blocks down from her B&B on Duval she spotted a small outdoor café that appealed to her. After snagging one of the last open tables on a busy Saturday night she ordered a bowl of conch chowder and a side order of plantains and ate while watching the constant parade of awe-struck, sunburned tourists and a few opportunistic locals shuffle by.

When she was finished she cut down Angela to Whitehead, leaving the Duval mob behind as she headed a block north to her favorite destination in Old Town, the Green Parrot. A deeply tanned singer-guitarist was on stage when she walked in; she stayed long enough for one drink, standing by the fully occupied bar, during which the singer played three Buffett tunes. Because she wanted to get an early start in the morning, she reluctantly left after one beer, but not before a portly man in his fifties wearing a T-shirt emblazoned with "GOD'S GIFT TO WOMEN" approached her and drawled, "Buy you a drink, darlin'?" She gave him a withering look before nodding toward the lettering on his shirt. "I never fall for false advertising," she replied archly before deftly moving away from him, toward the door.

*****

After a restless night's sleep – she had trouble turning off her mind as she went over the options the next day might bring – Marcia was up before dawn, headed back toward Cudjoe Key. A ragtag group of individuals was up early in Old Town as well, cleaning the streets in the day's first light after last night's festivities, trying to restore that Chamber of Commerce sheen before the next flood of visitors arrived.

She had the road to herself as she cruised north on Highway 1 across Stock Island, Big Coppit Key and Upper Sugarloaf Key. Several charter captains were already out on the Gulf as she approached Cudjoe, the early morning sky a flawless blue as the sun edged above the flats. If her hunch that a significant portion of the residents of Cudjoe Key were of retirement age was correct, she knew the active ones, the most likely candidates to have observed the comings and goings of Roberto Salazar, would be out early to beat the heat.

She turned left on Cutthroat Drive and parked a few hundred yards beyond where it intersected with Permit Lane. Grabbing a hat and her sunglasses along with a pen and pad of paper, she set out to find early morning walkers, runners or cyclists. She interviewed a couple of men walking their dogs first, who told her they were aware of the house further down the road but knew nothing of the owner. "We've never seen him," one of them replied.

She received similar responses from a retired commercial insurance executive, a jogger who was peeved at having his morning workout disrupted, and a cyclist carrying a small tackle box and fishing pole. All of them knew of the house – it was the largest on the key, the couple said – but none of them knew anything about the owner. Somebody wealthy, they opined.

After two hours of fruitless effort, she returned to her car and drove further north, to the last house on Cutthroat before Salazar's home. By now it was a little past ten, a decent enough hour to knock on someone's door, so she approached the two-story concrete structure, climbing the stairs above the unwalled ground level where a black Range Rover was parked to the front door and rang the bell.

A barefoot man with neatly trimmed white hair wearing orange swim trunks and a white T-shirt answered the door warily. "Yes?"

Marcia showed him her PI license and identified herself before continuing. "I'm working on a missing persons case and was wondering if you could help me out by answering a few questions."

"If it has anything to do with Irma, I'm afraid you came to the wrong place," the man stated with a distinct European accent. "I was in Amsterdam, watching football. I didn't return until November that year."

Marcia shook her head. "I'm was hoping to speak to your neighbor, but he doesn't appear to be home."

"Roberto?" the man offered in a neutral tone. "He doesn't spend too much time down here these days."

"Roberto Salazar?" Marcia asked.

The man nodded. "That's him. Is he the one who's missing?"

"No," she replied. "I'm trying to track down an associate of his, a young woman." She reached into her purse, withdrew a photo of Hazel and passed it to the man. "Do you know this woman?"

The man looked at the photo for a moment before nodding. "That looks like Hazel."

Marcia's heart jumped. "When was the last time you saw her?"

He thought back. "I think it was just before Irma. The two of them spent that summer down here. I remember they left about a week before I flew to The Netherlands."

"You haven't seen her since, Mr. ____?"

289

The man blushed with embarrassment. "I'm so sorry, Miss Alvarez. How rude of me not to introduce myself. I'm Jelmer van Basten." He continued. "Of course, I'm only here during the winter months, but no, I haven't seen either Roberto or Hazel since the hurricane."

"Not even to check on his house to see if it sustained any damage?"

Jelmer laughed. "That house is built like a fortress, two feet of reinforced concrete on every level. Despite the fact that the hurricane made landfall here, the only damage that house sustained was a few broken roof tiles." He smiled ruefully. "I wish I could say the same thing."

"Do you have any idea where he spends his time when he's not on Cudjoe Key?"

He nodded decisively. "In New York. He has business interests there, along with a residence. He told me once he loved the anonymity of living in Manhattan. He could go out on the streets and walk around without anyone recognizing him or bothering him. I figured his restaurant there must be quite famous." He smiled. "Restaurant owners are like rock stars these days – they even have their own cable television shows."

After she'd asked him a few more questions about how to get in touch if she wanted to follow up, she handed him a business card while extending her hand in thanks. "You've been a big help, Mr. van Basten. Thanks for spending some time with me. If you do see either Mr. Salazar or Hazel, please give me a call."

"It will be my pleasure, Miss Alvarez."

Back at her car, she decided to drive by Salazar's house one more time. The security gate and nine-foot wall surrounding the property hindered her ability to see much, but she felt she had to give it one more shot before heading back to Key West. With the exception of the foreboding wall, there was nothing she could see that differentiated Salazar's palace from other wealthy landowners in the Keys, but she felt a chill nonetheless.

She wondered what the weather would be like in New York in January.

*****

She searched frantically through the plastic garbage bag that contained what remained of her personal items: clothing, a few books, the last birthday card her mother had given her, a pack of bent and broken cigarettes. Finally, at the bottom, she found what she was looking for, an ornately carved pillbox that Roberto had given her for her birthday last year.

She opened it; it was empty. "Fuck!" she screamed, the sound reverberating in the compact space. She hadn't been paying attention; she was out of pills. Using her only source of light, the dimly-lit bulb on the table next to the couch, she stretched the cord as far as it would go, looking around the dank room where she'd been living these past few months, hoping for a miracle but failing to find one. She couldn't call Roberto and ask him to get her some more pills because he'd stopped paying for her cell phone after moving her from the apartment under construction above the bar where she'd been living to the basement below it just before Christmas.

She needed those pills to get well. Fast.

51

Marcia called Colleen on her way back to Key West and filled her in on what she'd discovered so far. "According to his next-door neighbor, he hasn't been down here for some time. I want you to get me reservations to New York for Wednesday. Plane and hotel. Try to get me as close to Soho as you can. You have the address of Salazar's loft, right?"

"I do. I'll get on it right away." She paused before continuing. "Will you be coming back tonight since you're finished down there?"

"No," Marcia replied. "I'm going to have a nice Cuban dinner at my favorite restaurant and then watch the freak show at Mallory Square before sunset. A little one-day vacation, sort of."

"Too bad," Colleen said cheerily. "If you were coming back today, you could join Gretchen and me for lunch tomorrow."

"Gretchen Schiller?"

"Yes. She called me at home last night to see if I was free. She said she's never been to Kitty's and wants to see what it's like."

The disappointment in Marcia's voice was evident. "Damn! She called you at home?"

"I gave her my cell number on Friday, in case she needed me for anything. Anything you'd like to say to her?"

"Just that I'm sorry to have missed her," Marcia replied.

"If you were on the road by five..."

Marcia cut her off. "Ain't gonna happen. I'm not leaving the Keys in the dark. I want to travel during the morning light, soak it all in. Who knows when I'll get a chance to get down here again?"

"Suit yourself. Anything else?"

"If I think of anything, I'll call you."

*****

Both of the major papers in the Tampa area, the *Tampa Bay Times* and the alternative weekly *Creative Loafing*, had sent reporters to Skipper's Wednesday to review the performance of the Last of the Mojitos. Each review was glowing, especially when it came to Lucien's playing. In fact, the review from the *Times* was picked up by the online version of *Rolling Stone* as a part of their recent concert review section. By Saturday Lucien had heard from a number of his friends in the music business, all wanting to congratulate him on his comeback. Lucien was puzzled by the number of people who had his most recent contact info – both cell phone and email – until he talked with Monroe Jessup, who readily admitted he had been approached by the Nashville crowd after the review had appeared online. "Sure, I gave them your number. Email, too. So did Blake. People are really glad you're back, Lucien."

"So am I," he admitted, his voice catching. "Feels real good to be playin' again."

"How's the band?"

"The keyboard player, Gabe Templar, used to play with Koko Taylor. We did a coupla Allman Brothers tunes the other night that he really kicked the shit out of. The other two guys are okay for local gigs, which is what we'll be mostly playin'."

"Any chance of going on the road?" Monroe asked. "I know I could find you a place or two in Nashville to play."

"Early days, Monroe, early days. Like I told the boys when they started to get ahead of themselves – best learn to walk before we try to run."

"If you change your mind..." Monroe let the thought dangle.

Lucien laughed. "Hell, Monroe, we don't even have anybody to haul our equipment yet, let alone a manager or bookin' agent. Let's see how it plays out the next few months."

"How about your daughter? Any news there?"

Lucien's tone brightened. "There is. I hired a private investigator down here who's workin' the case real hard. She's down in Key West this weekend, runnin' down a lead. I'm waitin' to hear back from her as we speak."

"She?"

"Marcia Alvarez. She's ex-military, used to be in Intelligence before she became an MP. Put in twenty years before she retired. She's tough as nails. I like her a lot."

Monroe hadn't heard his friend sound this upbeat in a long time. "That sounds great, Lucien. I'll be praying for you."

"I can use all the help I can get, Monroe."

They talked for a few more minutes, swapping tales about musicians, road trips and a number of incidents that always seemed to happen at a Waffle House when Lucien's phone beeped. "I got another call, Monroe. I'll talk to ya later." He rang off with Monroe and picked up the unknown local number. "Hello?"

"Lucien, it's Rick. You busy?"

"How come I didn't recognize your number?" he asked, perplexed.

"My phone died. This is Elaine's phone. Tate called and wanted to switch Monday's rehearsal to tomorrow night. Seems his granddaughter is in a school play on Monday night and his family will kill him if he doesn't make it." Pause. "You okay with the switch?"

"Let me check my schedule," Lucien replied, tongue firmly in cheek. In a moment he said, "I'm free. At your place?"

"Seven o'clock."

"See you then."

*****

Marcia spent the afternoon on the Conch Train, which she picked up a block from her B&B, touring Old Town, seeing many of the sights that made Key West one of the most unique spots in America. She was seated in the rear of the car next to an attractive young blond in a crimson and gray Ohio State T-shirt named Stacy, who introduced her companion as her boyfriend Jon. It was obvious by the enthusiasm of their comments as they passed various landmarks that this was their first visit to Key West.

The weather was unseasonably warm for January, mid-seventies, with a slight breeze from the north – a perfect day for sightseeing. As they cruised past the Hemingway house and museum, the driver related the story of why most of the cats at the house had six toes, Stacy and Jon hanging on every word.

Marcia pulled out her notebook and began jotting down things she'd need in New York. She wasn't sure she had a coat sturdy enough to withstand the northern weather, so she added it to a list that already included gloves and a wool hat. She hadn't been in a cold-weather climate since she was a teenager living with her father in Oregon – all her military assignments had been well south of the Mason Dixon line, and her post-military life had been spent in the Tampa Bay area.

She hopped off the train at the corner of Front and Duval and strolled over to El Meson de Pepe, grabbing a seat at the outside bar overlooking Mallory Square where she could smoke. She downed a bottle of Hatuey while studying the menu, finally deciding on *ropa vieja*. As she waited for her dinner to arrive, she watched with amusement as several chickens scurried along the brick patio, on the lookout for careless or sloppy diners unable to keep their food on the table, all of the hens robust through the breast, an indication of why they had chosen this location as their home base.

She ordered a second beer which arrived just before her meal, which she gobbled down with gusto, having skipped lunch. When she was finished she paid her bill and strolled among the performers and artists spread throughout Mallory Square who were attempting to entice the current crop of tourists arriving for the sunset to purchase their hand-painted T-shirts, island trinkets or, for the performers like the sword swallower and the wire walker, to contribute to their tip jars. A large cruise ship was just leaving the dock, providing another vista for the crowd to watch the sun sink into the Gulf. The warmth of the sun on her face as she lit another cigarette reminded her that she would soon be trading the tropics for the cold, gray landscape of New York.

She was coming after Hazel Devereaux.

52

During the week the No Name Bar was a dive on Third Avenue between 12th and 13th Streets that catered to a young party crowd, many of them students from nearby NYU. On Sundays it was an NFL bar, its two sections divided between fans of the Vikings, who controlled the front room, and fans of the Saints, who crowded into the back room, as they cheered on their teams. There were three floors above the bar, each of which contained a single spacious apartment, and a foreboding basement which hadn't been updated since its original construction during the latter part of the 19th century.

It was an odd choice for Roberto Salazar's first metropolitan New York purchase, given the two high-end restaurants he operated in Miami. The building was about to be sold but was not yet on the market when Salazar learned through his real estate agent that the owner, an octogenarian real estate investor who now lived in Savannah, had grown weary of repeated visits from members of the Ninth Precinct to the bar and wanted to cash out and leave that particular headache behind. Salazar swooped in with a generous offer above the asking price and, after negotiating a compromise over a few minor discrepancies, became the new owner of one of New York's older taverns.

This was no impulsive move by Salazar. He'd been planning such a purchase for months, looking for an established cash business to use as a springboard to what he envisioned as his northern empire, shifting the emphasis of his illicit drug enterprise from Miami, where his restaurants had come under increased scrutiny from various law enforcement agencies, including the FBI, to the nation's largest city.

His next purchase was his loft in Soho, followed swiftly by two other buildings, one in the West Village, one in Lenox Hill. Each of these buildings featured a restaurant on the ground floor and apartments above, much like the building which housed the No Name Bar. Within three years of his arrival, he was one of the new hot restaurateurs in the city, each of his tropical themed restaurants reviewed in glowing terms, resulting in months-long waits to be seated at each.

So when the suave, handsome Salazar landed in tiny Ozona at Kitty Galore's and had his breath taken away by Hazel's resemblance to his dead wife, she had little chance of resisting what happened next: a whirlwind courtship underpinned by visions of a life of leisure that rotated between the Florida Keys, Miami and Manhattan. It took a little longer than he had planned – she was at first suspicious of his motives and had to be convinced – but his persistence paid off when she finally accepted his suggestion she quit her job and accompany him to New York.

At first it was a fairy-tale existence: lavish dinners at exquisite restaurants, VIP treatment at the city's most exclusive nightclubs, a limousine at her disposal, day and night, vacations to St. Bart's and Tahiti. But it wasn't long before Salazar's concentration on his business interests and his predilection to spend time with business associates, some of whom she was sure belonged on wanted posters issued by Interpol, left her frustrated and angry at being left alone and ignored. When her complaints began to get more numerous and strident, Salazar resorted to a method he'd used reliably in the past to placate such revolts by previous female companions: enough opioids to mute any dissent and inhibit further discussion.

Hazel had resisted initially – her only previous drug experience involved smoking weed and an occasional hit of coke. She was wary of the promises Roberto made when he'd begun to supply her with a variety of pills to help ease the pain of their separation, but not strong enough to stand firm when she realized he wasn't going to heed her pleas to spend more time with her. Once she started taking the pills, it wasn't long before her life was like a runaway eighteen-wheeler on a hill that's lost its brakes, careening toward disaster, offering little hope to regain control.

She became increasingly listless and erratic as the pills took over her life. She stopped bathing and eating and, on most days, had trouble getting out of bed. Salazar wasted little time in moving her out of the Soho loft, making sure she was sufficiently anesthetized to preclude any complaints when he instructed Rex Goodwin, the manager at the No Name Bar, to gather her belongings and move her to the basement beneath the bar, where she'd be unable to embarrass him in front of his associates. He stopped payment on her cell phone, cutting off communication with what few friends and family she had, leaving her totally isolated in the dungeon-like basement below the bar. Through Rex, he made sure she had enough food to survive and access to enough pills to avoid going into withdrawal, but nothing else. What had begun as an idyllic miracle, the adventure of a lifetime for a woman whose life had contained more than its share of tragic episodes, had become a slow descent into hell. Hazel had become a prisoner in Salazar's world, with little hope of being rescued.

*****

Marcia was on the road by 9:00 Monday morning. Once again she stopped at Mrs. Mac's Kitchen in Key Largo, this time for a more leisurely sit-down breakfast of biscuits and gravy with a side of Canadian bacon, before continuing north toward home. She stopped for gas and a bottle of water at the first Naples' exit beyond Alligator Alley and pulled into her parking spot at Causeway Towers at a few minutes before six.

299

After smoking a cigarette in the parking lot, she unpacked her bag and treated herself to a long, soaking bath. She hadn't done that much driving over a weekend in some time and her joints were protesting the long hours she'd spent in the car. The sound of Tegan and Sara drifted into the bathroom from the stereo as she tried to turn her mind off from thoughts of Hazel Devereaux.

She wondered how the lunch at Kitty's earlier today had gone. To her, Colleen and Gretchen made an unlikely duo; besides the obvious difference in ages, Gretchen's life had been one of extreme privilege from the moment she'd been born, spent at country clubs and cotillions, in stark contrast with Colleen's origins in Inverness as the only child of a welder and a part-time cashier at the local Winn Dixie. Somehow, they had discovered common ground in a short period of time. Marcia was torn between a sense of gratitude toward Colleen and what she'd accomplished since she'd accepted the administrative assistant position and pangs of jealousy regarding the younger woman's relationship with her financial benefactor.

When the water cooled and the skin on her hands began to wrinkle she got out of the tub, put on her pajamas and fixed herself a peanut butter sandwich which she ate at the dining room table while she checked her email. Nothing much there, just a notice from her bank that she had an upcoming credit card payment due and requests for contributions from two political organizations. She shook her head; it was January. Didn't the begging for dollars crowd ever take a break?

She thought about calling Lucien to fill him in on what she'd found out about Hazel, but after weighing the pros and cons of an evening phone call decided to wait until morning. There was no rush, especially since what she'd discovered about Hazel and Salazar on Cudjoe Key was minimal. She'd already known about Salazar's New York properties, so the switch of her investigative focus to New York could only be viewed in the curious context of one or both of them preferring Manhattan over Florida in the middle of January. Who in their right mind, given those two options, when cost is not an issue, chooses the depressing gray landscape of New York over the exhilarating pastels, invigorating warmth and brilliant sunshine of the Keys?

Lucien had been tightlipped thus far in what he hoped to get out of Marcia's investigation. Would he be satisfied knowing where his daughter was and how to communicate with her if she managed to track Hazel down, or did he have something more elaborate in mind? Perhaps something along the lines of a more permanent family connection, driven by Lucien's delayed feelings of guilt over his decision to turn his back on his daughter, denying her both the joys and sorrows of a traditional family configuration in order to pursue his own desire to make music. From their few, brief conversations, Marcia thought he'd been consistent and sincere when he said he wanted to make up for abandoning his daughter. The consequences of his decision had weighed heavily on his soul. His pain had been and continued to be visceral and searing.

She shut off her laptop and deposited her plate in the dishwasher before heading to bed. Although she was exhausted, it was a long time before her hyperactive mind shut down and allowed her to drift off to sleep.

53

"I must admit you surprised me."

Gretchen looked inquisitively across the table at her dining companion. "How so?"

"This morning, based on what I've seen and heard so far, I thought you might be the best-dressed woman to ever eat lunch at Kitty Galore's," Colleen replied, shaking her head. "Then you show up looking like a coed on spring break from Wisconsin."

Gretchen feigned a look of disapproval. "You told me it was laidback here, so I wore shorts and sandals. I'm just trying to fit in." She smiled. "What were you expecting? A fur coat and pearls?"

Colleen raised her glass of wine. "You look wonderful. Thanks for asking me to join you today." She tilted her head in the direction of Gretchen's plate, which twenty minutes ago had been filled with hogfish and black beans and rice but was now empty. "Looks like you enjoyed your meal."

"It was delicious," she said, looking around at the other tables on the patio, which were all filled. "This is a pretty popular place."

Colleen nodded. "Marcia says it's even busier once high season starts."

"Speaking of Marcia, when is she coming back from the Keys?"

"She should be on the road now," Colleen said. "I suggested she leave at five this morning so she could join us for lunch, but she said she wasn't getting up that early for anyone," quickly adding, "No offense."

"None taken," Gretchen answered. "Five a.m. is much more suited to the end of the day rather than the start of a new one." She smiled impishly. "At least it used to be when I was a bit younger."

It wasn't difficult for Colleen to picture a young Gretchen Schiller arriving home after a night on the town as the sun came up. She smiled as Gretchen continued. "Did she find Salazar while she was down there?"

Colleen shook her head. "He wasn't there. According to several neighbors, he hasn't been there for some time."

"What's her next move?" Gretchen asked, leaning forward, elbows resting on the table, her eyes animated.

Normally Colleen would regard such a question as rude and intrusive, but coming from Gretchen, Marcia's new silent partner, she thought it entirely appropriate. "Salazar has real estate holdings in New York City. His next-door neighbor on Cudjoe Key seems to think he spends most of his time there these days."

"Really?" she said. "In Manhattan?"

Colleen nodded. "Yes. Marcia's flying there on Wednesday to see if she can verify it. He owns two restaurants, a bar and a loft the city."

A broad smile broke out on Gretchen's face. "Have you made a hotel reservation for her yet."

"Yes. She's staying at the Moxy on East 11th Street," Colleen said.

"Cancel it."

Colleen stared at her smiling companion, confused. "Why?"

"Because I own a townhouse on Central Park West that she can use instead." Her smile sparkled. "I only use it when I have to attend board meetings, maybe two times a year. It sits empty the rest of the time. I also subscribe to a car service that she can use when she's there."

Colleen was stunned into silence before finally stammering, "Are...are you sure?"

"Positive," she said with conviction. "I inherited the property when my first husband died. My attorney advised me to sell it, but that was the one time I didn't take his advice." Pause. "I'm glad I didn't. The value of the place has skyrocketed since then. It'll be nice to have someone use it, even for a few days. I can drop off the keys tomorrow and alert security that I'll be having a guest for a few days. This way if she gets a lead and needs to stay longer, she won't have to deal with rebooking her room."

Colleen was staggered by Gretchen's generosity. As if she read her dining companion's mind, Gretchen continued. "After all, we're partners now. Why incur unnecessary expenses if you don't have to? A hotel in the area you're talking about won't be cheap. Staying at my place is a no-brainer."

Colleen reached for her cell phone. "If you don't mind, I'm going to step outside for a minute and cancel Marcia's hotel reservation."

Gretchen smiled, rising to her feet. "Take your time. I'm going to head into the bar, have a look at all the stuffed animals and fish you were telling me about, then visit the ladies' room." She looked around and caught the attention of their waitress and motioned her over. "We're not done yet, just taking a little break. We'll be back." The waitress nodded without speaking and headed to greet a couple who'd just entered and were waiting to be seated.

As soon as Gretchen entered the bar area, her eyes scanning the long, narrow bar space, Gracie Fenton noticed. "Can I help you?" she asked, abandoning her conversation with Lucien Devereaux and Steve Morrison who'd been eating their lunch by the service bar. Both Lucien and Morrison swiveled in their chair to appraise the new arrival who had drawn such a quick response from Gracie. Each was impressed by their first impression of the statuesque redhead, who responded to Gracie's swift inquiry with a smile. "I don't think so. It's my first visit, and my dining companion suggested I check the decoration scheme in the bar."

At the mention of a dining companion, Lucien and Morrison spirits sagged a bit. Their thoughts ran parallel – it was too good to be true to think that a classy woman like this would be having lunch here, alone.

Gracie gave the ogling men a frown of disapproval before returning her attention to Gretchen with a smile. "If there's anything I can do, give me a holler. My name's Gracie."

"Gretchen Schiller. Pleased to meet you." She gestured at the monster stuffed grouper suspended from the ceiling. "Nice place you have here, Gracie. I can see why Marcia likes it so much."

It was Gracie's turn to look gobsmacked. "Marcia Alvarez?"

Gretchen nodded. "That's her. She talks about this place all the time."

Morrison, his nerve bolstered by the introduction into the conversation of a name he recognized, broke in. "How do you know Marcia?"

She looked at Morrison with interest. "We met at a charity function recently, Mr.____?"

"Morrison. Steve Morrison."

She appraised him more closely. "You look vaguely familiar, Mr. Morrison. Have we met before?"

Before he could answer, Gracie broke in. "He used to be an actor."

Gretchen nodded as Morrison turned crimson at Gracie's move. "That must be it. I do watch a lot of films." She studied his features, trying to remember where she'd seen them before. "What have you been in that I might've seen, Mr. Morrison?"

He warned Gracie off with a withering glance before speaking. "Uh, nothing you've ever heard of."

She smiled. "Try me." She waited expectantly, hands on hips.

Morrison wanted to wring Gracie's neck. It was just his luck to meet someone interesting and have her screw it up. "None of my films never had a wide release. They were all straight-to-video," he mumbled.

That piqued her interest. She leaned forward invitingly. "So, a porn star?"

Morrison's heart sank; he wished he could evaporate from sight. On the other side of the bar, Gracie couldn't keep the grin off her face. Even Lucien was looking at Morrison with renewed interest. Gretchen continued, interpreting his silence in response to her query as confirmation. "That's certainly nothing to be ashamed of, Mr. Morrison." She looked him over like she was judging a steer at the state fair. "I'm sure you have certain attributes you're quite proud of."

"Don't get him started," Gracie warned with a smile. "You may regret it."

Morrison's enthusiasm sagged. This wasn't going the way he'd hoped at all.

54

Just then Colleen poked her head inside the bar, looking for Gretchen, walking over when she spotted her, temporarily rescuing Morrison from further inquiry. "It's all taken care of," she said, addressing Gretchen.

"Good," Gretchen replied. Returning her attention to her new friends, she continued. "This is my friend, Colleen. Colleen, this is Gracie, Steve and...."

Colleen broke in. "Lucien and I have met."

Without breaking stride, Gretchen continued. "Colleen works for Marcia. She's the one who recommended Kitty Galore's to me." She turned back toward her luncheon companion. "Your timing is impeccable. Steve here was about to tell us about his film career."

Colleen gave Lucien a smile and turned toward Morrison with interest. She was a real film buff, but she didn't recognize the dark-haired man on the bar stool. He must work behind the scenes, she thought. She wondered why his face was so flushed; the air conditioning in the bar was cool enough to stiffen her nipples. "Are you still working?" she asked him.

"Retired," he said in a voice that was barely audible.

"Mr. Morrison was a porn star, but he's a bit reluctant to share any details of what must have been a fascinating career," Gretchen said, following Gracie's lead.

Two stools down, Reb Jadel caught the words" porn star", turning his head slightly toward the conversation to listen in, hoping not to be noticed.

It was Colleen's turn to blush. Like most adults in the Internet age, she was aware of porn but not a follower. She turned toward Gretchen and took the easy way out. "I have to get back to the office. I have a lot of work to do before tomorrow morning."

"Don't let me hold you up," Gretchen said brightly. "I'll get the bill." She smiled at Morrison. "I think I might stay a bit longer. This lunch has turned out to be more interesting than I thought it would be."

*****

"You walked off the course?"

Gretchen laughed at the look of disbelief on Lucien's face. "I had no choice. The man cheats at golf. I don't play with anyone who cheats."

"Not even the president?"

"Especially not the president," Gretchen said firmly.

After Colleen departed, Lucien and Morrison made room for Gretchen to join them at the bar. For the next two hours they exchanged stories like friends who'd known one another all their lives, Morrison revealing that he'd acted under the name Biff Bratwurst, Lucien talking about the time he had to bail an inebriated Mac Rebbenack out of an El Paso jail, and finally Gretchen relating her disastrous golfing date with the president.

Gracie hung on every word. Later that night she revealed to her boyfriend Hank that she had never ignored her customers as much as she had that afternoon. "It was one unbelievable story after another. I couldn't tear myself away. I know my tips suffered, but I don't care. It was one of those afternoons that comes along once in a lifetime."

One person who had missed the stories was Reb Jadel. Since he'd left a water heater replacement job before it was completed because it was his lunch time, he had to return to finish it. His boss, who was aware of Jadel's history of going to lunch and not returning, had threatened to fire him if the job wasn't finished by two o'clock. Gracie was pleased to see him go; one less customer that she had to serve meant she could listen to more stories.

It was nearly four by the time Gretchen reluctantly excused herself, saying her goodbyes. "It certainly was a pleasure meeting you all. I hope we can do this again soon."

"Me, too," both Lucien and Morrison replied simultaneously. They looked at each other, embarrassed, as Gracie laughed, addressing Gretchen. "Look what you've done now, Gretchen. I do believe these boys are smitten."

Gretchen laughed off Gracie's observation as she rose to her feet. "I doubt it. We're talking about a porn star and a musician. Few professions are less suited to genuine emotional attachment than those two. They sure are fun to talk to, though."

*****

The following morning Marcia arrived at the office before eight. As usual, the smell of a fresh pot of coffee greeted her as she entered the room. Colleen was at her desk and looked up from her computer as her boss walked in. "Welcome back."

"It's good to be back," Marcia replied with a smile. "How was your lunch yesterday?"

Colleen chuckled, remembering. "It was really interesting. You should've seen Gretchen in action." She then went on to relate how Gretchen had attracted a bevy of admirers at the bar after they had finished their lunch. "I went outside to make a phone call, and when I returned, she'd left the table and was in the bar, making new friends. I had to leave to return to the office; she may still be there."

"What kind of friends?"

"Lucien was there having lunch with Steve Morrison – he said he knows you. And that blond bartender…"

"Gracie?"

Colleen nodded. "The four of them were having a great time. You'd hardly know she'd just met them."

Marcia nodded. Gretchen had a unique ability to make anyone feel like they were the most interesting person in the room, listening attentively, asking all the right questions. That's what had happened to her at the Hearts Across The Bay event. "I'm glad she had a good time. I wasn't sure how she'd react to Kitty's."

"She loved it."

Marcia shuffled through the mail in her inbox that had accumulated since she'd been away. "Am I all set for tomorrow?"

"Yes, with one change. Your plane is still leaving at 10:45, but I canceled your hotel reservation."

Marcia looked up. "Why?"

Colleen smiled. "Because Gretchen told me to. She wants you to stay at her townhouse. I checked out the address – it's on the West Side, overlooking Central Park."

"She has a place in New York?"

"She inherited it when her first husband died. Two stories, with a car service and of course a doorman. I know it's not as close to Salazar's loft in Soho as you originally requested, but I figured having your own driver would more than make up for the difference in distance. She also said the driver would pick you up at the airport. He'll be holding up one of those signs with your name on it when you arrive." She smiled brightly.

"Show me where it is."

Colleen called up Google Maps and plugged in the addresses of Salazar's loft and Gretchen's townhouse. Marcia leaned forward, trying to estimate travel time. In a moment she stood up. "I guess if I have a driver it'll work."

Colleen smiled. "Aren't you glad she's your partner?"

Marcia nodded. "Having your own personal driver certainly beats walking or taking the subway. Especially in January. Which reminds me – I need to get a coat. Any idea where I can find a winter coat in Tampa?"

Colleen handed her a list of names and addresses. "I made some calls yesterday. I had to guess at your size, so I made sure each of these places had one size larger and smaller, just in case."

Marcia shook her head in wonder. This woman thought of everything. "Anything else happen while I was away?"

"Not really, just the messages you have in your hand."

"Thanks, Colleen. As usual, you've done well."

"Well enough to deserve a raise?" she asked with a mischievous smile.

"We'll talk about that when I get back from New York."

55

Marcia's flight to New York was uneventful. The plane was filled with suntanned families returning home from extended holiday stays in Florida, grim-faced businessmen following the stock market on their phones and members of the Iona College men's basketball team returning from a game in Tampa the previous night.

Because of her late reservation, Marcia was stuck in the middle seat between a taciturn film student attending NYU seated by the window and a large man with reddish-gray hair on the aisle who wasted little time introducing himself as Colin Stewart. The bulky Stewart proceeded to inform her that he was returning to New York after delivering a seminar in Lakeland and was on his way to present a similar talk to an association of dentists in Brooklyn. The man's breath told Marcia that his preferred mouthwash was produced by Jim Beam, further evidence she used to derail his sales pitch before he gathered too much momentum. "I'm not a dentist and I don't play one on TV," she explained in a tone that had an edge discouraging further discourse. "I'm really not interested."

As Colleen indicated, her driver, dressed nattily in a dark suit, white shirt, black tie and matching cap, was waiting for her at

JFK, holding a neatly printed sign that read **ALVAREZ**. After introducing himself as Claude and gathering her bag from the claim area, he led her to a black Mercedes S560 and opened the rear door for her as she eased herself in. She inhaled deeply as she buckled herself in – the sleek sedan smelled like it had just come off the showroom floor.

Before they departed, Claude shifted in his seat and inquired in a faint continental accent if she'd like to listen to any particular style of music. Marcia thought for a moment. "Anything but rap or polkas."

Claude's skill behind the wheel was impressive. He navigated the streets of Manhattan with the verve of a veteran cabbie, edging the vehicle through spaces Marcia was sure were too tight, pulling up to the front door of Gretchen's building at West 65th and Central Park West in under an hour. As the doorman hustled out to greet her and handle her luggage, Claude handed her his business card. "Any time, day or night, Miss Alvarez." He bowed from the waist. "Enjoy your stay in New York."

Marcia smiled. "I'll do my best. Thanks very much, Claude. How about eight o'clock tomorrow morning?"

"I'll see you then."

She followed a young porter to an elevator which took them to the entrance to Gretchen's townhouse on the fifth floor. After placing her bag in the master bedroom overlooking the park, Marcia tipped the porter, who bowed slightly, turned and departed without a word, closing the door behind him.

Gretchen's townhouse was spectacular, stretching two floors, containing three spacious bedrooms upstairs, three full baths, two up and one down, a mammoth walk-in closet off the master bedroom, a fully equipped chef's kitchen on the lower level and a balcony on each floor overlooking Central Park. After a quick tour to acquaint herself with the layout, she called Gretchen, who picked up on the second ring. "How do you like it?"

"It's spectacular," Marcia gushed. "I feel like Princess Di. I never dreamed it would be this roomy."

"You'll appreciate it even more if the weather stays bad. What's it doing now?"

"It's snowing, but just flurries, nothing that's sticking," Marcia said. "Gray and overcast."

"Of course. Are you planning to go out later?" Gretchen asked.

"It depends. I'm going to call Colleen, see if she has any updates for me before I do anything," Marcia said.

"When you're done with Colleen, check your email. I sent you a list of places nearby that deliver food," she said. "It'll come in handy if the weather stays like it is."

"I really appreciate that, Gretchen. I can't thank you enough for your generosity."

"Sure you can," Gretchen replied. "You can find Lucien's daughter."

Next, she called Colleen, who had nothing new to report. "How was the flight?"

"Fine, except for the asshole consultant in the seat next to me," Marcia said with a grimace. "He was huge, took up all of his seat and half of mine, plus he smelled like he'd prepped for the flight in the bar."

"Sounds horrible," she said sympathetically.

"I'd forgotten what flying commercial is like – screaming kids, women sitting with their dogs, flight attendants who think they're comedians. It's like my father used to say: flying in coach is the new Greyhound."

Dead silence. After thirty seconds, Colleen spoke. "Greyhound? What's that?"

Marcia smiled and shook her head. She should've guessed that Colleen was too young to know what Greyhound was. "The way the unwashed masses used to travel. Taking the bus."

After they finished their call Marcia checked her emails, deleting the spam before reading Gretchen's suggestions concerning dining options. She'd planned on eating in Salazar's two restaurants while she was here to get a feel for the atmosphere in each – Colleen had made reservations for tomorrow night and the night after that – but Gretchen was right. If the weather turned nasty, she now had some nice alternatives to venturing out into the cold.

She unpacked her bag, hung up the two pants suits she'd brought for the restaurant in the walk-in closet, grabbed her cigarettes and stepped out onto the balcony for a smoke, her need for nicotine overriding her aversion to the cold. As she shivered in the frigid air she wondered where in this vast metropolis Hazel Devereaux was and what she was doing. There were few reasons a born-and-bred southerner would choose to spend the winter in such an intemperate climate, she thought, especially given the other options available to her, Miami and the Keys. The clear favorite, the reason that led the pack in her mind, was the common denominator that their research had pinpointed as soon as they identified Roberto Salazar and traced his history from El Salvador to the U.S.

Drugs.

*****

He'd been able to fight those urges off successfully until last Sunday. As they had after most of their practice sessions, Rick Manning and Tate Baggot stayed behind after Gabe left and shared a couple of pipefuls of Rick's weed in the garage. When Elaine joined them and offered him a hit as they passed the pipe around, he surprised them all by accepting, drawing the soothing smoke deep into his lungs, savoring the familiar feeling of relaxation and calm, his well-intentioned defenses finally breeched.

After Tate left, Lucien made the big move, asking Rick in a shaky voice if he could get him some more. He grinned widely, walked into the house, and returned with a small mason jar filled with fragrant green buds, sticky with potency. He unscrewed the top and held it out to Lucien. "Take a whiff of this. It's what we've been smoking tonight."

Lucien inhaled deeply. He looked at Rick. "How much?"

315

Rick dismissed him with a flip of his wrist. "Don't worry about it. There's plenty more where that came from out at Fuego. The first sample's on me."

Heart pounding like an inexperienced teen, Lucien drove home in the right lane of SR 54, observing the speed limit manically as cars raced by him in the two lanes to his left. He held his breath as a car he was convinced was a cop roared up on him from behind and followed him, only a foot or so behind his bumper, for nearly a mile before pulling out and blowing by him, the driver flipping him the bird. When he arrived home, he parked his car and carried his guitar and the jar of weed into his apartment, unable to shake that old, familiar feeling that a cop was poised to knock on his door at any moment, ready to snap the cuffs on him.

Just like the good old days.

56

Because the basement beneath the bar had no toilet, Salazar had instructed Rex to allow Hazel to use the facilities on the main floor when necessary, with strict instructions to monitor her movements closely. The last thing Salazar wanted was for an emaciated, unwashed junkie to appear partially dressed in the bar when it was packed with patrons – it would be bad for business.

Rex bristled with resentment when his boss informed him that his new project would be to make sure that Hazel Devereaux didn't embarrass Salazar or his business as long as she was living in the basement. Managing the bar was what he did best, what he preferred to do. Babysitting an erratic drug addict was a waste of his time and talents, he thought. But fear of Salazar's mercurial temper kept him from protesting out loud, to his face.

Instead, he took his displeasure with his adjusted responsibilities out on Hazel. Bathroom visits were only allowed in the mornings, before the bar opened. Rex stood watch outside the door of the ladies' room; when she was finished, he escorted her back to the basement and locked the door. He delivered two meals a day, lunch and dinner, leaving a full tray and retrieving the tray used for the previous meal, which often was barely touched. No wonder she looked so thin, he thought.

317

He also delivered the drugs which arrived daily at the bar in nondescript packaging via courier. Salazar had instructed Rex to pass the packages on to Hazel without opening them, so he had no idea what was inside. When on one occasion he expressed curiosity to Salazar as to the contents, Salazar had favored him with a small smile. "It's better you don't know, Rex." He never raised the subject again.

When Rex went down to the basement Thursday morning for Hazel's daily trip to the bathroom, he found her sprawled on the couch that served as her makeshift bed, unconscious. He shook her; no response. He tried again, this time harder, but still her eyes remained closed, her body deadweight. Alarmed, he checked her pulse. It was faint, but still there. He pulled out his cell and called Salazar, voice tinged with panic. "Boss, she won't wake up. Should I call an ambulance? Or take her to the hospital myself?"

In a calm voice, Salazar responded. "No ambulance, no hospital. Stay by her side. I'll send someone over." The phone went dead.

Rex cursed loudly into the darkness after Salazar hung up on him. He was on probation, having been released from Fishkill Correctional Facility eleven months earlier after serving twenty months for a weapons violation. The last thing he needed was to be tied to the overdose of a woman with whom he had no connection other than his employer's request to watch over her. He had no plans to go back upstate because of this bitch. He paced around the dank room, anxiously checking his watch, waiting for help to arrive.

*****

Claude was waiting for her in the lobby of the building when Marcia exited the elevator Thursday morning, dressed more casually at her request in a pair of dark slacks, sweater and a dark blue ski jacket. She had explained her reasoning in a call the night before. "I don't want to look like I'm being chauffeured around town. I want to keep as low a profile as I can."

She smiled at his outfit as she approached, nodding in approval. "That's what I'm talking about."

Claude, who had deferred to her sartorial judgment while at the same time wondering silently how being squired around town in a high-end Mercedes wouldn't broadcast a sense of privilege, responded, his face expressionless. "Where to this morning, Ms. Alvarez?"

"The No Name Bar, on Third Avenue. If you can, find a spot to park where I can watch the entrance, see who comes and goes."

"Yes, ma'am."

It was snowing again, heavier today, big wet flakes descending from the overcast sky like ash from Mount Vesuvius, snarling the morning rush hour traffic. As they inched their way across town in stop and go fashion, Marcia wondered how anyone could possibly enjoy living here. The traffic was impossible, the weather cold and depressing, the sidewalks jammed with bundled up, sour-faced pedestrians in a hurry despite the inclement conditions. Her hunch that Hazel was somewhere in the city suddenly was no longer as strong as it was after her trip to the Keys. Southern women, especially those who've always lived in a state bordering on the Gulf of Mexico, would have difficulty adapting to such harsh living conditions. She knew she would.

It was less than four miles from Gretchen's townhouse to the No Name Bar, a trip that this morning took them forty-five minutes. After circling the block several times, Claude spotted a delivery truck pulling out of a spot on the east side of Third Avenue opposite the bar and, after a brief wait, expertly guided the Mercedes into the vacant slot. He turned toward the backseat. "Would you like the engine on or off, ma'am?"

Marcia looked outside. It was snowing harder than it was when they'd set out; there were few people on the sidewalk braving the weather. "Better leave it on," she advised, sliding over to a position directly behind Claude to get a better view of the entrance to the bar.

She'd done some research on her iPad last night in her room. From the bar website she knew that the place didn't open until noon each day, which meant the employees would begin showing up at about eleven. She was looking for anyone who arrived or left before then, people whose presence at the bar before it opened would raise questions. She checked her watch: 8:55.

Although she hadn't explicitly asked Claude to watch the place with her, she smiled when she noticed his head turned in the direction of the bar. She gave him a friendly tap on the shoulder. "You don't have to watch with me, Claude. If you have something else to do, by all means, do it."

Without turning around the laconic driver said simply, "Four eyes are better than two."

"I can't quite place your accent, Claude. Where are you from?"

"Mortsel, Belgium."

"Where is that?"

"Nine kilometers south of Antwerp."

They fell silent, each watching the far sidewalk as the snow continued to fall. From time to time Marcia had to wipe condensation from the window to keep her line of sight clear. Without taking her eyes off the bar, she retrieved her phone and punched in the number of her office.

Colleen answered immediately. "How's the weather?"

She could tell by the tone of her voice that Colleen was trying to get a rise out of her. Not today. "Cold and snowing," Marcia answered succinctly. "Definitely not beach weather. Anything to report?"

"Nothing new here as far as Hazel is concerned," Colleen replied. "I went to watch Lucien's band last night at Skipper's. They're really good!"

"How was the crowd?"

"Standing room only. My girlfriend told me it was a fabulous crowd for a Wednesday there. What are you doing today?"

"Right now I'm staking out the No Name Bar."

"In the morning?' Colleen asked skeptically. "What time does it open?"

"Noon," Marcia replied. "I'm hoping__"

Just then a cab pulled up and discharged a passenger with a sizeable black bag. The man shuffled to the front door of the bar and rang the buzzer."

"Gotta go," Marcia whispered excitedly. "I'll call you later."

In a few moments another man came to the door and opened it just enough to allow the man with the bag to enter. Marcia tried but couldn't get a look at either man's face. She glanced at her watch: 9:57. She jotted down the time in her notebook.

At precisely 10:48 a cab pulled up in front of the bar. Moments later the man with the bag emerged from the bar and got into the cab. As it began to pull away from the curb, Marcia tapped Claude on the shoulder again. "Follow that cab."

"Yes, ma'am."

57

The cab driver made a tight U-turn and headed north on Third Avenue before turning right on East 12th. Claude pulled out slowly and fell in behind as the cab drove two blocks to First Avenue, where it turned left and proceeded north past Mount Sinai Beth Israel Hospital to East 17th, where he turned left and drove slowly past Second Avenue, pulling over opposite Stuyvesant Square Park.

Claude pulled over to the curb several car lengths behind the cab. Marcia watched as the man with the bag exited the cab and entered a three-story brick building. "Wait for me," Marcia instructed as she hopped out of the cab, retrieving her phone from her purse as she hurried along the slippery sidewalk and entered the front door of the building.

She was met by a stoic security guard in uniform seated behind a desk who regarded her impassively as he said, "How may I help you?"

Marcia held the phone out. "The man who just entered the building, the one carrying the bag, dropped his phone in my cab. I'd like to return it to him. Do you know where he went?"

"That's Dr. Clark" the guard said, still evaluating her warily. "You can leave it with me if you like, Miss."

Marcia shook her head. "I'd feel much better if I could return it to him in person. Can you direct me to his office? It'll just take a minute."

The guard hesitated for a long moment, still unsure, before finally pushing a logbook across the desk toward Marcia. "He's on the third floor, Suite 302. You'll have to sign in first."

A broad smile broke out on Marcia's face. "Thanks very much, Officer." She bent down and printed the name Diana Spencer in the book, jotted down the time, then pushed it back in the guard's direction.

The guard glanced at the name, then pointed behind him to the elevator. "When you get to the third floor, turn right. His door will the second door on the left."

"Thank you."

Inside, the elevator looked like it had been installed a century earlier. Marcia punched three; after a few moments the car lurched upward, barely moving. Marcia wondered if she should have taken the stairs.

The name "John Clark, MD" was etched into the glass of the office door, which looked to be the same vintage as the elevator. She pushed the door open and found a receptionist, dressed in a crisp white nurse's uniform, regarding her with a smile. "Do you have an appointment?" she asked brightly.

"No. I'm not one of Dr. Clark's patients." She held up the phone. "He left his cell phone in my cab. I'd like to return it to him."

The receptionist extended her arm across the desk. "I'll give it to him."

Marcia pulled the phone back. "I'd really prefer to give it to him myself. It's snowing like crazy out there, which means I won't get many fares today. Perhaps the doctor might look kindly upon my effort to return his phone..." She let the sentence dangle, hoping the receptionist would grasp the implication.

She did. The dark-skinned receptionist smiled. "I know what you mean. My father drove a cab when he first came here from Karachi. I was raised on tips." She indicated a closed door behind her. "He's in there. I'll let him know you're here."

Marcia reached across the desk and touched the receptionist's hand with affection. "Thank you for understanding." She moved quickly to the door, hoping to make it inside before the receptionist had a chance to trigger any suspicion when she announced her arrival.

Too late. Dr. Clark, a balding man in his fifties, stared at her through thick-lensed glasses from behind his desk. "You're not my cab driver," he exclaimed, reaching for the phone.

"I'm sorry to have deceived you, Dr. Clark, but it's very important. A matter of life and death." She thrust her investigator's credentials across the table. "My name is Marcia Alvarez. I'm a private investigator, looking for a missing person."

The doctor examined her license for a moment before looking up. "You're from Florida?"

"Yes, doctor," she said, retrieving a photo of Hazel from her purse and passing it across the desk. "I'm looking for this woman, Hazel Devereaux. One of my sources indicated that she might be at the No Name Bar. I was there earlier this morning and I saw you enter the building before it opened. You spent about an hour there before you came out and left. I was wondering if you saw her while you were inside."

The doctor looked at the photo for several moments before looking at Marcia. "Why are you looking for this woman?"

"My client is her father," Marcia explained. "He's been looking for her for more than fifteen years." It was an exaggeration that hurt no one, followed by another, larger lie, relayed in a solemn tone. "Her father is dying. He'd like to find her so he can say goodbye."

The doctor looked at the photo again, rubbing his chin with his free hand. "I saw a woman this morning who looks like her, but I can't be sure. She's a lot thinner now."

"This is the last photo her father has of her. It was taken two years ago," she explained, pausing before rolling the dice with her biggest gamble. "He thinks she's been involved with drugs, so she might look different now. Please take another look," she pleaded, watching him closely for his reaction to her hunch.

Paydirt. The doctor's face softened as he glanced at the photo, then looked back at Marcia. "This could be her," he said with a degree of conviction. "I can't be positive – I only saw her once, today, for less than an hour, but it looks like her." He looked at Marcia again sadly. "What you're asking me to do, to pass on information concerning a patient, is strictly illegal." He paused, struggling to maintain his composure. "I lost my own daughter years ago to a heroin overdose. She was only seventeen. I know what this woman's father must be going through." He straightened in his chair. "I treated the woman this morning for an overdose. She's okay for the time being, but it's clear she's on a downward spiral."

"I'm so sorry to hear about your daughter, Dr. Clark," Marcia said softly. He tried to smile at her compassion but failed. Marcia continued. "Where in the building did you treat her?"

A look of disgust crossed his face. "She was in the basement, living in filthy conditions. No running water, no toilet, hardly any light. It was more like a prison cell than someone's room. Absolutely inhuman."

Marcia pressed him. "Was anyone with her?"

The doctor nodded. "She was with another man. He let me in the door and took me down to see her."

"Did you happen to get his name?"

"No. He never offered and I never asked."

"Can you describe him to me?" Marcia asked eagerly.

He thought for a moment. "He's a black man, late thirties or early forties, no facial hair, a little over six feet, with a muscular build. If I had to guess, I'd say he came from a Hispanic country. He had that accent that a lot of Spanish-speaking people have when they speak English, sort of singsong, if you know what I mean."

"That's very helpful, Dr. Clark," Marcia said. "Tattoos?"

He shook his head. "None that I could see, but it was very dark and he's a black man, so I could've missed them if he had any." He looked at her forlornly. "Anything else I can help you with today, Ms. Alvarez? I need to get back to work."

"Not right now, Dr. Clark. You've been a big help." She reached into her purse and withdrew one of her cards. "If you think of anything else, please give me a call, anytime, day or night."

He took it without comment and placed it in one of the drawers in his desk. He stood, offering his hand across the desk. "I hope this turns out well, especially for that unfortunate young woman."

"So do I, Dr. Clark. So do I."

58

Marcia could hardly restrain her elation as she climbed into the back seat of the Mercedes. Claude turned and gave her an inquiring look. "Home, Claude," she replied jauntily. "No rush."

Although she felt Claude to be trustworthy, she hadn't known him long enough yet to be comfortable with sharing sensitive information, so she didn't mention her discovery to him. As he approached the front of the townhouse, Marcia spoke for the first time after her instruction to head home, "I have a 7:30 reservation for dinner tonight at Café Tulum in Lenox Hill. What time should I expect you?"

Claude did some calculating in his head. "It's just on the other side of the park. Shouldn't take more than fifteen or twenty minutes, even with traffic."

"How about 6:45?" Marcia asked. "If we get there early, that'll give me a chance to look around a little bit."

"I'll see you then, ma'am."

In her room, Marcia dialed Colleen, who picked up immediately. "Good afternoon. Is it still snowing?"

"Like a motherfucker," she replied breezily. "Can't hardly see your hand in front of your face." Pause. "But it's not all bad," she teased.

"What do you mean?'" Colleen asked eagerly. "Did you find a clue?"

"You could say that. I might've found Hazel."

Marcia's bombshell left Colleen momentarily speechless. When she finally responded, it was with a single word. "How?"

"Sheer luck," Marcia admitted. "I was in the right place at the right time."

She went on to explain how it had happened. How she had the bar under surveillance when a mysterious visitor arrived with what looked like a medical bag and then left an hour later, how she and Claude had followed him, how Marcia had used her phone as a ruse to get in to see him, and how the doctor, when shown a picture of Hazel, had been reasonably confident that the woman he'd treated for an overdose this morning was Hazel.

"Overdose?" Colleen gasped. "How is she?"

"She was still alive after the doctor treated her," Marcia said. "She must've responded well to his treatment if he didn't recommend that she be transported to a hospital."

"So you haven't seen her in person yet." More of a statement than a question.

"No," Marcia replied. "But now I know where she is. All I have to do is figure out how to get to her."

Colleen was confused. "You said she was in a bar?"

Marcia corrected her gently. "Not just in a bar, living in the basement beneath the bar. The doctor said she looked like she was being held there against her will."

"Any sign of Salazar?"

"No, and I didn't expect to see him there. The place is a dive, definitely not the kind of place where a drug kingpin like Salazar would spend any time." She paused before going on. "Who knows? Maybe my hot streak will hold and I'll run into him at the restaurant tonight. Which reminds me: how did you get me reservations at two of Manhattan's hottest restaurants so quickly?"

"Gretchen," Colleen replied. "I told her Salazar owned two restaurants in New York that you wanted to scope out. She made a few calls and voila! You were in. Good move accepting her offer to be your silent partner, boss."

Marcia couldn't have agreed more. She'd be nowhere on this case without Gretchen's help. "She certainly has friends in high places. Lucky for us."

"Luckier for Hazel, if you can get to her somehow. Sounds like she needs someone to come to her rescue. What's your next move?"

"I'll see if I can find anything out at the restaurant tonight, then go back to the bar tomorrow when it opens, see what the employees have to say about a woman living in the basement. Maybe I'll get lucky again." She shifted gears. "How are things at the office?"

"As slow as you might expect, with you being out of town." She added hastily, "Which is good. It gives me more time to investigate Senor Salazar."

"Stay on that bastard," Marcia said. "I want to be able to bury his ass if I find him."

"I'll do my best." Colleen promised.

When she hung up with Colleen, Marcia shed her clothes and took a long, hot shower, warming her thin Florida blood under the steamy spray. Today was the longest time in her life she'd ever spent outside, in the snow. The only other place where she'd ever lived where it snowed was when she was a young girl in Oregon, but in all her time there she'd never experienced a snowfall like the one this morning.

When she was finished, she dried herself and donned an incredibly soft and comfortable robe she found hanging in the walk-in closet. She walked over to the window. It had stopped snowing but was still gray and overcast. How did people do it, she wondered. She hadn't seen the sun since she'd arrived; judging by the cloud cover and the local weather reports, she might not catch a glimpse of it during the length of her stay.

She walked over to the bed, grabbed her cigarettes from her purse and walked back to the balcony door, which she cracked a bit to let the smoke escape. As she smoked furtively, careful to try to expel as much of her smoke outside, she thought about what to do if she was able to talk with Hazel. Would she be receptive to her father sending someone after her? Or would she dismiss the effort of her long-absent father as being too little, too late? How would her addiction affect her thought process? Would she be willing to try to escape what her life had become, or would she be unable to overcome the grip Salazar had so masterfully placed on her life? Marcia shook her head. Trying to speculate as to the thought processes of a drug addict – particularly one she hadn't met – was a fool's errand. Each case was different, each blend of variables unique.

She flicked her cigarette over the edge of the balcony and checked the time: 2:11. Plenty of time for a nap to recharge her systems. She tossed the robe on a nearby chair and crawled naked beneath the silk sheets, drawing the comforter up tight to her chin. She set the alarm on her bedside radio for 4:00 and closed her eyes, visions of Hazel Devereaux in her mind as she drifted off to sleep.

The alarm interrupted a dream she was having with an improbable cast of characters, led by the mysterious Headfake, the man who'd brokered the deal to sell the D.B. Cooper ransom cash. In it he had reached out to Judy Ruliani, who in turn contacted Marcia, telling her that the deal was no longer going to be honored because the purchaser of the bundles of money had taken them to a second expert, who claimed the money was fake. He wanted his money back. According to Ruliani, that meant Marcia would either have to sell Alvarez Investigations to raise the required cash or dissolve the firm. Marcia resisted, resulting in Headfake taking matters into his own hands, using his mastery of the dark web to sell the business himself, without Marcia's knowledge or consent. When she arrived at work the next morning and tried to enter the office, she found that the locks had been changed and a notice attached to the door, certifying the sale.

At that point she woke up, disoriented and panicked. It took a few moments for her to confirm that she'd been dreaming. She looked around the spacious master suite. She was still in New York, still on the trail of Hazel Devereaux, still the rightful owner of Alvarez Investigations.

That's what you get for skipping breakfast *and* lunch, she told herself as she stood before the mirror, splashing water on her face, pinning the blame for the bizarre dream on an empty stomach. She retrieved the robe from the chair and walked down the stairs to the kitchen, where she spent a few minutes rooting through the cabinets and drawers until she found a jar of peanut butter. She spooned it directly out of the jar, not bothering with crackers or bread, careful not to ingest too much lest she ruin her appetite for dinner at Café Tulum.

She planned on treating herself to something special tonight.

59

"I'm usually a beer drinker, Claude, but I'd like to order some wine tonight. Can you help me out?"

Was she asking him about wine because he was a suave and sophisticated European? Looking at her in the rearview mirror, he replied in a neutral voice, "What are you planning to order?"

Marcia had studied the menu in the townhouse before they left and was prepared. "They have a shrimp dish that looks really good."

"With a sauce?"

"Yes, a red sauce with some heat, according to the writeup."

No hesitation. "Red sauce, red wine. Maybe a California zinfandel, if they have one."

"Their online menu brags about the size of their wine cellar," Marcia said.

"You should be all set, then."

They were in the Mercedes, heading east through the park on 65th Street, on the way to Café Tulum. The snow had stopped and the streetlights were on, casting oddly shaped shadows on the piles of slush lining both sides of the road. According to the temperature displayed on the dashboard, it was 23°F. Just before they exited the park they passed a horse-drawn carriage headed in the opposite direction. The couple in the back were bundled so completely that it was impossible to determine their gender. Marcia shook her head; must be a bucket list item for them to be out, exposed to the elements in this kind of raw weather.

Café Tulum was located in the middle of the block, its location indicated only by a sign hanging from an awning overhead that said simply **Tulum.** As she exited the car, she asked Claude: "What will you do while I eat? You're welcome to join me if you'd like – I'm sure they would prefer serving two rather than one."

Claude shook his head. "Thanks for the offer, Ms. Alvarez, but I ate my dinner before I picked you up." He indicated a newspaper and several magazines on the seat beside him. "I brought some things to read to pass the time. Just call me when you're finished."

As she planned, she'd arrived early to give her a chance to study the place to try to get more of a feel for its owner. A pleasant dark-haired man in his thirties greeted her with a smile as soon as she entered the restaurant. "Good evening and welcome to Café Tulum. Do you have a reservation?"

"I do," Marcia replied. "Alvarez, for one."

The host checked the book, found her name and then gestured toward the heart of the restaurant. "Follow me, please, Ms. Alvarez."

She followed the immaculately mannered host through the crowded, noisy floor to a small table against the wall near the rear of the space. As he pulled out her chair for her, she glanced around the bustling scene. Hers was the only unoccupied table in the room. The host handed her a menu, wine list, and a single printed sheet indicating tonight's special. "Would you like some water?" he asked.

"Please."

333

He bowed from the waist. "It'll be here right away."

She watched him withdraw a small device from his back pocket as he walked back toward the door, entering some information. Moments later a young Hispanic man was at her table with her water and a small dish of lemon slices. Nice touch, she thought. "Thank you."

Café Tulum was decorated like a casual tiki bar, with colorful pictures of Mexican seaside life on the upper areas of the walls and a variety of props, including several vintage life jackets and a small, hand-woven hammock suspended below. It fit the theme of the restaurant depicted on its website as one specializing in fresh, innovative seafood dishes native to the Yucatan Peninsula.

She glanced quickly at the sheet of specials, wondering if any of them were intriguing enough for her to abandon the choice she made before leaving home, quickly deciding they weren't. Next, she picked up the bulky wine list, thumbing through the well-worn pages until she found the sections devoted to reds, looking for the zinfandels. She found an interesting selection from a boutique vintner located in Calaveras County and, because she'd had unexpected success in her quest today to locate Hazel Devereaux, decided to order a bottle rather than a glass, reminding her usually penurious self that the hefty price tag for this dinner would be written off as a business expense.

Her waiter arrived ten minutes after she'd been seated and asked if she had any questions about the wine list or the menu. When she said no, he asked. "May I bring you something to drink?"

"You may," replied Marcia. "I'd like a bottle of the Stephen Millier zinfandel, the 2018."

He nodded approvingly, not bothering to write it down. "Do you need more time with the menu?"

She shook her head. "I think I'm all set. I'd like to start with an order of *ceviche*, and for my entrée I'd like the Shrimp Caliente."

"Excellent choices, madam. I'll be back with your wine in a moment."

When he returned with the wine, Marcia had a question. "Is Senor Salazar here tonight? I ate in his restaurant in Miami two weeks ago and was very impressed. I wanted to compliment him on the cuisine and service, but my server in Florida told me he was in New York. I was wondering if he's here this evening?"

He poured a small amount for her to taste, then looked at her with a sheepish grin. "You missed him by a day," he said apologetically. "Senor Salazar flew to Miami this morning."

Trying to hide her disappointment, Marcia managed a rueful smile. "Just my luck. Do you know when he'll be back?"

"That I cannot answer." In a conspiratorial tone and with a sly wink, he added. "As you might imagine, he doesn't share his travel arrangements with me." He indicated the wine. "Is it to your satisfaction, madam?"

"It's marvelous."

Her server smiled. "I'll return shortly with your *ceviche*."

So much for her string of good luck, she thought. However, she had been impressed that her server had not introduced himself to her or wore a nametag – she felt the trend in most restaurants for servers to identify themselves these days was ridiculous and unnecessary. She wasn't looking to make a new friend, only to receive competent service. If she wanted to know the name of her server, she could find it on her check at the end of the evening.

The contrast between Café Tulum and the No Name Bar was striking. The patrons in the restaurant were well-dressed, well-mannered and older, long removed from their dive bar days, if they had existed at all. The ladies' restroom was immaculate, with an abundant supply of soft, white towels and a variety of moisturizing creams on the counters surrounding the sinks to help combat the effects of the relentless New York winter on the female complexion. The only thing missing was a deferential attendant. Although she had yet to experience the interior of the No Name, something she planned to remedy tomorrow, she felt confident her visit would leave her unimpressed.

She devoured the *ceviche*, marveling at the fresh chunks of seafood, fresh onion, red pepper and lime juice. Equally impressive was the Shrimp Caliente that followed, the sauce as piquant as advertised, finely chopped pieces of *habaneros* adding just the right amount of heat without overwhelming the other ingredients in the sauce. The dish was accompanied with a tasty lime and cilantro risotto and grilled green beans adorned with shaved almonds which left her, regrettably, with no room for any of the delicious sounding desserts her waiter urged her to select. "Next time," she promised. Holding up her full wine glass, she continued. "No rush on the check."

Shortly after she finished the last dregs of the wine – she jotted down the name of the vintner for future reference – her server magically appeared with the check as if he'd been observing her, waiting for her to finish. She looked at the amount; it was the most she'd ever spent on a meal, by far, in her life. But she had no regrets as she handed the server her credit card. It had been the most impressive dining experience of her life. She added a generous tip and handed the signed bill to him. As he walked away, she made one last visit to the restroom – she had consumed an entire bottle of wine, after all. When she returned to her table she dialed Claude's number.

"Pick me up out front."

60

The following morning Marcia was up at dawn, waiting impatiently for the chance to call Colleen once she arrived at the office. She'd spent several hours the night before, lying in bed in the townhouse, too keyed up by the day's revelations to fall asleep, working on a plan to rescue Hazel. It was nearly midnight when she settled on what she believed to be her best option. There were a number of variables that rendered the plan risky, starting with verifiable confirmation that Hazel Devereaux was indeed living in the basement below the No Name Bar. She had to make sure Hazel was there first. She hoped she'd be able to accomplish that today.

To kill time, she turned on the television in the master suite and watched a local news program while she sipped her morning coffee, anxious to see what the weather would be today. A glance outside revealed thick cloud cover, a feature of the January skies in New York she was finding unrelenting and depressing. She idly wondered how the winter suicide rate in New York compared to the Scandinavian standard as yet another day without sun was predicted by a bubbly young redhead wearing a magenta dress that clung to her like a second layer of skin. Shapely young women in skintight outfits must distract the viewers from the dismal forecasts, she thought.

At eight she called the office. Colleen answered immediately. "Morning, boss. How was your dinner last night?"

"Outstanding, one of the best I've ever had. If you speak with Gretchen anytime soon, please tell her thanks."

"You can call her yourself if you'd like. When I spoke with her late yesterday afternoon, she hinted that she'd like to hear from you."

"We'll see how things work out today," Marcia said in a neutral tone, hesitant to commit to anything unless she was sure she'd be conveying positive news. "I have a plan that might work, but I'm going to need some help from your end to make it happen."

She explained the plan to Colleen. When Marcia was finished, Colleen's response was brimming with enthusiasm. "It could work, as long as you can confirm Hazel's in the basement."

"That's the key," Marcia agreed. "In the meantime, call Lucien today and see how he feels about the general concept of the plan. We need to know if he's willing to do his part if we're successful on this end. But no specifics until I confirm her location, okay? I don't want to build his hopes up, only for them to come crashing down if something goes wrong."

"Whatever you say, boss."

When their call was finished, Marcia dialed Claude, who answered on the first ring. "Yes, Ms. Alvarez?"

"Good morning, Claude. I trust you slept well."

"Like a baby, thank you. Where are we headed to today?"

"Back to the bar," she replied. "I want to be there when it opens at noon, but we'll need to make a stop on the way. I want to pick up a burner cell phone – do you know anywhere I can find one? In Florida I'd head to Walmart, but I don't know if they even have one of those in Manhattan."

"They don't," Claude said. "But I know a place not far out of the way to buy one."

"If we go there, what time should I expect you here if we want to make it to the bar by noon?"

Claude thought for a moment before answering. "I'll pick you up at 10:45. That should give us plenty of time to buy a phone and get to the bar by noon."

"Perfect. See you then."

*****

As Dr. Clark took his morning shower, he wondered again if he'd done the right thing the day before by supplying information to the private investigator inquiring about that woman in the basement of the bar. Too late now, he told himself – what's done is done and can't be undone. He justified confirming the woman's identity because he understood the grief of her father, a grief he would never wish upon another parent, a grief that had not lessened for him in twenty years.

He thought about notifying his client, the one who paid his bills discreetly in cash, off the books, but dismissed that thought immediately. He didn't want to upset the man who provided a tidy income for him on the side, money he shielded from his wife who suffered from an addiction to online shopping.

No, he decided. He'd keep his mouth shut, play dumb if anyone came around inquiring.

It was what he did best.

*****

Despite wearing gloves and a hat and being bundled up in the down-filled jacket she'd purchased in Tampa, Marcia was chilled to the bone as soon as she stepped outside the building. Although it was not snowing, the wind was brisk, from the north. By the time she made it from the doorway to the Mercedes idling next to the curb, her nose was red and running.

Claude noticed. "I'd wager you're looking forward to getting back to Florida," he said as she slid into the back seat.

"Shrewd observation, Columbo."

Her tone discouraged further comment. While Claude drove in silence, Marcia went over the few facts she knew ahead of her visit to the bar. The man she was looking for, Rex, would probably have to be finessed a bit in order to avoid arousing any suspicions that he might be tempted to report back to Salazar. She had to frame her suggestion regarding the cell phone as liberating for Rex rather than as a challenge to his loyalty regarding Salazar. As long as Rex viewed her proposal as a possible solution to his babysitting dilemma, her plan would have a chance.

Claude drove through the park, turning right on Fifth Avenue until he reached 49th Street, where he turned right again and parked in the shadow of Rockefeller Center. Marcia had decided to have Claude buy the phone as a precaution against being caught on video, so she handed him four crisp new hundred-dollar bills and watched as he disappeared inside a bodega.

Five minutes later Claude returned to the car and handed a bag to Marcia over the seat. "Your change is in the bag."

She looked at him intently. "Did you buy the minutes?"

As he fastened his seat belt, he replied without turning his head, "Just like you asked."

She tore open the packaging, retrieving the instructions on how to boot up the phone to make it operational. She plugged the phone into one of the charging ports in the back seat, using the charger Claude had purchased, entered Lucien's number and name as a contact, then put the phone aside, letting it charge. If she was successful in convincing Rex to go along with her plan, the phone would be fully charged, loaded with minutes, when she handed it over.

Claude found a spot to park on East 11th Street and pulled smoothly to the curb. Marcia checked her watch: 11:57. She put her hat and gloves back on. "Wish me luck. Hopefully, this won't take too long."

Claude noticed the phone on the seat, charging. "Aren't you taking the phone?"

Marcia shook her head. "I want it to be fully charged when I hand it over. If I need it today, I'll come back for it."

She walked down 11th to Third Avenue, walking briskly against the wind toward the bar, chin tucked into her chest. The "**OPEN**" sign was lit in the front window as she pushed through the doorway.

A man in his thirties with longish hair and a neatly trimmed moustache was behind the bar and looked up as Marcia plopped herself on a barstool. "What can I get you today?"

Marcia glanced at the bottles of beer lining the top shelf behind the bar. "You have Yuengling?"

The bartender nodded. "Draft or bottle?"

"Bottle."

He passed her a bottle and an iced glass and remarked conversationally, in his slickest bartender tone. "Have I seen you here before?"

Marcia shook her head. "This is my first time. Actually, I'm looking for someone," she purred in a seductive tone. "Perhaps you could help me out."

A broad smile broke out on the bartender's face as he offered his hand in greeting. "My name's Danny."

"Nice to meet you, Danny. I'm Diana. Diana Spencer."

He leaned forward, resting his elbows on the bar, the picture of confidence. "Who is it you're looking for, Diana?"

She gave him what she hoped was her most inviting smile. "I'm looking for Rex Goodwin. I was told he works here."

A hint of caution appeared in Danny's eyes. "What do you want him for?"

"I'm not at liberty to discuss that – it's confidential. But I think Rex will be pleased to see me." She broadened her smile. "Is he in?"

Danny thought she looked harmless enough. Besides, she hadn't set off the metal detector when she came through the front door, which meant she wasn't armed. He pointed to a narrow corridor at the far end of the bar. "Go down that hallway, past the rest rooms. His office is the last door."

"Thanks, Danny," she said as she rose to her feet, clutching her purse. "Will you watch my things while I'm gone?" She licked her lower lip slowly. "I'll make it worth your while when I get back."

Danny thought: is she too old for me to fuck? Deciding she wasn't, he smiled. "Of course."

She walked past two doors marked **FILLIES** and **STALLIONS** and knocked on the door at the end of the corridor. An irritated voice responded. "What the fuck do you want, Danny?"

"It's not Danny, Mr. Goodwin."

Rex's hostile tone turned apologetic at the sound of a female voice. "Sorry about that. The door's open."

Rex was seated behind a cluttered desk, the surface strewn with papers. The room was tiny, barely large enough for a desk and chair, a four-drawer filing cabinet and an unpadded guest chair. He got to his feet and indicated the empty chair. "Sorry about the mess. I usually don't entertain guests. Please, sit down." When she was seated, he continued. "What can I do for you today, Miss____?"

"Spencer. Diana Spencer. Actually, it's what I can do for you."

His dark eyes regarded her with interest. They were all alike, he thought, even the older ones: wondering what it was like to be impaled on a big black dick. This one looked a little weathered but doable. "I'm listening."

"I have a proposition for you," she began. "Something that will make your life a lot easier, a lot more enjoyable."

Here we go. "What kind of proposition?" he leered.

"I understand that Mr. Salazar has asked you to take care of a young woman, Hazel Devereaux. I also understand that it might

342

be the kind of assignment you'd like to be rid of." She held his gaze. "Am I right?"

Rex's eyes narrowed, fantasies of sex evaporated. "Who are you? Are you a cop?"

She shook her head. "I'm not a cop, Mr. Goodwin. I represent Hazel Devereaux's father. He's been searching for his daughter all over the country for fifteen years. My sources tell me she's in the basement below us, and that Mr. Salazar has assigned you to take care of her." She smiled in sympathy and rolled the dice. "Must be a pretty shitty assignment for a man like you to have to babysit a junkie, day and night. Must cut into your social life." She smiled again. "Am I right, Mr. Goodwin? Does it make it hard for you to tap some of that sweet NYU pussy that hangs around the bar?"

"What do you want?" His voice held a hint of violence.

"I want to do you a favor, Mr. Goodwin. I want to put you in a position where you will no longer have to be responsible for Hazel. I want you to be able to go back to managing the bar and chasing pussy like you were before. Is that something that might interest you?"

After a long moment spent digesting her suggestion, he responded. "I can't hand her over to you. Mr. Salazar wouldn't allow it."

She was elated. His answer confirmed that Hazel was the woman Dr. Clark had treated yesterday. She caught the uncertainty in his voice and pressed forward. "I'm not asking you to. All I'm asking you to do is to let me see her, let me talk to her for a bit to make sure she's okay. Her father has been frantic, wondering if she's dead or alive. If I could see her and tell him that she's alive, it would help a lot." She paused, then continued. "Do you have any children, Mr. Goodwin?"

"Not that I'm aware of."

"So it must be doubly hard for you to be her caretaker, never having had kids of your own."

"I don't see how this solves my problem," he said haltingly. "She'll still be here after you talk to her." He gave her a confused look. "How does that help me?"

"Once I determine that she's okay, that she's coherent and can respond to a few simple questions, I'd like to leave a cell phone with her, one that has her father's number on it. My client is convinced she'd be willing to come home if she had the opportunity, which would get you off the hook." She looked at him imploringly. "What do you say, Mr. Goodwin? Is this something you might be interested in?"

He shook his head. "Mr. Salazar said no phones. He'd never allow it."

"Mr. Salazar doesn't have to know," she replied smoothly. "I'm guessing he doesn't go down in that basement, because he's left that job to you. So unless you tell him she has a phone, how would he ever find out?"

She was right. Salazar hadn't been down to the basement a single time since he'd dropped her off nearly three months earlier. "I don't know…"

Marcia could almost hear the gears of his mind working as he weighed the pros and cons of her offer. She moved quickly, playing her final card. "You don't have to tell me today. I'll be back tomorrow. You have twenty-four hours to think it over. But if you do decide to let me see her and she accepts the phone, you'll be well compensated."

Appealing to his greed was a smart move. "How well compensated?" he asked quickly.

She smiled as she rose to her feet, preparing to leave. "Enough to impress a lot of college girls. Do you prefer vanilla, or are you more of a chocolate fan?"

61

The bar was still deserted when Marcia emerged from the hallway. Danny watched as she approached and gathered her things, retrieving her unopened bottle of Yuengling that he'd stashed in an ice tub while he waited for her to return. He opened it and placed it on a fresh coaster.

As she zipped up her jacket, she said apologetically. "I'm afraid I have to run. It was nice meeting you, Danny."

"But you haven't touched your beer," he protested, holding it up in case she'd forgotten.

She gave him her best smile as she dropped a ten on the bar. "I'll be back again tomorrow. If you have any customers between now and then, feel free to sell it." After a moment she added. "Or maybe you can drink it yourself."

*****

After the mysterious woman left his office, Rex considered her offer. Would it be so bad to let the junkie have a phone? More than once he'd wondered why Salazar hadn't just tossed her out in the street, especially after it became apparent that she craved drugs more than him. It seemed obvious that whatever his employer had seen in this woman when he brought her back with him from Florida had soured, so why didn't he just cut her loose? He suspected Salazar had a darker side, one where the taking of another's life was merely considered reducing overhead expenses. Why did Salazar insist on continuing to allow such a liability to hang around while at the same time avoiding her like the plague?

It had been a long three months, Rex thought. Maybe it was time he deserved a break from this shit.

*****

Back at the car, Claude greeted her cautiously. "How did it go?"

Marcia beamed at him. "Pretty well. I know that Hazel is in the basement – her handler confirmed it."

"Handler?"

"Salazar has one of his flunkies from the bar babysitting her, feeding her drugs, keeping her quiet. But I think I might've gotten to him with my offer."

Claude regarded the news stoically. "Where to next?"

"Back to the townhouse."

Marcia worked her phone on the ride, texting the news that she'd confirmed Hazel's location to Colleen and warning her to keep it to herself until she was, hopefully, able to see her with her own eyes tomorrow. After finishing the text to Colleen, she sent one to Gretchen, thanking her again for the use of the townhouse and using her influence to get her dinner reservations on such short notice.

She resisted the overwhelming temptation to let Lucien know what she'd discovered about Hazel today, reasoning that she could give him a more realistic reading of the situation if Rex accepted her proposal and allowed her to talk with Hazel tomorrow. She didn't want to raise his hopes too much, especially if she felt, after talking to Hazel, that his daughter still resented the man who'd waited so long to acknowledge her birthright and, despite her current bleak situation, wanted nothing to do with him. She knew little in life was certain; she also knew that it would be unconscionable to offer false hope to a man who, after much soul searching, had realized the most serious error of his past and was doing his best to make amends.

As he dropped Marcia off in front of the townhouse, Claude said, "Dinner tonight?"

"I have reservations for 8:00 at Isla Martinique, on Bleecker Street in the West Village," she said. "What time should I expect you?"

Claude did the calculations, factoring in Friday night traffic. "I'll be out front at quarter past seven."

"I'll see you then," she said as she exited the vehicle. The doorman held the door as she entered the building. "Good afternoon, Ms. Alvarez."

She blew by him with a curt wave, her mind embroiled with Lucien's situation, trying to account for the possible scenarios ahead contingent on Rex's response to her offer as she headed for the elevator.

Inside her room, she grabbed her cigarettes and, still clad in her jacket and wool toque, stepped onto the balcony for a smoke. Traffic below was beginning to thicken as the weekend loomed. Once again, Marcia wondered why anyone would voluntarily live in such a crowded pressure cooker, especially at this time of year. She knew she was luckier than most – she had her own car and driver to help her get around. What about all the people crowded into the subway on a day like this? No wonder she never saw a picture of any of them smiling.

Back inside, she doffed her jacket and hat and checked the time on her phone before calling Gretchen. She answered cheerily on the second ring. "How's it going?"

Marcia answered as she pulled off her boots and reclined on the bed. "Did you read my text?"

"I did. Sounds like you've had a pretty good couple of days."

"Yeah, I think so. But I still haven't laid eyes on Hazel, so I haven't cracked the champagne quite yet. I'm waiting to hear back from her guardian to accept my proposal, but I'm pretty sure he will."

"What makes you so sure he will?"

Marcia snorted. "This guy, Rex, fancies himself as a real player. He manages the bar, which is mostly a hangout for students from NYU. After talking to him for five minutes I pegged him as one of those guys who thinks he's God's gift to coeds, despite the fact that he's twice as old as they are. Keeping an eye on Hazel has put a real damper on his bar action, so my proposal should be attractive to his little head, which I'm pretty sure calls the shots in his world. It gives him some realistic hope that he can get rid of Hazel, which would let him get back to what he wants to do most: chase pussy."

"It sounds like you reasoned this very well," she said approvingly. "The road to a man's mind runs through his dick. It's always been that way and always will."

Steve Morrison, who was sitting next to Gretchen on her second-story porch, opened his mouth to protest on behalf of his gender, but Gretchen cautioned him with a stern look and her upraised palm. Not now, big boy. She continued. "How did you like your dinner last night?"

"It was outstanding," she gushed. "Claude suggested the perfect wine for my entrée, which was out of this world. The shrimp were Florida-sized and tasted fresh, like they'd been caught yesterday. And the service was probably the best I've ever had. The only downside of the evening was finding out that Salazar, the guy I was hoping to meet there, had returned to Florida the day before."

"How are you and Claude getting along?"

"Where did you ever find him? He seems way too qualified to be someone's driver on demand."

Gretchen chuckled. "Claude marches to the beat of a different drummer, that's for sure. He's a real Renaissance man, if you haven't already noticed. I met him at the Grand Prix in Monaco in 1995. He was driving for the Peugeot team, the only Belgian driver in the series that year. He spun off the track on the 22nd lap during the race but walked away unhurt. Later that night, at the champions' dinner, I struck up a conversation with him. He'd been close to Ayrton Senna, who died in a crash the year before in San Marino, and he still hadn't shaken the effects of his friend's death. He was questioning whether he wanted to continue racing, still hurting a year later. Long story short, I decided to go to the next race two weeks later in Montreal, where I spoke with him again. He told me that he'd lost the fire and was going to retire. I gave him my card and told him to call me if he was interested in coming to the U.S. Eleven years later, out of the blue, he called me; he's been driving for me ever since."

Marcia's astonishment was evident. "He was a Formula One driver?" After a moment she continued. "No wonder he handles these streets so well. What is he, late forties?"

"Try fifty-nine. He takes excellent care of himself, if you haven't already noticed. He also speaks five languages fluently."

"He barely speaks when I'm around him," Marcia said.

"Claude is a man of few words," Gretchen explained. "I've learned to pay attention when he does speak."

"There must be more to this story," Marcia offered.

"There is. Remind me to tell it to you sometime." She looked at Morrison, smiling seductively. "When I have more time."

62

The two women chatted for a few more minutes before they said their goodbyes. As soon as the call ended, Morrison spoke to Gretchen in a mock accusatory fashion. "What's this about men only thinking with their dicks?"

The two were enjoying gin and tonics on Gretchen's porch overlooking Clark Bayou in Tarpon Springs and had been in the midst of discussing possible dining options for that evening when Marcia called. Although he gazed out at the bayou and the immaculate grounds of Craig Park during the call, he listened intently to Gretchen's end of the conversation.

"Why, Biff," she said in her best Scarlett O'Hara drawl. "You of all people should agree with me on that. If men didn't think with their dicks all the time, your former profession wouldn't have existed. *And* I wouldn't have called you to have drinks on my porch. You can thank Gracie for that. If she hadn't outed you as Biff Bratwurst earlier this week at Kitty's, I never would've guessed you had such a fascinating past."

He was warming quickly to this sort of suggestive word play with this intriguing woman. "How's my future looking?"

"Steamy."

John Rucker was having a difficult day. He was on his third attempt at preparing a lemon aioli for next week's pan-seared trout special, but he wasn't meeting Nelson's exacting standards. "Light and tangy. Not heavy and drab. Try it again."

Rucker was having trouble concentrating because he was thinking ahead to tonight. He had been notified yesterday that the band scheduled to open the Friday night triple bill at the recently renovated State Theatre in St. Pete, now known as the Floridian Social Club, had cancelled at the last minute. This was the first concert in the new space after a two-year renovation project and the promoter sounded desperate on the phone: would Alien Colonoscopy be able to take their place?

John had been rendered speechless by the request but recovered quickly and told the caller of course; they would be honored. Next followed a frantic series of text messages and phone calls with Kieran and Evelyn, trying to persuade them to give up their Friday night plans. "Dude, it's the State. It's, like, Mecca. Besides, I already told them we'd do it." Once they agreed, he began blitzing every friend he had with text messages, urging them to come to the concert. Even a few of his friends from Boca.

His mind was miles away from his culinary responsibilities, unable to engage fully in the subtleties of blending herbs and spices. Tonight was their big chance, the first concert scheduled in the revamped space of what had long been the most popular and prestigious punk venue in the Bay area. Getting up on that stage before a packed house, with all the local media in attendance for reopening night, was all he could think about.

He was scared shitless.

*****

Lucien rose from his nap at a little past four. He had promised John Rucker he would attend the show tonight in St. Pete, so he took a shower and donned a flannel shirt and a pair of jeans before rolling a joint he planned to smoke just before he went into the theater. He tucked it into the breast pocket of his shirt and automatically checked his wallet for cash as his mind drifted as it tended to do when something was troubling him.

He wondered how Marcia was doing in New York as she searched for his daughter. He'd expected to hear from her by now and was trying not to think of her silence as something ominous or foreboding. He'd been acutely disappointed when she had told him she failed to locate Hazel in the Keys, so he was trying to keep his hopes in check while she pursued her latest lead in New York. He shouldn't be worrying about things over which he had no control, he told himself, but this was his daughter. The longer she remained estranged from him, the more terrified he was that their separation might be permanent. If so, the burden for that separation would rest squarely on his shoulders. The weed that he'd purchased from Rick – he'd insisted on paying for it over his friend's objections – helped, but he'd absorbed enough from several stints in rehab to realize that drugs only offered a temporary stay, not a permanent remedy to the problem. Finding Hazel was the only solution.

Tonight would be a great distraction, a chance to spend several hours doing one of his favorite things. The music would fill his soul, even the raucous, sometimes cacophonous brand of music put forth by Alien Colonoscopy and the other two bands on tonight's bill, JFKFC and Hell Camino. He was especially looking forward to watching John's band after speaking with him last night when John had called to tell him about the show. Who wouldn't be fascinated to see how Lady Vulva and Tornado Jones would interact with one another on stage?

He also was curious to check out the crowd. He felt certain that he would be the oldest one there, a notion that raised the memory of the night in 1992 when he attended his first Phish concert, primarily to check out the guitar work of Trey Anastasio. As soon as the house lights in the indoor arena dimmed, joints were lit and started flying around his vicinity at breakneck speed. But because at thirty-six he was older than the rest of the crowd by fifteen years and had come alone, the dopers took one look at his longish hair and figured he was a narc, never offering him a hit. The irony of that incident still produced a smile all these years later. He wondered if the punks would be less paranoid than those Phish fans had been.

Traffic headed south on U.S. 19 was horrendous, even for Friday during rush hour. It took him an hour and a half to get to Bodega on Central Avenue. Circling the block, he was fortunate to find a parking spot on Baum Avenue in front of the Green Bench Brewing Company before wandering back across Central to the tiny street-front window. He ordered a Cuban sandwich and a fresh orange soda made on the premises; because it was a pleasant evening, partly overcast, temperature hovering in the high sixties, he ate at one of the small tables on the sidewalk in front of the place, watching a steady stream of early weekenders drive by on their way toward the bustling downtown area near the bay.

When he was finished with his sandwich he walked back to his car and smoked the joint, his head on a swivel, looking out for the bicycle cops John told him patrolled the central corridor area every weekend. Although pot was becoming legal in more and more states, Florida had been dragging its feet after its medical marijuana initiative, Amendment 2 on the ballot, was approved by voters three years earlier. However, the state government seemed to be in no hurry to allow voters to cast their ballots regarding recreational use, so Lucien remained cautious.

He saved a small roach for later, placing it in a storage space between the two front seats before exiting the car. The Floridian Social Club was five blocks east on Central, a pleasant walk on this winter evening. Although the Beaux Arts building had a long history as the premier punk venue in the Bay area, Lucien was interested to see whether the renovated space might be the type of place Last of the Mojitos would be interested in playing. He loved Skipper's and what their management had done for the fledgling band by offering them a steady Wednesday slot, but he felt the band would have to expand its horizons if it wanted to stay afloat. If the Floridian's renovation was anything near the quality of what had been produced at the Tampa Theatre, it would provide a favorable alternative for expanding the band's fanbase beyond the elderly hippie demographic.

John had arranged for Lucien to get a backstage pass, so he proceeded to the Will Call window and, after waiting in a short line for several minutes, gave the pleasant young woman on the other side of the glass his name. "Lucien Devereaux, with Alien Colonoscopy."

As soon as the words spilled from his mouth, the woman gave him a puzzled look – aren't you a little old for this kind of music? – before rooting through a small pile of similar passes, finding his, attached to a complimentary lanyard, and passing it to him with a smile. "Enjoy the show, Mr. Devereaux."

With a deep breath, he draped the lanyard around his neck and displayed it to the security officer at the door, who politely asked him to empty his pockets and raise his arms above his head as he wanded him in front and back before allowing him to enter. "Enjoy the show," he said with a smile.

The weed was settling in his system, obscuring any thoughts of Hazel and her plight, leaving a lopsided grin on his face that wouldn't go away. He looked for an usher who could direct him to the backstage area, assuring himself that there would be plenty to drink – water, for him – to assuage the dry mouth he was beginning to experience.

Time to rock and roll.

63

The décor at Isla Martinique was similar to that of Café Tulum: an earnest effort to recreate the atmosphere of a beachfront tiki bar, complete with a weathered wooden skiff suspended from an interior wall that Marcia thought could've been used by Hemingway's aging Cuban fisherman Santiago.

As she was led to her table by the young, exotic-looking dark-haired hostess, Marcia once again noted the restaurant was full and that her table for one near the entrance to the kitchen was the lone unoccupied slot. It was Friday night, she reasoned as she settled into her seat; the place *should* be packed. She had to admit that, separate from his past as a drug lord, Salazar and the people employed by him did know how to pack a room by hiring inventive chefs who weren't afraid to take chances and professional servers who'd mastered the subtle skill of minimal intrusion into the dining experience.

For her entrée tonight she decided on broiled amberjack topped with a mango and papaya chutney and a side salad that came with an intriguing house dressing redolent of fresh ginger and lemon. No wine for her tonight – she wanted her head to be clear tomorrow when she returned to meet with Rex, plus she had her eye on an especially enticing dessert offering, trifle with a Caribbean twist.

She sipped her water and thought ahead to tomorrow. She was confident Rex would agree to her suggestion concerning the cell phone. She noticed the way his eyes lit up when she explained how the phone could be the return ticket to his previous life, before the arrival of Hazel at the bar. Three months of acting as her nurse had taken its toll on his sense of masculinity – his body language said it all. He wanted her gone.

Less certain in Marcia's mind was how Hazel would react. If she was still using drugs, trying to convince her to abandon the source of those drugs, supplied free of charge on a regular basis, would be a formidable task. Addicts prefer their drug of choice to all other enticements: family, friends, wealth, fame. All that matters to them is the next high and how fast they can get there. Given her addiction and the tenuous relationship between her and her father, persuading her to return to Florida to be with Lucien would be a Sisyphean undertaking, one that would require all her negotiating skills.

She hoped she was up to the challenge.

*****

In the dressing room, John paced like an expectant father, muttering inaudibly to himself, long strides covering the length of the compact space, crisscrossing back and forth. Lucien, standing near Kieran and the transcendent Lady Vulva, who was wearing an outfit that reminded him of a diaphanous moth, tried to ease his nerves. "John__"

"Tornado!" he snapped. "Dude, onstage I'm Tornado Jones!"

Taken aback, Lucien tried again. "My bad, Tornado. I wasn't thinking."

"No shit!" he spat out with venom.

Lady Vulva leaned over to Lucien and gave him a reassuring tap on the forearm. "Don't worry. It's nothing personal. He gets like that when we practice, too. You just have to roll with it. As soon as the stage manager pokes his head in the door and says 'five minutes', he'll be back to normal." She smiled. "Tornado Jones normal, anyway." She gave him a look. "Didn't you ever get nervous before a show?"

Lucien nodded. "All the time. I usually stuffed enough coke up my nose to make the nervousness go away."

Kieran turned and laughed ironically. "You obviously were paid much better than we are," he observed in his thick brogue.

The door opened and the stage manager walked in, clipboard in hand, headphones over his ears. "Five minutes, Alien Colonoscopy." Just as quickly he was gone.

Tornado turned to his bandmates. "Lots of energy," he said simply before leaving the dressing room, Kieran, Lady Vulva and Lucien trailing behind. They congregated backstage as the announcer for tonight's event, a disc jockey from one of the area's FM radio stations, tried to quiet the boisterous capacity crowd, who were paying little attention to his plugs for area businesses and his efforts to get them to text to a certain number for a chance to receive free tickets to a future show. They'd come for the music, not shameless shilling from someone old enough to be their grandfather. The level of decorum in the building was fading quickly.

The announcer sensed that. Using the sort of booming cadence popular with certain boxing announcers, he delivered the punch line the crowd had been demanding. "Ladies and gentlemen, Alien Colonoscopy!"

Tornado walked confidently to the front of the stage, strapping on his guitar and glancing at his bandmates before leaning into the mike. "We're Alien Colonoscopy, from Oldsmar" – a few scattered boos – "and we're honored to be the first act to play in this beautiful building." He smiled at the crowd. "It may be called the Floridian Social Club now, but to us it will always be the State!"

A huge roar of approval greeted the statement as he turned toward Kieran, who attacked the bass drum and floor tom with ferocity as they opened with the MC5 anthem, "Kick Out the Jams."

Lucien smiled at the choice. He was likely the only person in the building other than the announcer who was old enough to remember the MC5, but he thought the song was an inspired choice, recognizable to a few, easily mischaracterized by the majority of the audience as an original from the band. He watched in admiration as Tornado executed a blistering solo after the bridge. The crowd lapped up the band's intensity and tossed it right back at them, rewarding them with hearty applause when the song ended.

They wasted no time transitioning to the Sex Pistols' "God Save The Queen" – they'd been informed by the promoter during his initial phone call and again before the show that they were allotted a tight forty minutes, with no encore. Tornado, with help from the other two, had crafted an economic set long on playing and short on patter. "Nobody in their right mind gives a shit about what we have to say between songs," John had said when explaining his song choices. "They just want us to play fast and hard."

When the song ended, Tornado offered his lone exception to the "no talking" edict. He wiped his brow and stepped to the mike. "This next medley honors the punk pioneers of Florida. You know their names."

Two songs from Miami's The Eat, "Kneecappin'" and "Nut Cop", were followed in rapid succession by "Reinventing Axl Rose" and "Pints of Guinness Make You Strong" from Gainesville's Against Me. They closed the medley with "Shut Up", "Now You're Gonna Die" and "More Beer" from another influential Gainesville band, Roach Motel. Following raucous applause, they finished their set with extended versions of the Dead Kennedys' "Holiday in Cambodia" and The Ramones' "I Wanna Be Sedated" before closing out the show with Tornado's song "Nips Don't Lie."

The applause was solid as the band came bouncing off the stage, all smiles. Lucien offered Tornado a high five opportunity that he responded to with glee before leading the band down the hallway back to the dressing room, where a modest spread of cold cuts and cheese and a variety of cold beverages awaited them. The four spread out, Tornado and Kieran with beers, Lucien and Lady Vulva with mineral water.

Tornado – was it okay to call him John now that he was offstage? – looked over at Lucien, adrenaline still pumping. "What did you think?"

"I thought opening with the MC5 was a brilliant move," Lucien said as he reached for a piece of cheese. "Especially the guitar riff you added in the middle. I also loved the way the band jammed on the Dead Kennedys' song. I have to admit, I didn't know a single song in your Florida punk medley, but it was obvious by the crowd's reaction that they did. And that's what matters, not what an aging guitarist thinks." He paused before continuing. "You had the crowd with you from the start. You never lost them, so you never had to fight to get them back."

"Having only forty minutes helped," Kieran said. "Plus, Tornado put together a dynamite setlist. Throwing those songs in from Roach Motel, The Eat and Against Me was inspirational, a stroke of genius. I have to admit I was wrong – I didn't think the crowd would recognize such obscure artists."

Tornado smiled widely. "That's because you're a fucking mick who knows fuck all about punk music in Florida." He raised his bottle to his drummer. "But you're learning."

Lady Vulva took a drink of her water and made a show of sniffing the air before addressing the men with a knowing smile. "Is it just me, or are we being bombarded by an overdose of testosterone?"

64

The next morning Marcia was up early, too nervous to sleep. She'd been going over her plan to clinch the deal with Rex, to make him an offer he couldn't refuse. She made a pot of coffee and had a piece of wheat toast with peach marmalade for breakfast as the television droned in the background while she waited for the day's local weather report.

She retrieved her suitcase from the closet and removed a manila envelope, spilling its contents of $100 bills on the unmade bed. She'd brought $9,900 with her, all in hundreds, for what she described to Colleen as incidental expenses. Her final play, should Rex decide to resist her suggestion of leaving the phone, would be to sweeten the pot with cash – five grand up front and the promise of another ten should Hazel use the phone to reach out to Lucien. She carefully counted out fifty of the bills, secured them with a rubber band and placed them in the bottom of her purse beneath her wallet, keys, makeup kit, cigarettes, her phone and the fully-charged cell phone and charger she planned to leave with Hazel.

She'd pinned her hopes for Hazel's rescue on her reading of Rex as one of Salazar's rescue projects, someone from a troubled background tossed a lifeline by a seemingly benevolent savior, offered steady employment and a brighter future than the one from which he'd escaped. She also reasoned that what had first seemed to Rex as excellent compensation for his services had been recast, through observation and comparison of others on Salazar's payroll, as beneath what he calculated his self-worth to be. The success of her plan was riding on the hope that her initial payment of five grand in cash would be enough to convince him to reconsider that loyalty to Salazar. She hoped she'd read him right.

If she had and Rex accepted the phone and the cash, she thought she'd fly back to Tampa on Monday. She was homesick for sunshine and warmth, tired of bundling up every time she went out. How did people do that, day after day?

She took a long, hot shower and spent extra time with her makeup, wanting to look as good as possible for the hormonally overloaded Rex. She chose a pushup bra and a white blouse that buttoned up the front, allowing her to expose as much cleavage as she deemed necessary to help seal the deal. She slithered into a pair of skintight jeans and donned the knee-high leather boots that had served her so well thus far.

She stood before the mirror in the expansive master bathroom, smiling in approval. I'd tap that, she thought, before turning and retrieving her phone to call Claude, who answered on the first ring. "Yes, Ms. Alvarez?"

"Can you pick me up in front of the building at 11:45? We're headed back to the bar today."

"No problem."

"There's one more thing, Claude," she said. "Do you own a gun?"

There was just the slightest hesitation before Claude responded. "This is New York, ma'am. Even a Belgian pacifist owns a gun here."

"Good," she said approvingly. "Bring it."

*****

Marcia went downstairs early to have a smoke before Claude arrived. She was standing on the sidewalk when he pulled up. She tossed her cigarette away and waved him off as he moved to exit the car and open her door. Such a gentleman, she thought. No wonder Gretchen hired him.

As Claude was preparing to pull away from the curb, Marcia spoke up. "I forgot to ask you if you have ammunition for your gun."

Claude gave her a quizzical look in the rearview mirror. "What good is a gun without bullets?"

Saturday traffic was light, so Claude made good time, dropping Marcia off in front of the No Name Bar at five past noon. She hopped out of the car with the grace and agility of a young girl. "Wish me luck. I have you and your gun on speed dial if I need you. Stay close to your phone."

Danny was behind the bar again when she walked in, greeting him like an old friend. "No Yuengling for me today, Danny. I'm just heading back to see Rex. Is he in?"

He nodded wordlessly as she headed down the hallway. She rapped on the door.

"Who is it?"

"Diana Spencer."

"C'mon in."

She got straight to the point as she stood behind his guest chair. "Do you have an answer for me?"

He ignored her question, posing one of his own. "You said something yesterday about compensation. How much we talkin' about here?"

She smiled widely, unzipping her jacket and draping it over the back of her chair before settling into the seat, leaning forward suggestively so he could get a good look. "That depends on you, big boy," she purred. "I was thinking about two payments. The first one, if you allow me to see Hazel and hand her the phone, is here in my purse." She patted her leather bag. "In order to receive the second payment, she'll need to use that phone to call her father. You might have to help convince her to make that call." She looked into his eyes and held his gaze. "Do you think you can do that?"

"How much?" he persisted.

"Five thousand cash, today, if you take me to see her and let me explain to her about the phone. Another ten if you can convince her to make that call." She noticed his eyes had dropped to her cleavage and smiled to herself. Some men are so predictable.

He leaned forward as he considered her offer, resting his elbows on the cluttered desk. "How do I know I'll get the extra ten if she makes the call?"

She leaned forward a little more, exposing more skin and the hint of a nipple. "You'll have to trust me, Rex, but I can assure you my word is gold. I can send that second payment, a cashier's check made out to you, here to the bar if you'd like. Or you can give me another address to send it to if you don't want Salazar to know about our arrangement. It's your call."

He stood up abruptly and moved from behind his desk. Reflexively, she gripped her phone, poised to summon Claude, as he moved to her side and openly stared down her blouse as he leaned over, his face inches from hers. "Show me the money."

Relieved, she released her grip on her phone and grasped the envelope instead, exposing just enough so that he could see it. "It's in here. Fifty bills, five grand, but you don't get to see it or hold it until I talk with Hazel Devereaux."

He hesitated for a long moment before straightening up. "Follow me."

Heart racing, she followed him into the back room of the bar and down another narrow corridor to a door with a padlock on it. He inserted a key, releasing the lock, and opened the door. Flipping on a wall switch next to the door, he cautioned her. "Watch yourself. These steps can be slippery."

She followed him down into the dimly lit basement, a space littered with beer kegs, empty and full, her phone out, its light helping to illuminate the way. They walked past the kegs to a door at the rear of the space, where Rex inserted another key, unlocking that door, walking inside.

She followed him in. The room was small, maybe twelve by twelve, with a low ceiling. There was a single low-wattage light in the room, a lamp on a table next to a couch. On the couch Marcia could see a shapeless lump, covered with a threadbare blanket. Marcia hugged herself; the room was damp and cold.

Rex approached the lump and gave it a firm shove. The form beneath the blanket recoiled in protest at having been awakened. "Hey!" a thin female voice protested. "What the fuck?"

"You have a visitor," Rex said. "All the way from Florida."

He moved out of her line of vision as she turned over to get a look at Marcia. Hazel looked at the unfamiliar woman, trying to focus, then back at Rex. "Who's this?"

Marcia stepped forward, stomach churning. Even in the dim light she could see that Hazel was in bad shape. Her face and forearms were covered with bumps and open scabs, evidence of sustained drug use, and as the blanket fell away and she raised herself to a sitting position with effort, she could see that Hazel was emaciated. She looked like a refugee who hadn't eaten for days. "My name's Diana, Hazel. I'm a friend of your father's. He sent me here to find you and help you."

Marcia could see Hazel was having trouble grasping the situation. This was probably the first time she'd seen another person besides Rex in this room. "My father?"

"Lucien Devereaux. Remember him?"

She laughed harshly, which turned into a fit of coughing. When it subsided she continued in a bitter tone. "How could I remember him? I've never even seen the bastard. When my momma told him about me, about me being his kid, he told her to fuck off." She glared at Marcia. "We talkin' about the same Lucien Devereaux here, Diana?"

Marcia tried to deflect the woman's anger. "He knows he screwed up back then, and it's been driving him crazy ever since. He came to Biloxi, looking for you after your mother died, but you'd already left for Tampa. He followed you there and kept looking. He finally tracked you down and found out that you'd been working at Kitty Galore's, but he was too late again. You'd met Roberto Salazar, and then the two of you left town. But he kept looking. Once he realized how big a mistake he made when he chose not to listen to your mother, he never stopped looking for you. That's why I'm here."

Hazel struggled to try to digest it all. Marcia knew she was throwing a lot at the drug-addled young woman, but she had no choice. This would be her only chance to convince Hazel that she was here to help her, to get her out of this hellhole and back to Florida. Finally, the young woman spoke. "So how did you find me?"

Here Marcia played her final card. "Faye Tompkins. She had a picture of you and gave us a good description of Roberto. Once we identified the real Roberto Salazar, I went down to his house in the Keys, but you weren't there. One of your neighbors on Cudjoe Key, a Mr. van Basten, told me that Roberto spent a lot of time in New York. I caught a plane the next day. And here I am."

Hazel looked from Marcia to Rex and back again. "My father is paying for all this? How? According to momma, he never had a pot to piss in. Spent all his money on dope and booze."

"He turned his life around, Hazel. He got sober and stayed sober. He's in another band now, living in Tarpon Springs. He's doing really well. The only thing missing in his life these days is you."

Rex, who'd been silent during these exchanges, finally spoke, masking his own greed with feigned concern for her well-being. "She's not askin' a lot. She wants you to call your father. You can decide what to do after that." He gestured around the spare, depressing room. "If I were you, I'd listen to this bitch. Sounds like she's offerin' you a lot more than this."

Marcia winced at the characterization but withheld a retort. Instead, she addressed Hazel. "I have a phone for you," she said, withdrawing it from her purse. "It's all paid for, and it has your father's number listed as the only contact. He wants you to call him, Hazel. He's out of his mind worrying about you. He wants to hear your voice." She handed Hazel the phone. Hazel looked at it like it was foreign object she'd never seen before as Marcia bent to plug the charger into the outlet that powered the light.

Rex was growing impatient. He wanted his money. "We done here?" he asked Marcia belligerently.

"Just one more thing." Marcia bent close and whispered, her lips grazing Hazel's ear. "Call him and we'll get you out of here. Please." She straightened up and looked at Rex. "Promise me you'll make sure she's taken care of. Try a little harder to get her to eat, okay?"

"I guess I can do that," he mumbled.

Marcia gave Hazel one last glance before following him out of the room. He locked both doors and led her back to his office. She was barely inside the office when he slammed the door and wheeled around. "Give me the money," he growled.

Marcia extracted the envelope from her purse and handed it to him. She watched as he counted it and placed it back in the envelope before sliding it into his top desk drawer, which he locked. Satisfied, he looked up at her with a malevolent grin. "Ten more if she makes that phone call?"

"You have my word."

"Pleasure doin' business with you, Diana," he leered at her, his eyes once again moving to the exposed tops of her breasts. "Anything else I can do for you today?"

She wanted to be far away from his loathsome presence but couldn't resist one last barb as she put on her coat, grabbed her purse and headed for the door. "Save it for the NYU girls, Romeo," she tossed over her shoulder without looking back.

She walked by Danny, who was chatting with his only customer, a gray-haired man with a ponytail wearing a Yankees' cap. "No tip today, Danny. I'm afraid I'm fresh out of cash. Take care of yourself."

Outside the door, she dialed Claude. "Where are you?"

"Around the corner."

"Pick me up in front of the bar."

"Will I need my gun?"

Marcia laughed. "Not today, Wyatt. The coast is clear."

Two minutes later Claude idled up to the curb. Marcia got in. As they pulled away, Claude caught her eye in the rearview. "Who's Wyatt?" he asked in a puzzled voice.

Marcia laughed again. "I guess they don't teach much western history in Belgium. Wyatt is Wyatt Earp, a famous lawman and gunfighter here in the late 1800s."

Claude nodded. "Brother of Virgil and Morgan Earp. I thought it might be him you were referencing."

Marcia was astonished. "You know about the Earps?"

It was Claude's turn to smile. "Doc Holliday, too. I may not know much about American history, but I do know a little about American western films. *Gunfight at the O.K. Corral*, 1957, Burt Lancaster, Kirk Douglas, directed by John Sturges." It felt good to have a bit of fun with his passenger. He quickly shifted back to a serious tone. "How did it go in there?"

"Like a fucking charm," she exclaimed, following up quickly with, "Excuse my French. Hazel was in the basement. I was able to talk with her and leave a phone with her, just like I'd planned."

He mulled that over for a few moments before catching her eye again in the rearview mirror. "What's the next move?"

"We wait for her to call."

Epilogue

The large dining area on the top floor of Kitty Galore's was rarely open to the public. It took a special occasion for owner Florence Leaf to sanction its use, usually a wedding reception or retirement dinner or, occasionally, when extra space was needed to handle the overflow crowd during the restaurant's annual anniversary party each September.

Tonight, the occasion was special indeed. It was Gracie Fenton's 50th birthday, and Florence and Faye Tompkins had conspired to put together a birthday celebration that excited everyone in the Ozona community. Except, of course, those unfortunate employees scheduled to work that evening. For them, it was business as usual.

By the time Gracie's shift ended at 5:30, a crowd had already begun to gather at the bar, priming themselves before heading up the stairs to feast on chef Nelson Gregory's seafood buffet, which included all of Gracie's favorite dishes: peel and eat shrimp, broiled hogfish, oysters on the half shell, steamed clams, fresh corn on the cob and mountains of French fries and onion rings, along with a half keg of Big Storm Tropic Pressure Florida Ale, two bottles of Patron, a tub filled with assorted bottles of beer and a giant punchbowl filled with homemade sangria.

As her contribution to the festivities, Gretchen Schiller, who was there as the guest of Steve Morrison, had generously offered to hire a car service for all, to and from the restaurant, allowing the patrons to imbibe as much as they wanted without risking arrest on the way home. Because of Gracie's popularity in the community, the initial guest list had been enormous, worthy of a royal wedding. A committee of Gracie, Faye and Gracie's boyfriend Hank Milosic winnowed the list down to a more manageable list of forty attendees, all of whom responded they would attend the gala event. Nobody wanted to miss the party of the year in Ozona.

Most of the crowd had arrived and moved upstairs from the bar by 6:00, the time indicated on the invitations as when the party was to begin. Marcia Alvarez and Colleen McKinny were hung up on a conference call with a client as their driver cooled his heels in the parking area of their office, waiting for the call to end, and were among the last to arrive.

Gracie was in rare form, a child's birthday cap on her head, empty shot glass in her left hand, when she spied Marcia and Colleen walking into the room. "We were about to send out the National Guard," Gracie exclaimed as the pair entered the room. "You know what they say about all work and no play…"

Colleen pointed to Marcia. "Blame her. I tried to get her to leave at five, but she had to make one more call."

Gracie walked over and gave Marcia a big hug. "You're forgiven. Now get yourself a drink and start having some fun!" She careened off in search of the tequila.

Marcia looked around the room. She recognized Zach Rheinhart and Gwen Westphal seated at a table with Steve Morrison and Gretchen Schiller, engaged in a lively discussion, Statler and Waldorf, the two snowbirds from Minnesota who were among Gracie's favorite customers, Faye Tompkins and her husband Brad, talking with another of Gracie's favorites, Arnold Berman.

At a table by themselves, distancing themselves from the crowd gathered around the buffet table and selections of booze, were Florence Leaf and her husband, Walter Smart. Marcia was surprised to see Walter; when she'd stopped in last week for lunch, Gracie had told her that Walter hadn't been feeling well lately and probably wouldn't attend the party. Both were drinking bottled water; neither of them was smiling.

Marcia's eyes swept the room; she was relieved that Walter's son Trace wasn't in the room. Next to Reb Jadel, who also had been omitted from the guest list, Trace was the most obnoxious person in Ozona, his sense of entitlement inflated by his stepmother's status as the owner of Kitty's. He was loud, overbearing and rude, qualities endured by the staff in tortured silence whenever Florence or Walter were in the room.

In the other corner of the room, two acoustic guitars and two stools were set up. Gracie had told Marcia at lunch last week that John Rucker, the apprentice chef, and Lucien had agreed to play some songs. She looked guiltily around the room for Lucien and saw him speaking with Madeline Collins, Judy Ruliani's assistant. He hadn't noticed her yet, which was a relief. It was the second week of November, ten months after Marcia had returned from New York. She was dreading his inevitable question, the question he asked each time they spoke: had she heard anything from Hazel? Although she hadn't faulted herself for leaving Hazel behind and Lucien had never said anything that would indicate disappointment on his part, she felt guilty that she wasn't able to offer the answer he was dying to hear. She had stopped explaining that Hazel wouldn't call her – the only number she knew, the only one on her phone, was Lucien's.

John Rucker came up the stairs with a fresh platter of shrimp, which was the early favorite among the night's dishes, and exchanged his full platter for the empty one. Before he headed back to the kitchen, he veered over to Hank, who was calling the shots. "What time do you want me and Lucien to set up?" he asked, raising his voice to be heard above the raucous crowd.

Hank glanced at his watch. "It's nearly seven. Give it another half hour. Everyone should be well lubricated by then."

He pointed toward a couple in their fifties who were standing alone, off by themselves. "Do you know who they are, Hank?" he asked. "I've never seen them in here before."

Hank looked in the direction John was pointing, nodding. "That's Gracie's older sister Thelma and her husband Frank. They flew down from Chicago."

"They better pick up the pace," John observed drily. "They look like Jehovah's Witnesses at an orgy."

"Don't worry," Hank advised with a wink. "They're just slow starters."

Gracie was standing by the bar, being urged by Statler – or was it Waldorf? – to have another shot. She gave him a big smile and a sloppy kiss that caused him to blush before she obliged, pouring it and downing it in one smooth motion. Zach and Gwen came up to wish the birthday girl well. "You only turn fifty once," Zach said sprightly. "Try not to lose your momentum." Gwen gave him an elbow in the side and a disapproving glance. Zach yelped and rubbed her target area. "Hey! That hurt!"

"Good," Gwen said. "It was supposed to."

Before he descended the stairs with the empty shrimp tray, John headed toward Lucien and waited respectfully until Lucien noticed him and broke off his conversation with Madeline. He motioned Lucien aside, out of Madeline's hearing range. "Who's that? She's hot!"

"That's Madeline," Lucien explained. "She's that lawyer's assistant, the one that's on all the billboards and commercials. Judy Ruliani."

"Is she here with a date?" John's interest in the comely blond was naked.

Lucien smiled. "I think she came with her boss, so y'all might be in luck."

John gave Lucien a confident smile. "Luck's got nothing to do with it." He went to leave, then turned around, remembering why he'd stopped in the first place. "Hank thinks we should start playing in half an hour, at 7:30, okay?"

"Got it."

As John headed for the stairs, Lucien peered around the room, looking for Marcia. He hadn't spoken to her yet and wanted to say hello. Things had been going well for Lucien and the band. Summer had been a bit slow – all of the Bay area's outdoor venues suffered during the heat and humidity of Florida's summer – but word had gotten out that one of the country's best guitarists was playing in a band every Wednesday night at Skipper's Smokehouse, and the midweek crowds had been growing steadily since the end of September. In addition, the Last of the Mojitos had opened for Jimmy Buffett at his Tampa show last month. He was beginning to get that feeling he'd had before, that he and the band were about to break through to the big time: he felt they were ready to start touring larger venues, starting in the south, as a headlining band. He wasn't sure Rick Manning wanted to give up his day job quite yet, but in Lucien's mind they were good enough to give it a shot. He knew he was – he hadn't had a drink in nearly two years now and felt like he was twenty years younger. He still smoked weed, but only in moderation, only at night. It was under control.

He saw Marcia with her assistant Colleen on the other side of the room and started to head in their direction when his phone chirped in his pocket. He retrieved it and looked to see who was calling.

He stopped breathing as he stared at the screen. Still holding the phone in front of him, he raced down the back stairs, past a startled Faye Tompkins. He burst through the door into the parking lot in back of the restaurant, raising the phone to answer, still holding his breath, unable to get any words out.

A tiny voice emerged from the other end of the line, barely coherent, wracked with sobs. "Daddy? Daddy, is that you?"

He almost collapsed to the ground before finally finding his voice. "Hazel?"

"Daddy? I want to come home."

Made in the USA
Columbia, SC
01 October 2020

21833498R00224